On the First Day of Christmas
My True Love Gave to Me . . .

"*Lord Dunvegan*," Caroline exclaimed in breathless fury, "just *what* do you think you're *doing*?"

Geordie, who'd kissed a fair number of lasses in his time, was not as discomposed as she. Dizzy and dazzled he might be, but not discomposed. "Dinna ye remember?" he taunted brazenly. "I was explaining the word intimate."

"That was *not* intimate. That was . . . *licentious!*"

"Nay, lass, I canna agree. Here we are under the mistletoe. For me to kiss you under the mistletoe is a legitimate Christmas tradition."

"Lord Dunvegan, you are a boorish, shameless *libertine*, and if you *ever*—Christmas or not—manhandle me in such a manner again, I shall give you another."

"Another, ma'am?"

"Another of these!" Without a moment of hesitation, she raised her hand and slapped him very smartly across his cheek. Then she turned on her heel and stalked off down the hall, leaving him holding his burning cheek, utterly abashed. The rampaging mischiefmaker had run into the wall at last.

—From *The Girl With Airs*
by ELIZABETH MANSFIELD

A Regency Holiday

Elizabeth Mansfield, Monette Cummings,
Sarah Eagle , Judith Nelson,
and Martha Powers

JOVE BOOKS, NEW YORK

A REGENCY HOLIDAY

A Jove Book / published by arrangement with
the authors

PRINTING HISTORY
Jove edition / November 1991

ISBN: 0-515-10705-0

Jove Books are published by The Berkley Publishing Group,
200 Madison Avenue, New York, New York 10016.
The name "JOVE" and the "J" logo
are trademarks belonging to Jove Publications, Inc.

PRINTED IN THE UNITED STATES OF AMERICA

10 9 8 7 6 5 4 3 2 1

Contents

About the Authors

ELIZABETH MANSFIELD ("The Girl With Airs") is the author of 25 Regency romances, all published by Berkley, including one previous Christmas story, *A Christmas Kiss*. She has received the *Romantic Times* award for best Regency writer.

MONETTE CUMMINGS ("Proof of the Pudding") was the recipient of the Romance Writers of America Golden Medallion Award for Best Regency of 1985. Her previous books for Berkley include *Scarlet Lady* and *A Kiss for Caroline*.

SARAH EAGLE ("A Christmas Spirit") is the author of two Jove Regency romances, *The Reluctant Suitor* and *The Marriage Gamble*. She also writes for Harlequin as Sarah Hawkes and for Meteor as Sally Falcon. She lives and works in Little Rock, Arkansas.

JUDITH NELSON ("Christmas at Wickly") is a *Romantic Times* award-winning author who has published several Regencies, including *Beau Guest*, *Lady's Choice*, and *Patience Is a Virtue*. Her latest, *Instructing Arabella*, is due out next year. She lives in Lincoln, Nebraska.

MARTHA POWERS ("The Kissing Bough") is the Golden Heart Award-winning author of *Double Masquerade*, *The Runaway Heart*, and *False Pretenses*. She and her husband Bill have two children and a cat with an attitude.

The
Girl
With
Airs

Elizabeth Mansfield

✻ 1 ✻

ANYONE SEEING HIM would have known at once that the young man who wove his uncertain way down the dark street had been imbibing too deeply. He tottered unsteadily on his feet, clung to every lamp post he passed, and actually tripped and fell twice. His very appearance attested to his inebriated condition. He wore only one glove, his waistcoat was unbuttoned and his hat askew. Worse, his neckcloth, which he'd pulled from his neck (despite the care and precision with which his valet had earlier folded it in place), was clutched in his ungloved hand at one end while the other end dragged on the ground behind him. But at this late hour of the night, there was not a soul on Henrietta Street to see him.

Drunk as he was, he seemed to know where he was going, for he stopped before the most imposing house on the street—a grey stone townhouse with arched windows and a delicately ornamented roof pediment—and muttered, "Ah, thank goo'ness, here we are!"

He climbed the three steps to a green doorway illuminated by two brass coach-lanterns and proceeded to pound on the door, ignoring the lion's head brass knocker. "Geordie! Geordie, old f'llow," he cried in callous disregard of the sleeping neighbors, "open up!"

Several minutes passed before his repeated summonses were answered. Eventually, however, the bolt was turned and the door opened. A butler, wearing house-slippers and a woolen robe that he'd hastily thrown over his nightshirt, peered out into the dark. "Michty me!" the butler gasped, lapsing into his Scottish brogue at the sight of the fellow on the doorstep. Although he recognized the visitor at once as Sir Archibald Halford (for Sir Archibald's pronounced nose and slightly receding chin made his face distinctive), his presence on the doorstep at this hour—and in such a dishevelled state—was completely unexpected. "Sir Archibald, is it yersel'?" the butler asked, blinking. "What—?"

"Mus' see Laird Geordie," the young man said thickly, pushing his way past the startled butler. "Mus' see 'im righ' now!"

"But, sir, it's past two in the morning!" the butler remonstrated, his proper butler's English restored. "Surely you can't expect me to wake his lordship at this hour."

"Wheesht, McIver," came a voice from the top of the stairs, "I'm already awake. How can a body sleep through such a curfuffle?"

"Geordie! *There* you are. Thank God!" sighed the interloper, stumbling toward the staircase.

The young man at the top of the stairs, wrapped in a blanket from beneath which a pair of bare legs extended, was a very tall, rangy fellow with a head of wildly curling, shocking-red hair, and a handsome face that could have been described as innocently boyish except for a pair of grey-green eyes that looked out at the world with a knowing, amused shrewdness. George David McAusland, Lord Dunvegan (called Laird Geordie by his friends in acknowledgment of his tendency to lapse into his "Lallans" accent whenever he lost his temper or was in any way discomposed) looked down at his friend in embarrassment. "Could ye come back in the morn, laddie? I've a bit o' company in my bed, y' see . . ."

"No, I c'n not come back in th' morn," the drunkard declared, hanging for dear life on the newel post of the staircase. "I'm desp'rate! Wha's more important—my desp'ration 'r yer lightskirt?"

Geordie squinted down at his visitor through the gloom of the staircase, but the light from McIver's candle was too dim to make out Archie's condition. Nevertheless, since his visitor's words made it clear that something was amiss, Geordie ran down the steps two at a time. "Archie? What're ye doin' here at this hour? Have ye gone daft?"

Archie's lips trembled. "Good ol' Geordie. I knew you'd come through if I needed you."

"Needed me?"

Two tears ran down Archie's overheated cheeks. "I've been stabbed, Geordie. Cut down like a weed in a rosegarden. Dispatched, annihilated, and destroyed . . ."

Geordie peered at him closely. "Archie, me lad," he grinned in relief, "I do believe y're cupshotten."

The inebriated fellow straightened up in offense. "Never. Not me. Can hold m' liquor wi' the best of 'em. Stabbed in the heart is wha' I am." Wavering on his feet, he clutched at the newel post again. "She won't . . . have me, Geordie. She's given me . . . back . . . m' ring!" That said, his grip on the newel post weakened, his knees gave way, and he slid to the floor, unconscious.

"Will ye look at that, McIver?" Geordie muttered, staring down at his friend and shaking his head. "The lad's ploughed out."

"Ploughed out, my lord?" the butler asked in confusion as he knelt beside the fallen visitor. "But didn't he say he'd been stabbed?"

"Dinna be a gowk. He's just had a few too many. It's as I said. The poor lad's cupshotten."

Archie did not return to consciousness until the next evening. He opened his eyes and found himself in a strange bedroom. His stomach was growling, his tongue seemed coated with a bitter film, and something like a blacksmith's hammer was pounding in his head. He gingerly rose from the bed and stumbled out of the room. Not until he reached the stairs did he realize he was still in Geordie's house.

He made his way carefully down the stairs. At the bottom he discovered Geordie waiting for him. "Ye slept the day away, ye haveril," the Scotsman greeted.

Archie met his friend's taunting smile with a sheepish one of his own. "What's a haveril?"

"A half-wit. How much were ye fool enough to imbibe?"

Archie shrugged. "Only a few swigs. Someone must've contaminated my brandy."

"Blethers, man!" Geordie retorted bluntly. "Ye swilled down more than a few. But come into the sitting room, laddie, and sit yersel' down. Ye look worse than ye did last night."

One glimpse at the mirror that hung near the sitting-room door told Archie that his friend was not exaggerating. His eyes were bloodshot, his clothes wrinkled, his face unshaven, and his brow furrowed with pain. "I knew it," he groaned, turning away and dropping down on a wing chair near the fire. "I knew I was a lost soul. She's undone me."

The tall, red-headed Scotsman paused in the act of sitting

down on the hearth. "What are ye babblin' aboot, ye saphead? Who's undone ye?"

"Caroline, of course. Who do you think?"

"Caroline? Who's—?"

"Damnation, Geordie, you know who Caroline is! Caroline Woolcott, my betrothed." He put his hand to his forehead and shut his eyes in pain. "She's jilted me."

"Jilted ye? She couldna done!" The Scotsman sank down on the hearth and stared at his friend in amazement. "Ye became betrothed not a sennicht past."

"Eight days ago, to be exact," Archie moaned. "We were to be wed at Christmas." The poor fellow stared glumly at the glowing embers of the fire. "My life is over, Geordie. I feel like putting a bullet in my brain and ending it all."

"Don't be so daft," Geordie snapped. "Ye'll not be killin' yersel' over a mere lass. The world is full o' sonsy lasses."

"Confound it, Geordie, don't start with your damn brogue. What's sonsy?"

"You know what I mean. Buxom. Shapely. If ye put yer mind to it, you can find yersel' sonsy lasses by the dozen."

"Not like Caroline. Caroline is . . . exceptional."

"What balderdash! Every fool who falls in love thinks his lady is exceptional."

"No, Geordie, you're wrong there. Caroline truly is exceptional. Take my word. First of all, she's the loveliest creature I've ever seen, with hair like . . . like . . ."

Geordie smiled sardonically. "Hair like silk, teeth like pearls, lips like rose petals—"

"You may joke all you wish, Geordie, old man, but those cliches are nothing but the truth in Caroline's case. Her mouth is full-lipped and as cherry red as in the song! And her eyes are a kind of . . . of golden brown, if you can imagine it. And she has the most unbelievable eyelashes! And—"

"Have done, man! I'll take yer word that she's a beauty. But ye'll not make me believe there isn't another lass to be found with full lips and long lashes."

"But there's so much else about her! There's her voice—"

"I know. Low and gentle," Geordie supplied dryly.

"Exactly! And her laugh is like . . . like . . ."

"Like music?"

"Yes. Like music. And, speaking of music, she plays the

pianoforte *and* the harp, she speaks fluent French, she knows Russian, she can read the classics in Greek, she sketches and paints, and—"

Geordie held up his hands. "Wheesht, man, wheesht! She sounds a veritable paragon. As we say at home, an unco leesome lass. But if she's so perfect, why did she jilt ye?"

"I don't know, Geordie. I was too upset to take in what she was saying to me. I know I should have argued with her. Convinced her she was being hasty. Told her how much I love her and all that rot. But I'm not glib with the ladies as you are. I get all tongue-tied."

"Ye were evidently glib enough to win her once," Geordie pointed out. "Perhaps ye can do it again."

"I don't think so, old man," Archie said, sighing deeply. "She made matters sound quite final." He stared into the flames for a long moment. "Unless—" he said, raising his head and gazing at Geordie with eyes suddenly alight.

"Unless—?" Geordie prodded.

"Unless you were willing to speak for me."

Geordie blinked at him. "Me? Whatever are ye natterin' aboot?"

"You can do it, Geordie!" Archie said excitedly. "You could sell a sailor the London Bridge if you'd a mind."

"You *are* daft! I don't even know the lass."

"But you know me, don't you? All you need do is tell her what a fine fellow I am."

"Fine fellow?" Geordie sneered. "What I ought to do is tell her she's saved hersel' from weddin' a fool!"

"Please, Geordie! It won't be hard for you to convince her she's made a mistake. Everyone says you've a silver tongue. And that Scottish burr of yours is the perfect addition. It makes you sound so . . . so *sincere*. I've seen how the ladies flock round you when you speak. That's how I know you're certain to win over my Caroline."

Geordie rose to his feet. "Archie Halford, gi'e owre! Silver tongue, indeed. I can barely speak the King's English! Never have I heard so wanwytted—idiotic—a scheme!"

"You speak the King's English perfectly, and you know it. You only throw in your Lowlands brogue to remind us where you come from," Archie accused.

"How I speak has nothin' to do with it," Geordie retorted. "The whole idea is too silly to discuss."

"What's silly about it? Can't a fellow speak up for his friend? After all, what are friends for?"

"I never heard that interferin' with a man's romantic problems was a requirement for friendship," Geordie declared, striding to the door.

Archie rose from his seat and followed. "Geordie, *please*—" he begged.

Geordie stopped in his tracks and looked back at his friend with a glower. "Anyone with a thocht—a grain—of sense knows better than to entangle himself in his friends' affairs of the heart. If ye want to win yer lass back again, Archie, me lad, ye'll have to do it yersel'! Under no circumstances will I have anything to do with it!"

But Archie was not one to be easily put off. "Let's draw for it," he said, catching Geordie's arm and keeping him from leaving.

"Gi'e owre, laddie," Geordie said, pulling his arm free. "I winna be coaxed—"

"My roan against a mere quarter-hour visit with the lady," Archie persisted.

"Yer *roan*?" Geordie turned in the doorway in disbelief. "The thoroughbred roan ye just had from Tattersall's? That one?"

"What other roan do I have?"

Geordie gaped at his friend. "Y're worse than daft—y're fair loony!"

"I'm desperate, that's what I am." Archie pulled a deck of cards from the pocket of his wrinkled coat and riffled them. "One draw. What do you say?"

"The roan against fifteen minutes with yer lass?" He shook his head and rolled his eyes heavenward. "May the good Lord forgive me . . . cut the cards!"

❊ 2 ❊

TWO HOURS LATER George David McAusland, Lord Dunvegan, was on his way to pay a call on Miss Caroline Woolcott. It was not that he'd changed his mind about the foolishness of interfering in another man's love affairs. It was merely that he'd drawn a six, and Archie had drawn a Queen.

He was full of glum self-disgust as he strode down the street toward the residence of the unknown Miss Caroline Woolcott. His enjoyment of gambling was beginning to seem like a dangerous dissipation. Ever since he'd come to England, "Laird Geordie" had indulged himself in all the debauchery available to young men of wealth and leisure. It suddenly occurred to him to wonder what was happening to his character. Was he going to sink into the mire of debauchery like so many of his London friends?

Although he considered himself every inch a Scotsman, he'd been forced to live in England since 1811. Banished by his father to England to "get a bit o' civilizin'," he'd been living away from his beloved Scotland for the better part of six years, four spent at Oxford and the last two in London to acquire "town bronze." In the six years, he'd made many friends among the dissipated Corinthian set, had lost much of his Scottish burr, and had developed a taste for gambling and lightskirts. None of this would have pleased his father, who, fortunately, had no notion of how his son was spending his time and fortune.

As Geordie approached the Woolcott residence, he cursed himself under his breath for having been a "maggotty wanwyt." It was surely witless to have accepted Archie's wager. It was a fool's wager. But how could Geordie have been expected to resist it? Archie's roan was a thoroughbred!

He'd lost, and it served him right. He was indulging himself too much in the profligacy of London life. Just last week he'd lost at faro more in one evening than his rented house cost for a year, he'd run up a bill for spirits last month higher than his father would spend on drink in a decade, and he was permitting the opera dancer he'd taken to his bed a few times to become much too expensive in her demands. Some might call this town bronze; his father, he was sure, would call it debauchery.

In truth, he would be glad to see his banishment end. He was delighted that his father had given him permission to go home to Scotland next month at Christmastime. Once he got there, he intended to convince his father that he'd been civilized enough. If he could persuade his father to let him stay home, he would put an end to his gambling and wenching and settle down to a sane and proper life.

Meanwhile, however, there was the problem of what to say to the beautiful Miss Woolcott, at whose house he'd now arrived. He knocked hesitantly at her door, rehearsing in his mind the points that Archie had suggested he make to the lady. "Tell her that I'm a catch," Archie'd said. "Tell her Archibald Halford is a man of loyalty, faithfulness, with a kind disposition and an easygoing, generous nature. . . ."

But before Geordie could fully review the list of Archie's assets, the butler came to the door. Geordie handed the fellow his card. The butler studied the card, eyed Geordie suspiciously, studied the card again, and frowned. "You are Lord Dunvegan?" he asked.

"I am."

"You've called to see Sir Horace Woolcott, I expect. I'm sorry to have to inform you, my lord, that Sir Horace passed to his reward last year."

"It's Miss Woolcott I've come to see," Geordie explained.

"Oh?" The butler raised his brows. "Is Miss Woolcott expecting you?"

Geordie, not accustomed to being kept waiting about on doorsteps, felt his temper snap. "Wheesht, man, y're a pawky one. Just gi'e the lass the card. Let her ask the questions."

The butler, recognizing a voice of authority even when dressed in a Scottish brogue, admitted him, placed his card on a salver, and asked Geordie to wait in the library. It was not a long wait. Geordie had barely time to study the room—a high-ceilinged chamber with tall windows and book-laden shelves climbing to the rafters—before the butler returned. "Miss Woolcott will see you in the study, my lord," he murmured, and he led the visitor down a long hallway to the very last door. "Lord Dunvegan," he announced, and stood aside.

Geordie crossed the threshold and stopped short. As the butler discreetly took his leave, Geordie gaped at the young woman rising from behind a desk. She was not at all what he expected. She was certainly not a beauty. His impression was rather that of a schoolmarm than a pretty girl. Small and rather thin, her hair that Archie had so glowingly described was pulled severely back from her face in a tight bun, her supposedly golden brown eyes with their "unbelievablc lashes" were hidden behind a pair of large spectacles, and her gown, with its high neck, severe white collar, and long sleeves, did not hide the fact that her figure was almost flat. In Scotland she would never be called sonsy. Only her mouth, ripe and cherry red, lived up to Archie's besotted description.

"Lord Dunvegan?" she was asking as she came round the desk.

"Yes, ma'am. But I fear I've interrupted ye in your work."

"That's quite all right. I'd almost finished for the day. If, as I suspect, you were acquainted with my father, you've probably guessed I'm trying to finish his translation of the *Antigone*." She studied his face carefully—blinking in a puzzled way at the wild red hair and boyish face—before putting out her hand. "You *were* an acquaintance of father's, were you not?" she asked dubiously.

"No, ma'am," he said, taking her hand and bowing over it. "I'm a friend of Sir Archibald Halford."

She stiffened. "Of Archie's?" She removed her fingers from his grasp and peered at him through her spectacles even more closely. Then her brow cleared. "Oh, I see. I suppose he wants his letters back."

"Letters?"

"He only wrote three or four." She went back to the desk and rummaged through a drawer. "I don't know why I saved them. They aren't very good. He can barely spell."

He laughed. "I've never heard that poor spellin' is a reason for jiltin' a lad, ma'am," he said, following Archie's suggestion that he use his Scottish brogue to its fullest melodious effect.

She looked up at him sharply. "What did you say?"

"I said, Miss Woolcott, that I never heard of spellin' bein' a qualification for wedlock." He grinned at her in what he hoped was a disarming manner, but she responded with a forbidding frown. He shrugged. "Ah, well, I suppose it wasna worth repeatin'."

"No, it wasn't," she said icily. "Here are the letters. Take them, please, and go."

"I dinna come for any letters, ma'am. I came to talk to ye aboot yer feelin's for Archie."

"Did you, indeed?" The girl drew herself up to her full height. "That's a bit high-handed, is it not? You and I are not even acquainted."

"No, ma'am, we aren't. But I know Archie well, and I can assure ye that there isn't a finer fellow in all of London."

"Can you, indeed?"

"Yes, ma'am, I can. I truly believe that any lass would be fortunate to have such a fine fellow for her husband."

"Do you, indeed?"

Geordie paused and cocked his head at her. "Indeed, ma'am, it seems y're indeedin' me a thocht too many indeeds. Are ye meanin' somethin' special by them?"

"Indeed I am. They mean that I don't care for your presumption, my lord."

"Presumption?"

"Yes, presumption. That's the proper word, I think, for the interference of a stranger who accosts me in my own home and presumes to advise me whom to marry."

Geordie was not surprised at the girl's show of irritation. He hadn't expected this interview to be easy. But since he considered himself adept at dealing with the moods and whims of females, he was not discomposed. Besides, he owed Archie fifteen minutes of sincere effort, and fifteen minutes Archie would get. "I'm sorry, ma'am," he murmured contritely, "but how can ye say I accosted ye?"

"Perhaps you didn't accost me, exactly, but you did come in under false pretenses, did ye not? I was under the impression you were a scholar, come to discuss my father's writings."

"I never claimed to be a scholar, Miss Woolcott."

"That's true," she admitted. "I should have known at once that someone with your boyish demeanor and wild hair could not be—but never mind. Just go, Lord Dunvegan. I have nothing to say to you."

"As you wish, ma'am," he murmured, lowering his eyes and moving a few steps toward the door. "I only wanted to help

Archie understand ye, ye see. Archie is such a good sort. And he does love ye, lass. Fair sairy he is since ye returned his ring."

The girl's eyebrows lifted. "Fair sairy?" she asked.

"It means wretched. Very wretched." He threw her another of his disarming smiles. " 'Tis a Scottish phrase. I dinna seem able to keep the Lallans from my tongue, I fear."

"I think you are fully aware that your accent is charming," Miss Woolcott said frankly. She took off her spectacles and eyed him coldly. "But I'm afraid I'm not easily swayed by charm. You said you were going, did you not? Then I bid you good evening."

Geordie felt a wave of irritation. This was an icy, sharp-tongued female if ever there was one. What on earth did Archie see in her? Except for her eyes, of course. Archie had been right about her eyes. They were rather remarkable, the brown of her irises streaked with little glints of gold. And her lashes were, as Archie had said, unbelievably long and dark. But behind those eyes she had the nature of a shrew.

He would have liked to turn on his heel and walk out without another word, but he couldn't, in good conscience, take his leave yet. He estimated that not more than ten minutes had elapsed since this conversation began. He owed Archie five more minutes. That was the bargain. He had to try again. "Then ye have no kind word I can bring to the poor lad?" he asked with all the sincerity he could muster. "Ye offer him no hope at all?"

"None at all." She waved her hand dismissively at him. "Goodbye, Lord Dunvegan."

"I don't understand ye," he said, holding his ground. "Surely ye took him in the first place because ye recognized his fine qualities—his loyalty, his faithfulness, his generosity, his easy-going nature. What could have happened in a mere sennicht—a mere week—to cause ye to change yer mind?"

Something in his tone must have made her capitulate a little, for she lowered her eyes and sighed. "If you must know, my lord, I broke our troth because I realized I'd been hasty in accepting him. Yes, Archie is all you say he is. But I discovered, to my dismay, that he is a member of the Corinthian set, to which you, too, appear to belong. I do not approve of that set, I'm afraid."

"Oh? And why not, Miss Woolcott?"

"Because, among other disturbing things, they gamble."

"Gamble, ma'am? Is that so sinful?"

"I find it so. When I discovered Archie's gambling, I felt strong misgivings about him."

"But, ma'am, I and all the men I know, Corinthians or not, play at cards or roll the dice now and then."

"I don't doubt it." She eyed him with utter disdain. "It doesn't surprise me a bit to learn that Archie's friends are worse than he."

"If you mean me, ma'am, I'll not deny it. Archie is a saint compared to me."

"I'm quite inclined to believe you. But *your* sins, my lord, are not my concern. Nor do they lessen my misgivings about Archie's."

Geordie eyed her curiously. "Is that why ye jilted him? Because he gambles?"

"Not that alone. I think Archie is typical of all your set. You are all gamblers, lechers, and wastrels. Not one of you is capable of holding a serious thought in his head."

"Ye malign us, ma'am. We may not be able to translate the *Antigone*—"

"*Translate* it?" She gave a scornful laugh. "You can't even *read* it!"

Geordie felt a stab of revulsion. Who was this creature to decide she was superior to half the world? If there was anything the Scotsman could not abide it was a girl who gave herself airs. Why, it was entirely possible that Miss Caroline Woolcott was a bluestocking! "There's many a good man who canna read Greek," he pointed out mildly, trying not to show his disgust.

"And many a loose fish, too," she retorted.

"Ye might find, Miss Woolcott, that there's many a loose fish who *can* read Greek. I'd be careful of that sort, if I were ye."

She looked at him coldly. "I really don't think I need your advice on that head, my lord."

He ran his fingers through his curls in a gesture of defeat. "It seems I've been wastin' my time and yours, ma'am, if readin' Sophocles is what ye require in a husband."

"Fortunately, I do not need your approval of my requirements." She gestured imperiously toward the door. "Good evening, Lord Dunvegan."

He shrugged and took the two strides necessary to bring him to the doorway. But there he paused and looked back at her. "I wish ye luck in findin' a suitor good enough for ye, Miss Woolcott," he said with a brusque little bow, "though I dinna ken one man in all London who'd fill the bill. Good evenin', ma'am."

Back at Geordie's house on Henrietta Street, Archie was anxiously awaiting his return. Geordie found him pacing the marble floor of the entryway. Before the Scotsman could take off his hat, Archie ran to him and grasped the lapels of his coat. "Well? What did she say?" he asked eagerly. "Will she reconsider?"

Geordie loosed himself from Archie's grasp, tossed his hat aside, and fixed his friend with a glare. "Yer Miss Woolcott winna ever reconsider anything," he declared. "She's the most thrawn—perverse—female I've ever met. I dinna see why ye offered for the lass. Did ye never notice how she puts on airs? She's a sharp-tongued, sour, obstinate, flicherin' bluestocking, that's what she is!"

Archie's shoulders sagged. "Then I suppose I must assume your mission was not a success."

"A success? It was a damnable soor mishanter!"

"That, I take it, means a disaster?" Archie asked miserably.

"A *complete* disaster. But ye needna look so dour, Archie, laddie. If ye ask me, y're well rid of her."

❊ 3 ❊

DESPITE ALL OF Geordie's efforts to cheer him, Archie remained shrouded in gloom for almost a fortnight. He wallowed in his despair. He kept to his rooms, refusing to go out no matter what amusements Geordie or his other friends devised to distract him, and he fell into bed at night full of brandy and self-pity. "I will never," he moaned daily, "find another girl like Caroline. I will never, never fall in love again."

Geordie scoffed at him. "Hasna anyone told ye that never is a long term? Ye'll love again, laddie, as sure as the sun will rise in the morn."

But Archie was quick to point out that the sun did not rise in the morn. Every day of the thirteen that had passed since that infamous mid-November evening when Caroline had returned his ring had been cold, grey, and miserable. It began to seem that even the weather was conspiring against the hapless lad.

But, amazingly, December began with a burst of sunshine. As soon as Geordie saw the brightness of the sky, he took himself to Archie's rooms and hauled the fellow out of bed. "On your feet, Archie, lad," he ordered. "Ye need a thocht o' sunshine to drive the gloom from yer spirit."

The Scotsman had already selected a destination: Covent Garden. He had often found the square a delightful, cheerful place in which to stroll. Although at night the place was the haunt of drunkards and prostitutes, in the daytime, even in December, it was a colorful amalgam of homely delights. On this particular day, the sunshine had drawn out a good number of vendors and farmers selling whatever wares they could still amass. The flower stalls were piled high with holly, evergreen boughs, and mistletoe for Christmas decorations. The vegetable stalls were loaded with late-growing cabbages, radishes, leeks, turnips, and carrots. There were apple sellers in abundance. Bakers carried baskets and trays on their heads containing all sorts of pies and pasties. Booksellers filled their stalls with periodicals of all sorts. And circulating among them were strollers and shoppers ranging from tiny babes to old crones, from ladies and gentlemen of wealth and station to thieves and doxies. The brisk air rang with shouts, laughter, and the music of a hurdy-gurdy. It was just the place, Geordie believed, to shake Archie out of his lethargy, if only for the afternoon.

They were traversing the square toward a baker's stall, drawn by the tantalizing aroma of hot buns, when a large-bosomed, matronly woman, crossing in the opposite direction, stopped, stared at the Scotsman, cried out his name, and threw her arms about his neck. "Geordie, *dearest boy*," she cried, "what a lucky chance! I have *this very morning* sent a note round to you."

"Aunt Maud!" Geordie said in red-faced surprise.

Before he could disentangle himself from this unexpected embrace, a young lady tapped the matron's arm. "Mama, you are embarrassing my cousin," she whispered.

Geordie blinked at the golden-haired girl who'd just emerged

from behind her mother. "Is it ye, Bella?" he asked, for he had
not seen his cousin for several years. She had become, in the
intervening years, a very pretty lass, with apple cheeks, a
glowing complexion, lips that formed a bow over an appealing
over-bite, huge eyes, and a shape that was nothing if not sonsy.
Geordie beamed at her. " 'Tis a leesome lass ye've grown to be!"

"There, you see, Bella?" Aunt Maud said triumphantly to her
daughter. "He's not a bit embarrassed."

"No, of course I'm not," Geordie assured them, kissing his
aunt's hand and giving his cousin a brotherly embrace. "But
what are ye doin' in London? I thought ye were fixed in
Lancashire."

"We've only come to town for a short stay," his aunt said. She
then launched into a lengthy explanation of the purpose of their
trip, a purpose that could have been expressed in one word:
shopping.

While she droned on, Archie ogled Cousin Bella with open-
mouthed admiration. Then he tugged at Geordie's arm to remind
him he was there.

"Oh, sorry," Geordie muttered, and drew his friend forward.
"Aunt Maud, Bella, this is my friend, Sir Archibald Halford.
Archie, may I present Lady Teale and her daughter, Miss
Isabella Teale?"

"How do you do?" Archie murmured as he bowed over the
older woman's hand, while unable to take his eyes from the
younger.

Lady Teale did not miss the look in Archie's eyes. Nor did it
escape her that her daughter's cheeks turned a pretty pink.
"Geordie, my boy," she said loudly, "come take my arm. I must
speak to you. Meanwhile, Bella, dearest, do go and buy me
some apples. I have a positive yearning for them. I'm sure Sir
Archibald will not object to escorting you."

Geordie watched in some amusement as Archie tripped over
his feet in his eagerness to do Lady Teale's bidding. Then he
turned his attention to his aunt. "I say, Aunt, was that a whiddle,
or do ye sairly have something to say to me?"

Lady Teale drew herself up in mock offense. "Watch your
tongue, Geordie McAusland! I do not 'whiddle.' Of course I
have something to say to you. But first, tell me about your
friend. Who is his family? I wonder if they're connected to the

Dorset Halfords, who, I hear, are very well to pass. Well, speak up, boy! Are his connections people of . . . of substance?"

Geordie threw his aunt a look of glinting amusement. "I believe they are, ma'am. But aren't ye being a thocht aforehanded? Yer Bella hasna had a chance to say ten words to the laddie."

"Don't wag your Scottish tongue at me, boy," his aunt retorted, turning to look after the pair. "I know what I'm doing. It's best to be 'aforehanded' in these matters. But if his family is good, then you may bring young Halford with you when you come to me in Lancashire for Christmas."

Geordie stiffened. "Wheesht, Aunt Maud, I'm nae goin' to ye in Lancashire. I'm goin' home to Kincardine, to spend Christmas with my father."

"But that's just what I wrote about in the note I sent you this morning. Your father has given you permission to spend the holidays with us at Teale Court. It's all arranged."

"Arranged?" Geordie felt as if someone had landed him a severe blow to his midsection. "Ye and Father arranged for me to go to Lancashire instead of Scotland? Have I nothin' to say to this?"

"But, Geordie, dear boy, don't you *want* to visit us in Lancashire?" his aunt asked, her face falling.

"Dash it all, Aunt Maud, I've nae been home in six years! I've been lookin' forward to it more than I can tell ye. I've actually been countin' the days."

His aunt peered at him in surprise. "You can't mean it. What amusement can you find at home, in your father's gloomy Scottish castle amid all that fog and those murky moors?"

"There's amusement there enough for me."

Her ladyship frowned. "Really, boy, you're more difficult than your father. It's amazing how like you are to him. Oh, dear, how this does bring back memories! I remember how I warned my sister, when she ran off to wed her precious 'Laird of Dunvegan' thirty years ago, that she'd find the Scots to be a stubborn lot. 'We English,' I said to her, 'are a reasonable people, but not the Scots. The Scots,' I said, 'are intractable.' But off she went to Kincardine anyway." The memory of her dear, departed sister made Aunt Maud's eyes water. She pulled out a handkerchief from her bosom and sniffed into it before adding in a tremulous voice, "But your mother, bless yer, would never say a word against your father—or Scotland—till the day she died."

"Ay, my dear Aunt, you were right about the Scots," Geordie said, not permitting himself to be swayed by her memories or her tears. "We *are* a stubborn lot. Dead thrawn, as we say at home. So I hope ye'll not take it amiss when I tell ye that I winna be goin' to ye in Lancashire. I'm for home."

"Now, Geordie, there's no need for *you* to be intractable. You *are* half English, you know. And even your Scottish father has agreed that you should come to me. After all, it's only for the holidays. A mere fortnight. What objection can you have to postponing your trip home for a mere fortnight, especially since I need you so badly?"

Geordie was beginning to feel like a trapped rabbit. "Need me, ma'am?"

"Urgently. You see, Bella has invited some of her school friends to spend the holidays with us, and I can't possibly entertain young females without having a man or two about the house for them to flirt with."

"Dash it, Aunt Maud, is *that* yer urgent need? To have me provide entertainment for a clutch o' maggoty females? And are ye askin' me to believe that my father was willin' to put off my return for such a reason as that?"

"Of course you must believe it. Read his letter, if you won't take my word." She rummaged through her reticule, and pulled out the crushed and folded document. "Here. You'll find all you need right there on the very first page."

Geordie scanned the missive scrawled in his father's unmistakable, barely legible handwriting, his disbelief gradually weakening as his disappointment strengthened. His father had agreed with his sister-in-law that Geordie deserved a holiday in the company of lively young people rather than in the lonely dullness of Scotland. He also agreed that after waiting six years for the boy's return, he could certainly wait another fortnight. Geordie began to see defeat looming up ahead of him. His father wanted him to go to Teale Court, that much was clear.

But it was the second page that really raised his ire. *But I count on you, Maud,* his father had written, *to do for the boy what you did for me thirty years ago—find him a proper English lass to wed.*

"So *that's* the real reason for all this," Geordie growled, waving the paper in front of his aunt's nose accusingly. "You want to play matchmaker for me!"

"You weren't supposed to read that part," she said, snatching the letter from his hand.

"Meddlesome gowks, the pair of ye!" Geordie muttered.

To his surprise, his aunt burst into tears. "You're breaking my heart, Geordie McAusland, just b-breaking my old heart! S-six years you've b-been in England and not once have you come to s-scc me at Teale Court. Often and often I've b-begged you to visit, but have I ever c-complained at being so s-sadly neglected? No! Not once have I thrown it up to you! But this time I really counted on you. And now, with my heart s-so s-set on it, you're letting me d-down!" And she pulled out her handkerchief again and blubbered into it.

Geordie winced. "Aunt Maud, I dinna mean—" Awkwardly, he put an arm about her and patted her shoulder guiltily. "Wheesht, lass, dinna weep! I'll do as ye ask. If ye and my father insist, I'll come to ye at Christmas." He groaned inwardly at his weak-kneed capitulation to his aunt's tears, but if his father could be patient a while longer, he supposed he could too.

"Oh, Geordie, dearest," his aunt sighed, beaming at him through her wet lashes, "I'm so glad!"

But he would not take defeat without a last show of rebellion. "I'll come to ye, Aunt Maud, and flichter aboot wi' yer glaikit little visitors, but if ye think I'll have a buttertoothed English miss shoved down my throat, ye're out in yer reckoning. Do ye hear me, Aunt Maud? Matchmakin' I won't have!"

Aunt Maud, having won the first skirmish, cheerily waved off the rest. "So long as you come, Geordie, my love," she said, "we'll let fate take care of everything else." Then she kissed his cheek and turned to go and find her daughter. "I shall expect you on Friday week," she called back to him. "And don't forget to bring your friend."

Geordie did not expect Archie to accept the invitation to Lancashire without a struggle, but not only did Archie accept—he was overjoyed. "Nothing I'd like better than to spend Christmas at Teale Court," he chortled. "Why are you surprised? I have nothing to keep me here in town. Besides, your cousin Bella is a charmer. The girl has the most beautiful eyes. And her mouth . . . well, her mouth is like—"

"I know. Cherries." Geordie looked at his friend in disgust. "Archie, ye great gowk, can it be that ye've gone and fallen in love again?"

Archie considered the question for a long moment. "Y'know, old fellow, I do believe I have. Do you think, Geordie, that it means I'm flighty?"

❈ 4 ❈

GEORDIE PUT OFF the trip to Teale Court as long as he could, but by the end of the third week of December he could postpone it no longer. He and Archie packed their portmanteaux, piled them up on top of the Halfords' barouche (which Archie claimed to be more suited to long trips than Geordie's lighter phaeton), and set out.

The ride to Lancashire was endless, the barouche draughty, and Archie annoyingly cheery. It seemed to Geordie that he'd never suffered a more depressing trip. It was only when he reminded himself that every mile was bringing him closer to Scotland that his spirits began to lift. Lancashire, after all, was on the way north. Almost exactly halfway between London and Kincardine. If matters became unbearable at Teale Court, he'd simply steal out, rent a carriage, and drive himself home. The thought was soothing, and he was able to face the prospect of the next week with a lighter heart. After all, the possibility of escape is ever the consolation of the prisoner.

As they traversed the southern part of Lancashire, Geordie was surprised to note how the landscape—a stretch of moor covered with heather—resembled Scotland. But as they trundled further north, the view unexpectedly became less and less northern. The moors gave way to low wooded hills, charmingly picturesque, and to gentle valleys covered with neat fields edged by rows of trees and crisscrossed by bubbling little rivulets. In the midst of this English charm sat Teale Court, a solemn-looking manor house of limestone built in the seventeenth century. It was set on a slight rise and made a commanding presence in the landscape, with its impressive facade flanked by the two extended wings, which formed the court that gave the house its name. Archie gaped at the facade's double stairways that went off in opposite directions only to meet again at the doorway on top. "Look, Geordie, the stairs are just like ours at Halford Grange!" he said in tones of awe, as if the similarity of facade of the two houses had some sort of mystical significance.

Aunt Maud and Cousin Bella were waiting for them at the top of the steps. Aunt Maud enveloped her nephew in an enthusiastic embrace, while Cousin Bella, blushing shyly, offered Archie a trembling hand in greeting. Then the new arrivals, without being permitted to take the time to change from their travel dress, were borne off to the sitting room where several of the other guests sat taking tea. The two gentlemen were promptly introduced to the assemblage, a group that seemed to Geordie at first glance to be a rather colorless lot. It consisted of one elderly couple—Lord and Lady Powell, his aunt's dearest friends—and several young friends of his cousin Bella, none of whom was above twenty-five years of age. Aunt Maud introduced her young guests one by one. There was, first, a Miss Emmaline Dawlish—a young lady severely gowned in brown-and-rust striped muslin, with a horsey face and a deep, rumbling laugh. Beside her was her brother Douglas Dawlish, a serious young man with an already-receding hairline and a look of penetrating intellect. Next came Lady Jane Grevemont—a willowy, slender, delicate girl wearing a pale blue silk gown and a wan smile.

"The only one who seems to be missing," Maud said, concluding her round of introductions, "is Caro."

"Here I am," came a voice behind her, and all eyes turned toward a diminutive figure in the doorway. It was a young woman with a pair of brilliant brown eyes, glowing hair that curled round her face in an auburn cloud, and a lithe figure whose slim charm was emphasized by a clinging gown of rose-colored lustring. Geordie blinked at her in admiration, for in that lackluster company her luminous appearance lit up the room. But Archie, gasping audibly, threw his friend a glance of utter dismay. It took Geordie another moment before he realized that the girl in the doorway was Archie's erstwhile intended, the shrewish Caroline Woolcott.

"Ah, Caro, my love," Aunt Maud said in fond greeting, taking the girl by the arm and drawing her into the room, "you're just in time to meet my nephew and his friend. This is Lord Dunvegan, whom everyone calls Geordie. And this is—"

"I know the gentleman quite well, Lady Teale," Caroline said with perfect composure. "Archie Halford and I were once betrothed."

Aunt Maud's whole body tensed. "B-betrothed?" she gasped, horrified.

Bella's breath seemed to leave her body in a whoosh. "*Betrothed?*" she echoed in a whisper.

Lady Teale looked from her daughter to Archie in distraction. Poor Archie was red with embarrassment. Everyone else in the room was watching the scene in silent fascination. Maud, aware of the tension in the situation, knew she had to do something but had no idea how to proceed. She turned back to Caroline. "Oh, dear," she mumbled helplessly, "How very . . . awkward . . ."

"Not at all," Caroline assured her with a smile. "Please don't be afraid that Archie and I are in the least discomposed. Our short relationship ended without bitterness and is quite in the past. I see no reason for us to be awkward with each other; do you, Archie?"

Archie expelled a breath of relief. "No, not if you don't," he said, his brow clearing. He took her hand and bowed over it. "How good to see you, Caroline."

Lady Teale peered dubiously at the two of them for a moment, but promptly became convinced of Caroline's sincerity, for the girl truly seemed unperturbed by Sir Archibald's presence. Maud, like Archie, sighed in relief. "Then come, both of you," she said, putting an arm about the waist of each of the no-longer-betrotheds (while casting an it's-going-to-be-all-right look at her daughter over her shoulder) and leading them to the tea table. "Let's forget about it and all have some tea."

For Geordie, the tea party proved to be a very revealing gathering. It gave him a hint of the romantic undercurrents that would play themselves out during this holiday. The scholarly-looking Mr. Dawlish, for instance, immediately sat himself down beside Caroline and engaged her in deep conversation, making it clear to Geordie that the fellow intended to try to win for himself the girl that Archie had lost. Archie, however, gave no further thought to Caroline. He immediately sat down beside Bella, whose cheeks were still somewhat pale from shock, ready to use all his limited verbal powers to convince Bella that his former engagement to Caroline no longer had any significance for him. And, on the other side of the tea table, the horsey Miss Dawlish and the delicate Lady Jane Grevemont sat together, eyeing Geordie interestedly. Which one, the Scotsman wondered, did his aunt intend for him to pursue? Or was he supposed to flirt with both of them?

For the moment, however, he intended to flirt with neither one. If his aunt wanted him to flirt, he—if he were completely honest with himself—would have to admit that he'd prefer a flirtation with Caroline Woolcott to either of the others. But he didn't have to involve himself with any of them yet. There was time. Seven long days lay ahead of him.

With his teacup and saucer in hand, he stood apart, an observer rather than a participant. He watched Archie worming his way back into Bella's good graces. He watched Lady Powell trying to prevent her pot-bellied husband from overindulging in the iced cakes Aunt Maud had lavishly supplied. But mostly he watched Douglas Dawlish converse with Caroline. His eyes turned to them with annoying frequency. The subject of their conversation must have been serious, for their heads were close and their expressions earnest and unsmiling. Geordie wondered what it was that so engrossed them. Something scholarly, he had no doubt. Geordie himself would be perfectly capable of holding a scholarly discussion with her, he told himself, if she'd give him the chance. He gnashed his teeth, remembering how she'd assumed he hadn't read the *Antigone*. What did she think he did at Oxford, nothing but carouse?

Suddenly Douglas Dawlish rose from his seat to refill his cup. Geordie, almost without conscious intent, promptly strode across the room and took his place. The Scotsman was merely following an irresistible urge to speak to Caroline again. He took the vacated chair (much to Mr. Dawlish's chagrin), smiled down at the girl in a conciliatory manner, and said quietly, "That was very well done, Miss Woolcott."

She met his eye calmly. "What was well done, my lord?"

"The way ye dealt with the introductions. Ye rode over a difficult moment with great aplomb. Another lass might've asked Archie to remove himself from this gathering, which he, as a gentleman, would've had to do. Ye showed great forbearance."

"Did I indeed?" she responded coldly, lowering her eyes to her tea and stirring it vigorously.

He did not miss the coldness. "Are ye *indeedin'* me again, Miss Woolcott?" he teased, putting down his cup on a nearby table in order to enable himself to give full attention to charming her. "Does that mean ye still find me presumin'?"

"Very presuming," she said flatly.

"Indeed? In what way, ma'am?"

She looked up at him, scorn blazing from her eyes. "To offer me your approval is presumptuous enough. But what is worse, you evidently presume that because I showed forbearance toward Archie, I intend to show that same forbearance to you."

"Why should ye have to show *me* forbearance at all, ma'am? You and I were not betrothed."

"No, that would be so great an impossibility that it isn't worth speaking of. But you did insult me, my lord. In a most cavalier, cutting manner, and in my own home. Do you deny it?"

"Nae, lass, I winna deny it," he said, resolved to charm her out of her resentment of him. "I suppose what I said that night might be taken as an insult, but—"

"*Might* be taken as an insult? A satiric remark implying that I would not find a man in all of London I'd consider good enough for me can be taken as nothing else! Yet you apparently expect me to ignore it. Believe me, my lord, your high-handed attitude is no more pleasing to me now than it was when I saw you last. Therefore do not expect forbearance from me. I'm in no mood to forgive or forget."

Geordie, completely taken aback, ran his fingers through his wild red curls in a gesture of helplessness. "Wheesht, lassie," he said, resorting to his Lallans as he often did when stumped for words, "'tis a thrawn, grumly, capernoitie female ye are."

"To hide behind your Lallans tongue is both cowardly and unnecessary," the girl retorted calmly. "I don't have to understand those adjectives to know they are not complimentary."

"Not at all complimentary, ma'am," he admitted. "I said ye're perverse, ill-tempered, and irritable. Now ye've been truly insulted. So, like as no, ye'll now expect *me* to remove myself from this gathering, is that not so?"

"You flatter yourself, my lord. Your presence in this house is a matter of complete indifference to me. But if you think I take any pleasure in your company, you are mistaken. I think it would be better for the contentment of both of us if we do not, during the next few days, get in each other's way more than is necessary for good manners."

Geordie felt his fingers clench. It was amazing how this slip of a girl could infuriate him. He'd sat down beside her for the express purpose of performing an act of conciliation; he'd merely tried to compliment her. For this, she'd rewarded him with an icy put-down. She had an air of cold superiority that set his teeth on edge. Never had he met a female whom he'd taken in such dislike at first—and second—sight.

He rose to his feet, bowed a punctilious bow, and turned his back on her. If she wanted none of him, that was fine. He wanted none of her, either.

But he hadn't taken four steps before he was aware that Mr. Dawlish was quickly taking back his vacated seat. The fellow hadn't wasted a moment! He'd made for the chair the moment Geordie's back was turned. *What a deuced muckworm,* Geordie thought in inexplicable irritation. He disliked the fellow as much as he disliked Caroline.

But the thought was disturbing to the Scotsman. It was not like him. He rarely disliked people on first acquaintance. He'd always considered himself to be the good-natured sort who was willing to befriend a man on sight. Why was he now being so unfair to Dawlish? He despised the fellow, but there was no good reason for it. Dawlish had done nothing to deserve his disdain. He'd merely taken a seat beside the toplofty Miss Woolcott and was whispering into her ear.

Geordie, glancing at the pair of them with their heads together over their teacups, felt his fingers curl into fists and his teeth clench. He was aware that this was a strange reaction. Try as he would, he could find no explanation for it. But reasonable or not, he had an overwhelming urge to turn on the scholarly Dawlish, haul him to his feet, and land him a facer. What on earth was going on in this situation to make an easygoing, peaceful fellow like himself suddenly develop an urgent desire for an ugly, bloody brawl?

❀ 5 ❀

GEORDIE CAME DOWN to dinner early, in consideration of his aunt. He knew that pre-dinner gatherings were always easier for the hostess if a few of the gentlemen were at hand to greet the ladies as they made their entrance. On this occasion, however, the Scotsman seemed to be the most considerate gentleman in the house, for, apparently, no one else had yet come down. From the threshold, the large drawing-room looked deserted.

But as soon as he stepped over the threshold he saw his aunt. Maud was standing before the drawing room fire, staring thoughtfully into the flames. She turned quickly round at the sound of his footsteps, her face brightening. "How grand you look, dearest!" she greeted effusively. "Your London tailor has fitted your evening clothes to perfection. Do you realize, Geordie, that in those clothes, and with your curls brushed back so neatly, no one would take you for a Scot?"

"I dinna take that as a compliment, ma'am," Geordie retorted, only half in jest. "I like bein' a Scot. If ye persist in such compliments, I might take it into my head to wear my kilt to dinner."

"Oh, pish-tush. Your kilt, indeed. You'd not come to my table in that savage dress, and you know it."

"Aye, I would," he insisted, thickening his brogue to emphasize the Scottishness in him that she loved to disparage. "And as for my curls, ye ken, they winna be biddable for more than ten minutes. If it's my throughither curls that make me seem a Scotsman, then I shall look a Scot afore we go in to dine."

"Oh, dear, that's too true. Even as a child your hair was completely unruly. Those curls of yours do make you look like a wild creature sometimes. But never mind, you've a handsome enough face to compensate for it."

"I thank ye, Aunt, for I *think* there's a compliment lurkin' in there somewhere."

She laughed and poked him affectionately in his ribs. "Saucy jackanapes! But let's not waste time talking of kilts and curls. I

26

shan't have many opportunities like this to have a private chat with you, Geordie, so come and sit here beside me on the sofa. I have something important to ask of you."

"Ask away," he said, perching on the arm of the sofa.

She fiddled with the ruffle of her sleeve in hesitation before speaking. "Now, don't get up on your high ropes over what I'm about to ask," she began. "I have good reasons for asking. You see, I want you to pay particular attention to Miss Woolcott this week."

Geordie's eyebrows rose. "Miss *Woolcott*?"

Outside in the corridor, that lady herself had been about to make her entrance. She'd paused at the side of the door to pull up the shoulder of her modish, emerald-green jaconette evening gown (which she feared showed too much decolletage), when she heard her name. Realizing that her entrance at this moment would be interrupting a *tête-à-tête* (and might possibly be embarrassing to the speakers and to herself), she stepped back into the shadows and waited.

"Yes, of course it's Miss Woolcott I wish you to attend," Lady Maud was saying to Geordie at that moment. "Why do you sound so surprised? She is a charming girl, and so clever and beautiful—"

"Do you really think she's beautiful?" Geordie asked interestedly.

"Of course. Don't you?"

"Nae, not I. Her eyes may be braw, and she has a pretty mouth, but . . ."

"There are no buts about it," his aunt declared firmly. "She's the loveliest creature I've ever seen, except perhaps for your mother in her salad days. And I say that with full awareness that I'm placing her above my own adorable Bella. And your good friend, Sir Archibald, must have found her beautiful, or why would he have gotten himself betrothed to her? By the way, Bella tells me it was Caro who broke it off. I'm not sorry, for I don't think she and your friend were suited. But you, I think, would suit her very well."

"I? I'm the hin'most man in the world who'd suit her!"

But Maud paid him no heed. "She's all alone, you know," she rambled on. "Hasn't a soul in the world. Lost her dear mother when she was still in leading strings. She was brought up by her father, who was rather famous, they say, in scholarly circles. He almost made a bluestocking of the child, but he was wise enough to send her off to school, so she learned something of the ways of the world. I think she's turned out very well in the circumstances. She has brains and beauty and *savoir-faire* and, in addition, I believe she has an inheritance that will make a considerable dowry. What more, I ask you, can a man want? So, my dear one, you must make your best effort in that direction. I noticed that Douglas Dawlish is already smitten, so you mustn't let him steal a march on you."

"Dash it, Aunt Maud," Geordie growled, jumping to his feet and glaring down at her, "are ye playin' matchmaker after all? Dinna ye hear my warnin' on that subject?"

"I paid it no mind. None at all. You young people don't know what's good for you. You need a little guidance from an older, wiser head. Your father wants you to bring home a bride. And Caro Woolcott is prefect for you."

"Perfect?" The idea was so ludicrous that Geordie couldn't maintain his angry pose. He broke into a grin. "Ye've o'erslept on this one, Aunt Maud," he chortled. "Missed the boat entirely. Miss Woolcott and I are already acquainted, ye see. She finds me presumptuous and detestable, and I dislike her just as much."

"Dislike her? How can you possibly dislike her?" his aunt demanded.

"The girl puts on airs. If there's anythin' that drives me daft, it's a lass with airs."

Out in the corridor, Caroline Woolcott was seething with fury. Although she was familiar with the saying that eavesdroppers never hear good of themselves, it did not make what she'd overheard easier to bear. Shamed and humiliated, she was not comforted to realize that she shouldn't have eavesdropped in the first place. But a sound on the stairs stopped her ruminations and sent her scurrying across the hall to the library; it was bad enough to eavesdrop, but to be caught at it would be infinitely worse.

Meanwhile, back in the drawing room, Aunt Maud had risen from her seat in disgust. "Airs?" she snapped at her recalcitrant nephew. "I never heard anything so foolish! I've known Caro since she and Bella went off to school together, yet I've *never* seen the girl put on airs."

"For a' that, Aunt Maud," Geordie said with a careless shrug, "if ye're set on pairin' yer Caro and me, ye winna have any success. Nary a crumb. And as for the other specimens ye've collected here for the holiday, there's no hope for a pairin' there, either. I'm afraid yer efforts are doomed. Since I promised ye to help entertain them, I'll dance with the pallid one and ride with the horsey one. But as for Miss Woolcott, I won't even—"

But he was interrupted by the sound of voices in the hallway, and in another moment Bella, Lady Jane, and both the Dawlishes entered the drawing room, soon followed by Archie, Lord and Lady Powell, and a rather red-cheeked Caroline. Thus the *tête-à-tête* between aunt and nephew was, of necessity, concluded.

A determined Aunt Maud placed Geordie at the table with Emmaline Dawlish at his right and Caroline Woolcott at his left. On this first night with the full company present, the guests were all dressed in formal elegance. Caroline, in particular, was stylishly accoutered in a gown that was nothing if not dashing. Geordie could not help noticing that although the girl was not 'sonsy,' the skin of her shoulders and neck glowed enticingly in the candlelight. He noticed, too, that all the gentlemen at the table—even the elderly Lord Powell—eyed her with appreciation. Nevertheless, Geordie refused to admit to himself that she was beautiful. A voice in the back of his mind told him he was a liar, but all he would concede was that there was nothing of the schoolmarm in her appearance tonight.

Caroline, still fuming over what she'd illicitly overheard, completely ignored the Scotsman's presence at the table beside her. Except for giving him a curt nod in greeting at the outset and passing him a plate of steamed brussels sprouts during the second course, she never turned her head in his direction. She spent the entire meal exchanging lines of Greek poetry with Douglas Dawlish, forcing Geordie to confine his conversational banter to Miss Dawlish on his right. This he proceeded to do with good grace. After a while, however, he found the experience trying. Miss Dawlish, who insisted that he call her Emmaline, was not very talkative herself, but she had a tendency to laugh with donkey-like guffaws at the end of every one of Geordie's sentences, as if she was convinced that every remark he made—even a mild comment on the succulence of the lamb roast—was the epitome of wit.

Geordie made one attempt to talk to the standoffish Caroline. During a lull in her conversation with Dawlish, Geordie turned to her and asked pleasantly which of the Greek plays they were discussing. Douglas Dawlish answered for her. "None of them," he said with a prissy, superior smile. "We were speaking of the poetry of Anacreon."

"Who's Anacreon?" Archie asked from across the table, innocently wishing to join in what he believed was a bit of town gossip.

"We mustn't talk to these sporting fellows about the Greeks," Caroline said to Dawlish, throwing Archie a teasing smile. "They don't even know the *Antigone*."

Poor Archie reddened in embarrassment. "Didn't know you were talking about the Greeks," he mumbled.

Geordie seethed at their tone of superiority. "Dinna ye underestimate old Archie there," he said, hiding his irritation behind a broad smile. "He's forgotten that he did a translation of Anacreon at school. *The Grasshopper*, wasn't it, Archie?"

Archie threw him a look of gratitude. "Yes, I do believe it was," he said, going along with the bluff. Then he sat back and basked in Bella's look of admiration.

But Caroline fumed. She had not missed the byplay. That blasted Scotsman had interpreted her little, teasing remark as a jeer at Archie, which she hadn't at all intended. Why was it that the deuced Dunvegan always made her feel like a contemptuous, condescending prig? He had declared to his aunt that Caroline Woolcott was a "lass who put on airs," and now he was intent on proving it. Well, this Caroline Woolcott would like nothing better than to scratch his eyes out! Would he say *that* was putting on airs?

As for Geordie, he made no second attempt to converse with Caroline. She had proved once again that she was a toplofty prig, and he wanted no more to do with her. But after an hour of being in the exclusive company of the guffawing Emmaline, Geordie prayed for this endless dinner to come to a close. Only Bella, sitting opposite him, made the meal bearable by occasionally turning away from the eagerly chatting Archie to smile across the table at her cousin. Bella seemed to sense that Geordie was suffering, and her sympathetic smiles were a refreshing breeze in this desert of a dinner.

By the end of the second course, he'd given up trying to converse with Emmaline and was staring ahead of him, stupefied by boredom, when he saw Dawlish's hand reach over for a wine bottle. The scholarly fellow, deep in conversation with Caroline about the rhythmic quality of Sophocles's *stichomythia*, did not notice that Caroline's long-stemmed wineglass stood in his way. The back of his hand brushed against it, tipping its balance. Geordie caught hold of it before it toppled over, but not before a splash of red liquid spurted onto Caroline's bosom. Geordie righted the glass as everyone at the table gasped.

Poor Dawlish paled. "Miss Woolcott, what have I done?" he cried, picking up a serviette and making an awkward motion with it toward her chest.

Caroline stayed his hand, took the cloth from him, and dabbed at the spots. "It's nothing," she assured him calmly. "Only a few drops."

"But wine . . ." the fellow mumbled. "Doesn't it stain?"

"I'm certain it won't," she said.

"Bella," said Lady Teale to her daughter, "take Caro upstairs to Dorrie." Then she turned to Caroline with a reassuring smile. "My abigail, Dorrie, will know just what to do," she explained. "She'll have it clean in a trice."

"Thank you, Lady Teale," Caroline said, getting to her feet.

The gentlemen all rose as Caroline and Bella left the table. But before departing, Bella looked back at her cousin. "That was quick thinking, Geordie, my dear," she said with a proud smile. "If it weren't for you, Caro's beautiful dress might have been ruined."

Caroline paused in the doorway, struggling with herself. That deuced Scotsman's words to his aunt still rang in her ears. He'd insulted her in every way possible—from her appearance to her character—but she had to admit that the dastardly fellow *had* prevented an embarrassing catastrophe in keeping the wineglass from toppling over. She would appear churlish if she didn't offer him a word of thanks. Grudgingly, she swallowed her pride and forced herself to turn and face Geordie squarely. "Yes, Lord Dunvegan, Bella is quite right. I must . . . thank you."

Geordie grinned. He could hear the reluctance in her voice, and he sensed that somehow, in the unspoken battle between them, he had managed to win a round. He was not at all sure what the battle was about, but he *was* sure that this tiny victory felt good. " 'Twas nothin', ma'am," he said, the merest note of triumph in his voice. "Dinna gi'e it anither thought."

❊ 6 ❊

THE NEXT THREE days were enjoyable for almost everyone. Archie and Bella were happily discovering each other, inseparable except when the duties of the household kept her from his side. Douglas Dawlish, too, was eagerly pursing the yearnings of his heart, constantly following Caroline everywhere she went, sitting beside her at the pianoforte when she was asked to play, reading to her when she sat knitting, or chasing after her when she went for a stroll. As for Caroline herself, the Powells were convinced that she thoroughly enjoyed his attentions. And the two other young ladies of the party—Emmaline and Lady Jane—were also following their romantic inclinations; they continued to vie for Geordie's attention, each one pretending to wish the other the success that she wanted for herself. If the passage of the days was less fascinating for Geordie, no one else was aware of it.

On the whole, the days passed pleasantly. The weather was chilly but clear, enabling the party to ride on horseback over the gentle hills of the Teale estate or to take brisk walks through the extensive gardens. Geordie rode out with Emmaline each morning (Lady Jane being too delicate to sit a horse), and escorted Lady Jane (carefully swathed in voluminous shawls to protect herself against the wind) through the gardens in the afternoons, thus dividing his attentions equally between them. Lord Powell, with whom he played billiards in the late afternoon, liked to tease him about his even-handedness with the ladies.

"My wife and I are wagering on the matter," the cheerful old fellow confessed, laughing. "I've put ten guineas on the Dawlish girl, but Lucy claims she's too boyish and that you'll come to prefer the delicacy of Lady Jane and settle on her in the end."

"Yer wastin' yer time if not yer brass, Powell," Geordie retorted. " 'Tis not a winnable wager. I'll not settle on either one. I'm only playin' the gallant to please my aunt."

On the morning of the fourth day of Geordie's stay at Teale Court, the household woke to find that the air had turned icy cold, the sky was overcast, and the world was covered with a thin blanket of snow. The scene was lovely to the eye, but the cold prevented the assemblage from indulging in any outside activity. The gentlemen were disappointed, but the ladies were not perturbed. They gathered in the downstairs sitting room after breakfast, intent on making the Christmas decorations. Brimming with good cheer, they seated themselves round a large table and, abundantly supplied with greens and string, began to fashion ivy into festoons, holly sprays into wreaths, and evergreen branches into kissing boughs. (Only Lady Powell and Emmaline were set to making the kissing boughs, for they were the most adept at weaving the evergreen boughs into proper basket shapes—baskets that would later be filled with apples, tasseled with mistletoe, and hung in all the doorways.) The gentlemen, feeling themselves above participating in such trivial chores, wandered about the house complaining that they had nothing to do.

The ladies, however, freed from the constraining presence of the men, giggled and gossiped to their hearts' content. Lady Powell soon turned the conversation to the romances that she believed were blossoming beneath her very nose.

"What a very delightful grouping your mother has arranged for you and your friends, Bella," she exclaimed as she twisted an evergreen bough round itself to shape a basket. "She's provided a trio of delightful suitors for you all to flirt with."

"Suitors, your ladyship?" Bella countered shyly. "I shouldn't call them suitors. Just companions."

"Companions, indeed," Lady Powell scoffed. "You, Bella, should be the last one to call them that, when it's perfectly obvious that Sir Archibald is on the verge of offering for you."

"Goodness, Bella, is that true?" squealed her friend Jane. "Why haven't you *told* us?"

"But it's not . . . I mean he hasn't . . . That is, there's nothing—" poor red-faced Bella stammered.

"It's much too soon for such speculation," Maud said calmly, reaching for a branch of ivy. "They've only just met."

"Yes, but the signs are clear," Lady Powell insisted. "Just as they are clear for Caroline."

"For me?" Caroline asked, her eyebrows lifting. "Whatever do you mean, Lady Powell?"

"She means my brother," Emmaline said with a shrug.

"Of course that's whom I mean," Lady Powell agreed. "His intentions are obvious to all of us."

Caroline blinked at her. "But that can't be so. He's never indicated any such intentions to me."

"Come now, Caro," Lucy Powell insisted, "you can't pretend to be surprised. Not when the fellow's been chasing after you like a besotted puppy from the moment he arrived."

"We may have spent some time in each other's company, Your Ladyship," Caroline said in sincere denial, her eyes troubled, "but that's only because we have such a strong affection for Greek drama in common."

"I've heard of happy marriages with less in common than that," Lady Powell said coyly.

"*Marriages!*" Caroline gasped. "I assure you, Lady Powell, that marriage is the furthest thing from our minds. Truly! It's quite beyond the intention of either Mr. Dawlish or me."

Emmaline Dawlish gave her braying laugh. "You sound just like Jane, Caro. She also likes to deny that *her* suitor, Lord Dunvegan, has intentions toward her."

"*My* suitor?" Jane squealed again on an even higher register, color flooding her pale cheeks. "Geordie is *your* suitor, and you know it."

"Featherhead!" Emmaline said, patting Jane's hand fondly. "Hasn't the fellow taken you round the gardens every afternoon since he arrived?"

"Hasn't he ridden out with *you* every single morning?" Jane turned a pair of pleading eyes to Caroline. "You tell her, Caro. You, of all our friends, are the most perceptive. Tell her which of us you think Geordie is pursuing."

"I can't answer that, Jane," Caroline replied, her eyes fixed on the sprig of mistletoe she was affixing to the bottom of a basket. "I take no notice of the activities and intentions of Lord Dunvegan. His doings are of no interest to me."

Maud, at the opposite end of the table, leaned over to her friend Lucy Powell and laughingly whispered, "I think the lady doth protest too much."

Lady Powell blinked at her friend in disbelief. "Are you suggesting that Caro has an eye for your Geordie? That, my dear, is nothing but wishful thinking. I'm convinced she cares only for Dawlish."

But Maud shook her head. "I think you're out there, Lucy," she said with quiet self-assurance. "I've noticed that Caro shows interest in Douglas Dawlish only when Geordie is present to observe it. When Geordie is not there, Dawlish seems to bore her to death. Watch them next time, and see if I'm not right."

"Makes no difference if you are," Lady Powell argued in as firm a voice as whispering permitted. "Geordie is going to offer for Lady Jane, if he offers for anyone. I've wagered ten guineas on it."

Maud did not respond. Only the knowing smile that hovered on her lips for the rest of the morning told Lady Powell that her friend was not at all convinced.

Since the snow continued to fall all through luncheon, the entire party, gentlemen included, spent the afternoon attending to the decorations. The women continued to weave and braid, while the men set to the hanging. They tacked the festoons over the windows, hung wreaths over the fireplaces, and nailed baskets over the doorways. Amid much laughter and the shouting of orders and suggestions, the house rapidly took on a festive look.

Suddenly, above the merry din, came a pained scream. It issued from the throat of the delicate Lady Jane, who'd pricked a finger on the sharp spur of a holly leaf and discovered . . . *blood!* "Good heavens, I'm bleeding!" she cried, turning white.

Bella and Caro exchanged amused glances, for they were quite familiar with Jane's tendency to hysteria from their school days. So was Emmaline, who had no patience for her friend's histrionics. "Heavens, Jane, must you carry on?" she hissed. "It's only a little pinprick."

But Jane stared in horror at the bit of blood, now swelling into a huge drop. "I think I shall . . . swoon," she gasped.

"Don't you dare," Emmaline ordered. "You know you only do it to get attention."

The gentlemen came running in from various parts of the house, Lord Powell and Archie from the drawing room where they'd been hanging a festoon between the two windows on the west wall, Dawlish from the library where he'd been decorating the mantel of the fireplace, and Geordie from the dining room where he'd been nailing a kissing bough on the lintel of the room's high doorway. "What on earth's amiss?" Lord Powell asked.

"Poor Jane has hurt her finger," Maud said with the show of sympathy that was proper in a good hostess. "I think she's feeling faint."

"Yes," Jane said in a weak whine. "I ought to lie down."

"I'll take you up," the good-natured Bella volunteered.

"Oh, rubbish!" Emmaline swore. "She doesn't need to lie down."

"A little rest won't do her any harm," Bella said, patting her fragile friend's shoulder.

"Then let one of the gentlemen escort her," Lady Powell suggested with a matchmaking gleam. "Lord Dunvegan can do it. You'd like Geordie's escort, wouldn't you, Jane dear?"

But Jane was too upset even to redden. She accepted Geordie's arm, and with her head drooping against his shoulder, let him lead her from the room.

Maud, after watching the pair go slowly out the door, threw her friend Lady Powell a look of amused disdain. "Much good that little ploy will do you, Lucy," she said *sotto voce*. "A girl so lacking in spirit will never catch my nephew. You can kiss your ten guineas goodbye."

The wounded girl's progress up the stairs was so slow that it took fully a quarter of an hour before Geordie could return to his task at the dining room doorway. But when he got there, he found that Caroline had taken his place. She was standing on a stepstool, attempting to nail the kissing bough to the lintel above her head, but she was having extreme difficulty. Even when standing on her toes on the very top of the three-step stool, she couldn't reach the lintel. If she extended her arm to its utmost, the head of the hammer just touched the overhead beam. Geordie watched her struggle for a moment before making his presence known. "'Tis a wee lass ye are, Miss Woolcott," he said at last. "Here, come down and let me do it."

"I'm quite capable of doing it myself," Caroline muttered, wielding the hammer in a firm, upward swing that resulted in her banging her index finger painfully.

Geordie pretended not to notice her wince of pain. "I ken ye can hammer a nail," he said, "but since the stepstool isna adequate for a lady yer size, it'd be an easier task for me. Dinna be so thrawn this once, lassie. Come down."

Caroline glared down at him, ready to do battle. "If I remember our last conversation rightly, my lord, thrawn means perverse. I don't care to be called thrawn, nor do I like the epithet lassie. You can take your insults and . . . and go away!"

He did not move but continued to look up at her with what she interpreted as a leer. Despite the stinging pain of her finger, she made up her mind to show him that he was no better than she at any task. Once more she lifted the basket, once more she pushed the nail through the handle, and once more she swung the hammer with all her might. There was a very satisfactory thwack as hammerhead met nailhead, with no finger between them to blunt the contact. Gingerly she took her hand from the basket. To her delight, the kissing bough hung there quite securely.

Still poised on the top of the stepladder, she smiled down at Geordie triumphantly. "There, my lord, I've done it," she announced proudly. "Now, if you'd be so obliging as to step aside, I'll climb down."

"Nay, lass, I winna step aside. It wouldna be gentlemanly. Here, let me help ye down."

Without waiting for a reply, he boldly took hold of her waist and lifted her from the top of the stepstool. The act was so sudden it caused her to drop the hammer, which fell to the floor with a loud clump. Geordie ignored it, for he was utterly absorbed in the task at hand. The girl he was holding in the air, his two hands almost completely encompassing her waist, was feather-light, and her face, staring down at him in surprise, was—he had to admit it—breathtakingly lovely.

"My lord," she said somewhat breathlessly, "this is not necessary. I can climb down three steps. Please put me down."

But he didn't put her down. Something came over him—a whim that was not at all gentlemanly but that he found irresistible. He was not going to set her down until he was good and ready. He held her up in the air, his prisoner. " 'Tis a wee dautie ye are," he said, grinning up at her. "Light as a bubble."

Caroline was not amused. She didn't know what the word *dautie* meant, but she was sure it was another insult. And she didn't like being held up in the air like a plaything. "Confound it, your lordship," she snapped angrily, "put me down!"

"Aye, Miss Woolcott, I will. Soon as ye call me Geordie. I

dinna take kindly to yer *my lords*. They're as bad as yer *indeeds.*"

"Damnation, Lord Dunvegan, I won't be bullied! Put me down, I say!"

"Michty me, such a curfuffle owre naught!" he laughed. " 'Tis a stubborn lass ye are, to be sure."

"Is it stubborn to hold to a bargain? I thought we had agreed to keep a distance between us?"

"*You* agreed. I was no party to it." He lowered her to his chest and peered directly into her gold-flecked eyes. "Wheesht, my dear, is it so hard to call me by my given name?"

"Yes," she said stubbornly, trying not to notice that she could feel his heart beating—and hers, too. "To address each other by given names is too . . . too intimate for us."

"Intimate, is it?" Slowly he set her down, but he kept one arm tight about her waist, holding her pinioned to him. Everything she said infuriated him, but he didn't want to let her go. He felt like a small boy on a rampage of mischief that had become so uncontrollable that only crashing into a wall would stop him. "That is not my understanding of the word intimate," he teased, hurtling on down his mischievous path by pulling her closer. "*This* is intimate." And, with malicious zest, he kissed her on her cherry-red mouth.

Caroline was startled into momentary inaction. She had been kissed before, but never with such fervor. The sensation it produced was surprisingly pleasant, and before her brain reminded her that the man holding her so tightly in his arms was the obnoxious Lord Dunvegan, she quite enjoyed the taste of his lips and the feeling that the blood in her veins had turned to bubbling champagne. But then she remembered. This was the man who'd told his aunt that she was not beautiful, that she was full of toplofty airs, and that he disliked her intensely. Remembering, she wrenched herself free. "*Lord Dunvegan,*" she exclaimed in breathless fury, "just *what* do you think you're *doing*?"

Geordie, who'd kissed a fair number of lasses in his time, was not as discomposed as she. Dizzy and dazzled he might be, but not discomposed. "Dinna ye remember?" he taunted brazenly. "I was explaining the word intimate."

"That was *not* intimate. That was . . . *licentious*!"

"Nay, lass, I canna agree. Here we are under the mistletoe.

For me to kiss ye under the mistletoe is a legitimate Christmas tradition."

"In the first place, your lordship, the tradition does not go into effect until Christmas Eve. In the second place, even at Christmas such a kiss would be considered licentious. And in the third place, Lord Dunvegan, you are a boorish, shameless *libertine*, and if you *ever*—Christmas or not—manhandle me in such a manner again, I shall give you another."

"Another, ma'am?"

"Another of these!" Without a moment of hesitation, she raised her hand and slapped him very smartly across his cheek. Then she turned on her heel and stalked off down the hall, leaving him holding his burning cheek, utterly abashed. The rampaging mischiefmaker had run into the wall at last.

❄ 7 ❄

CAROLINE HAD NEVER considered herself a tempestuous sort. Even at school the girls used to tease her about the difference in character between her and her namesake, the wild Caro Lamb. She had always thought of herself as serious and studious, calm in times of crisis, and soft-spoken but firm. That had been her self-image, but the image was rapidly disintegrating because of these encounters with the dastardly Lord Dunvegan. He invariably left her with her emotions in turmoil. He was making her wild!

The kiss he'd so brazenly stolen in the doorway was the last straw! She seethed at the memory of it. The broiling fury inside her was so unsettling that, on passing Lady Teale in the hallway, she behaved with unwonted rudeness. It was behavior utterly unlike her. She hardly recognized herself.

The incident with Lady Teale occurred shortly after she'd slapped the Scotsman on his cheek. With the palm of her hand still burning, she was hurrying down the second-floor corridor to her bedroom when she encountered her hostess strolling in the opposite direction. Lady Teale stopped, smiled, and asked in perfect innocence, "I say, Caro, have you seen Geordie? I've been seeking him for the past quarter-hour."

"Yes, I've seen him," Caroline snapped, "much to my regret."

"Regret?" Lady Teale raised her brows in surprise. "What do you mean?"

"I mean, Lady Teale, that every time I see your deuced nephew, he says or does something rude."

"Geordie? *My* Geordie?" Maud's face fell. "You can't mean it, Caro. What can he possibly have done? I'm sure, whatever it is, it can be explained. It must be some sort of small misunderstanding. My nephew is the dearest creature in the world."

"Your nephew, ma'am, is a rackety make-bait!" Caroline burst out. And then, worse yet, she turned away, lifted her skirts, and ran off down the hall without so much as a word of explanation to the astonished Lady Teale.

It was inexcusable behavior. She had acted in a manner utterly unlike herself. The more she thought about it, the more she realized she deserved a good scolding. She would certainly have to take herself in hand.

Later that afternoon, after having thrown herself upon her bed and indulged in a healthy bout of tears, she grew somewhat calmer. She would simply dismiss Geordie McAusland and his insulting behavior from her mind. To dwell on the matter would simply heighten the importance of a rude but not significant incident. And as for her own behavior, she was well on the way back to her usual self-control. All she needed to do, she realized, was to make amends for her own rudeness. She would have to face Lady Teale and apologize.

Since it was already growing dark outside, Caroline surmised that the ladies would all be dressing for dinner by this time. It was a good hour for her mission. She went down the hall to Lady Teale's bedroom and knocked on the door.

"Come in," Lady Teale called from within.

But Caroline, pausing on the threshold, discovered that Lady Teale was not alone. Lady Powell, with two gowns spread over her lap, was perched on Lady Teale's bed. Lady Teale herself was seated at her dressing table, dressing her own hair. "Do come in, Caro," she urged, waving her hairbrush in Caroline's direction.

Caroline hesitated. "Oh, no. I . . . I didn't mean to interrupt," she stammered. "I'll come back later."

"Don't mind me," Lady Powell said, also beckoning her in. "You aren't interrupting. I was just asking Maud if I should wear my green sarsenet tonight or save it for Christmas Eve. We are quite done making these momentous decisions. If you wish to be private with Maud, I shall go at once."

"I don't need to be private, your ladyship," Caroline said, stepping in and closing the door behind her. "I only want to tell Lady Teale that I'm sorry I was so abrupt when she encountered me in the corridor this afternoon."

"I quite understand, my dear," Maud said kindly. "You were upset. You said that Geordie had been rude to you."

"Yes, but he is always rude. I should not have let myself become discomposed."

"Geordie rude?" Lady Powell asked in surprise. "How strange. I should not have thought it of him. I quite like the boy, myself. And Lord Powell was remarking just last night how fond he's grown of the lad. He says that the hour they spend playing billiards together has become his favorite time of the day."

"Aside from the time he spends with his wife, of course," Maud teased.

"Of course," Lucy Powell admitted, laughing.

But Caroline did not smile. "I didn't mean to imply that Lord Dunvegan is rude to everyone," she said tightly. "I admit that he can be quite charming to the world at large. It's only *I* who's been singled out as target for his rudeness."

"In what way is he rude to you, Caro dear?" Maud asked, putting down her hairbrush and turning toward Caroline with concern. "His Scottish ways are different from ours, you know. Perhaps he doesn't realize—"

"He realizes perfectly well what he's doing," Caroline said bitterly. "Hiding behind his Scottish brogue will not get him far with me! I know what he means when he calls me *thrawn* and *capernoitie* and *dautie*!"

Maud's eyes lit with amusement. "I suppose, my love, that you may consider calling a girl stubborn and irritable to be somewhat rude, but in combination with *dautie* it is not so dreadful, is it? I would not be insulted if a handsome young man called *me* a darling."

"*Darling?*" Caroline gasped. "Is that what dautie means?"

"Why, yes, of course. Didn't you know that?"

"No, I didn't," Caroline muttered, flushing bright red. "I . . . I thought . . ."

"Then it *was* a misunderstanding?" Maud suggested hopefully.

Caroline shook her head. "No, ma'am, not really. I may have misunderstood one word, but there were others I understood quite well. Your nephew was rude in ways I could not misunderstand. But I don't wish to refine on them or even to discuss them."

"No, naturally you don't," Maud said sympathetically. "Not with his aunt, at any rate."

"Not with anyone, ma'am. But just because Lord Dunvegan had been rude to *me* is no excuse for me to be rude to *you*, Lady Teale. I hope you'll forgive me."

"There's nothing to forgive, dearest," Maud assured her, getting up from her dressing table. "I took not the least offense." And she underscored her sincerity by giving the girl a warm embrace.

Caroline curtseyed to the ladies and took her leave. As soon as the door closed behind her, Maud whirled about and grinned triumphantly at Lady Powell. "There, Lucy! What did I tell you?" she chortled. "Am I not right?"

"I think you are, Maud," Lucy Powell admitted with a shrug. "Geordie must be taken with her if he called her a darling. I doubt if he used the word dautie to Emmaline or Jane. It seems neither Powell nor I will win our wager."

Maud beamed. "And Caro is certainly not indifferent to him, don't you agree? Her dislike of him is too intense."

Lucy nodded thoughtfully. "Yes, I do believe the chit is more taken with your nephew than she's prepared to admit. Poor Douglas Dawlish."

"Never mind Dawlish," Maud said, sitting down at her mirror again. "It's not Dawlish's father to whom I made the promise of providing a bride for his son."

"It was a rash promise, Maud," Lady Powell said, rising, gathering up her gowns and starting toward the door. "Caro may be attracted to your Geordie, but I doubt that they can mend their differences before the holiday ends."

"They will if I have anything to say to it," Maud declared firmly. "If Geordie David McAusland doesn't go home to Scotland betrothed to that girl, it won't be because I didn't try."

* * *

At the same time, in the opposite wing of the house, Archie was perched on Geordie's bed, watching as his friend gave the finishing touches to his evening attire.

"But why, suddenly, do you want to take off for Scotland?" he was asking worriedly. "Until this afternoon you seemed content enough to stay here through Christmas."

"I wasna content," Geordie muttered, frowning at his reflection in the little round mirror on the wall as he carelessly tied his neckcloth. "I was only bein' biddable."

"Then what's happened to make you want to stop being biddable? Why is it suddenly necessary to take off for Kincardine?"

"This is not my home, that's why. A body shouldna have to spend Christmas away from home."

"Come now, old man, you haven't been home for the holidays in six years. What makes it so urgent to go home now?" He got up, strode across to Geordie, and pulled the neckcloth from his hands. "Here, let me. You're making a botch of it."

"Only because this deuced keekin' glass is so small," Geordie said in sullen defense of his prowess with a neckcloth.

"The 'keekin' glass' was large enough for you yesterday." Archie pushed his tall, red-headed friend down on the nearest chair and began to tie the neckcloth. "Something's happened to upset you, I'm sure of that," he mused as he worked. "I only wish you'd tell me what it is."

" 'Tis nothin' worth the tellin'," Geordie muttered, shamefaced. "I made a glaikit ass of myself with a lass is all."

Archie's brows rose. "Did you? I don't believe it. Geordie of the silver tongue does not play the fool with the ladies." Giving a final pat to the now neatly-tied neckcloth, he sat down on the bed again and eyed Geordie curiously. "Who was it, old man? Lady Jane?"

"Nae, laddie, not she. She's a wee tapeless hersel'—foolish, I mean—so she'd not likely notice the foolishness of anyone else."

Archie nodded in amused agreement, but his expression promptly altered as he was struck with a dreadful thought. "Don't tell me it was Emmaline, because I won't believe it," he declared. "You couldn't have made a fool of yourself over Emmaline Dawlish."

Geordie shook his head. "Not Emmaline, not Jane, and not Bella. It was yer blasted Caroline. I'm sorry I ever was gowky enough to call on her that day in London. I've been payin' for that interview ever since."

"Paying for it? How?"

"In orra . . . all sorts of ways. Today she slapped my face. I can still feel the sting of it."

"Slapped your face?" Archie's eyes widened in astonishment. "Confound it, you clunch, what did you say to her?"

"It isna what I said. It's what I did." Geordie got up, wandered over to the window, and stared out into the twilight. "I kissed her."

"You kissed *Caro*? Good God!" Archie peered at Geordie's back with something like awe. "I didn't know you were capable of that much bravado. I never had the courage to do it, even after we were betrothed."

Geordie, surprised, turned and gaped at him. "Ye never kissed her? Why on earth not?"

Archie shrugged. "I don't know. She always seemed so . . . formidable, you know?"

"Aye, she is that. Formidable is the very word."

"Then why did you kiss her? You don't like her above half."

"I don't like her at all. I dinna ken why I did it. It cows a'! I was liftin' her down from the stool, and she glowerin' down at me all fire and fury, and the next thing I knew I had her in my arms, and my heart was makin' a chitterin' callishangle in my chest, and I kissed her."

Archie shook his head in confusion. "Strange behavior, I must say. If you ask me, old fellow, you like her better than you're willing to admit. So stop talking about running off to Scotland. Better to remain right here and see what comes of this."

"Nothin' will come of it but embarrassment and humiliation. She's ta'en with that gomerell Dawlish, and as for me, I cannot abide a lass who puts on airs." And with one last glance in the glass to check his neckcloth, Geordie started toward the door.

Archie rose to follow. "That's too bad," he murmured thoughtfully. "Any man with the courage to kiss Caro Woolcott when she's glowering at him might be the very man for her."

"Ye may be right, but that man isna I." Geordie paused in the doorway and looked back at his friend. "But, Archie, my lad, though I'm fair loath to admit it, I must tell ye that if I *were* betrothed to her, I dinna believe I could *keep* myself from kissin' her, formidable though she be." He threw Archie a sudden grin. "The lass is much more sonsy than I thought."

❋ 8 ❋

GEORDIE, AFTER ENDURING another evening of being completely ignored by Caroline, was more than ever determined to cut short his visit and go home to Scotland. Not that he blamed the girl for ignoring him (in fact, after the liberty he'd taken with her under the kissing bough, it was no more than he deserved), but without the challenge of exchanging banter with her, there was little to interest him here on his aunt's premises. Archie and Bella were too preoccupied with their mutual infatuation to spend much time with him, Jane and Emmaline embarrassed him by their not-so-subtle attempts at flirtation, his aunt was busy with Christmas preparations, and the snow was too heavy to permit him even his few outdoor activities. The only enjoyment he could look forward to was the hour he spent each day playing billiards with the elderly but unaffected Lord Powell. But pleasant as Lord Powell's company was, one hour a day of billiards was scarcely a satisfactory replacement for the company of his father in his family home in Kincardine at Christmastime.

However, the next morning, when he broached the subject of his departure to his aunt, she refused to hear of it. "Three more days, Geordie," she pleaded. "Only three more days! Tomorrow night is Christmas Eve! How can you be so cruel as to even *suggest* leaving me in the lurch for such a tiny stretch of time as that? What can three days mean to a young man in his prime? You have all of *life* stretching out before you—years and years and *years*! How can you begrudge your only aunt a paltry three days?"

So, with a shrug, Geordie surrendered again. The three days would seem endless, but they would pass. He could, he supposed, endure.

The snow, though still falling, had slackened enough that afternoon to permit those of the company who wished to face the elements to go out and find a Yule log for the Christmas fire. As soon as the expedition was suggested by Lady Teale, Archie and Geordie volunteered. Then Bella shyly asked if she could join them, her example promptly followed by the hearty Emmaline. Lady Jane, having recovered from the injury to her finger (and unwilling to surrender the field to her rival), bravely declared herself ready to make one of the party, even if it meant risking an inflammation of the lungs.

Caroline, determined to avoid Geordie's company, did not join the group. She remained silent as the Yule log party began to dress themselves for the outdoor expedition. But Maud, determined to nurture the match she envisioned for her nephew, kept urging the girl to join the others. Caroline resisted as long as she could, but eventually her refusals began to seem rude, and she reluctantly succumbed to the older woman's importunities. Her swain, Douglas Dawlish, as soon as he learned that Caro was going, decided that he, too, would make one of the group. Maud tried several ploys to keep him at home (like tempting him to go down to the kitchen to sample some of the Christmas baking), but she could not prevail upon him to remain behind.

It was a cheerful crowd of seven that set out to brave the elements. Dressed warmly in galoe-shoes, mufflers, and mittens, and suitably supplied with two saws and a hefty rope, they slogged through the snow that covered the east lawn with a blanket over a foot deep, and headed toward the home woods. But they didn't hurry. Even though the sky was relentlessly grey, and a bitter wind nipped at their cheeks, they felt giddily happy. As they floundered with clumsy gaiety through drifts that were sometimes as high as their waists, they paused to toss snowballs at each other, to pull each other down into the snow, and generally to cavort like children. Soon the icy air was filled with the mist of their breath and the ring of their laughter.

Geordie, being pelted with snowballs by Emmaline from one side and Jane from another, shielded his face with a protective arm and loped through the snow away from them. Momentarily blinded, he blundered into Caroline, causing her to lose her balance and topple awkwardly into a drift. He laughed for a moment as he watched her flail about helplessly, and then he bent down, took both her mittened hands in his, and hauled her to her feet. "There ye are, lass," he grinned. "No harm done." And he reached out to straighten her bonnet, a little mauve silk confection tied with blue ribbons, which had been knocked askew.

Caroline, who'd been occupied with brushing the snow from her face and hair, looked up in time to see him reach toward her. Instantly her eyes became alarmed, and she held up her hands to ward him off. "No!" she gasped.

He backed off at once. "Wheesht, lass, what's afrighted ye? I was only goin' to straighten yer bonnet."

"I can do it myself," she said coldly.

His grin widened. "Ye needna fear I was goin' to kiss ye again. Not after that blow ye gave me the last time," he teased, rubbing his cheek.

Her only answer was an angry glare, after which she turned away from him and stumbled through the snow to Douglas Dawlish's side, far enough away from Geordie to be out of his hearing but not out of his sight. Dawlish had paused under a tall oak tree (standing in lone splendor in the midst of the lawn) in order to lean on the trunk while he emptied his boot of a lump of snow that had fallen into the top, but as soon as Caroline came up to him, he straightened up and stepped toward her. Having felt a sense of competitiveness with the Scotsman from the first (though he didn't know why), he looked down at the girl with a frown. "Did that deuced maw worm push you down on purpose, Caro? I'll give him a piece of my mind if he did."

"No, of course he didn't," Caroline said. "Pay him no mind. Just take my arm."

Douglas was somewhat taken aback by her tone, but he offered his arm as directed. Caroline grasped it tightly, and after taking a quick backward glance at Geordie to make sure he was watching, smiled up at Douglas with flirtatious affection. "There," she murmured, shamelessly fluttering her lashes up at him. "Your strong arm will keep me from another tumble."

Geordie stared at the pair, his grin slowly fading. Something troublesome—a battle of emotions—was going on in his chest. What was there about Miss Caroline Woolcott that put him in turmoil every time he had even the slightest encounter with her? Was Archie right? Did he care for that toplofty female more than he was willing to admit? And even if he did, what good was it to acknowledge the feeling? The lass cared nothing for him. She evidently wanted that stick, Dawlish, and as far as Geordie was concerned, she could have him.

He was about to turn away when he heard a frightening sound—the awful crack of wood splitting. It was coming from the oak tree under which Dawlish and Caroline were standing. "Look out!" he shouted, wading through the snow toward them as quickly as he could. "The *tree!*"

The pair looked at him, confused. "The *tree!*" he shouted again, gesturing toward the branches above them, but he could feel the wind take the sound from his mouth and blow it away.

Dawlish backed away a few steps and looked up at the branches to see if he could understand what the Scotsman meant. "He's playing some childish trick on—" he said to Caroline, but he was interrupted by another cracking sound from above them. It was then that he realized that a huge branch—the one right above where Caroline was standing—was cracking off the tree from the weight of the snow on it. Dawlish froze in terror. Caroline, looking up, belatedly realized what was happening. But she had waited too long; the branch was already falling. In another second it would be right upon her. There was no time even to scream.

At that moment, Geordie hurtled himself upon her and rolled them both out of the way just as the huge branch came crashing down.

During the moment that followed no one moved. Geordie, with the breath knocked out of him, lay gasping. It took another moment before he realized that he was lying on top of a speechless, breathless Caroline, who was staring at him with eyes wide and mouth slightly opened to form an astounded, soundless O. He scrambled to his knees and, placing his hands under her arms, slowly raised them both to their feet. For a moment their eyes locked as they each expelled a long breath. Then she broke away and stared down at the fallen branch, wincing at the sight of her beribboned bonnet, which was crushed beneath it. The crushed bonnet made her shudder, and instinctively, she threw herself into Geordie's arms and hid her face in the capes of his greatcoat.

His arms tightened about her. "Wheesht, lassie," he whispered, his lips on her hair, "ye needna get yersel' in a curfuffle. All's well that ends well."

Before she could respond, Dawlish, white-faced and trembling, came up to them. "Caro? Are you all right?" he asked, taking her by the shoulders and turning her out of Geordie's hold so that she could face him.

"Yes, yes, I'm fine." She smiled up at him reassuringly. "The branch completely missed us. You needn't get into a curfuffle."

Geordie heard her use his Lallans word, but he did not smile. He felt too angry at Dawlish—and at her, too. It seemed to him that she'd turned from him to Dawlish much too readily.

By this time the others were crowding round, everyone talking at once. Archie pounded Geordie on the back, congratulating him on his quick thinking, while Jane and Emmaline enveloped Caroline in hysterical embraces. Only Bella was thoughtful enough to ask Geordie if he was unhurt. The Scotsman did not fail to notice that Caroline did not look in his direction but stood quite contentedly with Dawlish's arm about her, the center of attention. Disgusted, he reached down under the branch, pulled out her bonnet, pushed through the crowd surrounding her, and handed it to her. "Here, lass," he said. "I ken ye can put it on yoursel'."

Before she could respond, he turned about and strode off toward the woods. "I say, Geordie," Archie called after him, "where are you going?"

"To find a Yule log," he called back. "Is it no the reason we came out?"

Feeling unaccountably irritable, Geordie slogged off through the snow toward the woods at a purposeful pace. He didn't pause or look back until he found himself completely surrounded by trees. There within the woods the snow was much less deep, and he was able to move about more easily. His mood lifted again as he looked about him, for it was quite lovely under the trees. The wind soughed through the snow-covered branches above him, causing light clumps of snow to fall with unexpected, plashing noises. The evergreens were clad with white, while the deciduous trees seemed to have been sketched in by some unknown, heaven-sent artist who underlined their white blankets with thin black lines, gracefully etching them against the grey sky in indelible india ink. A frosty haze rose from the ground, making everything more than ten feet away almost invisible. It was a scene of wintry beauty, eerie with mist and magic.

The magic dissipated somewhat when Archie and Bella caught up with him, and they set out on the mundane task of finding a Yule log. By the time the rest of the group joined them, the three had found a fallen tree whose trunk seemed the right size. "Geordie says we just have to saw off a few branches," Archie announced to the others, "and then we can tie it round with the rope and drag it back."

Douglas Dawlish shook his head in annoyance. He was tired of hearing Geordie's name, tired of seeing his face, tired of the admiration with which his sister, and Archie, and almost everyone else in Teale Court spoke of him. Dawlish was not gifted with the talent for objective self-analysis, so he did not recognize that the cause of his animosity toward Geordie was an overwhelming jealousy; a feeling exacerbated by the Scotsman's courageous act a short while ago. Douglas felt keenly, in a buried part of his brain, that he should have been the one who'd saved Caroline, but he didn't acknowledge to himself his deep sense of shame. He only knew that he didn't like Lord Dunvegan at all, and he didn't want to do anything that the deuced Scotsman suggested. "I'm certain we can find a bigger log than that," he said scornfully.

"But, Douglas," Bella said mildly, "this one is perfectly adequate."

"A larger one might be too big for the fireplace," Emmaline pointed out.

"And the larger the log," Archie nodded, "the heavier to drag."

"There are three healthy men here," Dawlish insisted. "Surely we can handle a heavier load than this puny specimen."

"Blethers, laddie," Geordie argued with good-natured logic, "ye canna call this log puny. It must be seven feet long."

"And at least eighteen inches in diameter," Archie added.

"Well, I'm going off to see if I can find one that's two feet across," Douglas said stubbornly, and he stomped off into the trees.

"Really, Douglas," his sister called after him in disgust, "must you always override everyone else? Come back here!"

But Douglas had already disappeared into the mist, and no answer drifted back from the shadows into which he'd vanished.

"Oh, dear! He's certain to get lost," Jane murmured timorously.

"No, he won't," Bella assured her. "These woods are not extensive."

"But I suppose we'd better go after him," Archie said glumly.

"Aye, let's go," Geordie agreed. "Like as no, the lad'll find a better log than this."

"This one seems perfect to me," Emmaline grumbled. "My brother can be a bumptious idiot sometimes. I don't know what you see in him, Caro."

"I?" Caroline gasped, astonished, as everyone's eyes turned toward her. The girl reddened painfully. "But, Emmaline, I never—"

At that moment, however, a loud cry of pain issued from the darkness into which Douglas had disappeared. "Oh, my *heavens*!" Jane cried. "What was *that*?"

"It sounded like Dawlish," Archie said. "We'd better see—"

But Geordie had already set off at a run in the direction of the cry.

They found Douglas easily enough, just by following the sounds of his groans. They found him on the ground, lying on his side and clutching his leg. Geordie knelt beside him. "Is it yer knee, old fellow?"

Dawlish shook his head. "Broke my leg," he gasped, his lips white and his face clenched in pain. "Stepped in a . . . damned hole and . . . broke my damned leg!"

"Oh, good heavens, a broken l-leg!" Jane whimpered. "How very d-dreadful!"

"I wouldna jump to conclusions," Geordie murmured, easing the fellow onto his back and straightening his leg gently. "Let's have a look at it first."

"Are you a doctor, too?" Dawlish asked, a mixture of pain and contempt in his voice.

Geordie ignored his sarcasm. Motioning Archie to support Douglas's head and shoulders, he began to examine the leg, starting up at the thigh. At the first touch, Douglas winced and cried out. "Wait!" he gasped, white-lipped. "Caro . . . would you . . . hold my hand?"

Caroline knelt beside him. "Of course," she said, biting her lip. She pulled off her mitten and took his hand in hers.

"What a baby!" Emmaline muttered under her breath.

Geordie gave Caroline one quick, unreadable glance and then began to examine the injured leg by exerting a firm pressure at significant places along its length. He could find no sign of injury, however, until he tried to move Douglas's foot at the ankle. The movement elicited a loud cry of pain. That was the sign Geordie was looking for. He stood up and took a deep, relieved breath. "It's yer ankle, like as no. It might be broken, but more likely it's only a sprain. We'll see after we get ye home and cut off yer boot."

"It's broken," Douglas muttered dejectedly. "I know it's broken. How am I to get back with a broken ankle?"

"Archie and I will support ye while ye hop on yer good leg. Here, let's get ye up and try it out."

They started back, with Geordie taking one of Dawlish's arms and Archie the other, the injured man groaning with every hop. The four ladies followed in silent dejection, depressed not only by Douglas's pain but by the rapidly darkening sky, the cutting wind, and the snow that was now falling more heavily than ever.

By the time they emerged from the wood, Dawlish was exhausted and quite unable to go on. They set him down in the snow and tried to decide what to do next. "Shall the ladies push on to the stable and send a carriage?" Bella asked.

"A carriage could never get through the drifts," Archie said. "I'd give a king's ransom for a sleigh right now. If this were America, you'd probably have a sleigh in the stable. I hear sleighs are as commonplace in America as they are in Moscow."

"But this isn't America," Emmaline said drily. "Or Moscow."

"For a' that," Geordie suggested, "ye lassies can push on. No need for ye to hang about with us."

"Not on your life," Caroline said. "We may prove useful yet."

"What do you take us for?" Emmaline asked, offended. "Deserters?"

"Of course we'll stay with you," Bella added. "Even Jane agrees with that, don't you, Jane?"

"Yes, I do," Jane said staunchly. "Besides, it's getting too dark for us to go on alone."

That settled, they all looked back at Dawlish, sitting in the snow with his back against a tree, his arms crossed over his chest and his head lowered glumly. "I suppose we'll have to carry him," Archie said quietly to Geordie, "though it won't be easy through this snow."

"We can fashion a litter," Geordie exclaimed, his eyes brightening. "Did ye hear that, Douglas, lad? With a litter we can carry ye back like a sultan of Araby on a sedan-chair. All we need do is cut two strong branches for poles, and button my coat over them for a seat."

"Splendid idea!" Archie exclaimed, his expression instantly turning cheerful. They immediately set to work, and in a few minutes the poles were ready. Then Geordie removed his greatcoat and riding coat, laid the riding coat out on the snow, buttoned it, pulled the sleeves inside out within the coat and slid the poles inside the sleeves. He then put on his greatcoat and gloves and assisted Archie in helping Douglas to sit upon the makeshift seat.

As they were about to lift the poles, Archie in the front and Geordie in the rear, Caroline offered a suggestion. "Emmaline and I can hold the poles at the rear, Lord Dunvegan. Two women are surely strong enough to replace one man."

"But what for, ma'am?" Geordie asked her. "I don't need replacin'."

"Have you forgotten why we came? If Emmaline and I can help to carry the litter, then you, my lord, can drag the Yule log."

This suggestion met with universal approbation, and before long the whole party was on the move—Archie carrying the litter at the front, Douglas seated on the buttoned coat with his injured leg resting on a pole and the good one dangling, and Emmaline and Caroline behind. Jane marched alongside the litter, and last in the line came Geordie pulling the log. They were not as cheerful a group as when they'd started out earlier, but neither were they as glum as they'd been when Douglas's injury was first discovered.

When they came in sight of the house, Caroline beckoned to Jane and asked to be relieved. "I'd not ask it of you, Jane, except that there's something I must do before we get back. Holding the pole is not very difficult, and we haven't much farther to go. Besides, you've been so very strong today, I feel sure you can manage it."

"Yes, come to think of it, I *have* been strong, haven't I?" Jane said with a blink of surprise. "I didn't faint once, in spite of all that's happened." She took the pole from her friend and smiled. "I'm rather proud of myself."

Caroline smiled back at her. "I'm proud of you, too." Then, waving her on, Caroline turned and walked back to where Geordie was struggling along with the log. She took hold of the rope and fell in beside him. "That log must be very heavy to pull, my lord," she remarked with what she hoped was a tone of nonchalance.

"Did you think I needed help, ma'am?" Geordie asked coldly. "If that's why ye dropped back here, ye can go back to yer friends. I assure ye I'm doin' quite well."

"I know you are," she said. "I have another reason for wishing to walk with you."

"Oh?" He looked at her suspiciously. "And what may that be?"

She threw a hesitant glance. "I wanted to thank you, my lord, for all your acts of quick-thinking courage today."

"Ah, so that's it." And about time, too, he thought. "'Twas nothin' so courageous, ma'am. But if ye truly wish to thank me, ye can stop callin' me *my lord*, which I told ye afore I downa like."

"Very well, I'll call you Geordie, if it will please you. But you cannot deny that you were courageous. This afternoon you've been . . . well, almost heroic."

"Heroic, ma'am? *I?*" The corners of his mouth turned up in a little smile. He was beginning to enjoy this conversation. "Are these words issuin' from the lips of the same Miss Woolcott who called me a boorish, shameless libertine only yesterday?"

"And so you were, yesterday," she retorted quickly, but almost instantly regretted it. She had not come to insult him but to thank him. She had to try again. "Today, I must admit, I saw another side of you," she went on bravely. "It makes me think that . . . that I might have been mistaken about you. If I have misjudged you, my lor—Geordie—I am . . . very sorry."

"Ye needna be sorry, lass," he said with wicked amusement. "As Sophocles says, 'To err from the right path is common to mankind.' Like as no, he meant womankind as well."

She stopped in her tracks. "Good God! That's from the *Antigone*! Why didn't you tell me you knew it?"

"Why, ma'am, did ye assume that I didn't?"

She flashed him a look of burning anger, but then her eyes fell. "You are determined to prove me a toplofty prig," she mumbled, trudging onward. "Now, I suppose, you're going to tell me you've even read it in Greek."

"I have no intention of tellin' ye so," he grinned, enjoying himself to the hilt. "Do ye take me for a braggart?"

She stopped again, staring at him through the darkness and the blowing snow, overwhelmed by waves of anger and humiliation. For the first time, she realized fully what their relationship had been. From the moment of their first meeting, he'd done nothing but make a fool of her. Even now, when she'd come to him filled with gratitude, he'd turned the situation into farce. All her feelings of gratitude died abruptly. She now wanted nothing so much as to slap his arrogant face. "I suppose," she said icily, "that means you *have* read it in Greek?"

To the Scotsman, her discomfiture was sweet revenge. "Aye, I've read it in Greek. Many times. And," he added, rubbing it in, "the rest of Sophocles, too."

She thrust her part of the rope at him furiously. "That," she snapped indignantly, "is the most disgusting thing you've yet said to me!" And she stormed off toward the house with as much dignity as she could summon. But dignity was difficult to achieve while wallowing through the snow, especially when she could hear his hooting laughter reverberating in the wind behind her.

❄ 9 ❄

DAWLISH WAS CARRIED up to bed and the doctor sent for. The poor physician had to slog two miles through the snow to attend him. He pronounced that the patient was suffering from a sprained ankle, that the fellow should keep it bandaged tightly for a couple of weeks, and that he should not walk about on it more than necessary. If the doctor felt any disgust at having to come out in such weather to attend so minor an injury, his feelings were certainly assuaged by the large fee that Lady Teale bestowed on him.

Dawlish himself was both relieved and disappointed. It would have given him some sort of satisfaction—after carrying on as he had—to have suffered a broken bone, but on the other hand, he was grateful that he didn't have to spend the rest of the Christmas holiday in bed. He had been planning for several days to do something very special on Christmas Eve, and he would not have liked to do it from a bed of pain.

His plan was to make Caro Woolcott an offer. It was the first time in all his twenty-eight years that he'd felt tempted to offer for a lady. Never before had he found a girl so perfectly suited to his taste. No only was she lovely to look upon, but she shared all his interests and concerns. And, best of all, she seemed to return his regard. For, as he confided to his sister when she came to see him after the doctor's departure, there was little point in a man's making a girl an offer if she was likely to refuse him. "You do think, don't you, Emmaline, that Caro will accept me?" he asked his sister hopefully.

Emmaline studied her brother with unwonted sympathy, for he looked a bit pathetic as he sat on his bedroom chaise with his bandaged leg resting on a pillow. "Caro's said nothing to me on the subject," she told him frankly, "but she *has* been in your pocket ever since we arrived. I suppose that's as good a sign as any."

"Yes, I think so, too," Douglas smiled, leaning back against the chaise with his arms behind his head, suddenly the very model of confident manhood. "I shall put the question to her tomorrow evening. It's quite the ideal time, don't you agree? In that way, in later years, she and I shall always have a particular, personal feeling about Christmas Eve."

Emmaline nodded, approving of the romantic notion. "I wish you all the best, Douglas," she said. "Caro will be as fine a life's mate as any man could hope for."

With that, she left to dress for dinner. But as she passed Caroline's bedroom, she had a sudden urge to reveal to her friend the exciting surprise in store for her. "Caro," she chortled, popping her head in the door, "be sure to save your most fetching gown for tomorrow evening."

"What did you say, Emmaline?" Caroline said in an abstracted voice. She spoke from the window seat, where she'd been sitting for the past hour. She'd been staring out into the darkness, thinking about the Scotsman, George David McAusland, Lord Dunvegan, who wanted only to be called Geordie. He'd called her *dautie*, a darling, but it was he who was dautie. She'd spent the hour at the window glumly reliving the very unsatisfactory conversation she'd had with him earlier, berating herself for having misjudged him, and for having been so poor-spirited in the manner in which she'd owned up to that misjudgment. She hadn't even apologized, and an apology was the very least the fellow deserved after having practically saved her life that afternoon! Her mind was a tumultuous sea of confusion, in which feelings of shame and frustration tossed about with other, deeper emotions that she was afraid to identify. She'd been uncomfortably aware of those strange emotions even before the afternoon he'd kissed her, but the kiss has stirred them up to a troublesome pitch. She'd been trying to come to grips with those feelings when Emmaline made her abrupt interruption.

"I said," Emmaline repeated gleefully, "that you must choose your most fetching gown to wear to dinner tomorrow."

Caroline looked over at her in utter confusion. "I don't know what you're talking about, Emmaline, but don't stand there half-in and half-out. Do come in."

Emmaline whisked herself in and shut the door. "I shouldn't be telling you this, my love," she grinned, "but Douglas is planning a tremendous surprise for you on Christmas Eve. So you must be in your very best looks."

"Douglas is planning a surprise for *me*? I don't understand. What sort of surprise?"

"Surely you can guess. His intentions toward you are as plain as pikestaff. Even Lady Powell was hinting of it yesterday."

"I don't have any idea what you're babbling about," Caroline said impatiently, passing her hand over her forehead and attempting to clear her mind. "What was Lady Powell hint—" But then she remembered. "Good God!" she exclaimed, turning pale. "You don't mean—?"

"That's exactly what I mean," Emmaline said, her face glowing with excited anticipation. "You're going to get an offer. A Christmas Eve offer!"

"Oh, Emmaline," Caroline gasped, *"no!"*

Emmaline was taken aback. There was no mistaking that Caroline's response was not a happy one. "No?" she asked, her high spirits instantly deflated. "What do you mean, no? Don't you believe me? I'm not mistaken, Caro. Douglas does intend to offer. He told me so."

"Emmaline, please!" Caroline jumped up from the window seat and ran across to her friend. "Don't let him. He *mustn't*!"

"But of course he must. Everyone expects it."

"How can they expect it? They have no cause—"

"No cause? How can you say they have no cause? Why, you and Douglas have had your heads together constantly for the past four days!"

"But that was only . . . I never meant—! Honestly, Emmaline, how can you have believed I cared for him? Didn't you always say he wasn't my sort?"

Emmaline fixed Caroline with an angry eye. "Before this week, I didn't believe he *was* your sort, but even *I* became convinced you were taken with him lately. If you're now trying to tell me you won't have him, that's of course your privilege. It's entirely your affair. I don't want to hear it."

"But, Emmaline," Caroline pleaded, "shouldn't you warn him? If he knows he's misjudged . . . that I didn't intend—"

"I don't want to hear it," Emmaline repeated, turning to the door. "I shouldn't have said a word to you." But she turned back for a parting shot before leaving. "The truth is, Caro Woolcott, you've led my brother on in the most flagrant way. And if now you've changed your mind about him, you'll have to get yourself out of this coil without any help from me!"

Caroline, left alone and shaken, clung to the bedpost for a moment, trying to sort out the muddle in her brain. Slowly she lowered herself to the bed and leaned her forehead against the bedpost in despair. This was all her fault, that much was suddenly quite clear. She'd used poor Douglas just to taunt Geordie, and now Douglas believed she cared for him. He would make his offer, and she would have to hurt him. As if that were not bad enough, Geordie would see her doing it, just as he'd seen her do it to Archie. Geordie already disliked her, but how much *more* would he dislike her when he saw her act the heartless jilt *again*?

She couldn't bear the thought of it. How could she—and on Christmas Eve!—break one man's heart and disgust another? It was too dreadful to contemplate. She wished with all her heart that she'd never come to this place. She should have stayed at home in London. Although she'd have been alone in London, she would have been safe from this sort of emotional turmoil. Safe at home was where she wanted to be, more than anything.

Why not? she asked herself, sitting up with a start. She could bribe a stablehand to borrow one of the carriages and a pair of horses, and they could leave at dawn. She could be in London by

Christmas! In two days, she'd be safe, and she would have avoided all the pain and stress that remaining here would cause. It was a wonderful solution that would be better for everyone. Lady Teale and Bella might feel offended, but she would write and explain. Emmaline and Douglas would be grateful, for they'd quickly realize that she'd saved Douglas from the humiliation of having his suit refused. And as for Geordie, he would barely notice that she'd gone.

It was decided. She would go. All she had to do was to steal down to the stables and make arrangements. There was still half an hour before dinner was to be served—she could do it right now.

At that very moment, Geordie was paying a call on Douglas Dawlish in the opposite wing of the house. Already dressed in his evening clothes, the Scotsman had come, at his aunt's request, to see if the incapacitated fellow needed some help in going down the stairs to the dining room. He found Douglas in a surprisingly good mood. "I'm glad to see that y're takin' yer mishanter in good spirits, Dawlish," Geordie remarked.

"That's because I realize my accident—my mishanter, as you call it—could've been worse," Douglas said, taking Geordie's arm. "At least I'll be well enough on Christmas Eve to be able to go down to dinner and make my announcement."

Geordie was supporting Douglas's arm as the injured fellow limped to the door. "Announcement?" he asked.

"I'm sure everyone's guessed by this time about Caro and me."

"Caro and ye?" Geordie felt a sharp contraction in his stomach. It was so painful that he stumbled.

"Careful, old man," Douglas warned, steadying himself by holding on to the doorjamb. "If you lose your balance, you'll upset us both."

"Sorry," Geordie muttered, carefully leading him toward the stairs. "What is it ye were sayin' about ye and Caro—Miss Woolcott?"

"Just that I've chosen Christmas Eve to announce our betrothal. It's a most appropriate time, wouldn't you say? So festive."

Geordie couldn't bring himself to utter more than a grunt. His shock was so great that he could barely take it in. Caroline and

Dawlish, betrothed! The thought sickened him. How could she? The fellow was a maw-worm! Couldn't she see it? But what did he expect? The first time he met her, the girl had described the sort of man she wanted. Hadn't she said then that she disliked Corinthians and gamblers and only wanted a man who could read the *Antigone* in Greek? Well, she'd found one. He wished her happy.

By the time they reached the drawing room he was so tired of forcing himself to wish her happy that he was ready to strangle her. The girl was an idiot. Hadn't she realized that he, Geordie, was in love with her? Hadn't she sensed that all their encounters had been nothing but lovers' quarrels? Where was her sense?

He deposited the odious Dawlish on an armchair and let Aunt Maud take over the chore of fussing over him. Geordie himself was done with the fellow. Even if Douglas Dawlish toppled over on his face, Geordie wouldn't lift a finger to help him.

The smoldering Scotsman stalked across the room to where Aunt Maud's butler was passing around the pre-prandial sherries. He took one from the tray and drained it in a gulp. Then he went to the window and stared out into the darkness. What was he doing here? he asked himself. This "holiday" was becoming nothing but torture. He ought to be home, in Kincardine, instead of being imprisoned here, where he'd have to endure Christmas watching Dawlish and Caroline with their heads together. And what misery he'd suffer on Christmas Eve, when he'd be forced to smile through the recital of that muckworm's betrothal announcement. Dash it all, he told himself, he would refuse to listen to it. He wouldn't. He didn't have to stay there. He could just go home.

The idea was too tempting to push aside. Who would stop him if he just took his leave? Archie's horses and carriage were ready in the stables for just such a purpose. He could take himself to Scotland first thing in the morning. Since his aunt's matchmaking plan for him was not going to be fruitful, she would probably be willing to let him go. But her wishes really made no difference; he had no intention of asking her. Tomorrow, when she came down to breakfast, she would find him gone.

But if he was to leave at dawn, he'd have to go out to the stables at once, tonight, to make arrangements. There was still time to steal down there before dinner was announced. After all, one of the guests had still to make an appearance. Caroline. Caroline had not yet come down.

❄ 10 ❄

CAROLINE, DRESSED IN her dinner clothes and protected from the cold with only a shawl, stood in the draughty stable pleading earnestly with one of the grooms to take her to London. Behind her, a pair of horses pawed the ground in their stalls, the breath from their nostrils visible in the icy air. The wiry little groom standing before her also pawed the ground with his feet, not only to keep himself warm but because the conversation with the lady from the manorhouse was making him uneasy. She was making a request with which it was quite impossible to comply. "It cain't be done, m'lady," he said for the third time. "We'd never make it. An' I'd surely be sacked in the bargain, which I cain't nohow afford."

Caroline was unwilling to listen to reason. "Not even for ten guineas?" she asked plaintively.

"It's a deal o' money, miss, an' I'd like t' oblige yer," the fellow said, politely but firmly, "but the snow's too deep. We'd get mired fer certain."

She was unwilling to accept his argument. "But by tomorrow the sun will come out. You can see already that the sky is clearing in the south. You can even see stars."

"Even if the sun does show itself, miss, it'll take days fer the roads t' open. Three, at least. Four, if the cold don't break."

"But can't we just try? If we get mired, we can put up at an inn," she said in desperation, adding glumly, "at least I'd be gone from here."

"Are ye wishin' to be goin' off somewhere, Miss Woolcott?" came a voice behind her.

She wheeled about. "Lord Dunvegan!" she gasped.

"Ye promised to call me Geordie," he reminded her. "Why on earth would ye be wantin' a carriage, ma'am, and at this particular time?"

Her cheeks grew hot. "I mean no offense, but it is no affair of yours." Her eyes flitted over his elegant black evening coat, high starched shirt points, and beautifully-tied neckcloth—evening

61

clothes that seemed incongruous against the background of stalls
and straw. "I suppose I'm holding up dinner," she murmured
guiltily. "Did Lady Teale ask you to search for me? It was not
kind of her to send you out in the wind so lightly dressed. You
haven't even a hat."

"Ye dinna seem so warmly dressed yersel'," he pointed out.

She wrapped her shawl more closely about her, as if in
answer. "How did you think of seeking me here?"

"Sheer good luck," he said, forgetting his own reason for
coming and waving the groom away.

The little groom was eager to leave, but he looked questioningly at the lady to make certain she was willing to let him go.
She merely shrugged in defeat. The groom expelled a relieved
breath and quickly whisked himself out of their sight.

"Now, then, lass, he's gone," Geordie said gently, "so ye can
tell me what yer doin' here."

"Nothing that should cause anyone concern, I swear. If you'll
give me your arm, Geordie, we can go back to the house."

"Ye can take my arm, my girl, but we're not movin' a step 'til
I have an answer. Ye were arrangin' to loup the tether, weren't
ye?"

"Loup the tether?"

"Skelp. Run off. Disappear."

She dropped her eyes. "You needn't trouble yourself about it,
my lord. I couldn't loup the tether even if I wished to. The roads
are closed."

"But why would ye wish to, when yer betrothed is all set to
make an announcement to the world tomorrow eve?"

"My *betrothed*?" She stared up at him, aghast. "What are you
talking about? I have no betrothed. Who told you—?"

"The fellow himself. Yer own Douglas Dawlish. And he was
as merry as a mouse in the malt when he told me."

Even in the dim light of the stable he could see her face fall.
She turned away from him in obvious distress. "But I never
meant— Dash it all, this is a dreadful coil! He never asked—"

"Never asked? Ye mean he didna yet make ye an offer? The
fellow's a cod's head! But lass, ye needna weep owre it. I'm
certain he intends to."

She shook her head and made a helpless gesture with her
hand. "But I don't *want* him to offer, don't you see? If he does,

then I shall have to refuse him. Just as I refused Archie. And then you will think that I . . . I . . . ."

"*I* will think?" His breath caught in his chest. Her words were strange and quite unlike her. Ordinarily she behaved as if she did not care a fig what he thought. Geordie felt a little tremor in his blood, a little throb in his temple, a little lurch in his chest. Something was happening here, something unexpected and exciting. His brain did not yet understand it, but all his instincts were preparing for it. He took a step closer to her. "*What* will I think, Caroline?"

She turned her head and peeped up at him before turning quickly away again. "You called me Caroline. It's the first time you—" She stopped herself, choked, and then went on in a very small voice. "Everyone calls me Caro."

"I dinna like Caro. 'Tis too bruckle. Brittle." He took hold of her shoulders and turned her to face him. "Answer me, lass. *What* will I think if you refuse Dawlish's offer?"

"That I'm a heartless wretch," she said tearfully, lowering her head so that he could not see her eyes.

The admission touched him to the core. He could no longer hold himself back. "Wheesht, lass," he murmured tenderly, "how can I think that, when I love ye so?"

For a moment she did not move. Then a shudder shook her shoulders. "No!" she gasped.

"Oh, aye, lassie, I do. Top owre tail. I ken ye ha'e a need to be thrawn, to contradict everythin' I say, but ye canna contradict me on this. Who knows better than I what I feel?"

"But you told your aunt that you disliked me. I heard you."

"Did ye now?" He lifted her chin and made her look up at him. "Eavesdroppin', were ye?"

"Yes, I was," she admitted bravely, blinking back her tears. "And I heard you say that I was not beautiful, that I put on airs, and that you disliked me. Intensely."

"I lied."

A dizzying wave of joy enveloped her. "Oh," she breathed. "Oh, Geordie!"

But he was still too confused to feel joyful. He studied her face with an earnest intensity. "I only said those gowky things because you seemed so set on Dawlish. Did ye truly intend to refuse him, lass?"

"Yes, truly."

"But ye did flirt with the fellow, Caroline. Shamelessly. It made me wild."

She slipped from his hold and turned away in mortification. "I never meant to encourage him. It didn't occur to me that he might take my flirtations seriously. I only did it when . . . when a certain odious Scotsman was present."

"I'm afeart I'll nae understand females to my dyin' day," he muttered, taking her arm in a cruel grasp and pulling her round to face him. "I ken ye were runnin' off to avoid an offer from Dawlish. Were ye runnin' away from a certain odious Scotsman, too?"

Believing she'd made her feelings clear, she didn't understand his anger. "You're hurting me, Geordie," she accused, trying to loose his hold on her.

He let her go at once. " 'Tis a great gowk I am," he said, abashed. He turned away from her to one of the horses' stalls, where one of the animals, his head looking over the door, was watching the scene with interest. Geordie imagined the horse was eyeing him with knowing sympathy. "I'm a blasted wan-wyt," he muttered, patting the animal's nose. "Just because ye dinna care for Dawlish doesna mean ye therefore care for me."

"You *are* a great gowk," she said, coming up behind him. "You were never odious to me, Geordie, haven't you guessed that? I only pretended—to myself as well as to you—to find you odious. It was a kind of self-protection. I was afraid to let myself believe that such a tall, winning, beautiful Corinthian—with a head of lovely red curls and a brogue that would charm the birds from the trees—would ever take notice of such a little bookworm as I."

Though these words set his heart bouncing about in his chest, he did not turn. "Michty me!" he said to the horse. "Can the lass be so daft as to call hersel' a bookworm? Bookworm, indeed! But did ye hear yer yatterin' on about *me*? Do ye think it means she loves me?"

Caroline laid her hand softly on his arm. "Wheesht, laddie, what else can my yatterin' mean?"

He turned back to her at that and lifted her high in the air, swinging her round in triumphant if crazed delight. Then he lowered her gently to his chest. "Look at me, Caroline Woolcott. I am the same man I was when you ordered me out of your London house. Do you truly mean to say ye love me?"

Two tear-sparkled eyes looked into his. "Yes, I do love you. Truly."

"Harken to the lass!" he crowed, grinning at her foolishly. "Then like as no ye'd not object to my kissin' ye here and now? Ye've no idea how I've been achin' to do it. 'Tis an age since the last time." Without waiting for a response, he tightened his arms about her and, while the horse neighed in approval, repeated what he'd done under the mistletoe.

After a long while, a flushed and starry-eyed Caroline brushed back his tousled curls fondly and reminded him that there were people back in the great house waiting for their dinner. "I suppose we'd better go. We don't want your aunt Maud to be angry with us."

"My aunt Maud will be beside hersel' with joy. What with her Bella findin' a beau, and her other matchmakin' scheme lookin' successful, she's about to enjoy a completely triumphant Christmas. All ye need do is tell her that ye'll have me. Will ye, lass?"

She buried her head in his shoulder. "Aye, Geordie, lad, I will."

"Even if I sometimes gamble? Or if I occasionally refuse to read Greek poetry with you?"

"I'll take you just as you are, Geordie McAusland. Just remember to call me dautie every now and then."

He kissed her once more before they started out of the stable. "I had the distinct impression, lass," he remarked, slipping his arm about her as they walked, "that ye didna ken the meaning of the word dautie when I used it last."

She threw him a glinting smile as they stepped out into the frosty night. "It seems, my love," she murmured happily, "that I've learned a great deal since then. And none of it Greek."

Proof
of
the
Pudding

Monette Cummings

SHE MUST BE *quite the loveliest girl in London—in all of England—no, in all the world*, Deryk Richardson thought as he exchanged a happy smile with the Beauty who was now sharing a country dance with his best friend. Several of his friends cast amused but sympathetic glances his way. He did not notice. His attention was fixed on Christine.

In the candlelit room, her crown of golden hair shone as brightly as the silver threads embroidered through her white gown. She wore no ornament save a small string of pearls, but to his mind, the gleam of her hair put to shame the glitter of the jewels worn by many of the ladies—and not a few of the gentlemen—who were present at the last and more ostentatious ball of the Season.

When Christine spun about from the hand of one gentleman to another, the jeweled heels of her dancing slipper caught the light. Their twinkle, however, could not compare with the dancing light in her brown eyes each time she encountered the gaze of the man she loved.

He could hardly believe she was his. Deryk still recalled his uneasiness on the day last winter when she had run gaily across the frozen fields between their houses to meet him. She had been so absorbed in her news she had forgotten both hood and muff. Her face was glowing as much from excitement as from the chill of the day.

"You can never guess," she had said delightedly. "I know you cannot, so it would be unfair of me to ask you to do so. I am going to London for the Season, after all! Is that not the most wonderful news?"

Deryk's heart had sunk. Although he had known she wanted him to join in her happiness, to him the news had been worrying rather than wonderful. "Your uncle has decided to send you there to find you a husband," he said at last, seeing the end of his life-long hopes. "Someone who has a fortune and a title."

"Goose-cap," she said with a laugh, as she brushed back a

68

lock of hair that had come loose from its riband. "Although I suppose I ought to say 'gander-cap.' Is there such a word? At any rate, you know that Uncle Matthew could never find me a husband. Have I not already found my own, years ago?"

He took her chilled hands, first blowing on them to warm them, then kissing them before pulling her cuffs down over them. "I know, my dear—it is what I have wished, quite as much as you. More."

"That would be impossible, for it is all I have ever wished."

"I thought that your uncle was pleased, as well. He seemed to want the joining of our estates. But why should he send you to London, if not to try to find you someone better?"

"There *is* no one better than you, my love. They could not find one—not if they searched the world around," she had cried loyally. "And as for seeking a husband for me, I do not believe my uncle cares a whit whether I go to London or stay here at home."

"But if he does not care—"

"I think it is Aunt Clara who is responsible. She has been nagging Uncle whenever she can lure him out of his lair in the library. He almost lives there, as it is the one place she is not allowed to follow him. When he is not around, she has been constantly telling me that every young lady should have a London Season, no matter what sort of future she plans."

"My dear girl, you know I should never wish to stand in the way of your happiness. It is only that I cannot help the fear that, once you have reached London and had a taste of the life you will find there, you will no longer be satisfied to settle on a small estate in Sussex."

"You should know me better than to think such a thing of me, my dearest one." Christine looked carefully around to see that no one was near, for she would not wish a report of her unladylike conduct to reach her uncle's ears—or rather, her aunt's ears. For, if the tale was carried to him, her uncle would doubtless only have shrugged and asked what one could expect of young people. She knew it was Aunt Clara who wished her to marry someone more important than her dear Deryk.

She lifted her arms to lock them about her beloved's neck, her face raised to his. "I have been promised to you these past three years—much longer than that, in my heart—so there is no one who can come between us. Not even the Prince Regent, should he be interested." She laughed. "Come to London with me, and see that all the pomp can make no difference in my love for you."

So he followed her to the City. Before the Season was well under way, the hostesses of the *ton* had learned that if they wished the Beauty to attend their balls or breakfasts, an invitation must be sent to Mr. Deryk Richardson as well. Else, Miss Christine Douglas would regretfully be kept away by a sudden indisposition, although she might be seen elsewhere in his company on the same day.

It was not surprising that Christine should be pursued by a number of the beaux, but she had managed to hint each of them away before he had the opportunity to make an offer for her. Her aunt's thinking it might be the wisest thing to separate the two young people for a short time had been unsuccessful.

This evening, Deryk had already danced twice with Christine. He had been careful to choose two waltzes, so that he could hold her close to him, a bit closer perhaps than some sticklers would have considered proper. To beg the favor of a third dance would be to label the young lady as fast.

Until they were formally betrothed, two dances in an evening were the only ones the rules of the *ton* would permit them to share. And Lady Douglas watched her niece quite closely to see that she did not flout this or any other rule. Just as she watched to see that there were no clandestine meetings between the young pair—for she knew that the eyes and ears of the *ton* were sharp and its comments spiteful.

Although her aunt was pleased that her charge was a success, she was disappointed that the gallantries of the beaux had meant nothing to Christine. Had she known all the facts, she would have encouraged several of the more important ones to approach Sir Matthew with an offer for the girl's hand. But Christine did not confide in her aunt or anyone except Deryk.

Whenever she left her partner to form another figure of the dance, Christine smiled at Deryk around the shoulder of the gentleman opposite her at the time. Twice, she had dared to purse her lips as if sending him a kiss.

Her aunt would give her a scold for such outrageous behavior if it had been noticed—and Christine did not doubt that it had been, for she knew how sharp were her aunt's eyes. Aunt Clara might, and frequently did, share the gossip of the other chaperons, but she was able to do so without once losing sight of her niece. However, Christine loved Deryk so deeply—had done so all her life—that she would not mind the scold.

She was enjoying every moment of the Little Season, as she had done in the spring. It would have been impossible for anyone not to luxuriate in the thought that she was envied by many of the other young ladies, or that she was being pursued by such a bevy of handsome gentlemen. There was also the feeling that, perhaps, Deryk might be suffering a bit of jealousy even when she was dancing with his friends. He had no reason to be jealous, but he would be; just as she was jealous on the few occasions when he led out some other fortunate miss.

Still, despite her present enjoyment, she was counting the hours—even the minutes—until the coming of Christmas Day. It was the date of her seventeenth birthday. For many years she had been unhappy that there could not be a separate celebration of her birthday and that of the Savior. Of course, that sharing made hers a special day, but all her friends had parties and gifts at other times during the year, and she sometimes thought wistfully that it would be nice if she could do the same.

This year, however, would be different than the others, for she knew she would be receiving her greatest wish for that day. After a great deal of coaxing on her part, her uncle had promised her that her betrothal could be announced on Christmas. While her aunt was overseeing the packing for their return to London for the Little Season, Christine had dared to go into his library sanctuary, resolved not to leave him in peace until he had agreed to her request.

He had grumbled at first about being disturbed, telling her she was as bad as her aunt, never allowing a man a moment to himself. In his own selfish way, however, he was as fond of his niece as it was possible for so self-centered a man to be of anyone, and did not begrudge her happiness—as long as he need not take himself away from his own interests.

"So all your aunt's connivance to get you off to London and show you the world has not changed your mind," he had teased.

"Not in the least bit," she had assured him. "Did you think it would do so?"

"Not at all—I know you too well for that." In truth, he knew little about Christine's activities while she was at home, but it would have taken one even blinder than he not to know her feeling for their young neighbor. "But your aunt was so certain you needed some—I believe the term she used was 'town bronze.'"

"Aunt Clara may call it bronze if she likes; to me, it is only brass. In fact, now that I have seen all that London has to offer, I am more than ever determined to wed my dear Deryk."

"Since you know what you want, and you have had years to learn the worst—"

"And the best."

"—and the best about him, I suppose you must have your way. Your aunt will not like it, I am certain, for she has wished for better things for you. And if she finds someone more to her liking, I fear your Deryk must be put aside even now."

"You would not be so cruel as that to me," Christine had protested.

"Cruel—to think of your best interests?" It was his own best interest he was considering, of course; Clara would never leave him in peace if he allowed the girl to have her way in this.

"It would be the cruelest thing you could do—to come between me and the man I love."

"What can a chit like you know of love? Still, unless I receive a better offer for your hand—and it is beginning to seem that I shall not—your betrothal to young Richardson shall be announced after our Christmas dinner." That was the one day of the year that Sir Matthew willingly deserted his collection to entertain friends and neighbors. To announce Christine's betrothal at that date would relieve him of having to entertain them a second time.

She had kissed him and danced away to give Deryk the happy news, while her uncle returned to the examination of an ancient coin.

He had argued with his wife that, since Christine had made up her mind to marry Deryk, there was truly no reason for them to return to London. Lady Douglas, however, was still determined that the girl must have these last weeks of exposure to the *ton*. "There is still the chance of a better match," she had told him. "I know of one gentleman, at least, that the girl has not put off, despite her attempts to do so. You may yet hear from him." She could not find much about that gentleman to admire, but he *was* the nephew of an earl.

As he had always done before, Sir Matthew had given way in order to have quiet.

Since it had been proven to them that they had no chance with the lady, at least half the beaux in London this Season envied Deryk his coming good fortune. None, however, had envied him more bitterly than Virgil Clive. He had watched Christine longingly in the spring, lost sight of her during the summer, while she and her aunt had visited with relatives, and had followed her since she had returned in the autumn.

His sudden infatuation with the young lady was a source of amusement to the other unlucky beaux. Mr. Clive, who was beginning to rival the Prince Regent in girth, had never before shown an interest in any lady. None had been able to win him away from the gaming tables, not that many had tried to do so, for most of them found him a figure of fun.

When Christine first appeared at Almack's, Virgil had fallen in love with her at first sight, a state he would have laughed out of existence had it not happened to him. He had approached Lady Sefton and persuaded her to present him to the young lady as a partner for the waltz. Her ladyship, while hiding a smile at the gentleman's insistence, agreed to present him, for she knew him to be quite proficient in the dance, despite his size. The thought of being permitted to hold Christine, even under the watchful eyes of the Patronesses and at the prescribed distance, had indeed been a heady one, and he made no secret of his feelings for her.

Christine had not found the gentleman a figure of fun; in fact, the nearly breathless words of love from one she had barely met, and whose size made him almost grotesque in her eyes, had been enough to frighten her and repel her. Although she had been polite to him during the dance, she had insisted that he return her to her aunt's side as soon as it was ended, refusing his invitation to join him for a bit of refreshment, despite her aunt's encouraging smile to him.

Neither would she agree to dance with him another time. He was unable to see why she should have taken him in such aversion. Had he been too precipitate, he wondered, in telling her of his feelings? It was only that this feeling was so strange to him that he felt she must know it, so why did she not share it?

He had followed her from party to party all through the Season, attempting to win her favor. Evening after evening, he had begged—sometimes abjectly—for dances, always to receive the same answer, "I am sorry, sir, but I have no dances available tonight."

As popular as she was, Virgil knew that was not always the truth, for often late-comers had been granted dances that earlier had been denied to him. It was made clear to him—and to all the *ton*, doubtless sniggering at him behind their collective smiles—that Miss Christine Douglas did not wish his company.

"You are being impolite to the gentleman," her aunt chided.

"But, Aunt Clara, I cannot like him."

"Nonsense. Merely because he is not that foolish young man you continue to make eyes at. Behave yourself, my girl, or I shall be forced to speak to your uncle."

Christine, however, was adamant in her refusal to accept Virgil Clive's attentions.

He had accepted her decision with outward politeness, since he had no alternative. One could scarcely carry off the lady of his choice bodily, pleasant though such a thought might be. That was the stuff of dreams, not of real life. Abductors of young ladies were given short shrift in these modern times. A gentleman was expected to accept his defeat graciously. That there was nothing gracious in his acceptance was a secret from everyone.

But that was all in the past. Now Virgil was certain he possessed the key that would bring her into his arms rather than into those of Deryk Richardson.

Last night, after having received the customary rebuff by Christine, he had left the ball to pay his usual call at one of his favorite gaming hells. It was the sort of place where wealthy young gentlemen were encouraged to come, with the lure that they might be able to win great fortunes on the turn of a card.

Tales of such winnings were not rare, even in the more respectable gaming houses, and newcomers often found that they were winning quite heavily early in the evenings, but in the long run, only Virgil Clive and those of his ilk were able to show great profits. The others left the games poorer, if no wiser than before, only to be drawn there again when they were given the assurance—assurance which was as false as the promises they had received before—that their fortune would doubtless be better the next time.

Young Mervin Foxe had been one of these. Newly come to town, he had, like so many others, fancied himself as a superior gamester and had been steered with great ease to the plucking. Night after night, he had gamed recklessly, often so befuddled by drink that he was unable to see that the cards dealt to him were not the ones he would have received had he been in an honest game.

At last he had cried, "You gentlemen have won all my money, even the deeds to my estates. I have nothing left in all the world except this," and had flung an odd-looking coin upon the table. "I shall wager this against all you have won from me."

"That old bit of tin?" one of the winning players said scornfully. "You must think us fools to risk good money against that."

Virgil took up the coin and looked at it closely. Not tin, as the other had said; he thought it was silver. He had recently seen a sketch of a number of old coins and if this—bearing the profile of a young man with what appeared to be a helmet adorned with small horns—was what he thought it was, it was worth more than everything that had crossed the table tonight. If he had erred, he would have lost only the time it would take him to play for it. It was well worth the gamble.

Careful not to betray his thoughts, lest he arouse the greed of his companions and find one of them competing for his prize, he said casually, "Well, it is true that, from time to time, you have lost a great deal of blunt to me, Foxe. Not more, certainly, than many other gentlemen have done in similar games."

"That I can believe."

"And none have found reason for complaint. When a man wagers, he must sometimes expect to lose. However, since you feel as you do, I am willing to give you an opportunity to recoup your losses. One hand, for what you have lost tonight against this old charm."

"What about all you have taken from me in the past?" The young man had put away a great quantity of Hollands gin while the cards had gone about the table, but he was not so far gone in drink as to forget the large sums he had lost to this fat man in their previous meetings.

The other players jeered at him for wishing to spoil sport, but Virgil said, "You drive a hard bargain, young sir, but everyone at the table knows that I was never one to avoid a wager, even so one-sided a wager as this."

"One-sided—when you have won from me nightly?"

"But the odds were not so great in those matches. Still, if you win this hand, you shall have back what you have lost to me tonight and my vowels for your earlier losses, as well, payable by the end of the week. If you lose, I shall have only your little pocket piece to show for my time. What could be fairer than that?"

Companions, even those who were well-acquainted with this style of play, told him he was daft to make such an offer, but Virgil only smiled at them and began to shuffle the cards. He knew how much was at stake and he had no intention of losing this hand. That coin *must* be his.

Considering the manner in which Mervin Foxe was playing this evening, Virgil could doubtless have won the hand by dealing honestly, but he did not take the risk of trying to do so. Every gamester knew that there were times when fortune went against a man, and he would not chance having that happen to him tonight. When the game had ended, he scooped the old coin from the table and slipped it into his pocket as if he thought it valueless.

"As I said, your little charm is mine. Better fortune next time," he told the young gentleman, who rose unsteadily from the table.

"There will be no next time for me, Mr. Clive, thanks to efforts of you and your friends," Mr. Foxe replied, in a steadier voice than was customary for one in his state. It was as if the knowledge of his complete loss was enough to sober him. While other players chaffed at him for a poor loser, he left the building quietly, and it was not until morning that friends learned he had put a period to his existence.

Virgil Clive heard none of this until much later, and when he did hear, he only shrugged, not caring a whit for the fate of his late victim. If the man could not afford to lose, he should not have played. For himself, he had located the sketch he remembered and saw that he had not been in error about the worth of his new acquisition.

Such sketches, however, were sometimes unreliable and this was no time for him to be wrong about its value. To make doubly certain that there could be no mistake, he had taken the coin to a reputable dealer. The man looked at his caller with some suspicion, for—despite the correctness of Virgil's apparel and mien—the other knew this was not the type of person who frequented his shop. However, he gasped when Virgil drew the coin from his pocket and tossed it upon the table as if he had no suspicion of its importance.

The dealer snatched it up, examining it carefully and glaring at the man who would so mistreat a rare coin. "You, sir, should have more consideration for something so fine as this." He was so overset by the other's carelessness that the words were uttered before he realized the error of speaking in such a fashion to a potential seller. He hoped he had not given the other the idea that he might ask a good price for this item.

"Then it has some value?" Virgil spoke as if the answer made little difference to him.

"A silver drachma—a coin of ancient Greece—and bearing the face of Alexander the Great in his pose as the son of Zeus? You may be certain that it has. At least, I should say that it would possibly have some small value," he amended quickly, fearing that his earlier enthusiasm might have ruined his chances of persuading the owner to part with the coin for a fraction of its worth.

"I suppose there are not many of these about?" Virgil persisted.

The dealer attempted to speak casually. "Not as many as we dealers should like to see, of course. There are never enough coins for each dealer to have a supply of every coin minted." The truth was that, in all his years in business, he had only seen one other coin like this, and that had been in a private collection. It was more valuable than most of the others in his stock. "But certainly there are still enough like this one scattered about to keep the value low to please the average collector."

Virgil Clive had not spent the greater part of his adult life earning a dishonest living handling the cards and dice without being able to read the thoughts beyond his opponent's outer expression. Although this shop was well recommended for its fair dealing, the proprietor apparently thought he could cheat his caller; although, like a winning gamester, he would merely have called what he was doing a matter of good business. He had no way of knowing he was facing a past master of the art of deception. This was clearly a coin of great value—and Virgil knew exactly what he was going to do with it.

Despite all efforts of the dealer to purchase the coin from him—even going to the extreme measure of owning that it *might* be somewhat more valuable than he had first said—Virgil said, "No, although I promise to keep you in mind, should I decide to sell it. However, I am not a collector, and I do not believe I wish to part with it for the moment. It is merely a charm, of course, something I acquired to bring me good fortune."

That was true enough; he was certain that the coin could bring him all the fortune he would ever wish. "I should like, however," he continued, "for you to give me a paper stating that it is an authentic silver drachma—I believe that is what you called it. If there is a charge for preparing such authentication, I am willing to pay it. Within reason, of course."

The dealer made another strenuous effort to persuade the caller to part with his coin, but was overborne, and knowing that the success of his business depended upon the goodwill of possible clients, even such a man as this one, was finally persuaded to provide the required certificate.

Virgil wrote at once to Sir Matthew Douglas, describing the coin in some detail. He received an instant response, for—as he had anticipated—Sir Matthew had nothing of the sort in his collection. The gamester knew, too, that a collector of any sort, whether he collected coins, books, or butterflies, was as avid to add something rare to his treasure as was the worst devotee of a gaming house in search of that elusive winning hand.

Two days before Christmas, therefore, Virgil was on his way to visit the old gentleman. The silver coin, no longer to be tossed about as if it were unimportant, instead was safely tucked in an inner pocket which had been purposely made for just such a use.

He had deliberately not sent a reply to Sir Matthew's request as to the sort of price he wished for his find, knowing the uncertainty of obtaining it would increase the baronet's anticipation to possess such a rare coin. There would be time enough to name his price when he arrived; he would demand nothing less than the hand of Miss Christine Douglas in marriage.

The eagerness in Sir Matthew's letter was enough to tell him the baronet would agree to give him what he asked. He might make some objections at the outset, knowing that his niece's wishes lay elsewhere, but when he learned that the seller was obstinate in his price, Virgil knew he would be granted what he wished.

The sight of an inn near Sir Matthew's home reminded him that he must be somewhat travel-stained, although the usual mud of the road was frozen under a blanket of snow. A prospective suitor must look his best, for Christine was certain to be at home at this season. When she heard of his destination, Mrs. Barker, wife of the manager of the Twin Unicorns, a woman whose rotundity was a match for that of her visitor and which only served to emphasize her husband's extreme thinness, reminded him that he was only a short distance from his destination.

"Ah yes, that is what I thought, although I am not familiar with this part of the country. However, I should not wish to appear there in all my dirt," he implied. "Nor do I like to arrive so late in the day. It implies a wish to be put up for the night, which is not my intention. There is time enough for me to pay my call on the morrow."

He was eager to have the arrangement with Sir Matthew settled as quickly as possible, but it would never do to display such feeling. The fact that he had halted for the night so near to his objective would only serve to whet the old man's appetite.

Mrs. Barker nodded. Although her honesty had compelled her to remind the gentleman of how near he was to the Douglas estate, additional trade was always agreeable, and especially so during the winter when there were so many people who preferred to remain by the warmth of their own firesides. Also she approved of a gentleman who was so nice in his ways, one who was too considerate of another to break in upon his comfort.

"Well, we have just the room for you, sir," she assured him. "The best room in the inn, I may say. Travelers do not come this way often at this season, more's the pity to our way of thinking. They come so seldom, I must own, that we have often argued whether it would not be better for us to close the inn at this time of year. But what else would we do?"

"It is my good fortune that you have not done so," he said politely, although it meant little to him what might happen to any of the country folk. If this inn had been forced to close its doors, doubtless there would have been another not too far distant.

Mrs. Barker demolished that thought with her next words. "Yes, for you would find nowhere else to stop within more than a dozen miles. A long way in this weather. So, although travelers are scarce, we remain open for whoever may come, although with a smaller staff than we have in the summer."

"As long as you can provide me with a room and some food, I shall be content."

"That we can do, sir, and better food than you will find at
many inns. We have only one other gentleman here at the
moment—that is, he has not arrived yet, but we expect to see
him at any time. For the same reason as you. He always stops
here to refresh himself before arriving at the Douglas estate."

Virgil nodded absentmindedly. It was to be expected that Sir
Matthew might have some visitors for the Christmas season, but
none, he was certain, who would be as warmly welcomed as he.
He doubted any other would bring his hosts so alluring a gift.
Nor, he was certain, who would demand so alluring a gift in
exchange.

He allowed himself to be conducted to his room, unaware that
the innkeeper's wife had chosen this one not because it was
better than any other room, for they were all alike, but because
she felt that the springs in this bed *might* withstand the
gentleman's weight. In Virgil's opinion, it was much like any
other, save that this one was much cleaner than many to which
he had repaired at one time or another. The state of his
surroundings were always dependent, of course, upon the
condition of his purse—but after he had met with Sir Matthew,
he anticipated a great rise in his prospects. Then he would be
able to afford the best, no matter where he wished to travel.

He carefully put away the clothing he would wear on the
morrow and brushed the greater part of the travel-soil from his
present attire. Descending to the tap room, he was promptly
supplied with liquid refreshment by the owner and the promise
of good supper from Mrs. Barker, a supper which he felt was
long overdue in coming. The luncheon he had been served at the
last posting house had been meager and had done little to dull his
appetite. He could not know that Mrs. Barker was purposely
delaying serving the evening meal, awaiting her favorite guest.

The expected visitor did not arrive until darkness had fallen.
Already overset by the delay in having his meal, Virgil scowled
when he recognized Deryk Richardson. He told himself, however, that he should have expected the young man to be
somewhere in the neighborhood. After all, his pursuit of
Christine Douglas had been the *on dit* of London—as much,
Virgil suspected, as his own. He was aware, however, that
Richardson's home was nearby. Why should he come to the inn
rather than going there? Surely, he could rest with more comfort
in his own bed.

Was it possible that Richardson had heard something of the coin he had won? That he had stopped here in an effort to wrest it away from him? Unconsciously, he touched the spot above the secret pocket, as if afraid something might already have happened to it.

Unaware that the success of the other man's plans meant the ruin of his own, Deryk nonetheless greeted him warily, wondering what could have brought the fat fop to this part of the country. Virgil hid his true feelings to return the greeting as pleasantly as he could. He was only too well aware that Miss Christine Douglas had not objected to Richardson's suit, as she had to his own. All of London had been able to see that, of course, but he could not account for her taste.

He could see that there was little difference between them. He was as tall as the other man, his shoulders were as broad, although the other's waistline and limbs were too thin, Virgil thought. His own hair and eyes were almost as dark, and most observers—except for those he had bested with the cards or dice—seemed to find his features as pleasant.

His birth, most certainly, was better than Deryk's. He was the nephew of an earl—not the heir, of course, as his uncle had two healthy young sons. Yet he might still inherit; stranger things had been known to happen. Deryk Richardson could not boast a title anywhere in his family.

Then why should Christine prefer the other man? Was it merely because the Richardson and Douglas estates were neighbors, and a union between the two families would be advantageous to both? He doubted that was the reason, for he did not think Christine Douglas was the sort of young lady who would place the welfare of an estate above her personal choice for a husband.

Whatever the reason for her preference at the moment, however, it would not matter when Sir Matthew ordered her to wed the man *he* chose. Virgil's fingers once more hovered over the ancient coin in his pocket which would soon be exchanged for marriage lines.

Mrs. Barker beamed equally at the two young gentlemen, happy to have their trade. Young Mr. Richardson had been expected to come here, of course; he was in the habit of stopping at the inn when he arrived for his Christmas visit, although it was not more than a mile to his home. However, by spending the night here, he could be assured of seeing Miss Christine the moment she arrived tomorrow morning. Both of them had been in London, the woman knew, but as always when they were home, they spent every possible moment in each other's company.

By the elegance of his clothing and the carriage he drove—which, although the elderly earl did not know it and would never have approved of its use, displayed his crest—the other gentleman must also have come from London. He could not be a guest of Sir Matthew; through the years, she had grown familiar with all those who would be present at the Christmas revels. She knew the baronet never made alterations in his list of guests, except when he added the children or grandchildren of his old friends, and she doubted that he would have permitted Lady Douglas to do so—even to include some friends she might have made in London.

Mrs. Barker was not anxious to lose the gentleman's trade when money was so scarce; nonetheless, she found herself hoping that he would be on his way early on the morrow, so that the young couple could have several moments alone together. The need to watch over the baking of her pudding would be her excuse for retiring to the kitchen, and she would see that Mr. Barker stayed out of the tap room for a time. She was not too old to remember how young people liked a bit of a cuddle.

" 'Tis true Christmas weather," she commented, and Deryk grinned.

"That it is, Mrs. B. Perfect weather for the season. I traveled through snow for the past hour. A fall of an inch or two more, and I wager Christine will have to make use of the sleigh tomorrow. Not that she will object to that—somehow, the sleigh always seems to fit the Christmas season better than a carriage."

"Miss Douglas will not be at home for Christmas?" Virgil asked a bit anxiously. Perhaps his business with Sir Matthew could be handled more easily in her absence, but he would wish her to be there when it was settled, to hear her uncle's giving her to the suitor of his choice.

Deryk laughed at the question. He was so happy at the thought of his upcoming betrothal that he could laugh at anything. Even at the presence of this man, one he had always thought to be something of an overblown fop and whose presence so far from his usual London haunts was a mystery.

"Certainly, Christine will be home for Christmas. There is nothing that could make her miss the day—'tis her birthday, you know. Or perhaps you did not know; she does not make the fact known to everyone. And this will be the best Christmas for the two of us. You may not know it, Clive, but you will soon be able to wish me happy."

"Oh, Mr. Richardson, you cannot mean to say—'tis all settled, then?" Mrs. Barker cried, relieving Virgil of the necessity of replying for a moment or so.

"Well, there is just one detail left, then it will be as nearly settled as it can be before the banns are called. Christine may wish to tell you the news herself, but I am certain she will not mind when she learns I have already done so. She knows that I should like to shout the news to all the world. Before she returned to London last autumn, Christine received her uncle's promise that he was planning to announce her betrothal as soon as everyone has eaten their Christmas dinner."

Oh yes, Richardson could be certain that Sir Matthew would keep his promise to announce the betrothal, Virgil said to himself, while Mrs. Barker congratulated the young gentleman, her eyes brimming with tears of happiness for the young couple. But that betrothal would not be to Richardson, for all the attention the chit had given him this season.

How fortunate it was that he had decided to come at this time, before it was too late. He had thought at one time that it might be best to wait until after the holidays to approach the old gentleman, that the longer he delayed, the more eager Sir Matthew would be for his coin. His eagerness to possess Christine, however, was as great as he knew her uncle's wish must be to add the drachma to his collection, so he had decided to delay his visit no longer.

What a disaster it would have been to all his plans if he had held to his original decision to whet the baronet's appetite further by putting off his arrival until the new year. Once Sir Matthew had made his announcement of his niece's choice, even the opportunity of adding such a valuable coin to his collection might not have been enough to make him change his mind. He was doubtless the sort, Virgil thought, who felt that his word, once it had been given, could not be gainsaid.

"But you said something about Miss Douglas traveling by sleigh," he said aloud, wondering that they could not hear the changed beating of his heart when he considered how near he had come to losing everything for which he had gambled. "I thought perhaps she might be paying a holiday visit to friends or relatives elsewhere in the country."

"Oh, not at Christmastime, sir. That is her special day. Nothing would prevent her from celebrating it at home. But she will be coming here on the morrow, along with her maid," Mrs. Barker told him. "She always comes here to fetch the special Christmas pudding that her uncle prefers—has done so every Christmas since I married Barker and left service."

Virgil's glance showed his puzzlement, making Deryk laugh once more. *Must* the fellow continue to whoop in such an inane fashion, Virgil wondered, then comforted himself with the thought that he would be the one who would be laughing on the morrow. Also, he was beginning to doubt the other man would be so happy if he suspected the reason for *his* visit.

"Of course," Deryk said pleasantly enough, "being a stranger to these parts, you could not know. Mrs. Barker was Sir Matthew's cook before she married."

"And Sir Matthew always declares that Christmas would not be Christmas without one of my puddings. Not a plum pudding, although I always have those as well, for any guests who might arrive here at Christmastide and expect to have them. Miss Christine will take one of those for their guests. But Sir Matthew always declares that they are too rich for his digestion."

Deryk laughed at that, as well; even a discussion of his future uncle-in-law's fictional digestive problems could make him happy today. "Although why a man who can manage to eat several helpings of oysters," he said, "the same of roast goose, a pair of plump pigeons, and finish his meal with a glass, or more likely a bottle, of port, should find cause to worry about his digestion is a puzzle. I have never known him even to suffer from the gout, as do many men his age."

"Nonetheless, what Sir Matthew wants for his own dinner is my Queen of Puddings—and that is what he shall have, as he has always had since I was large enough to hold a spoon and follow my mum's directions for making it. A nursery pudding, some would call it, but 'tis good enough for everyone. And he will have it, as long as I am able to make it for him. I shall be awake early, so that it is ready when Miss Christine comes for it."

"But I was of the opinion that Christmas puddings were

always made months before the season," Virgil commented. He had once heard someone say this. Whether or not this was correct, he had no way of knowing, but felt that he must say something. Anything, so that he would not accidentally reveal his pleasure at the information that he had arrived here in time to prevent Sir Matthew from giving his niece to the wrong man.

"That is true if you are referring to plum puddings, which must be aged before they are eaten. Some cooks prefer to make them as much as a year before they are to be served, but I usually make them no more than three or four months before Christmas."

"But you said—"

"That I make both kinds of puddings, for both are popular. If the plum puddings I have made now are not eaten by guests, they can be stored as long as need be with no problem, as they will not be spoiled by keeping but will only be the richer by judicious applications of brandy. The lighter puddings are not the same, however; they must be made shortly before they are to be eaten, so I do not make them in quantity. Still, we follow the same plan in making up the lighter ones as is done when making the plum puddings. Everyone in the house must come to the kitchen and stir the mixture for good fortune."

"Then I shall be happy to comply," he assured her, having no intention of indulging in anything so infantile. However, he had no wish to give anyone a reason to think him other than an ordinary visitor. He knew now that his fortune was already assured. The fact that he had learned in time of the young people's plans showed him that nothing could go wrong for him now.

When Sir Matthew had the drachma dangled before his eyes and knew it could be his, he would be only too eager to meet the suitor's price. Both Christine and this young smart might protest as much as they would; Virgil *knew* that the old man would decide in his favor. Sir Matthew's passion for his collection was well known.

Desirous of completing his arrangements with Sir Matthew as quickly as possible, Virgil rose the next morning much earlier than was customary for him. When shaved—a task he had learned to perform for himself, as he seldom was able to afford a servant—he donned his new coat of crimson superfine with the biscuit-colored breeches—were they straining just a bit too tightly across his thighs these last few days?—the marcella waistcoat with its faint red stripe, and spent the greater part of an hour arranging his cravat beneath his second chin until its folds pleased him. Being something of a recluse, Sir Matthew might not be conversant with London fashions, but Christine would know, and when he was presented to her as her future husband, he wished to look his best.

As Deryk Richardson had predicted, it had continued to snow during most of the night, but now the air was clear and crisp. Virgil had no doubt that one of his horses would be able to make its way along the drifted road, but he would have to leave his carriage in the inn yard for the present. Ah well, Christine had already seen it, and it would be the ancient coin, not the crest on his vehicle, which would count with Sir Matthew.

It would be most inconvenient to have to ride, of course, for he had not thought to bring riding gear. Neither had he brought the handsome mount he had recently won from another gamester who had more hair than wit. He was beginning to wonder if the animal, for all its looks, was truly up to carrying his weight. It might be best to wager it against one which would suit him better.

Perhaps it might be an even wiser choice, when he had become Sir Matthew's nephew-in-law, to give up his gaming. It would never do for the future owner of so great an estate to spend his time in gaming hells, although he knew plenty of young toffs who did exactly that. There was no need to make such a decision at this time, however; he could see which way the wind blew.

The anticipation of his coming victory had made him extremely hungry this morning. When he demanded his breakfast, however, it was brought to him by a young female whose mobcap was sadly askew and whose voluminous apron was certainly made to fit Mrs. Barker's girth rather than her own.

The child was quite nervous at being pressed into such service. From the clatter she made in her handling of the dishes, he thought it probable that she was more accustomed to making beds and sweeping out the rooms than in waiting upon the visitors to the inn. Even the food, while plentiful enough, was scarcely up to what he had come to expect after last evening's feast.

"Mrs. Barker is not ill, is she?" he inquired, not truly caring what the answer might be, only eager to be on his way and fearful that the wench's clumsiness might result in some food being spilled upon his finery. If his wife was unable to serve guests, why should Barker not come out from his place behind the bar and see that everything was done as it should be?

"Oh no, sir, she'd not know what it was to be ailing, not that one," the tiny servant replied, so clearly overcome by the finery of this enormous man that she was nearly gabbling. "And even if she was, she'd still be up and doing today, if you was to ask me, which 'tis not likely you'd be doing, sir, but which I can tell you anyhow. 'Tis her morning for making the special pudding for Christmas, you see, and she be hard at her work since dawn in the kitchen, with no time even to do her usual cooking or to seeing to customers, which is why I be down here."

Oh yes, the special pudding, it had been called; he had forgot the woman had spoken of making it today. Still, it should make no difference to him what the creature was doing. Her first duty was to see that the inn's guests were properly served, and with food of the best quality. When she had told of her plan for making the pudding today, he had promised to come and give it a stir for good fortune, as she had clearly expected. He did not plan to do so, however. Why should he when everything was going exactly as he intended that it should?

He could hear Deryk Richardson's footsteps upon the stair, but did not wish to meet him this morning if he could avoid it. In the face of the fellow's happiness about his upcoming betrothal it was difficult for him not to reveal the fact that *he* was to be the lucky man. If Richardson suspected that Virgil had so valuable a coin in his possession, he might attempt to prevent the meeting with Sir Matthew. As the other entered the tap room, Virgil slipped into the kitchen.

"There you are, sir," Mrs. Barker exclaimed happily, for the making of her special Christmas pudding always gave her the greatest satisfaction of any part of her duties at the inn. "Come out to take your turn at stirring the pudding, have you?"

As she spoke, she was busily whisking egg yolks with extract of vanilla and preparing to add them to her mixture of bread crumbs, sugar, and milk. " 'Twill be only a moment or two more, sir, and you can have the opportunity to do so. It should be especially good fortune for you, sir, since you're the first to come."

"Oh, am I too early? The girl said you were busy with your work, but I had no idea how long it would be." He moved away, as if he intended to return to the tap room, the last place he wished to be at the moment, but was halted by Mrs. Barker's cheerful statement.

"Oh, no indeed. You are not too early at all, sir. The stirring must be done in the next few minutes, because the pudding will soon be ready to be put into the pan. If the others have not come out by that time, they will miss their turn."

"Well, do not hurry because of me. I can await your pleasure." Although he appeared to be giving her all his attention, he had stationed himself near the door, where he could listen to the conversation which was taking place in the tap room.

"Clive a slug-abed this morning, is he?" Richardson was saying with that laugh Virgil had already come to detest. "I thought he might be on his way to wherever he was going, but I suppose the snow has put paid to that."

"Oh no, sir, you are the one who is late. The other gentleman has already had his breakfast. And quite a meal it was, too. I dunno when we have had a guest who ate so much as he. As for going on, belike he can beg a ride with you and Miss Christine is she comes in the sleigh. He is going to the manor, too."

"He is? Well, this is not time for such as he to be about. And when he comes in, I shall tell him so."

Why should the fellow object to his presence? Virgil wondered. It must be that Sir Matthew had let slip the news that he was bringing the coin. But even Sir Matthew did not know what he intended to ask in return. Everyone in London, of course, knew how fascinated he had been by Christine. Could the young man suspect that he was also going courting? Would he demand that Virgil give up the coin so that it could be returned to Foxe's family?

Without it, Virgil knew he had no chance to win the young lady. Richardson was *not* going to take it from him. Yet, if it came to a confrontation, despite the difference in their sizes, he knew he would not be a match for the younger man. It would be best if he could hide the coin and retrieve it later.

"The pudding is all ready for the final stirs, sir," Mrs. Barker was saying, holding out the spoon to him. Why should the woman bother him with puddings at such a time, Virgil thought, about to turn away when he had an idea. What better hiding place could he find?

He took the spoon, stirring it about in the mixture, and with the dexterity he was accustomed to use in handling the cards, slipped the coin into the bowl, quickly stirring it out of sight.

"It is already beginning to smell delicious," he observed, returning the spoon. Privately, he thought it smelled of nothing at all, but he was certain the old woman must think she was making something wonderful. "I must confess to you, madam, that this is also my favorite pudding—and I shall insist upon purchasing it from you the moment it is done."

"But—"

"No, not a word. You may ask what you will for it, but I intend to have my favorite pudding, one I have not been able to find for longer than I can remember. So few cooks know how to make it properly. You would not be cruel enough to refuse to permit a stranger to have his wish—not at this season, would you?"

Without giving her the opportunity to say more, he left the kitchen, secure in the thought that his valuable coin was now safe and could be retrieved at his leisure. As he stepped into the tap room, Deryk said, "I wondered where you might have gone, Clive."

"I merely stepped into the kitchen to compliment the cook on the excellence of my breakfast." It was better not to mention the pudding, although he doubted anyone would suspect that he had hidden the coin in it. "Why should my absence concern you, sir?"

"I wished to ask why you are calling on Sir Matthew Douglas."

"Oh, that. It is a matter of business."

"At the holiday season? I cannot see Sir Matthew wishing to conduct business just now when he is planning his Christmas celebration. And I was not aware that you were involved in any sort of business." Any sort that an honest man would wish to share, he added silently.

Virgil laughed. "There are many things about me that you are doubtless unaware of, my friend."

"I do not doubt that, sir."

Seeing that tempers were rising—at least, he thought Mr. Richardson's was doing so—Mr. Barker said swiftly, "It don't matter what the reason, do it? Why not share a drink to celebrate the coming holiday?"

Deryk shrugged. "You are right, Barker. Whatever Mr. Clive wants, it cannot matter to me. A drink would be quite the thing. Still, it might be as well if we should wait until Christine arrives. Then, sir, you could have a glass to both of us."

"Yes, it would please me to drink to Miss Douglas's future." But her future would not be with him, he added silently.

Before either of them could say more, Mrs. Barker put her head around the kitchen door. "Oh, there you are at last, Mr. Richardson. I thought I heard your voice. What are you waiting for? You know this is the day. Did you forget," she asked Virgil, "to remind him that he was to come and stir the pudding?"

"Oh, that is my fault; I shall come at once," Deryk told her, and hurried off. As the door closed behind him, Virgil could hear him beginning to explain that he had involved the other gentleman in conversation and had forgot the time.

If Mrs. Barker had not brought up his coin in her stirring of the mixture, Virgil supposed there would be no danger of Richardson's doing so. Still, he would have felt happier if the other man had not gone near the kitchen.

Perhaps it was a good thing that Christine was coming to the inn today. He had thought to see her uncle and settle the matter before she knew he was in the area, but it was improbable that she could have any suspicion as to the reason for his journey. Unless Richardson had been told by someone, that would be a secret until he had spoken to the baronet. Then he could claim the bride he wanted.

If he knew young lovers—how he disliked the thought of the girl having a lover other than himself—Christine and Richardson would doubtless welcome the opportunity to dally here for a time. Once he had retrieved his coin, he could be on his way to the Douglas estate. By the time Christine was ready to return home, he and Sir Matthew would have reached an agreement and the girl would be his.

The tinkling of bells and the susurration of runners over the crisp snow heralded the coming of a sleigh. Deryk hastened from the kitchen to a tap room window and craned his neck to look out, although he must have known that trees would hide the approach of the vehicle until it had nearly reached the door of the inn.

"Christine is here!" he cried unnecessarily, as she stepped down from the sleigh and hurried to the door, followed by her abigail. The half-dazed look upon her face would have been enough to tell everyone the newcomer's identity. "My dear!" He caught both her hands and drew her toward him, but she shook her head slightly, looking toward the other occupant of the tap room.

At the sight of his beloved, Deryk had completely forgot they were not alone. He flushed slightly at having placed her in a position of embarrassment. Turning toward the other man, he made the introduction, "I believe you know Mr. Clive, do you not, Christine?"

Christine nodded briefly and extended her hand. Virgil bowed over it. He would have kept it in his plump grasp and raised it to his lips, but she withdrew it the instant he had touched it, leaving him empty-handed. If she noticed the elegance of his dress, she gave no sign—and he had chosen these togs especially to please her.

Aunt Clara would give her a scold, Christine thought, if she could have seen how rudely her niece was behaving toward the gentleman. But Aunt Clara could not know the shudders Christine was forced to repress when those fat white fingers curled about her own—like some great slug, she told herself. She could *not* pretend to enjoy his company. Too, she had been looking forward to spending some moments alone with Deryk, as they would have little time to themselves once the Christmas guests arrived.

Mr. Clive had spoiled that plan, and although he could not have know what she wished, she found it difficult not to blame him for his interference. Without a word to him, she turned away to greet the landlord, who was now returning to the room.

"I have told my wife you are here, Miss Christine," he informed her.

"Thank you, Barker. I had planned to leave home earlier, but I was delayed having to answer a great many questions about tomorrow's decorations—unnecessary ones, for they have done the decorations in the same way for years. They took so long that I feared I should be late. However, the snow was not too deep, after all, so we came quickly. And how have you been?"

Christine unbuttoned her pelisse and slipped out of it as she spoke. Of sapphire-blue velvet, lined and trimmed with sable, the garment was uncomfortably warm in the heated room. She also removed the matching hood, allowing her fair hair to fall about her shoulders. It may have been unfashionable to wear it loose in that manner, but she knew Deryk preferred to see it that way, and Deryk's wishes meant more to her than all the dictates of fashion. Besides, she had left London behind forever, so what did it matter what others thought of her?

Her abigail came forward quickly to take the garments and the large muff from Deryk's hands and carry them away to the other side of the room. The removal of her pelisse revealed her walking dress of darker blue, its skirts drawn up to keep them from dragging in the snow, and to show the matching, fur-trimmed half boots.

"You know how it is with me, miss. I'm always well, thank you, save for a slight touch of the rheumatics when the weather is wet." It was the same answer Barker had given her every time she had asked him in the past twelve years, but Christine greeted it as news and commiserated with him on his ailment, as she had always done.

There was a stir outside the door, a muttered order to the young servant to hold it open but to stay out of the way, and Mrs. Barker came into the room carrying a large pudding, still steaming from the oven. Until this moment, Virgil had forgot her remarks about making a pudding for Sir Matthew. He now realized that she intended to give *his* pudding to Christine.

That must not happen! If Christine carried home the valuable coin, Sir Matthew would have it to add to his collection, and *he* would have nothing.

Uncaring how rude he must appear, even to the girl he wanted, he rushed forward and took the pudding from the cook's hands, crying, "My pudding! How good it was of you to bring it to me at once. Have the cost added to my bill," and ran from the room, while everyone stared after him.

In his room, gasping for breath after his unaccustomed haste upon the stairs, he pushed aside the garments scattered across the bed and seated himself, the pudding beside him. Grimacing as the still-hot jam and sweetened meringue clung to his fingers, burning them until he wiped the mess away upon the coverlet, he methodically tore the pudding apart.

Ten minutes later, he sat swearing, surrounded by a mess of crumbs, none of them large enough to hide his valuable coin.

Unable to believe the truth, he rubbed each particle between his fingers again and again, until there could be no doubt. The drachma was gone!

"That thieving woman," he cried, throwing the dish across the room so that it shattered against the wall, smearing sticky crumbs in its wake as it fell. "She must have been watching and seen me drop it in while I stirred the wretched pudding, although I thought I was taking care not to attract her attention. She must have realized it was valuable and fished it out of that mess and kept it, thinking that I would not dare to complain. She is wrong. I'll have my coin if I have to choke it out of her. And she dared to permit me to say I should pay for this abomination."

He scrubbed the sweetness from his hands and brushed as many of the crumbs as possible from his coat and breeches, realizing as he did so that many of the jam-coated ones had stained the fabric. He swore heartily as he stomped down the stairs. The ruination of his best attire was another score to be held against the cook's account, and he would demand satisfaction for that, as well.

Approaching the tap room door, he could hear Mrs. Barker saying, " 'Tis a pity to make you wait, Miss Christine, but since that gentleman was in such a hurry to take away the pudding he ordered—"

"Acting as if he was half-starved, although I do not doubt he had already had a breakfast fit for half a dozen like him," Deryk commented. He had several times seen the other man at table, shoveling food into his mouth as if he did not expect another meal for many days. Last evening, for example, he had taken such large portions of the generous food Mrs. Barker had served them that Deryk had thought *he* must go hungry.

"Yes, it seemed that Nell had to make a score of trips with his meal. I know she is slower than treacle in winter, but she was running back and forth nearly all the time I was making my pudding. I never knew one man could eat so much. Though you know we should never begrudge anyone a mouthful of food, nor expect him to pay more just because he ate more than his share."

"We know that, Mrs. Barker," Christine said soothingly. "I do not doubt your roomers get better food, and more of it, than any inn in the country."

"True enough, " Deryk agreed. "I have eaten in many places,

even in London, where you would be ashamed to give their food to a dog."

"It is kind of both of you to say that, though I do like good cooking, as one can tell by looking at me. But what I mean to say, miss, is that I shall have to make you another pudding, although I shall be as quick with it as I possibly can."

Christine was seated near the window, her hand snugly held in Deryk's. "I assure you, Mrs. Barker, I do not object to waiting, in the circumstances." She and the young man exchanged conspiratorial smiles, thinking of the moments they could spend together.

Mrs. Barker smiled slyly. "No, I doubt you'd mind the waiting. Mr. Richardson told me your news, and I want to wish you happy—both of you."

"Oh, thank you, Mrs. Barker. It is so kind of you to say that. Of course I shall not mind the waiting for you to make a new pudding for me. I always enjoy my visits to your inn, and especially—"

She broke off, slanting a glance upward to meet Deryk's gaze, blushing slightly at its ardor, then looked away again. Recovering herself, she went on, "Betty can return home with the driver, to tell where I am, then send him back for us later. Uncle Matthew likes to have his pudding for Christmas Eve supper, you know, rather than for the next day's dinner, so there is time enough and to spare, and it will still be hot when it comes to the table. But how did it happen that you did not make two puddings this time. I know that you always have done, so that you may keep one here for yourself and for any guests you might have, as well as the one you make for Uncle."

"Oh, I did, miss; I did, as you say. But you see, that clumsy girl must try to bring it in after the gentleman took the other, though I told her not to touch it. As I feared, she dropped it—breaking one of my best plates, too, and making a mess of the kitchen floor. The pudding was ruined, of course. We had to throw it into the pigsty."

Virgil howled with rage and rushed past them, out the back of the inn, leaving the kitchen door ajar behind him. In a small pen, a brood sow and four good-sized younger pigs were gobbling down the broken pudding. The small eyes seemed to dare him to stop the feast. He attempted to snatch up the bit which was still uneaten, and barely succeeded in getting his hand out of the way of the mother's sharp teeth, while her angry grunt conveyed the message that she would be happy to add his digits to her meal.

The five people in the tap room exchanged glances. "I vow the man acts as if he is touched," Mrs. Barker declared. "Snatching the pudding out of my hands as if he had been starved for a week, and now rushing about the place and screaming."

"I am not surprised at anything he might do," Deryk said. "but yet—"

"Even if he ate a part of it, as I suppose he must have done, since he seemed to be so hungry, there was nothing in it that might have overset him. It was still hot, to be sure, but not so hot as make him run about and cry out. And nothing but the purest ingredients in the making. You could feed it to a babe—that is why they call it nursery pudding. Nor do I ever hide thimbles or things of that kind in my puddings, as you know, miss. There is too much chance of something being swallowed—especially when the pudding is eaten by small children."

"I know," Christine agreed. "It cannot be anything he has eaten here."

In her corner, Betty remained quiet and shrank back against the wall, hoping her mistress would forget that she had planned to send her home. Nothing nearly so exciting as this had ever happened in her brief lifetime, and she longed to be able to tell the other servants about it. Mrs. Barker could be heard panting and animadverting about the queer ways of some people, as she pulled herself up the stairs, clinging to the bannister.

The couple in the tap room smiled sympathetically, and Deryk commented, "To tell you true, I have always thought Clive was an odd sort."

"I must confess that I have never liked him," Christine said with a shiver. "There is something about the way he looks at me—and when he touches my hand I feel—I feel so—"

"I never saw that," the young man admitted. "I was too occupied in looking at you, of course, ever to see anyone else. You should have told me how you felt about him at once and I should have ordered him to stay away from you. You should never have been worried by that bag of—" He broke off, realizing that the term he had intended to use was not fit for a young lady's ears.

She placed her free hand over his hand which imprisoned the

other. "I should not have wished you to make a scene, for others do not seem to view him in that way. Either they appear to welcome him, or they poke fun at him behind his back. I appear to be the only one who fears him. But what can he be doing in this part of the country?"

"That is what I asked him, and he said that he had business with your uncle."

"That makes no sense at all. Uncle Matthew is not a man of business."

"And especially, he would not have business with a Captain Sharp." At her puzzled look, Deryk explained, "A man who cheats at cards."

Christine shuddered. "How dreadful. I had not heard that about him."

"No, those he cheats are seldom the kind to tell of being cheated. If they know of it, which many of them do not, for he and his kind are clever. But rumors get about."

"Then it makes even less sense for him to be here." A sudden thought struck her, and she said fearfully, "You cannot suppose that he is here to make Uncle an offer for *me*?"

"How could he do that, my dear one? The man has nothing which would tempt your uncle."

"I trust you are right, but Uncle Matthew did say that if he received a better offer than yours before Christmas, he would wed me to another. And Aunt Clara has been telling me I should encourage Clive. Perhaps *she* suggested he come down and make an offer for me."

He caught both her hands, cradling them against his chest. "I know your aunt would prefer you to take one of the beaux. But surely not *Clive*. And even if your uncle is ambitious for you, he said a *better* offer than mine, did he not? What could that fat fop offer to compare to my estates? He has no claim to his uncle's title, and no livelihood except gambling. I do not think Sir Matthew would think that acceptable."

"I hope that is so. But I cannot help worrying—"

"My dear girl, you must not. I am here, and I shall not allow that fellow to come near you. And if he dares to approach your uncle, I shall throw him out of the house."

Christine relaxed against him. "You would do that for me, would you not?"

"All that and more."

"You are right, of course. There is nothing he can offer. And nothing else matters but the two of us. After tomorrow, everyone will know that I belong to you—as I always have done, my dear one."

Deryk lowered his head toward hers, aware only of the invitation of her lips. Suddenly he caught sight of the abigail, who was sitting in the half-dark corner, her eyes wide with excitement as she watched their every move. "Did you not say you planned to send Betty home with a message to your uncle?" he asked.

"Oh, yes. With Mr. Clive running about as he did, I forgot about her." She turned to Betty and gave her the message to carry home. "Have the driver return for me—oh, say, in two hours. Or perhaps it would be better to say three hours. I should not like to cause Mrs. Barker to hurry, for she has had trouble enough today without my adding to it by expecting her to rush about. I shall still be home with Uncle's pudding in time for his supper."

Disappointed at being given no opportunity to learn more about the exciting events taking place at the inn, Betty drew her cloak closely about her and started from the room, stopping as she realized she still held her mistress's pelisse and muff. Placing them quickly on a chair, she hurried out to the sleigh, rousing the driver from his nap in the stables and giving him her mistress's orders. She had hoped to be allowed to remain long enough to see more of what was happening, perhaps to learn the reason for the London gentleman rushing about as he had done.

Was it because he was a stranger that he behaved in this way? Her mam had always told her that living in the city made a person queer-like, although she could not see that it had harmed Miss Christine or Mr. Deryk. Of course, they had only been visitors, with a good, solid country upbringing to keep them from doing anything so daft.

At least she could take home enough of a tale out of what she had seen to make her the center of attention in the Servants' Hall tonight, for not even the driver had heard or seen any of the things that had happened. He had been too deeply asleep to be aware of anything—besides, the gentleman had run out the other way, and so would not have been seen from the front of the inn.

As well as the story of the gentleman's strange behavior, she could verify the tales which had been going about the estate: Sir

Matthew *had* agreed to announce Miss Christine's betrothal on Christmas Day. That would be of interest to everyone in the household, but since it had been expected for months, if not for years, the other news would be far more interesting. If only she knew what it was all about . . .

When the abigail had gone, Christine turned eagerly to Deryk once more, but inched away from his offered embrace, leaving her hand resting in his, as Mrs. Barker could be heard coming heavily down the stairs. The woman was panting, less from exertion than from anger.

"Look at this, if you would," she declared, her chins quivering with fury as she exhibited a soiled coverlet. "That rascally—" She paused, unable to think of a proper word to describe her villainous guest. "Not one bite of my good pudding did he eat, I vow, after running off with it as if he had been starved. Just scattered it all about his room, like a madman. Smashed the good dish against the wall, he did. *And* wiped his hands upon my second-best coverlet. You can see the marks he made."

"I always thought there was something odd about him," Christine observed. "But to do something of this kind—and to your wonderful pudding. Not to mention the other damage he has done. . . . Your beautiful old plate and the coverlet. It is beyond understanding that anyone should behave in such a way."

"Well, I shall just tell Barker to inform him that we do not wish to have his kind at the Twin Unicorns. Who knows what he might do next? Set the place afire, perhaps, or murder us all in our beds."

"I doubt if he would do anything so bad as that. Still, you may be right about his being a dangerous man; it would be best not to have him here," Deryk said. Since Christine had confessed her dislike of the way Virgil Clive had looked at her, how she detested his touch, Deryk wanted to keep him as far from her as possible. And he should not be allowed to approach Sir Matthew. Especially if Lady Douglas had been encouraging him. If the Barkers would order him away, it would not be necessary for *him* to say anything to the man. But after tomorrow . . .

At that moment, Virgil slammed open the rear door and stamped across the tap room, bound for the stairs. Forgetting that she had thought it the best thing to have her husband speak to the gentleman about the mess he had caused in his room and the breakage of her property, Mrs. Barker reached the foot of the stairs before he did, panting with her exertion, and exclaimed, "Here, sir, what do you have to say about this?" She waved the soiled coverlet before him.

"Oh, that? I merely found I did not like your pudding as well as I had thought I would," Virgil said, attempting to pass her.

The woman placed herself firmly before him, effectively blocking the steps. "If you did not care for it, you had only to tell us so. We'd not have charged you for it. There was no need to treat it like this"—she waved the coverlet again—"or to grind it into my rug. Dear knows how I shall ever get that clean. Or to smear the walls with it. And to smash my good plate—one of the set my mother gave me when I first went into service. She meant them to be kept for my wedding, as they were. And even now, they are only used for special occasions."

"Oh, who cares a farthing about your mother's plate?" Virgil said furiously. The word "farthing" reminded him even more forcibly of his lost drachma, and increased his ire. "Whatever you think it worth, put it on my bill, and do not bother me about it now." He caught her by one shoulder, pushed her out of his way, and climbed to his room, ignoring her angry cries at his mistreatment. She need not know it yet, but he had almost decided not to pay any part of his bill. After all, she had no right to throw out the pudding that held his coin.

If she had purposely meant to cause him trouble, she could not have done so more easily. His plan for winning Christine had vanished with his lost treasure.

Or perhaps it had not. All might not be lost yet, he told himself. If he could convince Sir Matthew that he would soon have the drachma in hand, the old man might still be persuaded to grant his wish. Had he not won fortunes in the past without anything solid to show? He would do well to visit the old man this afternoon, while Christine was waiting for the other pudding to be made, but he could scarcely pay so important a call in his present dirt.

He flung aside his soiled clothing—why had the woman loaded the pudding with so much jam and the like? How was he ever to get it cleaned from his coat and breeches? Even his waistcoat showed a number of red stains. And these had been his best togs, freshly made to his measure by none other than Weston: clothing which he could ill afford, but which he had planned to wear to impress Sir Matthew and Christine.

"No use in asking the old besom to clean them," he told himself. "I doubt she'd know how to begin the task—nor would she do so, just now, if she could. One would think she had a right to comb my hair for such trifling matters as her dish and her carpet. After all, it is her business to serve all who come here, not to throw their treasures out for the pigs to eat."

The only other clothing he had with him was what he had worn during the journey. The garments were travel-stained, but with a good brushing they would have to do. He would not have time to drive back to London to acquire fresh clothing. In this weather, the journey would take several more days. Christine might be betrothed before he returned.

He strode about the room as he dressed, uncaring that he was grinding more of the spilled pudding crumbs into the rug. Indeed, he took a spiteful pleasure in doing so. How dared that creature downstairs speak to him as she had done? She—and everyone—would sing a different tune when he was wed to Sir Matthew's niece.

When he was cleaned to the best of his ability, he went to the stables, then found that, as he had feared, the depth of the snow made it impossible for him to drive his carriage. Even the elements seemed determined to thwart him. He located a much-worn saddle and threw it across the back of one of his carriage horses, an indignity the animal violently resented. Virgil had to struggle to tighten the cinch then searched for a mounting block, for he was unable to pull himself from the ground into the saddle without help. At least, he thought, the fact that he must ride would give him an excuse for looking less than his best.

Unaccustomed to being ridden by anyone, much less by the ponderous figure now bouncing about at every stride, the horse balked and made several attempts to throw him, but was finally convinced that no such tricks would unseat the man on his back. By the time they had reached the Douglas estate, weary from the load it was carrying and the depth of snow through which it must make its way, it was exhibiting a docility which did not fool Virgil for an instant. The cursed animal would doubtless fight his mastery all the way back to the inn. But that no longer mattered.

He had arrived, and now had only to convince the baronet of his ability to produce the coin.

When Mr. Clive was announced, Sir Matthew ordered that he be shown at once to the library where the coin collection was displayed, and came to the door to greet him. "This is wonderful news you bring me, sir," he exclaimed, clasping the newcomer's hand and drawing him toward a chair. "I know of no other collector who has a coin to equal yours. It will be the pride of my collection, which I shall show you later. I am certain you will find it as interesting as I do. You have had your coin authenticated, of course."

"Certainly, Sir Matthew. I should not have offered it to you otherwise." Virgil drew out the papers he had insisted the expert sign for him. At least, they had been spared the damage done by the pudding.

"Wonderful, wonderful," the older gentleman declared after perusing them. "I know this man's reputation; his word proves the truth of your claim. It must have pained him not to be able to persuade you to let him deal for you, for he could have earned himself a good profit from handling the matter of the sale. But you were wise to deal with me for yourself. Your letter, however, did not say what price you had placed on your coin. I cannot expect it to be other than dear, but it will be well worth whatever you ask. You will find that I am not one to haggle about an addition to my collection."

"I am happy to hear that, sir. My price for the drachma is your niece's hand."

Sir Matthew shook his head. "That is most unfortunate, my dear sir. You may not be aware of the fact that I have already promised my niece that I would announce her betrothal on the morrow. She wishes to wed Deryk Richardson, you must know."

"I can see no reason why you should not announce the betrothal as you promised—except that you will substitute me for Richardson."

"That might cause something of a problem," Sir Matthew said slowly. "The two have considered themselves promised since childhood. Christine will be most displeased if she does not have her way in this, and I dislike to make her unhappy." Let the fellow think he would never have considered accepting another offer for her.

"A young girl's fancy, I am certain, one she will forget once she is my wife. After all, as you said, they have known each other for years, so she might easily think herself in love, without ever having truly experienced the emotion. As her guardian, Sir Matthew, you know that you have the right—the duty, in fact—to choose the man your niece will wed."

"That is true enough. And it is what most guardians would do. Still, I must tell you that I have never denied Christine anything she wished." He almost believed what he said, not caring a whit for the girl's feelings, but hoping to get the coin without giving her up to this fellow. There might still be a chance to make a better match for her, short as the time might be. "Cannot I offer you something else in exchange for the coin?"

Virgil smiled. The bait had been taken and he knew he had only to reel in the old gentleman. On the morrow, Christine would be promised to him. "I am certain that if I wanted mere money in exchange for my coin," he said with a shrug, "I could find any number of collectors who are willing to outbid you."

"True enough—Cavendish, for example; he thinks his collection is better than mine, which it is not. But he could easily afford to make an offer I could not meet. It would be disastrous, for me, if you were to take it to him." He sighed, thinking of the outcry Christine would make when he told her of his decision. Still, she must make the best of the matter. "Very well, sir, my niece in exchange for your drachma. But only if it is as good as these documents say."

"I can assure you that it is."

"Done, then." The baronet held out his hand, and for the first time, Virgil showed some sign of unease.

"I did not bring the drachma with me," he owned, causing the other to frown.

"Why did you not bring it to me at once, instead of merely calling to tell me what you wished in exchange? You must have known that I would agree to meet your price, unusual as it is."

"I had little doubt that you would do so. But there was always a chance that you would have considered the price I named too expensive, and that I should have to take it to market elsewhere. The coin is not far from here, however. I can place it in your hand on the morrow."

"Good. I have promised Christine that I shall announce her betrothal after our Christmas feast. Bring me the coin by three of the clock, and you shall be the fortunate man. If you are not here by that time, it will be Richardson who gets her."

That threat should be enough to stir the man to action, Sir Matthew thought. Nothing like the fear of competition to bring him into line. He rose abruptly, signalling that the interview was at an end. There was no need for more talk until the man had placed the coveted drachma in his hand. It was not necessary for him to like his caller and he did not do so. The sort of price the fellow had demanded proved that he was no gentleman—and if there had been any other way of obtaining the coin, he would not have agreed to this fat man's demands.

Sir Matthew hoped Christine would not be too unhappy with his choice for her. But as the man said, it was his right to choose her husband—and Clive, little as he liked the man, could offer him something that Richardson would be unable to match.

Well-satisfied with the result of his talk with Sir Matthew, Virgil again struggled with his mount. Once he had managed to climb into the saddle, there was slightly less trouble than before, because the animal seemed to sense that it was returning to the stable where its mate was waiting. It was difficult to tell whether man or horse was happier to see the end of the journey. Virgil dismounted stiffly, vowing that, whatever the weather, he would never again ride the recalcitrant animal.

His only worry now was that he might not be able to take the drachma to Sir Matthew in time to foil Richardson's suit. He might offer to purchase the sow and her brood, kill them, and thus retrieve his coin. He doubted, however, that either of the Barkers would look kindly upon such an offer, so he must only hope he could find the lost coin in the time left to him.

Mrs. Barker had informed her husband of the damage done by the London guest, and the innkeeper faced Virgil upon his entrance to the inn, telling him that he was no longer welcome there.

"Do not be daft, man," Virgil told him in his loftiest tone. "This house is open to the public. You cannot refuse to permit me to stay as long as I wish. In any case, I shall be leaving on the morrow."

Uncertain of his exact rights in the matter and recalling the crest upon the stranger's carriage, Barker thought it wise to say nothing more to him, instead retiring to the kitchen in an attempt to soothe his wife's feelings.

"Crest or no crest, you should have thrown him out," Mrs. Barker said indignantly. "Either he is a madman, or he is merely destructive. In any case, we do not wish his kind of trade here."

"But the man is right—this is a public house. And if he should report that we had turned him away without just cause—"

"Just cause! You think that the ruination of my coverlet and carpet, not to mention the breakage of a good plate and the scattering about of one of my puddings so that we may have to have the bedchamber wall recovered—all that is no cause?"

"All inns have problems with careless guests—" he began, but was shouted down.

"Careless! There was no carelessness here. I am certain the man did all those things purposely. He may be a madman for all we know."

Aware that he would never win an argument with her, the innkeeper shrugged and returned to the tap room, taking refuge behind the bar. Since Christine and Deryk had just left, Mrs. Barker had no one to listen to her woes but Nell, who merely sniffed and said nothing. Mrs. Barker had boxed her ears soundly for the plate *she* had dropped—but clearly, her mistress could not do the same to a paying guest. Nor even order him away, it seemed. Life was quite unfair.

Before noon on Christmas Day, dozens of vehicles filled the stableyard behind the Douglas mansion. Most of them were sleighs, but an occasional driver had braved the weather in his strongest carriage. The house had been decorated from the holly-trimmed front door to the kitchen in honor of the festive occasion.

In addition to the usual display of shiny holly leaves and red berries, and the garlands that had been bound around the stair posts, several of the more sentimental young maids had fashioned ribands and greenery into a greater number of kissing balls than were usually seen, and had hung them in a great many strategic spots about the house. They were quickly discovered by many of the young callers, as well as by the pair for whom they had been meant.

The Yule log crackled in the huge fireplace, its resinous scent mingled with those of pine and cedar, of cinnamon, ginger, and other spices, of fine wax candles, of roasting meats whose odors wafted upward from the kitchen, of the port and brandy liberally given to all who wished them. The earliest arriving children had soon found and devoured the remnants of last night's pudding, without diminishing their appetites for the huge dinner to come.

This being a momentous occasion for the family, the long table in the Great Hall was covered with a fine cloth and laden with delicate china, crystal goblets, and silver, although with a plenty of spaces left for all the good dishes that would be brought in by a small army of servants. For the benefit of the many children amongst the guests, as well as for those who wished to make the journey home before night, and those whose appetites had been teased by the smells of good food, Sir Matthew had decreed that—for this occasion only—the mid-afternoon meal would be the true Christmas dinner.

A brace of roasted geese held pride of place, but a saddle of mutton, several kinds of fish, vegetables—both plain and in French sauces—and savories of various sorts were placed about the table, along with baskets of candied fruits and marchpane, Spanish olives, and every sort of bread and cake the master chef could devise. There were soups and raised pies, syllabub and rich cakes to come. If there was something lacking at the table, only the master knew of it.

He looked about the table, from which a single place had been surreptitiously removed when the butler realized that one additional setting had been laid. It would never do to have an empty chair at Sir Matthew's table. But who was missing? He knew the names of all of the master's guests, for he alone had been responsible for sending out invitations. Everyone who had been asked to dinner was here. One of the servants must have erred in preparing the table; he would speak sharply to them later, for such errors were not permissible when *he* was in charge.

"Where is that fellow Clive, who called yesterday?" Sir Matthew muttered. "He said faithfully that he would be here by three of the clock."

His question did not reach the ears of his guests, but two of the footmen overheard him and exchanged grins when the butler was not looking in their direction. So that was the fellow the master had expected when he had ordered a place laid out for an uninvited guest. The place the high-nosed butler had forced them to remove.

He would not be here, they knew. One of the visitors' coachmen, who came from the city and knew Virgil Clive by sight, had reported with a snigger that, when he had driven past the Two Unicorns, the man from London had been observed in the inn's pigsty, of all places. He had been struggling to ward off the playful attention of the young pigs and the wrath of their mother, as he stalked from one side of the pen to the other, stirring up the mire with his cane. The man must be touched— not at all the sort of person who would be welcome beneath this roof, they thought.

Unaware of what was delaying the man he expected, Sir Matthew shrugged. Clearly, Clive had no intention of keeping his word; it was possible that he had never owned the ancient coin of which he had boasted, and had merely pretended to the ownership to win her uncle's consent to his betrothal to Christine.

There was little of the Christmas spirit in Sir Matthew's heart as he took his place at the head of the table. And why was Christine not in her place at his right hand? he wondered. Richardson was absent, too. What sort of a celebration did they think this was?

Christine had been summoned to the kitchen, to find a stable boy from the inn awaiting her. "Mrs. Barker said I was to bring you this, miss." He pressed something small into her hand.

She looked at it curiously. "But what is it?"

"I dunno. It was found in the corner of the kitchen and she thought it might have belonged to you or one of the gentlemen who stayed at the inn." Mixed with the dust from the floor, there had been a crumb or two of what looked like her pudding, but Mrs. Barker had cleaned it carefully before giving it to him.

"Thank Mrs. Barker for her trouble," Christine told him, "and for bringing it to me. I think Cook might find you a bit of sweet for your Christmas."

As the lad ran off clutching his sweet, Christine went to look for Deryk. "Can this be yours?" she asked. "It was found at the inn."

Deryk looked at it carefully, then shook his head. "I have never seen it. It must be someone's old pocket piece. Doubtless, it had been lying in some dark corner for months."

"I should not think so. Mrs. Barker is very thorough in her cleaning. Do you suppose it could belong to—him?"

"To Clive? I doubt it. Or, if so, it is worthless. Still, it is an unusual piece. Shall we ask your uncle what he thinks of it?"

Christine nodded and pressed the coin into his hand. He approached Sir Matthew somewhat diffidently and said, "I dislike to waste your time, sir, but is this old thing worth anything at all?"

Sir Matthew seized the drachma, looking at it closely. "How came you by this?" he demanded.

"It was given to me," Deryk said. "I believe the landlady at the inn found it somewhere."

Could this be the coin that fellow Clive had promised to bring him? Sir Matthew wondered. If so, the man was criminally careless to have lost it, and certainly did not deserve to be given Christine.

"It—it may be of some value," he said slowly. "Of course, I should have to have it authenticated. Are you willing to sell it?"

"I cannot feel it is mine to sell," Deryk told him. Then, seeing the look of disappointment upon the older man's face, he said, "For my part, you may have it. Should you hear from the proper owner, you may be able to purchase it from him."

So that fellow Clive never truly had the coin, Sir Matthew said to himself. He thought that if he could deal with me, he could then get hold of the coin and make a profit from it. No wonder he could not face me again. And this man had been too clever to let him have it. Aloud, he said, "You are a good lad, Ri—Deryk. It will be good to have you in the family." He turned to face the diners about the table.

"As many of you have doubtless suspected," he told them, "this is more than our customary Christmas dinner. Today, I am pleased to announce the betrothal of my daughter Christine to our good friend and neighbor, Deryk Richardson."

Cheers and toasts to the happy couple rang through the hall. Sir Matthew sank back in his chair, ignoring the look of disappointment on his wife's face.

Lady Douglas did not object to the betrothal. She had hoped for a better match for Christine after the Season in London. Still, considering the way the pair had been smelling of April and May for the past months, it was by far the wisest choice her husband could have made for the girl. In her book, however, such an announcement should not have been at a dinner with only a few close friends present, but at a lavish ball, preferably in London.

All the members of the *ton* would have been invited; perhaps even the Prince Regent would be there to set the seal of his approval upon the match. Sir Matthew cared nothing for such things. He had done his duty, he told himself, handing the girl over to the man she wished.

Now—if he could avoid any further plans his wife might devise—he could again be left in peace with this new addition to his collection.

When the meal was over and the last toasts had been drunk, he took his leave of a few friends and made his way to the library, where all knew better than to disturb him. He sank into his favorite chair and dozed, dreaming of the sensation he would make among his fellow collectors with the rare coin which had come into his hands.

Throughout the rest of the house, the elders sought spots where they could sleep off the effects of so rich a dinner. Many of the children followed their example; others romped up and down stairs, getting underfoot.

The young people had organized a number of games, seeming not to notice how often, during the dances and the games, Deryk and Christine "accidentally" met beneath one or another of the kissing balls. Well, why should they not? Many of the others were doing the same—and, at least, the newly betrothed pair had a better reason for their kissing.

A
Christmas
Spirit

❅ ❅
❅

Sarah Eagle

In memory of my grandfather,
EDWIN JOHN HAWKES, SR.,
who was always Father Christmas.

WHY HAD HE been propelled to this benighted spot? Lord Lancelot FitzWalter wondered as he pulled his cloak tight against his throat. It was an instinctive gesture, not for protection against the dense fog or heavy snowfall. He did not feel cold, only irritation as he stood along the London highway in the swirling winds next to a stone marker that displayed the distance to Oxford.

If he was here, then Denham Abbey had a new master, but he was tired of paying for his past sins—most especially if it included miserable weather and shabby clothing, he decided as he inspected his person. Wistfully he recalled his favorite crimson velvet doublet and breeches, Flemish lace at the band around his neck as well as his cuffs and his knees above his bucket boots. The cloth cloak and shapeless hat that fell over his face were a far cry from his favorite chapeau with its elegant ostrich plume. They were all gone along with his shoulder-length curls. It was little comfort that he would have his possessions returned once his mission was accomplished.

The rumbling of carriage wheels close at hand diverted his attention from his former sartorial splendor. Though he could barely see a foot in front of his face, Lancelot stepped away from the mile marker and sauntered to the middle of the crossroads. His task undoubtedly was to greet these travelers and direct them to Denham Abbey. No one else was about on such a wretched night.

Opening the metal grating of the lantern to allow light to spill forth, Lancelot pondered the mysteries of love, sacred or profane, and the price men paid for it over the centuries.

❊ 1 ❊

"*DIGBY, I REFUSE* to listen to any further rubbish about goblins and hauntings at the dinner table." Ian Fitzwalter, the newly ascended eleventh Earl of Denham, gave his young brother a harsh look that drew his straight dark brows together at the bridge of his hawkish nose. He hoped his narrow face was in a suitable scowl, something reminiscent of Zeus in a fine temper, unaware the angular planes of his narrow face were thrown into high relief by the flickering candlelight of the drafty dining hall.

Unfortunately, the eleven-year-old boy was not quelled by the stern look from his usually affable brother. From past experience he knew any indiscretion would be forgotten as soon as Ian left the room and became immersed in his scholarly pursuits once more. "But, I know it's true. I tell you there *are* ghosts at Denham Abbey and one appointed 'specially—"

"Digby." Ian's brown eyes locked with his brother's guileless pair of the same color. After a moment's hesitation, Digby's sidelong look at the three ladies at the table confirmed the earl's suspicions. The boy was embellishing the tale in hopes of unsettling the female members of the family. Though Digby could have described something more grisly than an ancestor who selected a bride for the earl. Why not a screaming skull or chain-rattling spirit? The pinched faces of Mavis, the late earl's widow, and her sister looked more disapproving than frightened, however, and his sister Elspeth was used to the boy's wild starts.

This was the first time since the tenth earl's death that the family was together, but not the first instance for Ian to regret his half-brother's clumsiness of falling into the duck pond on a chilly October afternoon. Who would have guessed such a stout man would have a weak chest?

The last thing Ian wanted had been to take Gawain's place after he had succumbed to his fever; the new earl had much more important matters to occupy his mind. They certainly did not include entertaining his sister-in-law's troublesome sister and her ne'er-do-well brother during Christmastide—though their presence kept Elspeth from concocting elaborate plans for her debut in the spring, despite the need for mourning over Gawain's untimely death.

He could not be bothered with talk of balls and women's clothing when he had an important essay to write on the rape of Greek treasures from their homeland. His family simply did not realize the implication of Lord Elgin and other supposed archaeologists' acquisitive actions in the name of scholarship. How could he think of what gifts to give the servants on Boxing Day when he was in the middle of a crusade to stem the flow of pillaged works of art from their natural settings?

"Ian, dear, may we have your permission to withdraw?"

He looked down the table in surprise to focus on Elspeth's golden brown ringlets that matched the color of his own tousled hair. The sympathetic smile gracing her heart-shaped face made him realize that his thoughts had drifted away from the present company. "There is no need to withdraw. I doubt that either Digby or I shall be sipping brandy and blowing a cloud in your absence." He returned his sister's smile with one of apology and a slight shrug for his lapse. A movement to his right made him recollect the rest of his company. "Of course, Captain Merriam may have a preference."

"Nonsense, old man," Cecil Merriam broke in without hesitation, gracing all the ladies at the table with the toothy smile that never failed to annoy his host. What did the man have to smile about on every occasion, when he had just been invalided home from the Peninsula? He smiled as much as his sister Mavis frowned. And did he detect the captain's blue eyes lingering overlong on Elspeth's flushed face? "I would much rather join the ladies in the sitting room than remain at table."

Everyone else seemed agreeable to the captain's suggestion and quickly rose from the table. As Ian lagged behind the others, he wondered if they were anxious for some form of entertainment or were merely as eager as he to escape the chilled atmosphere of the vaulted dining hall. The barn of a room was the only remaining part of the original structure that was still in use, and poorly insulated. At one time it had been the central room of the Abbey, before Henry VIII had seized the property during his early marital dispute that changed the course of

English religion. One of Digby's ghosts could be the mother superior who had roundly cursed the king for his worldly appetites.

"Ian, come quickly."

The excitement in his sister's voice brought his attention back to the present, making him speculate on the possibility of Digby's apparition suddenly appearing amongst the suits of armor that lined the entry hall. The ominous silence that followed Elspeth's call made him quicken his steps. The sight that greeted him was a creature of this world, however; a cold and wet creature. That much he could discern as he crossed the polished wooden floor.

A lone cloaked figure stood surrounded by his family and guests. Both Mavis and her sister Chloe stood as stiff as pokers with their raven-headed curls together, giving the appearance of smelling something distasteful, while their brother next to them was still smirking. Elspeth had a firm grip on Digby's shoulders to keep him still, from what Ian was not sure. Was the boy going to attack the stranger? Ian met his sister's expectant look with resignation. She was waiting for the earl to act, to take the matter in hand. What did she want him to do? Blast his mother for remarrying just a few months before Gawain's death, and marrying a Scottish peer at that. He needed her here, not venturing north for six months to become acquainted with her new family.

To his relief the figure took the initiative, pulling back the hood of the damp cloak. The newest arrival was a dark-haired young woman who possessed very expressive gray eyes, and though just past the first blush of youth, was passably attractive despite her travel-worn appearance. Her gaze skated over the company, neither apprehensive nor bold, simply inquisitive— until she spied him. For a moment he thought she looked alarmed, but in an instant her expression returned to one of mild interest.

"Can we be of assistance, miss?" he asked softly, still wondering what was happening and why Dreyer, the butler, was hovering in front of the door. Instinctively he reached up to loosen his cravat, which seemed to be constricting his breath.

"I am sorry to be thrust upon you in this manner, but the coachman lost his way in the fog. We were directed to this house by a man at the crossroads," she explained in a cultured, well-modulated voice that belied her bedraggled appearance. "Could you give the coachman the direction to Oxford? I have no idea where we—" She broke off as the front door came open in a blast of frigid air, allowing two footmen to enter carrying her trunk. As they headed for the stairs under the butler's direction, she exclaimed, "Oh, dear, what are you doing?"

"Just what they should be doing," Elspeth said hurriedly as Mavis took a step toward the servants. Before the older woman could speak, she directed Dreyer to continue with transferring the visitor's trunk to the green room. "You should not be abroad on a night like this. As it is, you will undoubtedly come down with a chill if we do not get you in front of a nice warm fire. Do you agree, Ian?"

"Oh, quite," he responded automatically while attempting to suppress the groan that was building deep in his throat. How was he ever going to get any work done if the household continued to increase?

The sound of the coach pulling away from the front steps appeared to make up the young woman's mind. The dejected slump of her shoulder seemed to say she had no other recourse if the coachman was determined to stay. "I thank you for your kindness to a stranger. I am Miss Serena Dodd. I was on my way to spend the school holiday with my family in Oxford."

"You seem a bit past the age for school," Mavis murmured, dabbing at her pointed nose with her handkerchief while measuring the new arrival from her calf boots to the high collar of her brown cambric gown beneath the woolen cloak.

"I teach music at Miss Haversham's Academy," Miss Dodd returned quietly, but was forestalled in commenting further by Elspeth's intervention.

"Mavis, please," she hissed at her sister-in-law, clearly mortified by the woman's unabashed bluntness, making Ian wonder what had occurred before he came on the scene. "We have already been rude enough by not introducing ourselves to Miss Dodd. I am Lady Elspeth Fitzwalter. Shall we go in by the fire before we make the rest of the introductions?"

"Ah, you go ahead and entertain our new guest, my dear. I have a reference I need to check in the library." Ian saw his chance for escape and was ready to bolt. Miss Dodd had done him a great service by appearing suddenly. She would keep his sister occupied, protecting her from Mavis's sharp tongue.

"Well, that is my scapegrace brother, Ian, the Earl of Denham," Elspeth exclaimed with a resigned laugh, but did not admit defeat as she watched his retreating figure. "Ian, I expect you to join us for refreshments in a half hour. Now, Miss Dodd, you must come in and get warm while your room is being readied," she instructed her new charge, not the least put out that her brother did not acknowledge her request. "The journey from London must have been dreadful. Did you say a man directed you here?"

❋ 2 ❋

"*Lady Elspeth, I* cannot impose on your brother's hospitality this way," Serena exclaimed, reluctantly allowing her young hostess to lead her up the stairs. She was torn between seeking the solitude of her room and running after the grim-faced butler, who had reported the appalling news of the weather. "Surely the coachman and Dreyer are wrong and the road will be passable tomorrow. I should be able to continue on my way in the morning."

"Miss Dodd, it seems you were fortunate to make it this far in the storm without coming to grief. Black fog, how unusual," her hostess murmured with a frown of concentration. "I do hope Dreyer has already taken care of gathering the evergreens and holly," she continued, leading her companion up the stairs.

When they started down the upper hallway, she gave her guest a brilliant smile and a consoling pat on the arm. "We have plenty of room here, and though we are not terribly festive this year, you shall be with a family to celebrate the season. You need to rest after tending to those poor unfortunate girls who came down with the measles."

"You are too kind, especially when your family has had such a recent tragedy," Serena returned, matching her steps with her companion's.

She could think of nothing else to say and thought it best to remain silent as she followed her hostess down the winding hallway. Though the lady was only a year or two younger, Lady

Elspeth would be appalled if Serena blurted out that Denham Abbey was the last house in the kingdom where Serena would choose to stay. Drat the Benjamin twins for infecting half the school with measles just before the holiday. If Serena had left last week as she had planned, she would not be in this fix, staying in Ian Fitzwalter's home.

"Well, here we are at last," Lady Elspeth announced, opening the door at the end of the hall with a flourish. "I hope you do not become lost in this rabbit warren of ours. Every generation seemed bent on adding another wing as the Abbey itself fell into ruins. We had lived in a delightful house on Curzon Street in London with Mother, before her recent marriage. But, the solicitors advised Ian to take up official residence here for the winter, though I do not think Messrs. Palmer and Perkins know how drafty this place can be."

"I am sure I shall be very comfortable," Serena whispered, but wondered at her ability to lie. The room seemed to have been part of a century-old renovation, if not older, and decorated at that time. It was covered in a vile shade of green from the faded velvet hangings on the bed and windows to the worn embroidered upholstery on the wing chairs near the fireplace, the only hospitable spot in the chamber.

"I am sorry that this is the best we have to offer, but with Mavis still in residence and her family visiting, all the best rooms are taken," Elspeth explained as she lit a brace of candles near the bed. Her lips suddenly curved into a mischievous smile. "To be honest, I am delighted to have another female for company besides my sour-natured sister-in-law. Please, must we be so formal? I think we shall be great friends, and being Elspeth and Serena will make it much easier," Elspeth said with a winning smile that suddenly turned into a wicked grin. "Did you really think Mavis was Ian's wife?"

Serena could feel a rush of heat to her face under Elspeth's amused gaze, uncertain where to look as she tried to forget the inexplicable feeling of disappointment that had assailed her earlier. She recalled her blunder and the acerbic reply from the lady on the matter. "It seemed logical when you introduced her as the countess," she managed weakly, trying to suppress the thought of her own impertinent reply—a reference to the lady's advanced years in relation to the earl. In their surprise, and Elspeth's and Digby's amusement, no one questioned that she knew the earl's age to be twenty-eight, exactly six years her senior.

"Well, I shall leave you to get settled," her hostess announced, biting her lower lip to contain her amusement. Her brown eyes were empathetic. "You will need your rest tonight because I plan to secure your help with the decorations tomorrow. We may be in mourning, but I refuse to have Christmas without the traditional greens and Yule log. I have already enlisted dear Captain Merriam."

"I would be happy to help in any way to repay your hospitality," Serena replied with a warm smile that barely stayed in place as her hostess swept from the room. Once the door closed behind Elspeth, Serena flung herself into the closest chair in a manner that would have earned a scold from Miss Haversham. "Why did I have to come to *his* house?"

Serena buried her flushed face in her hands with a groan of despair, but it did not erase the face of Ian Fitzwalter from her mind or her memory. She was a lovesick, gawky twelve-year-old child again, forever inventing excuses for an errand to her father's study at the moment the object of her affection was scheduled to arrive. Whenever her father's students came for Sunday luncheon, she had never been able to eat a bite because her heart was pounding in her throat. Her reason for existing was the moments she had been allowed to gaze on Ian Fitzwalter's golden brown curls and classically handsome features. The same features that had not changed that much in the intervening ten years.

But Ian Fitzwalter was no more aware of her existence than he had been then, and now he was an earl. Serena sat up and straightened her shoulders at the thought. She was making too much of ancient history.

Ian had not been aware of her worship until she overheard some of his classmates teasing him about his constant shadow. Even then, she was not sure he understood their meaning as he laughed at their jokes. At the age of eighteen he had already begun to assume the scholar's cloak of vagueness—so similar to her late father—that was alternately endearing and infuriating. She understood the young men's jibes and had been humiliated, however. From that moment on, she had avoided the company of Ian Fitzwalter.

"You are being as missish as any of your silliest students, my girl," she told herself firmly, and walked to the heavy curtains that cloaked the windows. Pulling back the dusty drape and wiping the condensation from the pane, she could see only her own reflection; a drab schoolmistress. Nothing could be seen in the opaque darkness beyond. Dreyer had spoken the truth of a black fog that obliterated the snow and surrounding landscape.

"Get to bed, and stop being such an idiot," she murmured, recalling the other members of the Denham household. She would need a good night's sleep to deal with the countess and her sister after her rag manners this evening. That seemed much more daunting that Ian Fitzwalter remembering a schoolgirl's infatuation.

❊ 3 ❊

A SHARP KNOCK on the door roused Serena from a half-formed dream of jeering schoolboys. Could it be morning already? she wondered, sitting up and rubbing her eyes as she called for the maid to enter and build up the fire. The only answer was a second knock at the door. Serena blinked and looked around the pitch-black room. Why was it still so dark? Had the weather become even worse? The fire was smoldering on the grate, she noted, still trying to clear her sleep-fogged brain.

When no one answered her second call, Serena groped for the flint box on the nightstand. By the light of a single candle she quickly spied her wool robe at the end of the bed. Pulling on the garment and securing the sash at her waist, she headed purposely for the door. Somewhat irritated at the hesitant servant for not answering her call, Serena tugged open the door and was surprised to discover no one in the hallway—not even a twig of discarded wood on the floor.

Though eager for the warmth of her bed, she was stopped by a rustling sound. As she stepped forward again and peered down the hall to her left, she thought she saw a movement at the turning to the main corridor. Used to nocturnal inspections of the students' sleeping quarters, Serena did not hesitate to investigate once she retrieved the lit candle next to her bedside.

As she rounded the corner, she was glad for the warmth of her serviceable nightclothes and clutched the lapels of her robe tight against her throat. She could see her breath in small white puffs as she cautiously made her way, her ears alert for any sound. Straining her eyes to see into the darkness at the end of the hall near the head of the stairs, she was startled by a whimpering noise that sounded close by, almost next to her.

Keeping a firm grip on the candlestick, she turned to look at the shape next to her. In the flickering light she could discern the outlines of an ornately carved chest mounted on a matching stand, flanked by two matching chairs. The whimpering came again from near her feet.

Without hesitation, she knelt to investigate.

"Well, what are you doing under there?" she asked, letting out the breath she had been unaware of holding until that moment. Another whimper answered her question as the small white Scottish terrier stared back at her. When she held out her hand for inspection, the dog's tail thumped against the wall while he gave her hand an inquisitive sniff.

"Hsst, Spenser, where are you? Spenser? Hsst?" a voice whispered as Serena coaxed the animal out into the open.

"Are you Spenser?" Serena asked her companion in a whisper, scratching behind the dog's ear, then neatly snaked her arm around his plumb waist. "Shall we find out who is looking for you?"

The searcher was easily discovered once Serena rose to her full height with Spenser tucked against her side. A door was now open halfway down the hall, and Chloe Merriam was peering around the door frame, but looking in the opposite direction.

"Spens—"

"Is this what you—" Serena's question was cut short by a squeak of surprise from the other woman. "I am sorry I startled you, but I think I found your dog."

"Oh, dear, I thought you were Digby's ghost," Chloe exclaimed, her voice returning to a breathy whisper as she clutched the door frame for support. She gave Serena a malevolent look, her plumb hand clutching her scantily clad bosom in her distress. With a nervous glance over her shoulder, she seemed to pull herself together. Though she had barely said a word earlier in the evening, Serena had not guessed the woman to have such a nervous disposition.

"Thank you for finding my dog. I hope he was not making a nuisance of himself," she murmured, and reached for the dog.

"I do not think he was the one who disturbed me," Serena returned absently, the sight of the other woman's ridiculously diaphanous gown making her mystery visitor seem unimportant for the moment. The sheer blue material was hardly something a young unmarried woman would wear in any weather. No wonder she was shaking, Serena decided as she started to hand over her furry burden, though Miss Merriam's mane of dark hair might offer some warmth. Between the frigid air and her fright—"Did you say a ghost?"

"Never mind. I shall take Spenser now," Miss Merriam hissed when Serena did not relinquish her hold immediately. "Miss Dodd."

Serena was not listening to the other woman's harsh command. Footsteps sounded in the darkness near the head of the stairs and moved steadily closer. Did ghosts whistle? Before Serena could chastise herself for the fanciful thought, the earl stepped out of the shadows.

The sight of the two women brought him up short, cutting off his cheerful tune on a soar note. His glance flickered from Serena to Chloe and back again in confusion, then two lines etched his forehead as his dark brows drew together. "Is something amiss?"

"I was simply returning Miss Merriam's dog to her," Serena explained, managing to find her voice first as she allowed the other woman to take the animal. Perhaps the wiggling animal would help cover the woman's poorly concealed curves.

"Gotten loose again has he, Chloe?" His tone was abrupt, hardly sympathetic to the woman's distress in misplacing her pet. He kept his eyes trained on Serena's right shoulder as he continued to address the other woman. "I thought I suggested getting a leash the last time this happened."

"Y-yes, you d-did, Ian," the woman answered quickly, seeming to move closer to Serena as she spoke. "It was s-so f-fortunate that M-miss D-dodd f-found him."

Serena wondered if Miss Merriam's voice was wobbling from the mortification of being discovered practically unclothed, or if her teeth were chattering from the cold. Or perhaps it was apprehension at the earl's autocratic behavior. What possessed the man to treat the poor creature in this cold manner?

"Indeed. You had best go off to bed before you catch a chill then. I would not want you to be stuck in bed when your sister is ready to leave."

Chloe's eyes widened at his curt words before she burst into tears. She was not a woman who should cry in public from the horrible gulping sounds that she made. For a minute she stood immobile, her ample chest heaving as she made the most abominable noises. When the earl thrust a large white handkerchief under her nose, she snatched it from his hand and brushed past Serena to run down the hall.

"But where is she going?" Serena asked, perplexed by the situation as she turned to see Chloe disappear through another doorway. She thought they were standing in front of Miss Merriam's room.

"To her room where she belongs," Denham returned with a nod of his head in the direction of Miss Merriam's flight. "Was there something you needed, Miss Dodd?"

"No, not really, but I am afraid I do not understand." She quickly ran over the recent scene in her mind, but still could make no sense of it. Nor could she understand Denham's lack of kindness. "You do not like her dog?"

"The dog is not the problem, and certainly not something I wish to discuss in the middle of the night," he stated in a firm voice, raising his hand to massage the back of his neck. He addressed his remarks to Serena's toes.

"Well, I see," she returned, stung by his continued arrogance, and was suddenly embarrassed by her unkempt appearance. How did one seem dignified in a mended wool robe with her hair down about her shoulders? Perhaps she needed to seek Miss Merriam's advice. She was also tired and wanted her own bed, but not without a word to a man who had clearly not learned how to deal with the female species since leaving Oxford. "No matter how late the hour, some people remember their manners. There was no call to be so abrupt with Miss Merriam over such a minor problem."

"Miss Dodd, I am always abrupt with Chloe when she loses her dog near my bedchamber at such a late hour," he said in clear round syllables, as if talking to a very young child. "Especially when she seems to make a habit of it. I think this is the third or fourth time I have come up from my study to find her lurking in the hallway."

"Oh, dear." She suddenly had a clear picture of what he was implying and felt the heat rushing to her face at her stupidity. He raised one eyebrow to show she had finally understood his meaning, and she was appalled at what he was suggesting. Surely Miss Merriam could not be trying to compromise him in his own house.

That disagreeable, conceited oaf had been the object of her youthful affections? she thought wildly. She had to admit that he was still a good-looking man, and his figure had matured nicely into broad shoulders and narrow hips. His personality, however, had gone for the worse. Apparently he had no more use for females—or understanding them—now than he had ten years ago. She almost pitied Miss Merriam for her obvious efforts and lashed out without thinking. "Why would a young lady go to so much trouble over a man with no more finer feelings than you possess? There must be any number of men who would treat her more gently and respect her dignity. Good night, milord."

Serena turned on her heels before he could respond, anxious to reach the solitude of her room. What had she done? She had been terribly rude, although it was not proper for Ian Fitzwalter to suggest to a respectable young woman that his guest had loose morals—even if he was an earl. Surely he did not think she was of a like mind, especially when so shabbily dressed in comparison to Miss Merriam? Why had she ever gotten out of bed to investigate the knocking on her door, especially in a strange house?

As she rounded the corner to her room, she glanced back without thinking. Her embarrassment at her idiotic behavior increased tenfold at the sight of the earl still standing in the middle of the hall, his mouth hanging open.

Lancelot sneered from his hiding place in the shadows, watching his brainless descendant's imitation of a frozen buffoon as the young woman disappeared from sight. The newest earl was an idiot! He had two women all to himself, and he let both of them get away without so much as a pinch or a tickle under the chin. What had happened to the FitzWalter bloodline since his last two visits in, what was it, 1694 and 1735? Those gentlemen had known what to do with lively females.

And given Ian's opportunity, Lancelot would have taken decisive action. When he first spied the plump, black-haired jade scampering down the hallway, he knew exactly what the sly boots was about and decided to spice up the evening a bit more. The results had been mildly interesting, but the lad was a sore disappointment. What does the dolt do? He hands out handkerchiefs and talks like a bloody Roundhead. Lancelot grimaced in disgust. Granted one of them was a watering pot and the other a bit shrewish, he acknowledged as he recalled the recent tableau, but Miss Dodd had been magnificent in her anger.

He preferred his ladyloves to have a touch of temperament, especially when soothing her back into good humor could be so invigorating. Now, if the schoolmistress would only borrow one of the sniveling one's nightdresses . . . He could not waste precious time woolgathering; he needed to bring Ian into line, away from that blasted scratching and solitary reading in the study. And right now was the moment he would begin showing his displeasure.

Ian stood staring at the empty hallway for a few minutes, still trying to understand when he had lost control. At the sight of Miss Dodd standing with Chloe he had been relieved that Mavis's continuing plan to ensnare a title for her younger sister had failed yet again. He tried to act the part of an outraged but calm nobleman. He thought that was how an earl was supposed to act. How had he become the villain of the piece?

Running a weary hand over his face, he walked slowly into his chamber. As the younger son, he had never expected to inherit and spent little time bothering with the tiresome expectations of polite society. Even with his limited experience, he knew he would have to apologize for his ungallant comments to Miss Dodd. No gentleman would talk of such indelicate matters as an attempt to compromise him no matter what the provocation, he acknowledged walking into his bedchamber. Just as he reached for the latch to close the door, a cold blast of air swept through the room, slamming the door shut.

"What the devil?" he exclaimed, looking around to discover the source of the icy gust. The sight of one latticed window opened wide to the night air had him cursing under his breath as he stomped across the room. He latched the window into place, then studied the damp patch of snow on the carpet, wondering if he would ever understand women. Perhaps he was spending too much time studying extinct civilizations and needed to familiarize himself with the living instead.

❊ 4 ❊

THE CLOCK IN the entry struck ten as Serena descended the stairs the next morning, trying to formulate a proper speech of apology for the earl. It had not been her place to reprimand anyone on proper behavior, especially her host. Apparently she had been teaching young girls for so long she was beginning to treat everyone like her students. She was not positive what prompted her outburst, certainly not her maidenly modesty. More than likely it was embarrassment for being so slow to understand the situation.

She was still attempting to resolve the problem as she followed the footman's directions to the morning room. Much to her relief, only two male figures were at table.

"Miss Dodd, this is delightful. We do not normally have the pleasure of a lady's company at this hour," Captain Merriam exclaimed, rising to his feet as she crossed the room. "Right, Digby?"

"Tha's right," the boy managed around a mouthful of toast. "Others never show their face 'til noonday."

"But I thought your sister would be starting early on decorating the Abbey for our celebration tonight," the captain said, stepping over to hold out a chair for Serena as Dreyer hovered with the teapot.

"Ian says Elspeth won't forsake her beauty sleep, no matter what she plans to do," her younger brother assured the captain, more interested in slathing more jam on his toast.

"Oh, has your brother already eaten?" Serena asked as innocently as possible, unfolding her napkin with great concentration. If she was going to make her apology, she would like to get over the rough ground as quickly as possible, and hopefully without any witnesses.

"He prefers the company of ancient Greek relics to us, I am

afraid, Miss Dodd, and has taken his usual tray in the study," the captain answered while Digby concentrated on his food.

"I understand. My father was much the same when he became preoccupied with his work. Mother always claimed he would never have remembered to eat without someone reminding him," she said, remembering her mother's affectionate scolding.

"I cannot vouch for your appetite if Digby continues talking about his ghost." The captain had a twinkle in his blue eyes, though his face was purposely serious.

"Ah, Cecil, he isn't a mean ghost," Digby shot back, but he had a speculative eye on Serena.

"A ghost? Truly?" She tempered her voice with the right blend of interest and disdain as she returned the captain's amused look. One small boy was no match for her three years' experience with Miss Haversham's wily pupils, as well as two brothers and three sisters of her own. "Didn't Miss Merriam mention a ghost last night?"

"Oh, yes, Will the footman told me all about the ghosts at the Abbey, especially Sir Lancelot," Digby informed her, his face so earnest as he warmed to the subject that she had to suppress a smile.

"Sir Lancelot? You did not tell me he was one of King Arthur's noble knights," Cecil prompted as the boy paused, almost waiting for the adults to stop his tale.

"Oh, no. This Lancelot isn't a knight. He's an ancestor. According to Will, they call him Sir Lancelot 'cause Lord Lancelot Fitzwalter's such a mouthful."

"Where does this particular Lancelot do his haunting?" Serena asked when Digby stopped to fortify himself with a mouthful of ham.

"At the Abbey now, I hope, since Ian isn't married," he continued, forgetting himself enough to wipe his mouth with his cuff. "He should be here to help Ian find a wife. That's what Lancelot does, finds a wife for any earl who comes into the title without one. He was killed the night before his Christmas wedding, fighting the Roundheads to save King Charles."

"A noble knight after all, poor sod," Cecil added, unconsciously rubbing the fresh scar along his jaw line. "Then the gentleman has been around for a few years. Quite a better spirit to have lurking about than a headless monk or a moaning lady. What do you think, Miss Dodd?"

"Oh, quite," she assured him in the same dignified manner. Digby looked crestfallen that his ghost was not so spectacular. "Think how discomforting it would be to have all those noises in the middle of the night, the jangling chains and the knocking—"

"The knocking what, ma'am?" Digby's anxious question broke into Serena's disjointed thoughts.

She looked at her two companions, wondering if she was being foolishly superstitious about the phantom knocking on her door last night. The noise had merely been the settling of the old house, and she had been restless sleeping in a strange bed, just as she determined last night. "The knocking of the shutters and loose windows, of course. But I do not think we shall have too much to worry about with Sir Lancelot. He seems to be a quiet ghost so far."

"I know," Digby acknowledged with a sigh of regret, "and Will says no one has seen the screaming nun among the ruins in over a hundred years either. Ian doesn't believe any ghost exists, 'pecially Lancelot, 'cause a self-respecting ghost wouldn't be playing Cupid, whatever that is."

"Oh, am I too late to join you?" came Elspeth's breathless voice from the doorway, cutting off any further discussion of unearthly visitors.

"Not at all, my dear Elspeth," Captain Merriam exclaimed, scrambling to his feet so quickly he almost knocked over his chair.

Serena watched the pair with interest. Elspeth demurely lowered her eyelashes under the captain's warm smile as he crossed the room in two strides and escorted her to a seat next to his own. Apparently this pair did not need the services of the family matchmaker, she decided, and attempted to keep from smiling. Digby was not pleased to lose his companion. He rolled his eyes when the captain requested the honor of filling a plate at the sideboard for Elspeth, something he had not done for Serena.

For a moment she considered the possible match. Though she had only met both Elspeth and the captain the previous night, Serena was accustomed to sizing up people quickly. The young lady was cheerful, intelligent, and unspoiled by the attitudes of the *ton*. Captain Merriam's dark good looks were a pleasant foil for Elspeth's delicate beauty. She did wonder how such a seemingly pleasant man could be related to the countess and Miss Merriam.

The thought of Chloe reminded Serena of her mission. Ian Fitzwalter probably did not like his work interrupted any more than her father had, but she wanted to get the interview over with. There was no telling how long the weather would prolong her stay at the Abbey, and she wanted to be on speaking terms with her host for the duration.

No one would notice her absence from the table, she thought with a wry smile. Elspeth and Cecil were attempting to discuss the day's activities, then their eyes would meet. They would stop and smile, forgetting about conversation and the prolonged preparation of Mrs. Easterby's plum pudding momentarily. Abruptly one or the other would recollect themselves, and the halting conversation would begin once more. From the mutinous look Digby was sending the couple across the table, he would make an excellent chaperon in her absence.

As she murmured her excuses, Serena wondered if the rest of the family was aware of Elspeth's and Cecil's attachment. The previous night there had been no indication of any personal interest between the two. Now they almost seemed to be taking advantage of a stolen moment together. Serena giggled as she left the morning room. She might not reach home for her holiday, but her stay at Denham Abbey was not going to be boring, even if Digby's ghostly friends did not pay a visit.

❄ 5 ❄

"OH, IAN, I hate to trouble you, but I would like this letter franced," Chloe said in a breathy voice that never failed to annoy him. She had also drenched herself with the overpowering musky perfume that always made him want to sneeze.

Ian looked up from his manuscript without bothering to mask his annoyance. Did Mavis stay up throughout the night thinking up ways to bring her sister to his attention? Did she think he was so absentminded that he would not notice and marry the first available female in his path? His sister-in-law must dread losing her active position at Denham and retiring to the dower house more than he thought. Surely that structure was more hospitable than the Abbey, since it had only been built a century past. Messrs. Palmer and Perkins apparently suspected this acquisitive side of the countess, since they had instructed him to take up residence at once.

"Give me the letter, Chloe," he said in resignation, hoping to make the interview as short as possible. If he took care of the letter—no matter that it would not be sent until the weather improved—then she would go away.

"Oh, thank you," she gushed in gratitude, scampering around the massive mahogany desk as if she were a child instead of a woman well into her twenties. She leaned over the leather arm of his chair to place the pink square in front of him.

He held his breath as the double dose of scent from Chloe at his side and the letter in front of him tickled his nose. While he scribbled his initials, he wondered if the woman had any dresses that did not display most of her upper body. He was aware that the classical Greek style of dress was becoming fashionable, but he had seen ancient statuary that had more covering than Chloe Merriam.

"Oh, goodness," exclaimed another voice from the doorway, and Ian looked up in time to see Miss Dodd stumble awkwardly into the room. He jumped to his feet in relief at the diversion and almost knocked Chloe to the floor.

"Miss Dodd, are you all right?" he asked while trying to untangle himself from Chloe's clinging hands. Impatient with the woman, Ian grasped her shoulders and practically lifted her to one side.

"Yes, Lord Denham," Serena responded quickly, looking back over her shoulder as if she might find some obstacle at her feet or someone standing behind her. "I must have tripped over the rug. I was not sure if I should disturb your conversation with Miss Merriam and must not have watched my footing."

"You should not have been hesitant. Chloe was merely having a letter franced," he explained quickly, noting the high neckline of Miss Dodd's gown with approval. "She undoubtedly has something more exciting planned now that her errand is finished. Right, Chloe?"

"Well, really," the woman responded with a loud sniff and toss of her curls as she stomped to the door. When she reached the threshold, she turned and directed a resentful look at the pair standing in the middle of the room. Without another word she walked out of sight.

"Ah, Miss Dodd, you seem to have arrived at the right moment once again," Ian exclaimed, smiling in delight over ridding himself of Chloe so easily. "I must thank you for your help, but I also must apologize for my unseemly behavior last night."

"You need to apologize, but why?" she asked, her eyes widening in surprise. "I was the one who was impertinent. It was not my place to read you a lecture on manners. That is why I came to visit you this morning, to beg your pardon."

"Shall we both blame it on the late hour of the night and weariness from a long day?" Ian was amazed how well the matter was working out. Miss Dodd seemed to be a levelheaded, reasonable woman, and very attractive in her blue kerseymere dress. He had not noticed yesterday that she was such a handsome woman, in a quiet understated way, or the light scent of lilac that clung to her trim figure, and her hair smoothed into an elegant coil.

"Oh, yes, your work. I do not want to disturb you any longer, now that we have settled the matter so agreeably," she stated with a slight smile, glancing at the manuscript pages scattered over the surface of his desk.

"I assure you the disturbance was timely," he returned, and wondered why he was so reluctant for her to leave. "Perhaps I should formally request your services as my official protector against romantic-minded females. With you by my side—"

A clattering of metals near the fireplace drowned out the rest of his words, causing both Ian and Serena to start in surprise. He turned quickly to see the source of the disturbance. The crossed rapiers that had previously hung on the paneling now lay on the floor along with the silver platter and two cups that had been displayed on the chest beneath them.

"This place seems to be coming down around our ears," he murmured as he crossed the room to assess the damage.

"Perhaps your ghostly matchmaker does not approve of your practical suggestion of having a protector against romance," she remarked from close by his side.

"So, Digby had been at it again. I must talk to that boy about his wild tales," Ian commented with a frown, and walked to the bell pull to summon Dreyer. He tugged on the embroidered strip of cloth and studied Serena as she surveyed the rubble on the floor. The thought of her half smile and twinkling eyes helped him come to a decision. "Miss Dodd, I was joking about needing a protector, but you could be of service with my brother. I should like to explain about Lancelot, if you will excuse my plain speech on the matter."

"You mean there really is a Lancelot?" Her eyebrows rose in surprise as he nodded and pointed to a small painting hanging just below where the rapiers had hung.

"He was a younger son at the time of the Civil War. From the accounts in the family history he was wild and reckless, exactly the type of Cavalier that Cromwell found so distasteful," Ian explained, crossing to Serena's side. He looked over the slender, dark-haired young man in the painting, dressed in crimson velvet and lace, a large hat decorated with an ostrich plume in one hand. Ian did not like to acknowledge the family resemblance in his ancestor's narrow face that was surrounded by long, shoulder-length curls. "Digby has only heard a fictitious account that has been passed down by superstitious servants. Lancelot broke his neck the night before his wedding, falling from a second-story window."

"Surely, Lord Denham, that is not the full tale, or you would have told your brother by now," Serena prompted when he finished, and he turned away from the portrait to study her face.

Ian smiled slowly in response to the spark of amusement in her gray eyes. "You have a quick mind, Miss Dodd. After my indiscretion last night, I was reluctant to speak on another indelicate matter."

"I have been instructing young ladies against the wicked world for three years now and do not think this piece of family history will shock me unduly." Though her face was solemn, he noted she was nibbling her lower lip in an interesting manner to keep a smile at bay.

"You are a very sensible and intelligent young woman, Miss Dodd," he commented, bowing slightly in compliment to her pragmatic attitude. Almost wistfully he wondered why there were so few women in the kingdom who were of a like mind, instead of an over-population of nitwits like Chloe Merriam. "It seems that our Lancelot was a reluctant bridegroom because he did not want to . . . um, limit himself to one lady, especially a young girl of seventeen. He went *visiting* the night before his wedding, and unfortunately that lady had a jealous and suspicious husband."

"Oh, dear, I can see why you have not told Digby the real story as yet. That poor girl," Serena murmured, giving the smiling face of Lancelot a reflective look.

"Not so poor, actually, though Lancelot's companion that night was her cousin. The bride married Lancelot's older brother less than a year later, and soon after became the Countess of Denham," Ian concluded.

"Good heavens, then she is your grandmother, a number of times removed," Serena exclaimed, finally allowing her smile to break free. "It seems that Lancelot did her a great service that tragic night."

"Yes, he did. I knew that as a reasonable lady you would understand my problem," he responded and wished that he could detain Miss Dodd longer. He found her quiet manner and quick mind very refreshing. "As a sensible person, you can understand that Digby is so impressionable now." He broke off as the butler quietly entered the room. "Ah, Dreyer, have this mess cleared away and bring in some tea."

"I really must not keep you," Serena stated, stepping away from the debris, all traces of humor gone from her face.

"Oh, must you? I had hoped you would join me for some refreshment," Ian said quickly, wondering once again why he was so anxious to detain her. He frowned slightly as he noticed the rigid set of her shoulders and straight back.

"No, I cannot. I have promised your sister my help with placing the greens, and I must speak with the coachman about the roads. Excuse me, Lord Denham."

She was gone before Ian could say another word. Why had she wanted to leave so quickly? Absently he stepped out of Dreyer's way as the servant inspected the damage. He sat behind his desk but did not even glance at his papers, his thoughts preoccupied by Miss Serena Dodd. What had caused the change in her attitude from shared amusement to chilly politeness?

As he lounged back in the leather upholstery, Ian knew that he would never understand women in a million years.

"Practical, sensible, reasonable, indeed," Serena muttered under her breath as she hurried away from the study. She knew that she was all those things, so why did she dislike the earl's comments so much? Perhaps she was still tired from yesterday's journey and the lack of sleep. Why else would his words disturb her so much? And why did she keep remembering his warm smile of greeting after her precipitous entrance into his study?

All the fanciful talk of ghosts and romance must be softening her brain. Her steps faltered for a minute, and she stopped in the middle of the entry hall. The army of empty armour that lined the walls seemed the perfect setting to consider Sir Lancelot. For a moment she looked back toward the study, remembering the feeling of being pushed as she stood on the threshold. Then she laughed at her foolishness. She *had* caught her foot on the rug.

A slight chill skated down her back, and she decided to seek out Elspeth's company before she began imagining the knock on her door had not been the house settling, or the rapiers had not fallen off the walls because of a loose nail. Soon she would be imagining that the echoes of her footsteps sounded like laughter.

❈ 6 ❈

"*ELSPETH, WHAT IS* that contraption?" Ian exclaimed as he followed the others into the sitting room after dinner. His tone was a mixture of amusement and exasperation as he walked toward the object that was suspended from the timbered ceiling near the windows. Dreyer was lighting the candles that circled the four-foot leafy sphere with apples suspended from ribbons within the circle.

Serena sat down on the end of the green-striped settee to watch with interest as her hostess hurried across the room with Captain Merriam at her heels. Elspeth had outdone herself during the day, directing Cecil, Serena, and Digby—as well as every available servant—where each stem and leaf should be placed. By the time they were done, every bannister and mantel, practically any available space, had been draped with evergreens and holly. The old walls of Denham Abbey seemed more cheerful with its garlands, or it may have been the extra candles that Elspeth had requested.

Though it was a somber evening compared to Christmas Eve in the boisterous Dodd household, the company had been pleasant thus far, everyone seeming to put his best foot forward. The earl had joined the company before dinner in a cheerful mood, announcing that he had finished his article—unaware that Serena had kept the others away from his study. Then he assembled the servants before dinner and read the Christmas story from the scriptures since the steady snowfall prevented anyone from attending midnight mass in the village.

The reading seemed to have influenced the countess and her sister; both ladies made pleasant small talk throughout dinner. Even Spenser was well behaved, staying close to his mistress's side. Serena waited expectantly for Ian's comments as he inspected his sister's contraption with rapt interest, undoubtedly giving it the same concentration he would a piece of Grecian sculpture.

"Do you like it, Ian?" Elspeth asked anxiously as he finished his scrutiny.

"Well, my dear, I am not sure. Exactly what is it?" her brother asked with his eyes still trained on the object. He propped his elbow in one hand and rubbed his chin with the other, closing one eye for a new perspective. "And what is that hanging from beneath?"

"M-mistletoe," Elspeth replied, looking across the room at Serena for support before lowering her lashes to study the toes of her kid slippers.

Serena decided to come to her new friend's rescue as the countess and Miss Merriam rose to join the gentlemen. Elspeth's cheeks were now deep red, and she was looking everywhere but in the direction of Captain Merriam.

"It is a kissing bough, Lord Denham. My family has one every year, and I was forward enough to ask your sister for a little touch of home," Serena pronounced, linking her arm through Elspeth's. The young woman squeezed her arm in gratitude for the small fabrication, since the bough had been Elspeth's idea. "We liked to have a special place for Father Christmas to leave our presents."

"Very ingenious, Miss Dodd," the earl agreed, but the considering look he gave his sister made Serena wonder if he had noticed the growing rapport between the captain and Elspeth.

"Did you request that my grandmother's harpsichord be brought down from the attic as well?"

"No, that was my idea after Elspeth mentioned missing the carolers this year," Captain Merriam announced, giving the lady a generous smile before turning his attention to Serena. "I thought we would ask Miss Dodd to lend her talents to help us pass the evening."

"A splendid idea, Cecil. How fortunate we have a music teacher among us," the countess murmured with a smile barely curving her thin lips, running a disdainful eye over Serena's pink satin gown. "Chloe just loves to sing. Would you mind accompanying her, Miss Dodd?"

"I think we should all join in and give Elspeth a true group of carolers," Ian said quickly before anyone else could respond. The look he gave his sister-in-law seemed to dare her to say another word. "Shall we all gather around the harpsichord and give Miss Dodd our requests? I shall take precedent and asked for 'The Boar's Head.' Anyone else?"

"Oh, what fun. Thank you, Cecil and Serena," Elspeth exclaimed, clapping her hands like a small child given a special treat. "I would like 'The First Nowell' and 'The Holly and the Ivy,' please."

"What about the 'Wassail Song' or 'I Saw Three Ships'?" The captain readily joined in when his sisters remained silent.

"Before we overcome Miss Dodd, I have my own surprise, and I shall need your assistance, Cecil," Ian proclaimed, clapping his hands for attention, much to Serena's relief as the others bore down on her. "While Miss Dodd becomes accustomed to a new instrument, Cecil and I shall retrieve my small offering for the evening."

"What about me, Ian?" Digby chimed in anxiously.

"Yes, you may come along since this is a gentlemen's project." With that he lead his small band out of the room.

"What do you suppose he is doing, Mavis?" Chloe asked in a loud whisper as Serena took her seat at the harpsichord. "Should I go and—"

"Now, Chloe, you would not want to ruin Ian's surprise, would you?" Elspeth broke in ruthlessly from where she stood next to Serena, sending her new friend a speaking look. "There is no telling what he is up to. I think some years he has taken more delight in the festivities than Digby."

"Here we come, ladies," the earl announced from the hallway just seconds before he entered the room. He was grinning from ear to ear as he crossed the threshold, effortlessly carrying one end of a tremendous log on his right shoulder, Cecil hoisting the other end and Digby close at their heels.

"Oh, you remembered the Yule log," Elspeth exclaimed, skipping across the room while Serena began playing the appropriate processional. "Shame on Dreyer for telling me there was no time to find one before the storm. You had it all along. Now we shall have good luck throughout the new year."

"Indeed," Ian answered as he signalled Cecil to lower his end to the hearth. "This prime piece of ash should probably burn until Twelfth Night and a month beyond. I instructed Dreyer to hide it in the cellar to dry out and to keep it away from the inquisitive eyes of a certain young lady. We shall have it alight once Digby runs to fetch Dreyer and Will the footman."

"This is turning out to be such a lovely Christmas, not at all the dreary holiday I imagined. Oh, thank you, Ian," his sister stated, kissing him on the cheek. Then she turned hesitantly to Captain Merriam to do the same.

"Elspeth, what are you doing?" her brother exclaimed loud enough to be heard in the village.

Serena stopped playing on a discordant note, rising quickly to her feet. Both the countess and Miss Merriam were already moving away from the harpsichord to join the trio in front of the fire. Ian was glaring at his sister, who remained close to Captain Merriam's side.

Digby ran back into the room with Dreyer and the footman close behind. The boy skidded to a stop in front of his brother to look questioningly at the silent adults. "I thought we were going to have carols."

"Not now, Digby," Ian snapped without turning his head.

"I would like to pay my addresses to your sister, Denham," Cecil stated in a steady voice, and reached for Elspeth's hand as he spoke.

"Has the whole household gone mad with romantic nonsense?" Ian grit out between clenched teeth. His gaze rested on Serena as if she was the only person who could answer his query.

She was afraid to speak, in case her defense of the captain made matters worse. Elspeth was already pale, clutching Cecil's arm as if in need of his support to stand. The countess and Chloe were watching Ian's angry face in avid fascination, neither uttering a word in case his ire turned on them. But a whimpering noise from Spenser, clutched tight under Chloe's arm, drew Ian's attention to her and her sister, the countess.

"Well, madam, is this part of your plan? If your sister cannot succeed with the earl, you will try to get your hands on the Fitzwalter money through your brother instead?" Ian's face was rigid with indignation as if he was sure there was a conspiracy afoot, not just something he imagined in a moment of rage.

"How dare you?" his sister-in-law practically snarled before turning with a flip of her skirt and walking regally from the room. She only paused for a moment on the threshold with a curt command to her sister, who quickly trotted after her.

"Ian, what is happening? Why aren't we going to sing carols?" Digby tugged at his brother's sleeve in a bid for his attention.

"Digby, I think you and Elspeth and I should go upstairs while your brother has a talk with Captain Merriam over a soothing glass of wine," Serena broke in before Ian could say a word. She could tell from his expression that he had been about to say something cutting to his younger brother, and was relieved that she had intervened.

When Serena put a comforting hand on Elspeth's arm to draw her away, the younger woman began to protest. "Oh, Serena, I cannot—"

"Nonsense, my dear," Serena stated, ruthlessly interrupting the young woman. After three years at Miss Haversham's, she knew what was best for distraught young ladies and how to avert disaster. Elspeth's presence would only fuel her brother's irritation. "It will be much better if we let Ian and Cecil have a long chat while we go upstairs and have a nice cup of chocolate to help you sleep."

"Serena is right, sweetheart," Cecil concurred with a comforting pat on her hand. Serena knew that he would like to kiss the girl, but did not dare under her brother's watchful eye.

"Come along, Digby, the gentlemen need to have a private discussion," Serena instructed, and placed a firm hand on his shoulder.

"But I don't understand what's happening. Nobody tells me anything," he complained, but walked along at her side just the same. "All I'm supposed to do is be quiet or go away. I don't think anyone would notice if I disappeared."

As Serena guided her charges across the entry hall, trying to soothe them both, she nodded to Dreyer, who had quickly shepherded the footmen from the sitting room as soon as he sensed trouble and was now hovering just outside the sitting room door. With the uncanny perception of a veteran servant, he was already carrying a tray with a crystal decanter of crimson liquid and two glasses. After giving Serena a solemn nod of acknowledgment, he walked calmly into the sitting room to serve the gentlemen.

❋ 7 ❋

DENHAM ABBEY WAS so quiet it seemed uninhabited when Serena walked down the stairs two hours later. No one was in the lower hall, so by instinct she crossed the entry to the sitting room, wondering if Ian and Cecil were still there. She had promised a tearful Elspeth that she would check on the gentlemen personally before she went to bed.

The sight of a cleared hearth made her breathe a sigh of relief. It seemed to denote a return to normal, though she was not sure what that was in the Fitzwalter household. Someone had put the Yule log in its proper place, and the bright blaze was lighting the room. Most of the extra candles had been removed, and the ones remaining were burned down almost to the sockets.

"Lord Denham?" she called softly, wondering if she should try his study. "Ian?"

"Here," came a response from the far end of the room, near the windows. The curtains had been drawn aside, and she could see the outline of a figure framed in the window enclosure, the snow continuing to fall outside.

"Is that my serene Miss Dodd who kept her head when everything else turned to chaos?" Ian asked as she moved closer. In the dim candlelight she could see that he was holding a glass in his hand and was swaying slightly on his feet. "You may not want to keep me company, my dear. I am just a bit well to live after my discussion with the good captain."

"Has he deserted you already?" she asked hesitantly, wondering if she should go or stay. She had never had to deal with someone who was bosky and was not sure she wanted the experience now, despite her promise to Elspeth.

Ian's bark of laughter did not reassure her until he spoke. "I have not thrown him out into the snow. After a lengthy discussion on what is best for my sister, he has gone off to sleep," he explained, weaving his way toward the harpsichord and the decanter sitting on top of it.

"Are you planning on having another glass, Lord Denham?" she asked in hopes that he might think better of the idea. What had he and Cecil decided about Elspeth?

"Yes, I think I shall. But must we be so formal, Serena? You called me Ian just a few minutes ago, and I think I like that," he remarked while pouring a generous portion of wine into his glass. "Would you like to join me in a toast to the holiday and the possibility of my sister's engagement some six months from now?"

"Yes, I shall," she declared in answer to the challenge in his smile. She knew she had taken him by surprise when he paused to give her considering look. Then he turned back to the decanter and poured a second glass for her. Neither of them spoke when he handed her the glass. He simply touched the rim of his glass to hers, letting the peal of the crystal echo across the silent room.

He remained mute, turning back to the window and staring out into the night. Serena moved slowly to his side, not finding the silence between them awkward but comfortable.

"What is your family like, Serena?" he asked suddenly after a lengthy silence. "You must have learned your deft touch in volatile situations from them."

"You are very perceptive, Lor—Ian," she responded, thinking of growing up in the small house surrounded by her brother and sisters, sometimes longing for the peace and quiet of a night such as this. "I am the oldest of six and began helping my mother with the babies when I was five. We all managed in a little house not far from the university. Papa was always immersed in a book or busy with his students, while Mama and I watched out for the little ones."

"Good Lord, your father was Dr. Sedgewick Dodd. I was

sorry to hear he had died. I was very fond of him," he said softly, but did not wait for her to comment before he continued. "I remember that little house and Sunday luncheons. Mrs. Dodd had the sweetest smile in the world and nothing ever seemed to bother her, even the professor coming home with six or seven boys without advance notice. There was one little girl with great big eyes who never spoke a word, but simply sat watching the others as they gamboled about like eager puppies."

Serena was dismayed that she suddenly felt tongue-tied. She was horrified that he would remember his friends' teasing at any minute. She wanted to stay and leave at the same moment, fascinated and afraid of what he would say next.

"That was you. I should have remembered those expressive eyes," he said quietly, looking directly at her and holding her in place when she wanted to flee. "How do you do it, Serena? Always so calm and knowing exactly what to do each minute?"

"Ian, you are becoming fanciful. Remember the ill-bred young woman last night who wanted to teach you some manners?" she asked with a shaky laugh. Her heart was beating rapidly, and she suddenly felt flushed all over, but warned herself against the warm regard in his eyes. It must be a trick of the dim light.

"Nonsense, a momentary aberration. You were quick-witted enough tonight to keep me from planting my fist in Cecil's face," he returned, his soft smile only increasing her heartbeat. "I need to know how you manage it. Ever since Gawain's death I have been stumbling through life, hoping that each day I do not make a giant blunder that will ruin us all. I have an estate to run that I know nothing about, and my mother has left Elspeth and Digby in my care until she returns in the spring. Every day it seems to become more complicated."

"That is all anyone can do," she murmured and took a step back as he seemed to move closer. "You simply take each day and situation as it comes. Then you make the best decision to resolve the problem. Tonight you compromised with Cecil, and tomorrow you will have a nice long talk with Elspeth about the need to wait until after she has had time to think over the matter."

"Tell me, my dear, was the kissing bough really your idea?" he asked abruptly, cocking his head to the side as he considered the matter. A slight smile played across his lips that Serena did not trust.

"No, it was Elspeth's," she managed in a whisper of sound. She knew she was being foolish; even in his cups Ian would not think of kissing her. He wanted nothing to do with romance. But a second later he proved her wrong by placing an arm around her waist.

"Have I surprised you, Serena? If you stand under the mistletoe, a gentleman is obliged to kiss you," he murmured and bent his head to brush his lips against hers. "That was not so bad, was it?"

"No, Ian," she barely managed, pressing one hand against his chest and trying not to spill her glass of wine in her other hand.

"Then I should like to try again, now that I have the hang of it," he explained before claiming her lips again.

Wildly she thought he did not need any practice; he was very proficient. Then with a sigh she gave herself up to the moment, knowing she would regret her foolishness later, but wanting to experience the delightful taste of his kiss and the feel of his arm tightening around her waist. But it was over much too soon.

"I shall not beg your pardon for this, Serena, because I enjoyed that very much," he stated matter-of-factly as he stepped back, though his voice was slightly hoarse. "In fact, I am not sure I shall remember this in the morning, which will be a damn shame. Please consider it a heartfelt thank you for your help tonight. Now run along before I decide I need more practice."

She did not hesitate and turned on her heels before she did something outrageous. With every step away from Ian she was tempted to go back and throw herself into his arms. Only the thought of Chloe Merriam's foolish behavior kept her from so much as looking back at the man standing in the shadows. As she crossed the threshold, she thought she heard him speak but knew that he could not have said, "Pleasant dreams, my sweet Serena."

From where he sat near the fire Lancelot grinned in approval, wishing he could share some of Ian's excellent claret. The boy was beginning to show promise after all, and Lancelot was not sure that he was responsible for the transformation. Miss Serena Dodd seemed to have a magic all her own, but he was determined to help her in such a worthy cause. Once he had the earl betrothed, he could return to his cozy niche until the powers that be called him forth to be of service to the FitzWalters again.

❋ 8 ❋

"BUT, IAN, I'M tired of having nothing to do. The snow has stopped, so why can't we go outside? Couldn't we explore the ruins?" Digby implored his brother for what seemed the hundredth time in the few hours since Ian rose from his bed at noon. "You said we would study them one day. Why not today?"

"Digby, well over a foot of snow has fallen in the past two days." Ian leaned back in his leather chair as he gave the explanation slowly, knowing that Digby should have it memorized by now. "We shall have to wait until there is less snow. There is nothing but drifts out there now."

"But that might not be 'til spring," the boy protested, kicking his foot against Ian's desk. "By then, Mama and Elspeth will have dragged me off to London again."

"Digby, it is not my fault it has snowed. There is nothing more to say on the matter," Ian finally snapped in exasperation, rubbing his hand across his forehead. He simply could not reason with the boy, especially with his head beginning to pound once more.

"I'm never allowed to do anything," Digby grumbled with a mutinous look on his round face, but did not argue after seeing his brother's sudden scowl of disapproval. He flung away from the desk and ran out of the room.

"Damn and blast," Ian muttered, wondering if he should go after his brother. He thought he had seen tears beginning to form before the boy turned away. For a moment he considered it, then slumped back in his chair once more, knowing he would only make matters worse in his present frame of mind. He was still feeling some of the effects of his decadence the previous night and wondering—a little sullenly—how Cecil could be so cheerful today since he had drunk more than his fair share.

"Undoubtedly because Elspeth is still speaking to him today,"

Ian muttered morosely. Contrary to his expectations last night, he did remember everything that had taken place when Serena returned to the sitting room. He almost wished his prediction to her had come true; it was agony to remember the sweetness of the moment and know that was precisely the reason the lady wanted nothing to do with him today.

After the promise of the night, today had been a disaster thus far—the only bright spot was Mavis's pithy note reporting that she and her sister were keeping to their rooms. Once he was presentable enough to venture out of his room, Ian found himself tripping over Cecil and Elspeth in every corner of the house. Wherever he went they would be sitting close together, whispering and laughing over absolute twaddle. It might not have grated on his nerves so badly if Serena had not been pointedly avoiding him.

Every time he entered a room, she was leaving; if he was going up the stairs, she was coming down. He was sure she had not lingered in one place for longer than two minutes, unless there was another person present. That was how he kept stumbling over Elspeth and Cecil. Serena was not allowing a chance for any personal discourse by making sure there was always a third party at hand, even going so far as to seek out Mrs. Easterby in the kitchen to inquire how she prepared the Christmas goose.

He could not fathom a solution to the problem. There was no doubt in his mind that he had offended her by kissing her, the last thing that he had intended to do. But would she believe him if he told her his intentions were honorable after such a short acquaintance? He was not sure he believed it. Until two days ago, the only women who held his interest for any length of time were from a civilization that had died out over a thousand years ago and were now immortalized in marble.

Bitterly he wondered if the men of Athens understood women any better than he did today. He stared at the neat pile of manuscript pages on the desk in front of him, but took no joy in the fact that his latest essay was ready for publication. All he cared about now was Serena and her opinion of him. Did he dare acknowledge he remembered their whispered conversation beneath the kissing bough, or should he continue to pretend ignorance?

He was still mulling over the question an hour later as he

entered the sitting room and tried to restrain a groan of frustration as he spied Elspeth and Cecil on the settee in front of the fire. Serena sat primly across from them, her smile seeming to falter the moment he stepped across the threshold.

"Shall we go into dinner, since I understand Mrs. Easterby has outdone herself for today's festive banquet?" Ian asked with no real interest in food.

"Lead on, my good man," Cecil pronounced heartily with a mock bow, offering a hand to assist Elspeth to her feet. "I understand that my sisters are still barricaded in their rooms, but what about Digby?"

"I saw him run up to his room about an hour ago," Serena remarked, her gaze never straying from Cecil and Elspeth. "Has anyone seen him since?"

"Perhaps he has fallen asleep," Elspeth added, and slipped her hand from the crook of the captain's arm. "I shall run up and see what is keeping him. He hardly ever forgets a meal. The rest of you go into the dining hall, or Mrs. Easterby will be having fits."

Ian stepped forward to escort Serena into dinner but was not surprised to see her move closer to Cecil. The captain looked nonplussed for a moment and quirked a questioning eyebrow to his host. Ian gave a quick nod, trying to mask his look of disappointment. Something in his demeanor must have given him away, for the other gentleman gave him a commiserating look over the top of Serena's bent head as they walked past.

He walked slowly behind the couple toward the dining hall, stealing the opportunity to watch Serena unobserved. They could not go on like this, he decided. Once dinner was through, he would request a private interview with her. Unfortunately he had no idea what he was going to say. Life had been much simpler when his work was his only interest.

"Ian!" The quiver in Elspeth's voice warned him that something was wrong even before he turned to see her distressed expression as she ran across the entry hall. "Ian, Digby is not in his room and Dreyer has not seen him for over an hour."

The words were barely out of her mouth before the butler approached from the kitchen quarters. "M'lord, I have checked all the rooms on this floor, and there's no sign of the boy."

"Damn and blast." Ian was sure he knew what the foolish child had done. He should have followed Digby when he left the study, but it was too late now for second thoughts. "Dreyer, check with the other servants as well as the outside entrances for any fresh footprints. I shall be in the study looking over the old maps of the Abbey ruins to organize our search."

"You do not mean the boy has ventured out in this weather," Cecil exclaimed as he followed close at Ian's heels.

"That is what I fear," he replied without slackening his pace until he reached the map cabinet opposite his desk. He yanked open two drawers before he found the drawings he sought. Once the parchment was free of the drawer, he carried it to his desk and smoothed it across the wood surface. "What is left of the old Abbey is in this area close to the house," he explained, pointing out two sections of the structure to his companion. Then he grabbed at a loose piece of paper and drew a rough sketch of the area. "You search this area to the left, and I shall take the other side and the cellar."

"If Serena saw him an hour ago, he might not have been gone too long," Cecil commented as he studied the diagram of the building. When Ian did not answer, he placed a hand on his shoulder in sympathy. "Small boys have a special guardian angel to keep them from harm. You and I survived to become adults, so we shall undoubtedly find him in the midst of a great adventure."

Ian tried to smile at the captain's good intentions, but he kept remembering that he was responsible for the boy running away. "Well, we cannot find him standing here, so we had best get started." He turned on his heel and strolled over to his desk to retrieve his father's dueling pistols. He did not say a word as he loaded the guns, more worried about his brother than he cared to admit, and handed Cecil one of the pistols.

As he crossed the entry hall, Ian looked around for Dreyer, then stopped in his tracks at the sight of the two women on the stairs. His eyes never left Serena's face as he growled, "What do you think you are doing?"

"We are going with you," Serena said quietly, and secured the hood of her cloak. She continued down the stairs, but her heart was in her throat while she pulled on her gloves as if she were preparing for an afternoon drive. Stopping on the bottom step, she looked directly into Ian's glaring brown eyes, silently daring him to refuse her help.

She was prepared to do battle with him over the matter. Her

motivation was not only to help find Digby; she needed the activity after moping around from room to room all day. What else was she supposed to do? She had no idea how one should act after being kissed by a gentleman, especially one who said he would not remember anything the next morning. Unfortunately she did and was greatly embarrassed by her wholehearted response the previous night.

What if Ian did remember suddenly? She had not dared talk to him today, afraid that something she said would remind him of their whispered conversation beneath the kissing bough. Never mind that she had lain awake half the night remembering the magic of his embrace. It seemed that she was no wiser than the silly twelve-year-old girl who had loved Ian Fitzwalter from afar. Only this time her heart was in more serious danger of being broken. He had kissed her out of gratitude, nothing more.

"Sir, we found his footprints outside the dining hall doors," Dreyer called as he rushed toward them in an uncharacteristic show of exertion. Behind him were two footmen carrying coats and blankets.

Serena let out the breath she had been holding when Ian turned away without a word to let Dreyer help him into his greatcoat. As he shrugged into the garment he began giving orders. "Cecil, you take Dreyer and Will, and John will come with me and Serena. Follow the route I showed you, and if you find him, fire a shot."

Serena was startled when Ian came to her side and grasped her hand. His face gave nothing away, but he tightened his grip before he headed toward the dining hall. When they reached the outside door, Ian took the lead, still keeping a firm grip on her hand. The bitter sweep of the wind took her breath away the moment she stepped through the door. Picking their way carefully through the uneven drifts, they crossed the open area that separated the ruins from the rest of the house.

The remaining walls were uneven, some with only a few feet of masonry while others towered over their heads. As Ian moved to the right, Cecil led his group through a corridor that was still standing to their left. Rocks and fallen timber hindered their progress, and the light was beginning to fade as dusk approached. Serena held tightly to Ian's hand, not wanting to relinquish the contact. She could not imagine what Digby was feeling if he was lost in this labyrinth alone.

"Dreyer, we shall need the lantern now," Ian ordered, and stopped to allow the servant to pass him. The pathway ahead led into another hallway with a doorway on each side. "Light the way, but go carefully."

Serena tried not to shiver as she watched the older man move ahead, and was glad for the comforting arm that Ian placed around her shoulders. For a moment she let her head rest against his shoulder, savoring the moment. When she tried to pull away, he stopped her by placing his hand gently against her hood.

"Not yet. Dreyer will signal when he is ready," he murmured, and wrapped both arms around her trembling body. "Thank you for coming, Serena."

She tilted her head back to see his expression more clearly, but it was difficult in the failing light. What could she say? She could not tell him that she had fallen in love with him once more in a matter of days, and she wanted to be by his side during this small crisis. Before she could speak, he touched her lips with the tip of his glove.

"Not now," he murmured, a slight smile playing across his lips. "Later we shall have a nice long talk about last night."

Dreyer's shout from ahead gave Serena no time to reply. She was still trying to fathom's Ian's words as he took her hand and walked ahead. There was no time to dwell on what he could mean because Dreyer was gesturing toward the doorway on the right, where a wooden door was still in place. As they came closer, she could tell what had excited the butler; a flickering light was coming from the room beyond.

Serena wanted to laugh and cry with relief as Ian led her into the room. The room was almost habitable, with the ceiling mostly intact, its stone flooring littered with debris but free of snow, and the massive stone fireplace was in use. Digby lay wrapped in a blanket on the brick hearth, fast asleep.

Ian was across the room in a single bound, kneeling down to scoop the boy up into his arms. He enclosed the child in a fierce hug and looked up at Serena with a grin, unashamed of the tears that were beginning to form in his eyes. Digby sputtered awake at the rough handling, shaking his head and blinking owlishly at the three adults standing over him. Then a grin split his drowsy face.

"You *did* notice that I disappeared," he exclaimed, throwing his arms around his brother's neck. "Oh, Ian, you knew I was gone."

"This is exactly why I need you to marry me," Ian said in a ringing tone, looking up into Serena's startled face with a fierce frown. Then he turned back to his brother, swinging him to his feet and holding him in place by the shoulders before giving him a shake. "If you ever pull a stunt like this again, you scapegrace, I shall beat you within an inch of your life. Do you understand?"

"Oh, yes," Digby answered, but he could not erase the happy grin from his face.

Serena was beginning to wonder if she had imagined Ian's words. She must be dreaming. There could not be any other reason for Ian Fitzwalter, the Earl of Denham, to mention marriage. Suddenly she felt the need for support and reached out blindly. Her gloved hand came into contact with the warm stones of the fireplace, and she gladly leaned against it. She watched with detachment as Ian handed Dreyer his pistol, still keeping one hand on Digby as if he thought the boy might run away again.

The report of the pistol snapped her out of her lethargic state. She was acting ridiculous. Ian did not know what he was saying, or perhaps he remembered the kiss and felt obliged to make the offer to an unchaperoned young woman who was his guest. She did not have time to dwell on the matter in the chaos of the next few minutes as the other searchers rushing into the room. Elspeth knelt down to join her brothers, and the three of them almost tumbled to the floor at her enthusiastic embrace.

Everyone was laughing and crying and talking at once until Dreyer reminded the earl that Mrs. Easterby's dinner was waiting. Digby protested loudly—ruining the effort by giggling—as Cecil swung him over his shoulder to lead the procession back to the house. Serena stepped quickly away from the fireplace, hoping to catch up with Elspeth for the walk back. She did not dare look in Ian's direction, which was her undoing.

She was only a foot away from her goal when he captured her arm, holding her in place as the others disappeared from sight. Though she stopped, Serena did not have the nerve to look up and was disgusted with herself for her lack of courage. It would be best to get this misunderstanding out of the way. Ian must understand he was not obliged to make her an offer, but she shied away from the actual words.

"Are you going to stare at the floor much longer?" he asked

with laughter in his voice. "We could be here for a long time, even if I have to hold you captive."

No sooner were the words out of his mouth than the door in front of them slammed shut. Both of them were momentarily stunned. Ian recovered first, stepping forward to test the latch, which would not budge. He turned back to her with a smile. "See, even the spirits are on my side. Perhaps it is Lancelot himself, bless his romantic soul."

"I thought you did not believe in romance or ghosts, especially matchmaking ones," Serena dared to say, finally looking up from studying his boots. The warmth of his gaze increased the rate of her pulse, and she almost began to think foolish thoughts again, just as she had the previous night.

"I did not believe in much of anything until a few days ago, not until I became bewitched by a pair of expressive gray eyes," he began, and took two steps forward to grasp her hands. A teasing smile curved his lips as she tried halfheartedly to pull away. "Surely, my dear Serena, if I have imagination enough to envision ancient civilizations, then I can also visualize a family ghost, especially since spirits are known to be restless during Christmastide."

"Ian, this is—"

"Hush and let me speak. You have seen what a muddle I have made of my life on my own in the past few days," he stated with a slight grimace, his expression turning anxious for a moment. "If it had not been for the snow, I am sure Elspeth would have eloped as a result of my stupid outburst. Then tonight Digby ran away to see if I would miss him. How am I going to cope with all this without you in my life?"

"Ian, I am only a simple music teacher." The look in his eyes told her differently, but she could not forget his sister-in-law's haughty snubs. "You need someone who can act as your hostess, someone who is used to the *ton* and the dictates of society."

"What fustian is this? Was last night so distasteful that you cannot bring yourself to consider my offer?" He did not bother to hide his smile, and she looked away. But he would not allow her withdrawal, tipping up her chin with his forefinger as he pulled back her hood with his other hand. "I have no use for an empty-headed society hostess. Instead I want a lady to stand by my side, a lady who will pull me away from my work so that I do not neglect my family. A lady who would fill the house with children who possess solemn gray eyes and carefree hearts. Is that too much to ask?"

"No," she barely managed to say with a tremulous smile before he crushed her to his chest. She gladly surrendered, knowing that she had begun to love him years ago without understanding it. Perhaps others might think he could have made a better choice, but no one could love him more than she.

"Does this mean you will accept my offer of marriage?" he said anxiously, rubbing his cheek against the top of her head.

"On the condition we wait until spring for the wedding," she stated firmly, because one of them had to be practical.

"Until spring?" he almost shouted, then grasped her shoulders and held her at arm's length. "Do you think I am so impressionable I may find another lady in that time?"

"I hope not, but that is the same stipulation you gave Cecil last night. He has known Elspeth longer than you have known me," she explained, trying not to smile at his scowl of displeasure. "And I think your mother would like to be here for your wedding."

A slow grin lit up Ian's face, but before he could utter a word an eerie laugh echoed through the room. Serena stepped quickly into her betrothed's embrace before she looked over her shoulder to discover the source of the disturbance.

The laughter came from the shadows beyond the fireplace, and a man stepped out of the shadows. He was wearing plain yeoman dress: a smock and a shapeless hat pulled low over his face.

"The man at the crossroad who directed my coach here," Serena murmured, and almost swallowed her words as the figure transformed before her eyes. In place of the rough clothing there appeared a crimson doublet, trimmed in lace at the neck and cuff as well as at his knees above his knee boots. His hat was replaced by a handsome head of shoulder-length ringlets, and in his hand was a wide-brimmed hat trimmed with a white ostrich feather. "Lancelot."

As she whispered his name, Lancelot's form seemed to shimmer. He executed an eloquent bow with a flourish of his hat, blowing her a kiss as he rose to his full height. Then he was gone.

"Oh, Ian, what is to become of him?" Serena asked as she rubbed an errant tear from her cheek.

"You should not fret, my love. I think he is happy in his own way," he answered with conviction. "Traveling from century to century in aid of his family undoubtedly suits Lancelot's adventurous spirit better than being a lost soul in purgatory for his sins. Besides, you might be seeing him again in the future. According to the family legend, Lancelot also watches over the daughters of the household, protecting them from rakes and scalawags such as himself."

"Is that why you gave Cecil your provisional approval?" She dared to tease him, becoming secure in the warmth of his love.

"I still have my reservations on that matter until spring," he admitted reluctantly, "but I think we can discover a place more comfortable than a tumbled-down ruin to discuss that, and a few more interesting matters—such as this." He bent his head and claimed her lips to demonstrate his meaning.

"Ian, what are you doing?" Serena gasped a few minutes later as he swung her up in his arms and walked to the door that somehow had swung open without them noticing it.

"I am carrying home the most precious Christmas present I have ever received," he announced as he walked through the door with a very satisfied smile on his face. "This year we had the perfect exchange of gifts, my sweet Serena. I gave you my love and received yours in return."

Christmas
at
Wickly

❋ ❋
❋

Judith Nelson

EDWARD, EARL OF Wickham, was not amused.

He had bounded up the steps of Wickly Manor that first day of December with the same enthusiasm he'd shown since his arrival home nearly two months earlier. Enthusiasm collided with shock once he threw open the manor door, however, and shock was soon replaced by consternation.

The pile of bags littering his Great Hall stopped him short. Wickham watched in astonishment as two of his footmen labored up the wide staircase that was the manor's showpiece under the weight of an obviously heavy trunk. A "what the devil—" had just exploded from his lips when he realized he was not alone.

A pair of calm brown eyes in a thoughtful face surveyed him; the woman to whom they belonged was seated tranquilly on one of the long padded benches that spotted the hall. The book in her hand indicated she had been reading.

The earl had barely absorbed her presence, and started toward her with a demanding, "Who *are*—" when an older woman entered the scene from the drawing room door across the way.

"Edward!" The older woman came forward to give the earl a peck on the cheek. Since the new arrival was dwarfed by the earl's imposing height, Wickham had to bend to receive her kiss. His arms enclosed the small woman as his shocked mind registered her appearance in his recently inherited and—until her arrival—quiet, well-ordered home.

"Grandmama!" he sputtered.

The old lady leaned back within the circle of his arms, and smiled archly up at him. It was clear from her expression that she recognized his surprise, and enjoyed it.

"So good to see you, too, Edward," the dowager countess purred. Edward flushed, aware that his astonishment had sent his manners begging.

"Of course—" he stuttered. "Delighted—not that I expected—"

"No." The word was spoken abruptly as she shook her head,

her brows drawing together. It would have been apparent to anyone who knew her that she had a bone to pick with someone; it was just as apparent to the someone standing before her that the bone she wished to pick was with him. "I know you did not. Which is why I am here. Having received your note saying you were back in the country and would visit me when it was *convenable*"—her emphasis on the word made it clear what the dowager countess thought of *convenable*—"I decided—"

She broke off suddenly, turning to smile at the woman still seated in the hall shadows, watching them with interest.

"But there!" The dowager countess patted her grandson's arm in a meaningful way. "We shall have a comfortable coze, just the two of us, in a few moments. For now, let me make my young friend and traveling companion, Miss Cassandra Worthington, known to you. Cassandra—" The countess held out a beckoning hand, and the young woman came forward obediently. "This is my grandson, Edward. Wickham, you know."

Cassandra held out her hand and the earl took it with a slight bow. "Miss Worthington," he said, straightening to look down at her from his superior height. She was a pleasant-appearing woman, not beautiful, but with a face that spoke of character. She was dressed modestly but in good taste, had soft brown hair, and intelligent eyes that suggested a great deal of humor. The cut and quality of her clothes made it apparent she was not a paid companion. The earl ran through his mental list of distant relations. Worthington. It had been a long time—had he forgotten? Should he know her? Worthington. Worthington. Try as he might, he could not think of any familial connection with that name.

"We have not met, my lord," the lady said. She smiled as he gave a slight start, embarrassed she had so easily read his expression. "But your grandmother has told me much about you."

"Oh?" The word was noncommittal, and Wickham once again turned his attention to his grandmother.

"Yes," the dowager countess confirmed. "And little of it good. For when a grandson returns after ten years out of the country and does not even stop in London to visit his grandmother, but instead posts down to Wickly so that that grandmother is *forced* to follow him into the country if she wishes to see her nearest and dearest relative—"

The earl, aware of the amusement in Miss Worthington's eyes, and aware, too, that his grandmother could continue in this embarrassing vein for hours, cleared his throat.

"I believe, Grandmama," he said, his voice firm, "that we were to have this conversation in private."

If his statement was meant to put either the female speaker or listener out of countenance, he was doomed to disappointment. His grandmother was not the least discomfited, and Miss Worthington, her eyes alight, said only, "Quite right, my lord. It is so disagreeable to be scolded like a scruffy schoolboy in public."

The earl, who had not heard himself compared to a scruffy schoolboy for some years, and who did not like it any more now than he had then, stiffened but said nothing. The young woman turned to the dowager countess and, with a curtsy, said that if Lady Wickham did not mind, Miss Worthington would retire to her room now to change for supper.

"But of course," the dowager countess said. "Smythley will show you to your room, my dear."

As if conjured by magic, the earl's estimable butler appeared from the shadows. Wickham wondered how long he had been there as the bowing Smythley said, "If you will follow me, Miss Worthington." The lady went up the stairs in the butler's stately wake and the earl, watching, shook his head. Surely it was the lighting that made it appear as if the lady mimicked the butler's solemn posture and tread, not out of maliciousness, but from a joy of the ridiculous. He was still trying to decide when his observation was cut short by his grandmother.

"Well, Edward?" the old lady said.

"Well, Grandmama?" His smile was one of reluctant admiration, and the countess's chin rose. Without another word she turned and walked into the drawing room. The reluctant earl followed her.

"You what?!"

If the earl had been disconcerted to find his heretofore peaceful hall turned chaotic minutes earlier, his consternation was nothing compared to the irritation he felt now. It seemed, his grandmother informed him, that his home would soon be invaded—his word, not hers—by any number of those persons considered the cream of London society who the dowager countess had invited to Wickly for Christmas. To that end she had thoughtfully—at least, *she* seemed to think it very thoughtful of her—posted down to their ancestral home, bringing Miss Worthington to help her with the preparations for the coming holiday. She'd thought it only fair, the dowager countess said, smiling up at her oh-so-frowning grandson, that she tell him, before the guests arrived in a little less than three weeks, that his house would soon be filled to overflowing with people he hadn't seen for a very long time, or had never met.

"You—" The earl seemed to choke on the word as he stared at her. He made a hasty turn about the room, running his hand through his hair in aggravation. "You—"

"You sound just like your grandfather." The dowager countess was reminiscent as she sat by the fire, basking in its warmth. The firelight threw her patrician features into sharp relief, and the crackling flames were reflected in the highly polished wood that defined the room. Plentiful sconces were now being lighted by an unobtrusive servant, and the earl, waiting for the man to leave, wondered dismally what had happened to the tranquility he had previously felt in the room.

"Your grandfather used to take just that ferocious tone with me whenever I did something he might not quite like," the countess continued, ignoring the carefully blank-faced footman.

"Might not quite—" The Earl of Wickham took several more restless steps about the room. A meaningful glance at the footman dismissed any need to light more candles at that time, and with a bow James retired. After the footman quit the room, the earl returned to stare at his grandmama in bafflement. His memories of his grandfather were vague, and he wondered if the previous earl had had any more success in dealing with the lady than he himself was having.

"Tell me, madam," Edward said, moving to the fireplace to lean back against the mantelpiece, "did his ferocious tone have any effect upon you?"

"Not in the least," was the cheerful reply, and the old lady's eyes sparkled. The earl, torn between the urge to scold and the urge to applaud her insouciance, compromised with a rueful grin.

"Well." His voice held a decidedly milder note as he looked affectionately down at the woman who had championed so many of his causes when he was small. How long ago that all seemed!

"Be that as it may, my dear grandmama, I really must insist. Whatever plans you have put forward to invite these people to Wickly for Christmas must be put at an end—"

"Put at an end?" The dowager countess laughed, a triumphant sound that brought a quick frown to her grandson's face. "Do not be ridiculous, Edward. As if I could! Only think a moment. You must see that I cannot."

The earl's eyes narrowed and his frown deepened. It was clear he saw no such thing. "I beg your pardon?"

The words were civil, but the tone incredulous. The dowager countess's smile increased. It was apparent her grandson had not had his will crossed by an expert for quite some time, and the sooner that happened, the better she felt it would be. Luckily for him, she thought, *she* was just the one to do it.

"I can't," she repeated. "Only think what people would say! You've been gone much too long, dear boy, if you don't remember how these visits go. Some of our guests no doubt are already on their way—stopping at their own estates, or visiting here and there with other friends for a few days. Everyone will have made their plans, refused other invitations. No, no—it's much too late to uninvite them, and we can hardly turn them away when they arrive at the door, can we?"

There was something in the earl's face that suggested he would not find that nearly as difficult as his grandmama thought, and for a moment the dowager countess held her breath. Suppose—just suppose . . .

The grandson who stood before her now obviously was not the young man who had left the country ten years earlier. That young man had been much more amenable. Suppose she had pushed too far . . .

"You—" The earl's eyes, narrowed before, opened almost to goggling as he comprehended the full impact of her words. "How dare—how could—" He took another turn about the room.

"Why you should think I would care to spend my first Christmas back at Wickly with a houseful of guests I do not know," Edward began. The dowager countess, deciding this was not the moment to report she had not considered his wishes in the least when she invited the guests, lowered her eyes. In a carefully neutral tone she informed the room at large that had her grandson come straight to London upon his return, instead of traveling directly to Wickly, he would now know and welcome these people.

"Ahhhhh." The word was low, and comprehension lit his eyes. "I see."

Not sure whether she *wished* him to see or not, the dowager countess remained silent.

"I did write you," he said. The words were half-indignant, half-apologetic.

His grandmama snorted. "An impertinent little note, saying nothing of importance other than that you hoped for my good health and knew that we should meet sometime in the future! When it was more *convenable* for you!"

Something about the emphasis on "convenable" had the earl tugging at his cravat; it had grown suddenly tight. "I planned to come to London when—"

"When you were good and ready!" The countess finished the sentence for him, and gave him her most powerful glare. "Never caring that your aged grandmama might depart this earthly coil any day, without once more seeing her long-absent grandson—"

The earl laughed. "Doing it up a bit too brown, my dear," he told her, fond amusement lighting his eyes. "Everyone knows you'll outlive us all!" He moved forward to kiss her cheek and take her hand.

"I am glad you are here," he said. "Until I saw you, I did not realize how much I have missed these past years. My family, Wickly . . . I suppose I tucked it all away because of the hurt it brought when I thought about it—"

His words broke abruptly, and he straightened to stare off into the fire. "For years I dreamed of this room, warm, inviting as it is now, but then there was nothing here for me—"

"Your family was here." His grandmother's voice was soft, and after a moment he looked down at her as if he had returned from someplace far away. "No one asked you to leave."

The earl shrugged, the motion emphasizing his well-muscled shoulders. Unlike his grandfather, father, and brother, Edward was not a burly man. It was apparent, however, that there was strength in him; strength of body and strength of mind.

"No," he said, "of course not. Robert and I got along well. But I was the second son. I would always be the second son. I did not wish to live my life dependent on my brother's sufferance—"

"So to prove you were your own man in your own right you went off to India and made a fortune," his grandmama ended for him. "Which was a very good thing, because an estate such as Wickly requires a fortune. Not that it doesn't pay its own way, because it does, but still—" Another thought entered her mind, and her brow furrowed. "Although you could have come back, now and then, to visit. Why you had to go and stay and not come back—" Her voice took on the quarrelsomeness of someone hurt by another's actions, who would never say just how much those actions had pained her. The earl took her hand again.

"I really am pleased to see you," he said, his smile so like his grandfather's, father's, and brother's that it made her heart ache. "But as for your guests . . ."

Twenty minutes later Edward sat in the chair across from his grandmother feeling as if the world, which had tilted at her arrival, was now totally askew. These were not *her* guests coming to Wickly for Christmas, the dowager countess informed him, they were *his*. Some of the prize beauties of the country would be there, with their mamas, and a few with their papas as well. Plus a few of the dowager countess's intimates, who just happened to be the influentials of London society who could do him a great deal of good.

The earl interrupted her cataloging of the coming guests with a frown. "Beauties?" he questioned.

The countess appeared not to hear.

"Beauties?" he repeated, louder. Her look of innocent inquiry sent a cold chill down his back.

"Grandmama!" All trace of amusement was wiped from his face as he stared at the old lady. "You have not—you would not—"

"Would not, dear boy?" she prodded, when he appeared unable to continue.

"You would not try to turn Wickly into a marriage mart within two months of my return to the country—"

Something in the countess's face suggested she would, and he glared at her in disbelief. "This passes all bounds!" he roared. The sound did not discompose the countess in the least, although in other quarters it had been known to make grown men cringe and hastily check their work to make sure they were not the cause of such anger. "This is exactly why I did not come to

London at once—to avoid a constant parade of simpering little misses whose sharp-eyed mamas are on the lookout for a catch such as the Earl of Wickham! I have enough to deal with in fitting into my new title, finding my feet, without dancing the pretty for a pack of marriage-minded young women all bent on establishing themselves as best they can! I won't do it, I tell you. I won't."

"Oh?" The countess was all polite interest. "I see. You have, then, formed another plan to ensure the succession? Perhaps you have someone joining you shortly—a fiancee, perhaps even a wife—whom you have forgotten to tell your grandmama about? Or there is a lady upon whom you have already settled your interest, who returns your favor, but you've not yet asked her—someone you knew before you went away? Although who would wait for *you* for all these years, I don't know. And I wouldn't think much of her intelligence if she did!"

The earl, grim-faced at the beginning of her speech, grinned at the barbed ending. The countess sniffed. "You may glare or grin at me all you wish, Edward; neither will work any more now than they did when you were twelve. I do not know what you have been about these past—what is it? Thirty? Forty years?"

"Forty?!" All trace of the earl's grin vanished. "Forty indeed! I am just turned two and thirty!"

The countess bit back a smile at his quick offense, and sniffed again. "Two and thirty! Past time for the Earl of Wickham to be setting up his nursery."

Edward pointed out that he had not been the Earl of Wickham for more than eight months; that the news of his brother's untimely death had not reached him until then; and that if his brother had set up his own nursery, as he should have, they would not even be having this conversation—

Too late did he realize the trap he had laid for himself. He tried to turn the direction of her thoughts, but his grandmama pounced on his words.

"Precisely!" she said. "And if Robert had not been so distraught when Elizabeth and the babe died in childbirth, he might have done so. Married again, and had two or three sons running all over the property, and keeping him out of boats he should not have gotten into. But no! No matter how many times I tried to talk with him about it, he would only say that after his passing you would secede him. I always thought—when he grew older, perhaps, and the sorrow had grown dimmer . . . But then the storm came up when he had taken that curst boat out . . ."

The old lady's voice broke, and she covered her eyes with one hand. The earl came forward to press her shoulder in comfort, and after a moment she raised her tear-glazed eyes to smile waveringly up at him. "It is no joy, Edward," she said, "to outlive not only your children, but your children's children, as well."

"I am sorry, Grandmama." He squeezed her shoulder again.

"That is why I would like to see you established," she said. "I want to dangle a great-grandchild on my knee before—"

"Nonsense!" The word was bracing. "Didn't I just say earlier I expect you to outlive us all?"

This time the dowager countess did not smile. Instead she patted his hand, and the look she gave him was half command, half entreaty. "Don't you see, Edward?" she asked. "I do not wish to outlive you. Not as I have outlived your grandfather and your parents and now Robert. I do not wish it at all! While Robert preceded you and might still, in time, be brought to find someone else, there was no reason to press you to find a mate and marry. But now—" Her voice broke again, and she stared off into the fire. The earl ran a harassed hand through his hair.

"Now," she said, "there is reason."

"But Grandmama—" The hand attacked his hair again. "I'm sure that—in time, yes—but I've only just returned, and I thought—later, I supposed . . . In a few years, after I had the estate in order, perhaps then . . ."

The countess frowned at him. "Do you remember the Darpools, Edward?"

Confused by the conversation's abrupt turn, he stared down at her, blinking. "Darpools?" The name registered in the hazy corners of his memory, but he could not pull it out. "Darpools. Aren't they—?"

"Distant relations," the countess supplied.

"Yes." He remembered now. "Of course. Some sort of cousins, aren't they?"

"The worst sort," the old lady said. "Poor as church mice, and no more intelligent than that table there." She pointed to a cherrywood side table that held the earl's brandy, and thought a moment. "Which may insult the table."

"I see." He said the words automatically; it was clear he did not.

"You will meet one of them this holiday."

"I will?"

"Clarence." The dowager countess said the name and dismissed the young man with a wave of her hand.

"I see." Again he did not. "But—" He could not help asking. "If you so dislike this young man . . ."

The countess stared up at him in astonishment. "I don't dislike Clarence Darpool," she said. "He is a most amiable young man. Lovely manners, and I do believe a kind heart."

"Then—"

"But such a slowtop! Oh, my, Edward—*such* a slowtop. I cannot, I *will* not, abide the notion of him—or his older brother, who does *not* have lovely manners, and may be missing a heart altogether—as Earl of Wickham. And should you die before you have a son to follow you, that is just exactly what will happen. The men in this family have such a bad habit of dying at the most inconvenient times, and you'd leave no one closer to you by blood than those Darpool cousins, and that awful entail says Wickly must pass to a male member of the family, and— Oh, Edward, should it pass to a Darpool, I do not believe I could bear it!"

The earl, attuned to the sudden passion in his grandmother's voice, gazed at her in consideration. He knew of the entail; it had not overly concerned him, because he had believed that in time . . .

Still, it was apparent the matter concerned his grandmother a great deal.

"You are very serious about this, aren't you, my dear?" he asked, his own voice grave.

"I am!" The words were vehement. "You must *try*, Edward. When our guests come, you really *must* try! I have brought Cassandra with me to see that all is in order when the others arrive, for she is a very helpful and organized young woman, is Cassandra. And I have invited young ladies whose presence will make our Christmas party the envy of many—most of them have very good connections. They are young ladies known for their looks and amiability, and I flatter myself that I have even invited one or two with intelligence, which I find most attractive in a woman, and I hope that you, too . . ."

She paused, and looked up, her eyes once again filled with entreaty. "Tell me you will try, Edward. Just try—"

She stared at him as hard as she might, but she could read nothing in his expression. It occurred to her that her grandson must be an excellent card player, for he was able to keep his face blank, and his eyes and thoughts hooded.

The most he could be brought to say after considerable coaxing was a noncommittal, "We shall see."

Supper that night was a strained affair. The earl sat frowning at every dish set before him, and the dowager countess sat frowning at her grandson. Only Miss Worthington appeared to have no more on her mind that her dinner, which she attacked with considerable relish, commenting from time to time on the tastiness of this dish or that. At one point she glanced up to find the earl's dark gaze upon her, and she smiled, her eyes twinkling.

"I assure you, my lord," she said, "I am not the enemy."

The words, said in jest, were met by a stern stare and a stiff "I beg your pardon?"

"Well, I rather think you might," Miss Worthington said agreeably, helping herself to a comfit from a dish directly in front of her, the earl and his grandmother previously having refused the treat. "Leaving me to make all the dinner conversation myself—"

"I hardly think," the earl said, the words dry, "that remarking on the abundance of peas at my table qualifies as conversation."

"Ah." The lady nodded approvingly. "If you were not speaking, you were, at least, listening—"

"Let he who has ears, hear," the dowager countess interjected darkly. The earl and Miss Worthington glanced at her in surprise. Miss Worthington, after several moments of silence, uttered a polite "Quite."

"The thing is," Miss Worthington continued, smiling at the earl as she selected another sweet, "I am not one of the young ladies coming here to win your approval—well, I am not a young lady at all, which should have been your first clue. I am well past the age of all that! Why, I must be only a few years younger than you." Not knowing why he frowned so fiercely at her words, or why his grandmother laughed, Miss Worthington paused before adding, "I am here to help your grandmama any way I might, and to help chaperon my niece, when she arrives with her mother—"

"Aha!" said the earl.

Miss Worthington blinked at him in surprise. Now it was her turn to say, "I beg your pardon?"

"You have a niece!"

"In point of fact," the lady said, "that is not unusual. I might—although I do not—have several."

"And your niece is coming here."

Miss Worthington blinked again, and nodded.

"I imagine she is very beautiful, your niece."

"A diamond," Miss Worthington assured him, a slow smile starting to form on her lips as she caught the direction of his thoughts, "of the first water."

"Aha!" The earl said again.

"Unfortunately"—Miss Worthington's voice was tranquil as she once again surveyed the sweet tray—"my niece already considers herself in love, and has not the slightest interest in you. It is most trying for her, but what can one do? And besides"—she made her selection and popped the tidbit into her mouth, swallowed, then continued—"she considers herself much too young for you. So you really do not have to look for threat from my family at all."

The dowager countess, brooding over her wine, took a sip just as Miss Worthington concluded her last two sentences, and choked. A thoughtful Miss Worthington rose to pat her on the back before returning to her seat.

"Too young—" The earl's face was incredulous. "Miss Worthington, I can only assume you joke!"

"Oh, no," the lady assured him. "You must realize, my lord, that at eighteen, forty seems older than—"

"I am," the earl said, his jaw tight, one hand clenching and unclenching at his side, "just turned two and thirty."

"Oh?" The lady tilted her head to the side, considering. Her eyes were opened very wide, and his color had heightened considerably before she added, "And looking not a day over," in a far from convincing tone.

"Then why you thought I was forty—"

Miss Worthington considered again. "I believe," she said,

turning to the dowager countess, "it was something you said when you asked my age, and I said I was just turned eight and twenty."

"Forty or two and thirty," the dowager countess said, signalling the footman to refill her wine glass, "it makes no difference."

Miss Worthington, watching her host, could not help but smile. The earl's expression made it quite apparent that in his mind, at least, it made a great deal.

After supper Miss Worthington excused herself, saying she was sure the earl and his grandmother had a great deal yet to discuss. She was right, but since the earl could not seem to find the right words to discuss it, and since every argument he put forward was foiled by a stronger argument from his grandmother, he soon bid the countess good night and made his escape to the library, his favorite room at Wickly and a sure solace. Unfortunately his favorite chair by the fire was occupied when he strode into the room, his brow dark. That brow did not lighten at the sight of the woman there.

"My lord!" the lady said.

"Miss Worthington."

She smiled. "Giving up so early, are you?"

His frown remained. "I do not know what you mean."

"Only," she said, voice and face friendly, "that it seems very likely that your grandmother has bested you in some argument and you have come here in search of peace—"

"—which I did not find." He ended the sentence for her, and her face made it apparent the lady took his meaning. Annoyed with his own rudeness, the earl bit his lip and half turned as Miss Worthington said, "Ahh," as if she'd just expelled a long breath.

Her next words were soft. "Touche, my lord."

"And I did not argue with my grandmother." Much, he added mentally, with complete disregard for the truth.

"Oh." Miss Worthington considered him carefully for several moments, then smiled. "Couldn't find the words? That can be most frustrating, when one wants to say terribly cutting things but keep them icily civil, and the words will not come—"

"Miss Worthington!" The lady looked questioningly at him as his nervous hand disarranged his hair for the twelfth time since the ladies' arrival. He was frowning. "Do you always do that?"

"Do what, my lord?" She appeared perplexed, and he tugged at his hair again.

"Read a person's mind like that! It is most unsettling."

"Oh." The lady rose, biting back a smile. "I am sorry, my lord. I did not mean to unsettle you. My sister-in-law is always telling me that I have a terrible habit of plain speaking, coupled with a most regrettable sense of humor, and apparently I have once again proven her right. You wish to be alone. I find that at this moment, so do I, so I will just take my book—" She reached for the volume she had placed on the small table by her chair when he entered; it slid from her grasp and both of them bent to retrieve it. Their fingers touched and Miss Worthington withdrew her hand, leaving the book for the earl to recover.

"Chaucer!" he said in surprise as he glanced at the cover. The lady's smile was rueful.

"I am quite found out," she said. "I beg of you, my lord, tell no one."

"What?" He was surprised at her book choice, and puzzled by her words. Miss Worthington laughed.

"I am already well on my way to being known as an eccentric in society, my lord," she told him. "It is my regrettably plain way of speaking, coupled with the fact that I have neither beauty nor money to temper it." At his look of inquiry she laughed and said he had been too long gone if he'd forgotten their society forgave the very rich and the very beautiful much. Smiling, she added, "Do not, I pray you, make known my book choice and let them add bluestocking to my name!"

The earl turned the book over in his hands; now it was his turn to tilt his head sideways, considering. "Would that be such a terrible thing, Miss Worthington? To be thought intelligent?"

Her bubble of laughter rose, and it occurred to him, in some distant corner of his mind, that he liked the sound. "My sister-in-law," she told him solemnly, "assures me it is fatal."

"Why?"

She met his clear gaze with one of her own, and her chin rose. "Why, my lord, do you so resent my, as you say, reading your mind?"

"I don't resent—" he started, taken aback.

Miss Worthington smiled at him. It was a knowing, disbelieving smile, and he felt his color rise again—something he thought had happened rather too much that night. She held out her hand. "My book, my lord."

He gave the volume to her. "Your book, Miss Worthington. And oh, Miss Worthington—"

Almost to the door, she turned back toward him, waiting. One eyebrow was raised in surprise.

"Good night."

Again that clear gaze, followed in short order by a slight curtsy and an equally clear "Good night."

If the earl had thought his Great Hall turned upside down the day of his grandmother's arrival, that flurry of activity proved to be nothing compared with the upheaval in his home that followed.

Preparing Wickly for guests apparently was not, as he had vaguely assumed, a matter of laying in a rather larger than usual amount of food and airing a few beds. Under his grandmother's supervision and that of the efficient Miss Worthington, footmen were set to polishing silver and chandeliers, maids scurried everywhere with dustcloths and fresh linens, and candles were checked and rechecked.

Two days after the ladies arrived he wandered into the morning room in search of the tranquility he'd known there only a week before, and instead found Miss Worthington industriously twisting silvery paper into cunning shapes. A number of small packages surrounded her, and when he asked what she was doing, Wickham was stunned to find she was wrapping *his* Christmas gifts for *his* guests.

"Oh." The earl quirked an eyebrow as the absurdity of the situation struck him. Here was a woman he barely knew wrapping presents for people he *didn't* know, or hardly remembered—people coming to his home whom he had not invited, and did not particularly care to see. Yes, he thought, such a scenario clearly indicated the master hand of his grandmother.

"And am I a generous host?" he asked.

Miss Worthington, giving the final package in her lap a finishing twist as she placed it on the table, smiled at his tone. "Quite," she assured him, eyes twinkling.

"And do I have good taste?" It was that half-teasing, half-self-mocking tone again, and Cassandra laughed.

"Exquisite," she assured him, the slightest dimple showing in her cheek. He hadn't noticed that dimple before, he thought, picking up several pieces of her work to observe them more closely.

"And what exquisite gifts am I so generously providing for these visitors my grandmother has invited to make my home theirs?"

Miss Worthington, rescuing her work from his hands before he could undo it, said that the ladies would receive beautifully painted fans, while the gentlemen would be heartily pleased with their snuff boxes.

"Ah." Wickham nodded. "I *am* a generous soul, aren't I? Hand-painted fans and snuff boxes; perfectly correct, yet nothing scaly about them. What good manners I have, to be sure!" At her laugh he smiled and asked, "And do I have you to thank for my good taste and generosity, Miss Worthington?"

She smiled back, explaining that she had gone with his grandmother to make the purchases, but it was really the dowager countess who had made the final selections—

Her words were cut off as the earl's grandmother entered the room and, hearing Miss Worthington's last sentence, finished it for her. "Yes, yes," the countess said, waving a languid hand to dismiss their coming guests in favor of what she considered a more important topic at the moment. "It's more than most of them deserve, of course, but I wanted it to be clear that the Earl of Wickham can be most generous. Now, Edward, run along and quit bothering Cassandra. I'm putting her in charge of decorating the manor, you know, because the dear girl has the most talented hands. Soon there will be holly, ivy, evergreen boughs, and mistletoe everywhere, and—"

Wickham, wondering if he should first make it clear to his grandmother that it was *his* house, and he was not to be told to "run along," or if he should first address the fear inspired by her last words, focused on the fear.

"Mistletoe?" he asked. The forboding in his voice made Miss Worthington smile, and it was clear she enjoyed the spirited exchange he and his grandmother entered into concerning that mystical plant. When it was just as clear the earl had been rousted by his indomitable grandmama, and was on his way out of the room, Cassandra stopped him by asking if a proper Yule log had yet been procured.

"Yes," he said, looking toward her. The earl was fonder of Yule logs than of mistletoe. "In fact, I have been quite looking forward to it. Yule logs have not much come my way since leaving home."

Miss Worthington smiled. "The Yule log is one of my favorite customs," she said. "There is something so comforting about it—the idea of light and warmth, amidst winter's cold."

"Yes, well!" The dowager countess, her mind on other things, dusted her hands together briskly. "You both may have your Yule log, if it pleases you so, but for me, dear Cassandra, do not forget the mistletoe!"

The earl saw an opportunity to get back a bit of his own, and his eyebrow rose as he asked teasingly, "And who amongst our coming guests is it you wish to catch under the kissing plant, Grandmama? Is it someone of whom I would approve?"

The countess gave a beatific smile. "Silly boy!" she said. "I've had my days under the mistletoe, and enjoyed them immensely, thank you. No, no—this year the only person I hope to see caught early and often until each of the berries on each of the plants is gone is you!"

Wickham, feeling his color rise as he heard Miss Worthington laugh, thought of someplace else he was meant to be, and fled the scene.

"Tell me, Miss Worthington . . ." the earl said abruptly three hours later. He had come upon the lady in the drawing room, artfully arranging holly in one of the great glass bowls that dotted the many small tables there. Cassandra started, for her mind had been elsewhere and she'd thought herself alone. Immediately he apologized and she shrugged, saying it was nothing.

Gazing around, Wickham found the room more festive than he could ever remember seeing it. Cassandra watched him in silence for several moments before asking if there was something he would like changed.

"What?" The question seemed to surprise him, and hastily he shook his head. "No, no! You have done a lovely job, Miss Worthington. I don't remember when I've seen Wickly look so—happy. . . ."

Miss Worthington gave a pleased nod. "I am glad my work meets with your approval, my lord. You have a beautiful home.

It is a pleasure to ready it for Christmas." For some reason her words, obviously sincere, pleased him immensely, and he smiled as she went back to her holly arranging, moving to another table with a basket containing the vegetation on her arm. When he did not seem inclined to leave, she looked up and said, setting down the knife with which she'd been trimming holly branches, "Was there something, my lord?"

"What?" He had watched her work with interest, approving the quick, sure moves she made, and the artistry with which she filled the bowls. "Oh. Yes."

"My lord?" she prompted, when he showed no further inclination to begin. The earl asked if she would care to be seated, and without comment she slipped into one of the high-backed chairs that sat on either side of the floor-to-ceiling windows that looked out onto the east gardens. The earl took the other chair and, clearing his throat, began.

"I was wondering, Miss Worthington," he said, seeming to choose his words with care and some embarrassment, "if what you said that first night, at dinner, was said out of pique or was true."

"My lord?" Her head was tilted to the side, waiting, her gaze clear. She was a calming sort of woman, he thought.

"When you said your niece was not one of those coming for my—ah, approval—"

"Oh." She smiled. "That, my lord, was true."

"Then why—?"

She raised an eyebrow. In the face of her questioning look he found it difficult to proceed.

"Why then," he asked, "are you here, and why are your sister-in-law and niece coming, if your niece does not wish to be the Countess of Wickham?"

"Oh." She seemed to find it a surprising question, but was not averse to answering it. "I am here, my lord," she said, "and my sister-in-law and niece are coming, because we were invited. By your grandmother. An invitation from the Countess of Wickham is highly valued, you know."

"Well, yes," he said, not realizing quite how it sounded. "Of course. But if you knew her reason and really did not wish to be part of it—"

The lady grinned. "Is it so difficult to believe, my lord," she asked, "that not every woman in London spends all her waking and sleeping moments scheming to be your countess?"

"What? Oh. No, of course not." Too late he realized how he must appear. "Not at all! It's just that—that—"

Miss Worthington laughed. "If it makes you feel any better, my lord, my sister-in-law *is* coming with the fond hope that once you meet my niece you will fall madly in love with her, and the silly chit will return your feelings, and the two of you will live happily—and wealthily—ever after."

"Oh."

"My niece is coming because I told her she must, and because your grandmama has invited Clarence Darpool, that amiable twit Letitia—my niece—at present imagines herself in love with."

"I see." He wondered why he said that when he actually did not see at all, and sought further enlightenment. "But why did you tell her she must come, unless you, too, hope—"

"Hope?" For a woman who earlier had divined his meanings so easily, it occurred to the earl that Miss Worthington was being most obtuse now, and he frowned.

"Hope?" the lady repeated. "Oh! You mean, do I hope that you and Letitia will fall in love?" At his nod she laughed. "Oh, no, my lord! Believe me, no! I did not wish it before and now, having met you, my mind is quite set against it. You and my niece would not suit. Never!"

The earl, who moments before would have believed his fondest wish granted to find that even one of the young ladies coming to his home was not interested in entrapping him in matrimony, now found himself perversely annoyed to discover the lady in front of him dismissed him as a possible suitor for her niece's hand.

"I see," he said, voice and backbone stiff. Miss Worthington gazed at him in mild surprise.

"I thought that would please you, my lord," she said. "After all, you have made it quite clear you do not appreciate your grandmother's interference in inviting your coming guests to your home."

"Of course it pleases me," his lordship said in anything-but-pleased tones. "It pleases me very much. Although I still do not understand why, if you have decided I am such an ogre, you have come."

Watching him, Cassandra realized she could soothe his

wounded ego by assuring him that she did not consider him an ogre; oh yes, she knew she could. She was sure he was waiting for her to disclaim, and she was sure her sister-in-law, in the same situation, would have made haste to do so, saying it was the right thing to do. It was regrettable, Miss Worthington mused, that she did not more often feel moved to do the right thing. . . .

Instead, she smiled brightly and said, "I have come, my lord, because I am so dishearteningly tired of the price of coal. And peas."

"Coal?" For a moment Wickham thought he could not have heard right. "Peas?" The lady's nod confirmed he was not experiencing a hearing loss, and he sat back in his chair, staring at her. "I beg your pardon . . . I do not seem to understand. . . ."

Miss Worthington reached across the space between them and patted his hand as it rested on the chair arm, assuring him there was no reason he should. When he continued to stare at her askance, she sighed and said, "You would not understand, my lord, because of your great wealth, how enormous a burden can seem the price of peas."

It was apparent he was waiting for her to continue, and Cassandra smiled. "This does not concern you in the least, my lord," she said. "There is no reason you should understand—or care. But the thing is, when my brother died ten years ago, when Letitia was only eight, and I was about to make my own debut, he left his affairs in something of a muddle. I put my own plans aside for long enough to help Alicia—my sister-in-law," she said, at his look in inquiry, "—learn to hold house, and somehow, well—either I am a very poor teacher, or Alicia is a very poor pupil, although she does try, poor dear, I know she does—I have stayed. . . ."

"And your own season?" he said, when she seemed to lose herself in the sentence. Cassandra smiled.

"I would not have taken," she said. "It was no great loss."

"You might have surprised yourself, Miss Worthington."

The lady laughed. "I hardly think so. I seldom do. Anyway . . ."

"Anyway?" the earl prompted. Miss Worthington went on to say that this year she and her sister-in-law had decided to rent a house in London to launch Letitia into the *ton*, for the child was so beautiful it really was a shame for her not to have a London Season when she wanted one so much. They'd rented their home in the country to a scholar looking for a quiet place to work on a book, and with that money and the income they received from the small estate, plus the amount Cassandra had managed to save for them over time and Cassandra's own modest inheritance, they'd come to London. And everything was going well, it really was; Letitia and Alicia were enjoying themselves immensely. It was just that everything cost a little more than Cassandra had planned; coal, and candles, and the dreadful price of peas, while as for clothing—

She broke off at the expression on his face, and looked questioningly at him.

"My lord?" she asked.

"Letitia and Alicia," he said, "are, you say, enjoying themselves immensely. What about you, Miss Worthington?"

"What?" Her surprise made it apparent the question had not been put to her before. She thought for a moment, then laughed.

"Well, my lord," she said, eyes twinkling, "I am at present immensely enjoying knowing that that funds-eating house in the city is closed up for a month while we're gone—Letitia and Alicia soon will be visiting friends before coming here—and I enjoy knowing that every time I feel warmth, like I feel now"— she nodded toward the cheery fire burning in the grate—"I am not feeling another of our hard-earned pounds going up in smoke. Oh!" She thought of what she'd said, and blushed. "That is—not that I am happy to think that it is your pounds being made use of, my lord! Please do not think—"

The earl held up one hand as he continued to survey her. "Do you not enjoy the parties too, Miss Worthington?"

She smiled and said she was sure they were very nice; she had met some delightful people, like his grandmama . . .

The earl, whose last conversation with his grandmama had been anything but "delightful," blinked but said nothing.

She actually enjoyed the country more than town life, Miss Worthington told him, adding with a twinkle that Alicia told her it was *fatal* to admit such things. But, Cassandra grinned, she really could not help herself; she liked to putter in her garden, and to take long walks, where she could stride right out and not be constrained by city rules about not leaving the house alone. And when she took a city maid with her, Miss Worthington said, the woman wanted to do no more than *dawdle*, not really *walk*—

Miss Worthington smiled apologetically. "I am sure, my lord, that that is much more than you ever cared to know. Actually, I have much enjoyed seeing the sights of London— and oh, the lending library! *How* I have enjoyed that!"

"More than trips to the hatmakers and dressmakers, Miss Worthington?" He said it to tease, but the lady appeared embarrassed. Glancing down at her gown she said that while she must, of course, present a certain appearance for Alicia and Letitia, it seemed so much more important to spend the greater amount of clothing funds on their clothes, because they did both so love lovely things—and besides, who knew? In a world where anything might happen, she couldn't help but think that both Alicia and Letitia might contract eligible matches, for Alicia also was a beautiful woman, and—

The earl, who knew less about lady's dress than many of his cohorts, said hastily that he thought she looked quite well; he had not meant to imply otherwise. Miss Worthington's gaze was one of evident skepticism, but she let his statement pass as another thought struck him. Curious, he asked, "Do you not think you yourself might contract an eligible match, Miss Worthington?"

She laughed. "Now you are teasing me, my lord," she said, wagging a finger at him in mock reproach. "And it is too bad of you! I told you when we first arrived that I know myself to be beyond all that. You have only to look at me to see I was born to be an aunt."

She was smiling at him, her head up as she invited him to agree. Thus it was that the earl considerably surprised Miss Worthington—and himself—with his reply.

"What I see when I look at you, Miss Worthington," he said, after several moments surveying her, "is a remarkable woman!"

Wickham, unsure why those particular words had come out of his mouth at this particular time, was also unsure just what reaction the remarkable Miss Worthington would have to his statement. What he *wasn't* expecting—and he *was* sure of that—were the peals of laughter that burst from her lips after one long, incredulous glance in his direction.

"No, really—" he began.

"No, really, my lord," she echoed. "Of all the whiskers!"

"I assure you, Miss Worthington—"

His assurances were interrupted by the appearance of his grandmother at the door of the drawing room, demanding to be told what was so funny. Cassandra, her face merry, rose from her place by the window and returned to her holly basket, informing the countess that her grandson was getting back a bit of his own for all the plain speaking she'd done earlier in the week. The countess frowned.

"If that young jackanapes has been rude—" the dowager started, glaring direfully at the earl. Miss Worthington assured her it was no such thing; in fact, Wickham had entertained her immensely. The "young jackanapes," so bemused by Miss Worthington's reaction that he failed to recognize his grandmother had just called him "young," was heard to mutter that he had not meant to be entertaining.

"Oh, but you were, my lord," Miss Worthington assured him. "You were!"

Glancing at his grandmother, the earl said that he hoped they would have the opportunity to continue their conversation later. Miss Worthington, laughing, shook her head and said that she, herself, believed their conversation quite finished.

"Oh, my lord!" Miss Worthington said the next day as she met the earl in the hall as he emerged from his library. She again carried her workbasket, and the artistic arrangements the earl now saw in his hall, making the wide area even more welcoming than usual, showed that she once again had been busy. Several sprigs of holly and a generous supply of evergreen peeped from the basket on her arm as she said, "I was wondering if you wished for a bit of greenery in your library, to mark the season?"

It was clearly a question, and he was pleased that she'd asked before acting—something he was sure his grandmother would not have done. He nodded, saying that that would be very nice. With a smile Cassandra started toward the library door, stopping only when she realized he followed her.

"My lord?" she asked, head tilted to the side in that considering way he was starting to recognize.

"I have forgotten something," he replied, reaching past her to open the door. "I will only be a minute."

Miss Worthington surveyed him through her calm brown eyes but said nothing as she preceded him into the room. Setting her basket on a large oak table that sat beneath the west windows, she started to work. However, after several moments in which he had done no more than watch her and lean his shoulders back against the door as he did so, the lady turned and said, with a slight smile, "It appears, my lord, that what you have forgotten is to leave."

Wickham grinned. "I would continue our conversation from yesterday in the drawing room, Miss Worthington."

"Oh?" The lady picked up a snippet of holly and placed it in a small bowl before turning to a large porcelain vase that sat at the center of the table. "Odd. I, on the other hand, would not."

"You seemed to have great difficulty believing I meant what I said, Miss Worthington."

The lady smiled. "Let us just say, my lord, that I know a whisker when I hear one."

"Meaning?"

"Meaning, my lord, that I have over time since coming to London—and even in the retired country—heard several women referred to as remarkable. They have been women of great beauty, like my niece—many young men have, this past season, assured her she is most remarkable. Or they have been women of great wit—although that is not always admired, I find, so I should, perhaps, clarify with great wit *and* great fortune. Great fortune among the *ton* must always be deemed remarkable. What they have *not* been, my lord, is women with plain brown hair and plain brown eyes and little height and a regrettable sense of humor that makes them see the ridiculous just when those around them would *most* hope the ridiculous would not be seen, and no more talent granted them than the ability to hold house and carry on a reasonably intelligent conversation."

The words were said matter-of-factly, even lightheartedly. They were devoid of rancor, and the earl, watching her, was moved to ask if the men of England had grown so blind while he was away that they no longer saw to appreciate such things.

Miss Worthington laughed. "Now you *are* roasting me," she said. "I know it. For I have just told you that they are *far* from blind—oh, far, far from it. And soon, when your guests arrive, you shall see what stirs the blood of Englishmen. In fact"—she fished in her basket, reaching under the evergreen—"I rather thought it might help you if I made a list. . . ."

Miss Worthington had indeed made a list, a list of every one of the guests coming to the earl's home. It was a very thorough

list, filled with the main attributes of each of the impending
visitors, their familial connections, their likes and dislikes as
they were known to the lady, and—he shuddered at the
thought—the various accomplishments of each of the young
ladies his grandmother was bent on making known to him in the
hopes he would take a bride.

Miss Sophia Symington, the list said, was a dark-haired
beauty much admired by the town bucks. Her smile was said to
be pure delight, and many were the London hostesses who
enlivened their small, convivial dinner parties by asking the
beauteous Miss Symington to sing.

Her mother, Mrs. Amelia Symington, held a deep aversion to
dogs (so, cautioned Miss Worthington's list, he might like to
disinvite his setter from accompanying him into the morning
room, as it often did, when the guests were there).

The earl, reaching down to scratch the ears of that friendly
setter, who now sat at his side as he perused the list, frowned.
Without meeting the woman he already knew he preferred the
dog to Mrs. Amelia Symington.

Miss Tuttleton, the list continued, was thought by all of
London to be a most high-spirited girl, forever ready to take the
lead on the hunt or the dance floor. She would arrive with her
proud parents who—and this was hinted at most delicately—
were determined, now that their daughter was midway through
her third season, that she would not see a fourth as a single lady.

The earl shuddered.

The Honorable Elizabeth Chatsworth, known for her wit and
poetry, would arrive in company with her mother. Her father,
Viscount Chatsworth, had hied off to his own estate in high
hopes of a peaceful holiday, now that his wife and daughter were
invited to Wickly (that latter information the earl would learn
later; it was not included in Miss Worthington's helpful note).

By Letitia Worthington, her niece's name, Miss Worthington
had penned, "Beautiful. Quite." He grinned, and read on.

Penelope, granddaughter of Lord and Lady Harling, two of
his grandmother's oldest friends who would be accompanying
the girl to Wickly, received the comment, "A tall, good-natured
girl, who likes horses. I like her very much. You might also."

"Oh, I might, might I?" the earl said to the setter and the
empty room, crumpling the paper after reading the few remaining comments about the other guests—Clarence Darpool and

Viscount Chively, both younger than the earl and both invited to help make the numbers at table more even, and because Clarence Darpool was a distant relation and Viscount Chively the dowager countess's godson. Also coming was Lord Worthhope, one of the dowager countess's oldest friends, invited for her entertainment. Pondering the information, Wickham spared a moment to wonder what it was that made him so unappreciative of Miss Worthington's helpfulness in this matter, when she had obviously put so much thought and work into her list.

The days between the arrival of his grandmother and Miss Worthington and the arrival of his other guests passed with more speed than the earl thought possible, each day developing its own rhythm. With his servants bustling and his grandmama more than ready to brangle with him at every turn, the earl drifted more and more into the company of Miss Worthington. He liked to watch her work. He liked the way she settled the concerns of his housekeeper with good sense and a smile. He liked the way he could depend on her to see the humor in the strangest things.

He had several times coaxed her away from her duties—something it was remarkably hard to do, for Miss Worthington was a disciplined woman who tended to task—to ride with him on mornings that were cold but clear. They cantered over his lands while he told her of this or that improvement that he planned to make. He had had no one other than his bailiff to discuss his plans with since his arrival at Wickly, and he found Miss Worthington an attentive and intelligent audience. The questions she asked were to the point and thoughtful, and several times prompted him to rethink his ideas.

She was not above teasing him when he started to take himself and his ideas too seriously, and he found—rather to his surprise—that he enjoyed that, too. He looked forward to their rides together, and came by degrees to be more than a little dissatisfied on the mornings the lady declared herself too busy to ride that day.

Miss Worthington also enjoyed the rides they took together, but for another reason.

Their high-spirited gallops—to say nothing of the races they ran—reminded her, she said, of her childhood. She had not enjoyed herself so for years.

"Oh?" Wickham, bending forward to pat his horse's neck after just besting Miss Worthington in a half-mile run to the forked tree, looked up with interest. It did not surprise him that Miss Worthington did not keep a riding horse in London, for from what she'd said of their circumstances he would imagine it more than their budget could bear. But surely—

"Don't you ride, then, when you are at your home in the country?" he asked.

She laughed, and patted her own horse approvingly. "Ride?" she repeated. "Well, yes, I do—if you can call it that! But our stables boast nothing as fine as this lovely lady. We have one old riding mare my brother bought for Alicia shortly before he died. Poor horse—it does the best it can. It was nine years old when Richard purchased it, and he bought it for its mild manner and slow gait—which has grown slower over time!"

At the earl's look of inquiry, she smiled, "Alicia," she excused, "was always a nervous rider."

"But not you, Miss Worthington?"

Her smile broadened as her eyes grew reminiscent. "My father," she said, "kept wonderful horses! Richard, too, when he was alive. In fact, Richard probably put much too much into his stables; more than he could afford. I found that when I— Well."

She gave herself a shake, and the earl could almost guess what went unsaid. Richard Worthington would not be the first man to overextend his financial resources, no doubt believing he could rebound with several canny deals. Richard, however, had died before those deals were made, leaving a wife, daughter, and sister to try to salvage what they could. The earl frowned, and it was several moments before he realized Miss Worthington continued speaking.

"We were forever tearing about the countryside when we were children, Richard and I," she said. "It brought Mother's reproofs down upon our heads, for she said Richard positively *encouraged* my hoydenish ways. She straightly forbade him to do so."

"And?" he prompted, when she stopped.

"And of course we paid not the slightest heed to her warnings!" Cassandra giggled. "We just tried to see that every time I tore my dress or took a tumble, Mother didn't find out about it. At least," she amended, her smile softening, "she never let on that she knew. I imagine she did. We later learned Mother had been something of a hoyden herself, when she was child."

"I wish I could have met your family," Wickham said, reaching out to rest one gloved hand on her wrist. She stared down at it for several moments before looking away.

"I wish you could have, too," she said quietly. Then, to change the mood, she applied her heels to her mare's sides, and was off.

"Race you to the far fence," she called back, and this time, with the element of surprise on her side, Miss Worthington as she told everyone at Wickly who would listen (and that was everyone there, it seemed; the earl soon learned that Miss Worthington had become a fast favorite with his household)—won.

Although he didn't think about it much on purpose, in some corner of his mind Wickham was aware he was growing more and more to look forward to the evenings, when Miss Worthington put aside the many tasks she's assumed for the dowager countess and joined him in a game of chess—she was really quite good!—or a companionable evening of reading, always ready to discuss his book or hers, or the one his grandmother read.

He had asked her one night where she had learned to play chess and she, in the process of removing one of his pieces from the board, said absently that she'd often played with her grandfather.

"Your grandfather?"

"Yes," she said, looking up to smile into his eyes. Her grandfather had lived with them the last years of his life. Confined to his chair and his bed, he found the days long, and had taught Cassandra to play chess with him, to while the hours way.

"I see." The earl made his next move, only to have Miss Worthington quickly claim that piece, too. "And you were—how old—when you learned to play?"

"Twelve," Miss Worthington said.

The earl sat back in his chair and his eyes narrowed. "Do not," he threatened, heedless of the smile his words brought to his grandmother's face as she watched them from her place by the fire, "tell me that here you are, destroying all my defenses, yet you have not played chess since your grandfather's death!"

Miss Worthington giggled. "I would like to tell you just that, my lord," she said, "if only to humble you for the high-handed manner in which you won your race yesterday—by pretending your horse was injured and then, when I was quite stopped and had turned around and was coming back toward you, by taking off at high speed!"

"Edward!" the dowager countess scolded. Wickham flushed, and Miss Worthington grinned.

"Alas, I cannot," Cassandra continued. "When at home I play each week with the village vicar. He lost his wife three years ago, poor man, and is so lonely. A game of chess does us both good."

"I see." The earl moved his king, and sat back again to regard her. "Your grandfather and the village vicar, along with your sister-in-law and niece. It would seem, Miss Worthington, that you have been taking care of a number of people for a very long time."

The lady shrugged. "Each of us, my lord," she told him, "does what she can." She pushed one more piece forward, and grinned again. "Check!"

When the two had arrived the earl had thought it would be forever before they left, but now it surprised him to realize they'd been at Wickly over two weeks, and those for whom his grandmama and Miss Worthington had been preparing soon would be with them. It surprised him even more to realize he would miss his grandmama and her guest (could it be *especially* her guest?) when they were gone.

The earl was once again out with his bailiff when the first of his Christmas visitors arrived, and so once again was taken by surprise at the amount of baggage and commotion that greeted him upon coming through the Wickly Manor front door.

The difference this time was that no restful lady sat, book in hand, quietly surveying him; instead there was general confusion, and the chattering of what seemed a thousand voices made him wish to beat a hasty retreat. It was too late, however; his grandmother had spotted him and came forward to present him to Sophia Symington and her mother, who took instant exception to the dog at his heels. From nowhere Miss Worthington appeared to lead the setter away, talking kindly to the dog even as she hissed an "I told you so!" at the earl.

He wanted to hiss back that he had not yet known he'd been

invaded, but his grandmother's voice, recalling him to his new guests, stopped him.

"My lord!" the dark-eyed, dark-haired Sophia said, and as Wickham gave her his full attention, he had to admit Miss Worthington was right. The girl was beautiful, and had a pleasant voice.

"What a lovely home you have!" Miss Symington said. Then she giggled. With every succeeding sentence that came out of her mouth, she giggled again. The dowager countess, watching, imagined that there were many young men who found that sound delightful. The twitching muscle in her grandson's cheek suggested he was not one of them, and with a sigh she led him away to meet Miss Tuttleton.

As soon as possible the earl retreated to his room, saying he had not meant to meet his guests in all his dirt, and would be more presentable when he saw them at dinner. The spark in his grandmother's eye made it clear she knew the real reason for his escape, but was constrained by their guests from calling him the coward she knew him to be. He was thankful for that as he settled himself by the fire burning in his bedchamber fireplace and, feet propped on the small stool before him, contemplated the flames. Mentally he counted the days until his home would be his again, with the new guests gone. The number was too high, and it was all he could do not to groan. Why his grandmother had to interfere with his life . . .

Closing his eyes, Wickham prayed for good weather and open roads well into the new year, so that none of the newly-arrived Wickly guests would find themselves snowed in before he could wish them Godspeed and send them on their way. Then he prayed that when he joined his guests for supper that evening, he would see them in a different light. Alas, the earl would find later that night, the answer to some prayers seems to be "no."

In the drawing room before supper he looked in vain for Miss Worthington, but she did not appear as he made his bow first to one guest and then another as his grandmother led them up for introductions.

"You remember Clarence Darpool, Edward," the dowager countess said as she arrived at his side, a young man and two women in tow.

Wickham looked at the easy-going and somewhat vacuous face before him, and lied. "Of course."

"Good of you to invite me, my lord," Darpool said, shaking the earl's hand with what Wickham felt was undue enthusiasm. "Very good. Didn't much fancy ducking down to my brother's place, you know—a real nip-cheese he is, and not a bit of fun as we're like to have here."

"I'm glad you could come," the earl returned, realizing that once one set one's feet on a path of untruth, it was most difficult to recover from it.

"And this," the dowager countess interrupted, when it seemed Clarence would talk on for some time, "is Mrs. Worthington, Edward. And her daughter, Letitia."

"Ahhhh." The earl bent over Mrs. Worthington's hand and then over Letitia's in a way that made Mrs. Worthington's heart swell with pride. His critical appraisal made it apparent the earl found nothing to despise in the younger Miss Worthington's appearance. The girl really *is* a diamond of the first water, the earl was thinking, remembering how Miss Worthington—the *other* Miss Worthington—had described her on the list with just two words: Beautiful. Quite.

And knows it, he silently added, as his eyes met Letitia's, and found calm self-confidence there.

"You have a lovely home, my lord," Letitia said, looking at the rose-colored walls and drapes with approval before glancing down at her own gown of only a slightly lighter shade. "And this room, especially—it is almost as if it were decorated for me!"

Her approving smile suggested she favored that idea, and before he had thought, the earl blurted out that the walls had been that color for years—probably had been that color before she was born.

"Oh!" The young lady's surprise made it apparent she had previously not given much consideration to the idea that a world existed before she was born; Wickham, stifling a smile, looked in vain for her aunt, to share the joke. Into the silence spoke Clarence Darpool who, with soulful enthusiasm, made it known that if he had a house, he would change the wall colors daily to match Miss Letitia's every gown and every mood.

"You *would*?" said both the earl and Letitia—the words the same, their meanings different.

"Yes," Darpool affirmed, "except for one room, which I would leave forever violet, to remind me of the glory of your eyes."

"Oh, Clarence!" sighed the younger Miss Worthington.

"Yes," said the dowager countess, revolted, as she took her grandson's arm to move him on. "Oh, Clarence!"

Supper that night found the earl seated at the end of the table, with Sophia Symington on his left and Letitia Worthington on his right. Between the giggles of one and the speculations of the other as to which of her gowns would most set off the dining room to advantage, Wickham found the meal interminable. He was more than a little relieved when the ladies departed, leaving the gentlemen to their port. He kept his male guests lingering over that as long as he could, rising with reluctance to suggest they join the ladies in the drawing room. When he finally handed the last of his guests their candles for the night and bid them sleep well, he was sure he had aged three years and would be one hundred and twenty-three by the time the holiday was over.

After asking his grandmother with some acidity if he could disown her—a question that made the old lady laugh heartily as she climbed the stairs to bed—he made his way to the library. Shutting the thick oak door behind him, he leaned against it for a moment, one hand reaching into his pocket for a handkerchief to mop his brow. That accomplished, he turned toward the fire and looked straight into the amused eyes of Miss Worthington—the *elder* Miss Worthington; the one he was coming to think of as *his* Miss Worthington.

That train of thought brought him up abruptly, and he frowned. The lady, misinterpreting the frown, grinned.

"Giving up so soon, my lord?" she asked.

"There you are, you coward!" he replied. She looked at him in surprise.

"I beg your pardon?"

"Just what do you mean, not joining us for supper and that interminable evening in the drawing room?"

Cassandra laughed. "The numbers at table were so uneven, my lord. I offered to absent myself and your grandmother, knowing how I love a good book, took pity on me and said that this night I might do so." She held up the book she had been reading, and he frowned at it, too.

"Besides." She grinned. "I also said I had a most tiresome headache."

"Do you?" His concern made her grin grow.

"I did after spending an hour in Amelia Symington's company, after *you* deserted your grandmother in the hall. Happily," she chuckled, reaching down to stroke the ears of the setter who lay companionably at her feet, its head resting on her crossed ankles, "the cure of not sitting down with Amelia at supper has quite restored me. Not that I should say so, of course."

"Well, I don't see why Grandmother should be so considerate of you, when I have had to endure a most trying evening."

The lady laughed again. "It is because, my lord," she said, "your grandmother is not doing her best to get me married. You, on the other hand . . ."

"After a meal I thought would never end, when we joined the ladies in the drawing room—Sophia Symington sang!" he told her.

Miss Worthington managed, with great effort, to still the laugh his expression invited. "Oh," she said. "She is said to have a beautiful voice, you know. She has had lessons."

"And has she had lessons in giggling?" His look of ill-usage was so strong that this time Cassandra could not contain herself, and laughter bubbled up.

"I do not believe," she managed, "that she has needed lessons in that."

"You neglected," he said, frowning down at her, "to put the giggle on your list."

"She cannot help it," Miss Worthington excused. "And besides, I once heard a young man call that giggle most enchanting."

The earl was clearly disbelieving as he eased into the chair across from her, giving a pat to the dog, who had lain his head briefly on the earl's knee, then circled three times in front of the fire, settling there with a sigh of pure contentment. Wickham's gaze was pensive as he watched the animal. "Miss Tuttleton," he told the room, "played the piano."

"Oh, dear!" Cassandra's eyes held both sympathy and amusement, and the earl felt his shoulders start to relax. She was such a calming woman.

"Three pieces, each longer than the last."

"Poor man."

"Does she have *any* sense of rhythm?" he demanded.

Miss Worthington turned her laughing eyes to the fire. "She, too, has had lessons," she told him.

"And *then*—" he continued, his sense of ill-usage once again strong, "Lady Elizabeth recited one of her poems."

"The one about ivy and a tall, tall tree?" Cassandra asked.

Wickham nodded, indignation apparent. "It should be titled 'Ivy and a Long, Long Poem.' What does she *mean*, with all that folderol?"

Miss Worthington shook her head. "I haven't a notion," she confessed. "Although I believe she does it very well."

"And then what must my grandmother do but say that Lady Penelope and your niece must entertain us some other evening, and I suppose I'm to find a harp about someplace—who knows where, for we do not, thank goodness, keep harps at Wickly— but I am to find one because Lady Penelope's grandmother tells me most fiercely that her granddaughter *plays*."

"She does," Miss Worthington said. "Quite well."

The unfairness of it all struck him, and he brooded for some time before adding, as an afterthought, "Oh. And your niece is to recite a poem."

"What?"

"Your niece." The earl, noting with satisfaction that he had at last jolted her from her laughter, felt better. "She is to recite a poem."

"Letitia docsn't know any pocms!"

"Yes." The earl nodded. "I overheard her tell her mother that. Mrs. Worthington, not wanting her daughter to be outshone by all the other young ladies, merely informed her that you will teach her one."

"I—"

"Do you know any poems about gowns?"

"About—" She stared at him as if he'd grown another head.

"Your niece was one of my supper companions, Miss Worthington," Wickham said. "I gathered from her conversation that she would be most interested in poems about gowns."

"Oh, dear!" Cassandra's face was rueful. "She is so very young, you know. And so fond of pretty things—"

"Your niece," the earl said, not mincing words, "is a beautiful ninnyhammer."

"Well," said Miss Worthington, firing up on Letitia's behalf, "your cousin Clarence Darpool is a handsome clodpate!"

"He is," agreed the earl promptly. He grinned. Miss Worthington, taken aback for a moment, soon started to laugh.

"Oh, dear!" she said, wiping her eyes with a wisp of handkerchief she had tucked up her sleeve. "Listen to us! People are what they are, after all. To prove it, here we sit! Although I still think it unkind of you to desert your grandmother and guests so early—"

"Desert?" Wickham showed surprise. "I did no such thing! They've all—thank heavens—gone to bed."

"What?" Now it was Cassandra's turn to be surprised, and a quick glance at the clock turned her surprise to dismay. "Oh, my! I had no idea—I so lost myself in my reading. My lord, I am so sorry, when you've obviously come here looking for a quiet place and here I sit—I will go at once!"

She rose to accomplish the action, but the earl took her hand and held it a moment before raising it to his lips to brush a kiss upon her palm. Miss Worthington stared at him.

"I am glad you were here," he told her. "I missed you tonight."

"My lord—" She pulled her hand free and took a step back.

"Don't go."

"I must!"

"We could play a game of chess."

"No!"

"Why?"

"Because only think how improper your guests would think it if they knew we sat up until the wee hours together, playing chess after they'd gone to bed." It was clear the earl was going to make known his opinion of what his guests could do with such thoughts, and without thinking she placed a finger to his lips to still him. "And because it is late, and I have told your grandmother I will help her tomorrow, so I must get my rest now, and because . . ." She was almost at the door now, for she had been walking away from him as she spoke. Her words were muffled as she reached for the door handle.

"Because?" he questioned.

"Because," she said, turning back with a smile that this time, unless he deceived himself, was slightly strained, "because if what you have told me is correct, it will take me a very long time tomorrow to locate a poem Letitia might memorize with any enthusiasm. For the life of me, I cannot think of a poet who writes solely about gowns!"

His shout of laughter followed her down the hall, and at the sound of it, Cassandra found herself smiling.

Much to the earl's surprise, the time with his newly arrived guests passed more quickly than he had imagined possible. Several days he took the gentlemen in the party hunting, only to find, upon returning, that the ladies had been busy adding to the mistletoe Miss Worthington had already spread throughout his house.

Since, to his jaundiced eye, the purpose of mistletoe seemed to be so that watchful mamas could point out the presence of their daughters under the magical plant to the earl so that he might claim a kiss and pick one of the berries, he did not much appreciate that. He did, however, appreciate the activities the capable Miss Worthington planned for the guests, which kept them from aggravating him as much as he had feared.

Only last night the younger ladies, Mr. Darpool, and Viscount Chively had—with much laughing and giggling—presented a highly entertaining farce for those assembled, basking in the applause and laughter they'd received. A quiet word to Mr. Darpool elicited the information that the play had been Miss Cassandra Worthington's idea and—Jove!—hadn't it been a good one?

Who had written it? Well, Mr. Darpool rather thought Miss Worthington had penned the script, not that they'd exactly kept to it, you know, each person had wanted to add his or her bit, and Miss Worthington had assured them that was all right; in fact, had left it up to them. And they had put *hours* in on it. . . .

A thankful earl assured his guest that was quite apparent, and mentally blessed Miss Worthington for her effort. So that was what had occupied the younger members of the party the last few evenings, and saved him from night after night of Miss Symington's songs and Miss Tuttleton's piano performances, and the certain insistence of Lady Harling that he find a harp.

As for the mistletoe, well . . .

After his guests were abed, Wickham spent several nights ridding the blasted plants of their berries, since once all the berries were gone the mistletoe lost its power to promote a kiss. He was discovered in that occupation one night by Miss

Worthington, who had taken a message to the cook in the kitchen as the rest of the party retired to their respective beds.

"For shame, my lord!" she said, coming up behind him and nearly startling him out of his wits as he stood in the drawing room doorway picking five of the seven berries that remained there from the plant. "And all this time your grandmother has thought the mistletoe berries were disappearing because of naughty footmen catching the housemaids in doorways!"

"Miss Worthington—" he stuttered. "I did not see you—"

"I know." Her eyes were laughing. "That is quite obvious!" She paused before adding kindly, "Your grandmother will just have more mistletoe brought in, you know. She likes this custom prodigiously—she and Lord Worthhope."

"Lord Worth—" Wickham started, and his eyes widened. "Why, that old dog!"

Miss Worthington laughed. "They enjoy themselves, my lord. It is good. It is Christmas."

"Well, *I* don't enjoy it!" his lordship said. "It seems I can hardly stand anywhere in my house without seeing a young lady standing nearby under mistletoe—and her sharp-eyed mother there to point the fact out to me if I look away!"

Miss Worthington's rich laugh was heard. "I know, my lord," she said. "I have derived much enjoyment this past week watching you scurry through doorways before your female guests even see you near the plant."

"Have you, Miss Worthington?" The question was dry, and her eyes twinkled. "Had I known you were on the lookout to find me under mistletoe, I might not have—scurried, I believe you said."

Ignoring her protests that she, herself, had in no way wanted to find him under the mistletoe, and that he had willfully misunderstood her, the earl broke off one of the pieces above his head that still contained a kiss-claiming berry, and held it over her. The startled lady moved as if to step aside, and he followed her.

"Will you pay the forfeit, Miss Worthington?" he asked, and there was something in his eyes that she had not seen before, if you did not count that night in the library—which she didn't. She certainly didn't. Something that—

"My lord," Miss Worthington demanded, eyeing him narrowly, "are you intoxicated?"

Wickham's shout of laughter was heard and brought a quick scolding that he would wake the house. In amusement he assured her that that night he had had no more than a very little wine. But, he added, moving toward her, there was something most intoxicating in the air.

Miss Worthington, watching him closely, was so surprised that she could do no more than gape as he bent forward and placed a soft kiss on her cheek. "My lord!" she gasped as he removed the mistletoe's remaining berry.

"My lady!" he replied, with a courtly bow. When he straightened Miss Worthington had fled, and the earl's laughter floated down the hall again.

He was not laughing two days later, however, as he stalked into his grandmother's bedchamber after one brief rap. The old lady's maid "tsked, tsked" at such unseemly behavior and the dowager countess, after considering him from head to toe, said, "So nice to see you, Edward."

"Hmmph," said the earl, and threw himself into a chair by the fire. The countess signalled her maid to leave and, when the woman had departed, said with great goodwill, "Such pretty manners you have, my grandson."

The earl grunted again and his grandmother, starting to be rather alarmed by his moroseness, rose and walked toward him. "Well, for goodness sakes, Edward," she asked, "what is it?"

The earl transferred his gaze from the fire to his grandmother's face.

"It being the day before Christmas, Grandmother," he said, "I thought I would give you your gift. This scheme of yours, to attract me to one of the young ladies under my roof—well, it has worked. I find myself most sincerely attracted."

"Oh!" When he remained silent, the countess asked if she was to know the name of this lucky young lady.

"Miss Worthington," he muttered, once again scowling at the fire.

"Letitia Worth—"

"No, no!" The earl waved Letitia away with impatience. "Not *that* Miss Worthington! Heaven preserve me, no! *My* Miss Worthington. The one who came with you. Cassandra."

He had expected the news to surprise, even shock her, and so was not prepared for the slow smile that spread across her face, or for the way she took his hand, which had been fidgeting on the arm of the chair, and placed it between both of hers, looking down at him with pride.

"My dear," she said, giving the hand a squeeze, "I am so glad."

"What—" he began, read the message in her eyes, and shot out of the chair, glaring down at her.

"You *planned* this!" he said, incredulous.

His grandmother laughed. "Let us say I hoped." She gave his hand another squeeze and he snatched it away from her.

"You *planned* this!" He took a half-turn around the chair, stopping behind it to lean on the chair back and gape at her. "Of all the— And then you invited those other people here—and—and—*why*?"

"Why did I invite the others here, my dear?" his grandmother said, trying to follow his train of thought. "Why, for contrast, of course! Sometimes when one has an original under one's nose, one needs something—or in this case, several someones—to compare to, to be aware of the value of the original."

"You, madam, have your nerve!" Wickham thundered in what for a moment seemed to her to be the very voice of his grandfather. The dowager countess looked at him with pride. He prowled the room like a restless tiger, glaring her way from time to time in a manner that made her work hard not to laugh. At last he stopped and said, in a voice of command. "Tell me this, Grandmother. Was *she* in on it, too? Did you plan this with her?"

"She?" For a moment the countess was honestly puzzled, and the honesty of the emotion in her face did much to ease his temper. "Oh, Cassandra!" the countess said, at last divining his meaning. "Of course not! Silly boy! She would not have come if I'd told her!"

"Yes, well . . ." Mollified to know he had not been mistaken in Miss Worthington in that way, he lowered his long length back into the fireside chair, once more returning his gaze to the flames. "She might as well not have, for the way she treats me now."

"What?" That did bring a frown to the dowager countess's forehead, and she sank down onto the stool at her grandson's feet so she could better observe his face as she urged him to tell her all about it. The earl did, starting with the night Miss Worthington had found him removing the berries from the mistletoe—a story that brought reproof from his grandmother for such actions—and ending with how the lady had been avoiding him ever since. She no longer seemed to visit his library, except when he was known to be out hunting or riding, and when they were in company together she kept her niece or sister-in-law, or one of the other tiresome young ladies and their equally tiresome parents, between them.

"Oh!" The countess's forehead relaxed, and she gave a little laugh her grandson could not help but think ill-judged. "Is that all?" She rose from the footstool and walked to her dressing table, there to fiddle with one of her earrings. Wickham frowned at her.

"All, Grandmother?" he asked. "The lady of my choice holds me in aversion, and you say 'Is that *all*'?"

The countess glanced at him in surprise. "You were not used to be such a dramatic young man, Edward," she reproved, once again returning her attention to her earring. "Of course Cassandra is avoiding you. That is to be expected."

"It is?"

The countess nodded. "Of course. You have surprised her."

Not nearly as much as he had surprised himself, the earl wanted to say, but did not. Instead, he listened as his grandmother told him Cassandra considered herself responsible for her sister-in-law and niece.

"Yes, yes," Once again the earl waved Letitia and her mother away with impatience. "That is very clear."

"She will not," the dowager countess said gently, watching him for the effect of her words, "marry as long as she feels the two of them have no one to look after them."

"Oh." It was clear Wickham had not considered—and did not relish—this latest complication. "But—" He looked at his grandmother for guidance, and was not disappointed.

"I have always thought," the dowager countess said, picking up her powder brush and moving it gently across her face, "that Clarence Darpool and Letitia Worthington would suit most comfortably. *They* certainly seem to think so!"

"Yes, but," the earl objected, thinking aloud, "Cassandra has suggested Letitia's mother does not relish the thought of her daughter marrying a penniless younger son—"

The dowager countess put her brush down with a loud sigh, and informed him that Clarence Darpool would not be a penniless younger son if *someone*—perhaps a rich relative—were to become his patron and settle a comfortable living on him by finding him something to do.

"Ahhh!" It was clear the idea took root, for the earl was frowning deeply. After a few moments of thought, however, he raised his eyes to his grandmother with one last objection. "Yes, but Grandmama—what *can* young Darpool do?"

The dowager countess took his arm and, when he had risen unresisting to his feet, let him escort her down the stairs to dinner, patting his hand as she did so and saying, "We shall think on that, Edward. Oh, my, how we shall think!"

Try as he might, the earl found it hard to believe his grandmother was thinking of anything other than merrymaking that evening. He sat watching her at dinner, waiting for some sign that she had hit upon the perfect solution to his problem, but no sign came. Instead she laughed and flirted (outrageously, her disgruntled grandson thought) with Lord Worthhope, and quizzed young Mr. Darpool, to her right, on what he would most like for Christmas. Since she looked so pointedly at Letitia Worthington when she put the question to him, it was not surprising that the inarticulate young gentleman turned bright red and choked on his dinner. That made the dowager countess laugh harder. When she caught her grandson's frowning eyes upon her, she merely smiled like a cat in the creampot, and gazed past him.

The dowager countess had decreed that tomorrow they would all attend Christmas services and then would spend the day quietly, as her own father in her youth had decreed Christmas Day must be spent in his house. The earl wondered if that was why his grandmother had decided to have such a rollicking good time this night. He also wondered *why* she had decided to follow her father's example, when she had more than once told him she had not particularly enjoyed it as a child, but he had not asked her. Nor, as far as he knew, had any of their guests; the old lady was held in such awe that no one had the temerity to question her. The earl supposed it had something to do with memories, and a few of his own came to visit as he thought of other Christmases spent in part in this room, with other family members and guests. For a moment he pictured the faces of those dear to him who were now gone; involuntarily he looked down his long table, past the boar's head, the Christmas goose and Christmas turkey, with all the accompaniments a bountiful host could provide, to Cassandra Worthington.

She sat, chewing placidly, while she lent an indulgent ear to one of Viscount Chively's involved explanations of the joys of astronomy. The topic provoked keen enthusiasm in the young man, and he could talk on the subject for hours with only the slightest encouragement. Cassandra must have felt Wickham's eyes upon her, for she glanced up. He smiled and so did she, then colored, as if she had just remembered something.

Miss Worthington returned her attention to her tablemate, taking care not to glance in Wickham's direction again, and his smile turned to a frown. He really, he decided, must speak to his grandmother about these deuced seating arrangements, which always seemed to put Cassandra—for so he had begun to call her in his mind—as far from him as possible. A brief word after dinner imparted the knowledge that it was Cassandra herself who kept switching the young ladies at his left and right, and that knowledge did not give the earl good cheer. *That* he sought in a steaming wassail bowl which he prepared in full view of all his visitors, the gentlemen taking the most interest in the proceedings and offering the most suggestions. When it was ready he did, as host, deliver a cup to each of his guests. When he came to Cassandra, seated by his grandmother, he handed her the cup, saying, as meaningfully as he felt he could, with so many ears about, "To your very good health, Miss Worthington."

Her "And to yours, my lord" was so automatic, and so devoid of feeling, that he passed on with his forehead furrowed, not hearing, as his grandmother did, the much more heartfelt, though softly delivered "And to yours."

Cassandra, looking up into the dowager countess's eyes, colored at the understanding there, and rose, setting down her wassail with an "I fear I have the headache—if you will excuse me, my lady—" just as the younger members of the group called out for choral rounds and someone to lead them.

Spying Miss Worthington on her feet, Lady Penelope called, "Oh, yes, Miss Worthington, do lead us," before Sophia Symington, feeling anything to do with song must perforce belong to her, could rise.

"What?" Cassandra turned, surprised, as Lady Penelope and Letitia bore down on her, calling, "Please, Miss Worthington," and "Oh, yes, Aunt Cassandra, please do; you have such a lovely voice!"

They were seconded good-naturedly by Clarence Darpool and Viscount Chively who had never heard Cassandra sing, but who could be depended upon to second the younger Miss Worthington on anything. Cassandra, not knowing where to look, was further discomposed when the earl added his entreaties.

"No, really—" she started as Amelia Symington was heard to say—loudly—that it was no wonder the poor woman didn't care to sing, with Sophia there for comparison. Nodding graciously to Cassandra, Amelia said they all quite understand her reluctance, and she could be dismissed; Sophia would lead them in song.

Alicia Worthington fired up at that, letting it be known that Cassandra was thought by those at home to have the best voice within miles. And, she added, a dangerous glint in her eye, she did not quite understand just where Amelia Symington found the audacity to *dismiss* Cassandra in the Earl of Wickham's home.

The earl did not know the answer to that question, either, but before he could say so Mrs. Symington escalated the battle with Cassandra's sister-in-law by ignoring the latter part of Alicia's comments and attacking the former.

"No one," she informed those present, nose in the air, "has ever said within how *many* miles of the Worthington home."

"Why—" Alicia said, starting toward her rival with two spots of color burning bright in her cheeks. Cassandra, with a comic glance of dismay toward the earl, caught her sister-in-law's arm and agreed to lead them in carols, if they would all join in. After pressing Alicia gently into a chair as far removed from Amelia Symington as possible, Cassandra led the group in several songs, with Miss Tuttleton providing a loud if not tuneful accompaniment.

When there was a pause in the singing Mrs. Symington, with what she felt was a point to prove, suggested that Miss Worthington sing them something quite alone.

"Alone?" Cassandra repeated.

"Yes, my dear." Mrs. Symington smiled her most superior smile. "I am sure we would all be most delighted to hear the best voice within miles of home—*your* home, that is."

The earl, moved by the look on Cassandra's face, was about to say he believed they'd had enough singing for the evening when Letitia, with an encouraging smile for her aunt, said in a carrying voice, "Sing 'The Coventry Carol,' Aunt Cassandra. Like you always do, each Christmas."

"But—"

"Yes, Cassandra," said her sister-in-law, holding her handkerchief in readiness. "Do." She turned toward the countess, seated several chairs away, to explain that she did not really believe they could have Christmas Eve without Cassandra's gift of "The Coventry Carol."

The dowager countess smiled her encouragement and Cassandra, seeing no way out, motioned to Miss Tuttleton that she would sing the song *a capella*. The earl, tearing his eyes from her with difficulty after the first few notes, was more than a little pleased to notice that the smug smile on Mrs. Symington's lips was beginning to fade. Had his attention remained on the older lady, he would have seen the smile was quite gone by the second verse, and by the third Amelia was looking a little green, as did her daughter, who recognized talent when she heard it.

The last *"by by, lul-ly, lul-lay"* seemed to echo in the room for several seconds after Miss Worthington uttered it, and several of the ladies had recourse to their handkerchiefs before loud and long applause greeted her performance.

Cassandra, unused to being the center of attention, blushed as her niece and sister-in-law rushed forward to embrace her. Alicia Worthington could not forgo one "I told you so" look directed toward Amelia Symington, but otherwise was most gracious as others came up to add their words of praise. Several people asked why they had never heard Miss Worthington sing in London, but she only smiled and shook her head. There were others, she said, much more fitted for center stage than she.

The earl, coming forward at last, raised Cassandra's hand to his lips and bowed deeply, straightening to look down into her eyes in a way that made it hard for her to breathe.

"Remarkable, Miss Worthington," he said, the words reminding her of a previous conversation. Her color heightened. "Truly remarkable."

Looking around at the warmly approving faces that surrounded Cassandra, Amelia Symington yawned loudly, and said she did believe it was more than time for bed.

The next day the earl was pleased to find Miss Worthington alone in the hall, standing by the large fireplace where the Yule log burned, staring into the flames. She was clearly awaiting the rest of the party and transportation to church, for she already wore her cloak. The lady was so lost in her own thoughts that she did not appear to hear him until his "glad Christmas" wishes drew her head up in surprise.

"Oh, my lord"—her color rose again—"glad Christmas to you, too, my lord. A very joyous day."

"I believe," he said, his tone whimsical, "that it would be a better Christmas for me were I this day to hear you call me by my name."

"My lord?" Miss Worthington questioned.

"No." He shook his head. "I know that is not it."

"Edwa— I mean, Wickha— I mean, my lord!" The usually composed Miss Worthington stuttered. He regarded her with interest.

"You almost had it," he encouraged. The lady frowned at him.

"I have told you, my lord," she said, "that it is most unkind of you to tease me this way."

"You have?" He cocked his head to the side, considering. "I seem to have forgotten that. Why?"

"Because," Cassandra said, fixing him with a stern eye, "you know very well that that is not why I was invited here."

"But you were," the earl protested. "My grandmother told me so only yesterday!"

"Your grandmother told you that I was invited here so that you might tease me unmercifully?" Miss Worthington scoffed. "I think not, my lord!"

"No, no," he protested. "The teasing part comes naturally. The other part is about being invited here for me to marry."

"I thought so," Miss Worthington said, reacting to the first two words of his statement. "For we all know that you—" As the other words filtered into her mind her eyes widened and her jaw dropped, to be quickly closed again.

"My lord," Miss Worthington said severely, "you must *stop* teasing me. And this is a most improper conversation. As you know, I am here to help your grandmother and to shepherd my niece—"

"—who finds me quite old," he finished for her, reminding her, when she seemed about to deny it, that she had imparted that information to him herself. Miss Worthington bit her lip.

"As do, I am sure," he mourned, "all of the other young ladies."

"Miss Symington does not seem to find you old, my lord," Cassandra reminded him.

"Miss Symington," he told her, "giggles."

"Elizabeth—"

"—is more interested in ivy and tall, tall trees."

"Lady Penelope—"

"—plays the harp." The earl gave a visible shudder.

"Miss Tuttleton—"

"—*tries*"—how he emphasized the word!—"to play the piano."

"I did not come here, my lord, as one of the young ladies to meet you."

"No," he said, "and thank goodness for that. For I am quite decided, you know, that a young lady will not do. Well," he amended, gazing down at her, "not too young a lady."

"I," said Miss Worthington, looking firmly away, "am quite on the shelf, my lord."

"No, are you?" He asked with such polite interest that her lips twitched in spite of themselves. "How very nice for you, I'm sure! May I join you there?"

No, Cassandra said crossly, no, he could not. And they must not go on in this vein, because—because—

"Because?" the earl questioned.

"Because it is quite impossible!" the lady cried. "I could not think of marrying, even if I wanted to—which of course I do not. No," she said resolutely, looking away from his disbelieving eyes, "I do not! I have obligations. People who depend on me. I cannot just consider my feelings—" She realized that was the wrong thing to say the moment she'd said it, and tried to call the words back as the earl pounced on them.

"You do not understand!" she said in exasperation. "It is impossible! Besides"—she put up a hand to halt his words as a babble of voices came from above them, and the sound of feet was heard on the stairs—"others are coming!"

The earl, with nothing good to say about the interfering others, said nothing. In fact, his grandmother noted he had little to say throughout the rest of the day for, hunting now in earnest, he was kept from his prey by Miss Worthington saying, upon their return from church, that she rather thought she was developing the headache, and would retire to her room for the afternoon—which the earl later found would also stretch into the evening. Several of the other ladies chose to do the same, finding that the countess's decree that they should have a quiet day was much to their liking after the rigors of town life and the courting of an earl. Although all but the elder Miss Worthington appeared at supper, the guests chose to make an early night of it. The earl, following his visitors up to bed, sat for several hours in his room staring into the fire and wondering when his tiresome love would begin to believe he was not teasing her but was, instead, most sincere.

Picking up a book that lay on his bedside table he found it held little interest for him, and thinking he might find a better diversion in his library, he slipped from his room and went quietly down the stairs. He paused only when he'd reached the bottom step, for it was then he realized he was not alone. Miss Worthington had pulled up a stool by the Yule log fire and sat in the hall, back to him, humming the carol she had sung the night before as she stared into the flames. There was something about the way she sat that spoke of a need for privacy, and he had turned to go when the squeak of the second stair made her aware of his presence.

"Oh, my lord!" she said, rising.

He turned again. "I did not mean to disturb you," he said quietly. "I came for a book—"

"Please." She motioned him toward the library. "You will not disturb me. I came for a memory."

He had taken several steps toward the library door but stopped at that, looking down at her, admiring the way the flickering flames highlighted the subtle red tints in her hair. "A memory, Miss Worthington?"

She smiled, leaning her head forward until it rested against the outer stone of the huge fireplace. "I have always loved the tradition of the Yule log, my lord," she said. "When I was a child, my brother Richard and I would go with Father and the men to drag the biggest Yule log we could find into the house, and Mother would have us sit on it, each in turn, to make our wishes for the new year." She laughed. "I always wished to be tall, and look what it got me!"

He smiled as she continued. "Later, when the log was lit Mother and Father would talk to Richard and me of the beauty of light in darkness, of warmth in winter, of how each of us must carry our own Yule logs within us, to stave off winter's chill. So now, each Christmas, I like to sit awhile after everyone has gone to bed and pull out my memories like the shiny bright gifts they are—"

Her voice caught, and without thinking he reached out to place a hand on her shoulder. "You are very lucky in your memories, Miss Worthington," he said.

Her own hand rose to cover his. "Yes," she said, once again staring into the fire. "I am."

"Someday," he suggested, "your own children will have such stories to tell."

"My own—" She looked up, startled, and became aware that her hand still covered his on her shoulder. Hastily she moved away. "Perhaps Letitia's children," she said, lightly. "I believe I have told you, my lord, that it is my firm conviction that I was born to be an aunt."

She swept him a graceful curtsy and departed. As she rounded the first bend in the stairs she heard, faint but distinct from below her, a soft, "Oh, I think not, Miss Worthington. I think not."

Hand to her throat, Cassandra continued up the stairs. That night she lay for hours, thinking, in the darkness. When she arose the next morning there were dark smudges under her eyes, and the earl overheard Alicia tell the dowager countess at breakfast that it was so odd for Cassandra to seem so preoccupied and—well—sad. Usually she among them most loved Christmas.

The dowager countess, noting similar dark smudges adorning her grandson's face, smiled inwardly and said nothing.

Although the dowager countess had decided they were all to spend Christmas Day quietly, she did not mean for the quiet to last. The day following Christmas she'd planned a huge party for the Wickly guests and many neighbors from the area. It was to be a costume party, she said, and to that end she'd opened the attics of Wickly to the visitors, to the delight of the ladies in attendance, and even, it must be told, to the pleasure of the gentlemen.

Cassandra, who had been busy with the countess all morning going over last-minute details for the party, was just leaving the small sitting room where they'd met when the older woman asked, "And have you picked out your costume for the party yet, Cassandra?"

Miss Worthington said tranquilly that she had had no time, but that Alicia had promised to find her something, since her sister-in-law so delighted in such things.

"Well, and I am sure Alicia has quite good taste," the dowager countess said, smiling at some inner thought, "but if you do not yet have your heart set on what you are to wear, I wonder if I might suggest something?"

Cassandra, surprised, said that well, yes, of course, if her ladyship wished . . . In short order she found herself following the countess up the stairs to the old lady's bedchamber. The countess was talking all the time.

"You may not have noticed it, Cassandra," the countess said as she opened the door to her bedchamber and led Miss Worthington in, "but we are almost of the same height, you and I."

No, Cassandra realized, she hadn't noticed it. The dowager countess always seemed so much larger; it was the way she could fill a room with her presence, Cassandra supposed.

Realizing that the other woman awaited an answer, Miss Worthington said, "Why, so we are."

The countess smiled.

"I do not believe I ever told you, Cassandra," she said, walking to the cupboard where her dresses hung and throwing open the doors there, "that I knew your grandmother."

"You did?" It was clearly a surprise. The countess smiled again.

"Yes, we were great friends. As a matter of fact, she once did me a signal favor."

"She did?"

The countess was rummaging in the cupboard and her words were muffled. "Yes." She turned and eyed Miss Worthington considerably. "You are very like her, you know."

"I *am*?" It was that surprised look again; Cassandra did not know she was like her grandmother, who had died ten years before she was born. She liked the idea of it, though, and an answering smile formed on her lips. "Tell me about her."

"She was very beautiful—" the countess started.

"Oh." Cassandra bit her lip, disappointed. "I thought you said I am very like her."

"But you are!" Now it was the countess's turn to be surprised.

"My lady, please," Cassandra said, looking away. "I have more than once seen myself in a mirror. Plain brown eyes. Plain brown hair. Not much height—"

"Ahhh." The countess nodded. "You look, my dear, but you don't see. As I was saying before you interrupted me—"

Abashed, Cassandra begged pardon. The countess continued.

"She had a sort of way about her—calm good sense, and she looked at the world through laughing eyes. Several of the young men fancied themselves very much in love with her, including the man who would later become my husband."

"They *did?*"

The countess laughed. "Yes, my dear, they did. And that is the signal favor your grandmother did me—she married your grandfather! And left me to comfort Wickham, after dropping a hint in his ear that he was a fool to pine after her when someone who would be better for him was so close at hand." She paused in reminiscence. "She was one for plain speaking, your grandmother. It is a trait you inherited."

Cassandra bit her lip again. "Perhaps," she suggested, "it did not land my grandmother in the briars quite as often as it does me!"

"Oh, no!" The countess shook her head. "It landed her there quite often, but little did she care. How I treasured that woman! The world has not been quite the same since she went out of it. That is why that day, when I saw you in the lending library, I looked at you so strangely, for it was as if your Grandmother Cassandra stood there, her smile polite but puzzled, as yours was. And then when we talked about books—she also loved books, did you know that?—and were forever meeting at this ball or that, I thought—"

She peered back into the cupboard and Cassandra, a slight frown furrowing her forehead as she remembered the earl's words on Christmas Day, prompted, "You thought, my lady?"

"Aha!" The countess changed the subject as she found what she sought. "Here it is, the very thing! My dear, I would be so pleased if you would wear this tonight."

Cassandra's eyes opened wide at the gown the countess now held before her. Obviously a cherished relic of a bygone day, it had an embroidered and quilted petticoat topped by embroidered gold fabric that fitted over a large hoop. The gown's skirt spread wide from the narrow waist, and was gathered and draped at the side to reveal a heavily embroidered underskirt of silver. The bodice was fitted, with a square neck, and the long sleeves also were heavily embroidered.

"My lady!" Cassandra breathed.

The countess smiled in remembrance. "I was wearing this dress the night—" she began, then stopped. It seemed for a moment that her eyes misted before she said, with another smile, "It would please me no end, Cassandra, if you would wear it tonight."

"But it is so fine—" Cassandra started.

"No finer, my dear," the countess said simply, "than you."

"Oh, my lady—" For some reason Cassandra wanted to cry. "It is too good of you."

"Please, Cassandra," the countess said. "Oblige me in this. It would make me so very happy."

"It would?" Cassandra looked with longing toward the dress. Just once, she thought, just once, for one night, she could be the princess in the fairy tale. Not the sensible, what-is-the-price-of-candles-and-how-will-we-afford-peas Cassandra, but a woman dressed in silver and gold. She had never in her life gotten to be the princess. . . .

"I would be honored, my lady," Cassandra said. The countess clapped her hands.

"We shall powder your hair," the old lady said, "for the wig I wore with the dress is gone. We wore our hair piled high on our heads then—my maid will know. She was with me then, too. Oh, Cassandra." She smiled a misty smile. "You have made me very happy."

Cassandra, staring in dazed wonder at the dress that was to be hers for a night, managed to say that she was very happy, too.

Cassandra's happiness grew that night as she descended the stairs in the countess's wake, the old lady having decreed that they would make their entrances last, after all the other Wickly guests were assembled in the hall. There had been the buzz of cheerful conversation as they made the turn in the stairs, but as they came down, one by one the voices stilled as those gathered below stared at the visions before them.

The gown Cassandra wore shimmered in the candlelight; it was as if the tiny flames that seemed to live in the diamond and gold necklace the countess had lent her for the night were reflected a thousand times in the stiff and heavily embroidered dress. Her hair was powdered white and the countess, at the last minute, had stuck a sprig of holly amidst the high-piled curls. Cassandra's eyes sparked and the earl, watching her, caught his breath.

Cassandra did not know it, but the countess's dress of black shot through with silver, also flowing over a large hoop and fitted at the waist, was a perfect foil for the picture she presented.

"Aunt Cassandra!" she heard Letitia gasp, followed by "Cassandra, my dear!" from Alicia, and a "By Jove!" from the less-articulate Mr. Darpool. She smiled, and the motion seemed to release those below who, until this last entrance, had been heartily pleased with their own costumes of heavy brocades or striped silks. The men, their hair powdered, wore coats heavy with braid; a few had even found braided waistcoats to match.

Now more than one lady was asking herself how she missed such a treasure in the attic as Miss Worthington moved forward, her skirt swaying and glinting in the light.

"Remarkable, Miss Worthington," the earl said, catching her hand and bringing it to his lips. "Simply remarkable." The lady, blushing, moved on.

It was during the dance that followed the huge dinner that Wickham, spying Clarence Darpool standing off to the side with a look of despair and adulation on his face as he watched a laughing Letitia go down the floor with Viscount Chively, approached his young relative and said pleasantly, "She is very lovely."

"Yes." Clarence sighed. "She is."

"Going to marry her, are you?"

Clarence, startled, started to stutter. Nothing could make him happier—it was his greatest wish, but . . . A man in his situation, without funds . . . He heaved a mournful sigh, and returned to watching Letitia with an expression that put Wickham forcibly in mind of his setter when the dog fancied himself in love.

"The thing is, Darpool," the earl said, "I've been thinking I need a man—a man I can trust, you know—to look after a little property I have in Berkshire. And I thought—who better than a relative? It's a snug little estate, lovely manor home, and I'd want to pay you a living for your trouble, of course—"

Clarence, who had been listening with only half an ear at the beginning of the earl's speech, was paying full attention at the end. "Wickham!" he said.

The earl looked at him.

"Do you mean—?"

The earl looked at him again.

"Sir!" Clarence's shoulders went back, and it seemed he had trouble breathing. "Are you saying—that you wish—"

"I wish you to live at my Berkshire property and look after it for me," the earl said, growing quickly tired of these transports. "For which you will be paid a good living. More than enough to keep a wife. And a mother-in-law," he added, as an after-thought, to rid himself of another problem.

"A mother-in-law—" Clarence repeated.

"You would not wish Mrs. Worthington to live alone?" Wickham inquired, incredulous.

No, no, Clarence said, of course he would not. Of course not. It was just that, Miss Worthington—Miss Cassandra Worthington—who would she live with, if not Mrs. Worthington? Not that she wouldn't be welcome in his home, too. Of course she would. A very good sort, was Miss Worthington . . .

The earl, stifling a smile to hear how quickly his home had become Mr. Darpool's, agreed. "Yes," he said. "A very good sort. And I have great hopes Miss Cassandra Worthington will not be your concern."

"Will not be—" Clarence stood looking after him in surprise for several moments, trying to puzzle that last statement out before, with a whoop that considerably startled those standing near him, he turned and half ran onto the dance floor, catching Letitia up and carrying her off so that Viscount Chively, turning back to his partner after their separation in the dance, was surprised to find himself dancing alone.

The earl, meanwhile, was stalking the elder Miss Worthington. She was not hard to find, for all eyes seemed to turn toward the lady in the golden dress, whether she was dancing or stood chatting with someone near the wall.

"My dance, Miss Worthington," Wickham said as he came up beside her, bowing.

"Oh, my lord." She smiled uncertainly at him, checking her card and looking around. "I believe Mr. Darpool—"

"—is elsewhere engaged," the earl finished for her. "He has relinquished his dance to me."

"Oh. Well." Again the uncertain smile. "In that case—" She laid her hand upon the arm he presented to her, and waited for the earl to lead her onto the dance floor. Instead he walked her around the dancers and out the door of the ballroom, one of his hands firmly covering hers as he led her down the hall toward the library.

"My lord!" Miss Worthington said, her steps hurried to keep up with his long strides. "My lord—"

"A moment, my dear," he said, smiling down at her in that disturbing way as he opened the library door and all but pulled her through it. Once inside he released her and took several steps back to lean slightly against the mahogany desk as he watched her.

"My lord!" Miss Worthington said, smoothing down her skirt with fingers that shook slightly. "I must protest—"

"And so must I, Miss Worthington," he interrupted, "for you have been avoiding me all night. And for days past, as well."

"I—" Miss Worthington said.

"It is enough to make a man feel unloved," he complained. She looked at him.

"And it is certainly no way to treat the man you are going to marry."

"But we are not to marry, my lord."

"But we are."

Cassandra looked away, unaware, as he was, that she was twisting and knotting the handkerchief she held in her hands. "I have told you, my lord. I have—obligations—"

"Your niece and sister-in-law."

She nodded, her nervous fingers continuing to reveal the pain this conversation caused her.

"They are taken care of."

"*What?*" Now he had her full attention; her eyes were wide and her mouth hung slightly open. He grinned when she closed it.

"Clarence Darpool," he said, "has, unless I very much miss my guess, just asked your niece to marry him."

"Clarence Darpool!" She half-laughed, half-cried the name.

"You know his circumstances. Now I shall have one more person to look after!"

"Clarence Darpool," the earl told her, each word deliberate, "has just come into a very nice living."

"He—has?" There was that look in his eyes that distracted her, and Cassandra had to force herself to attend. "But how——?"

The earl's grin grew, and she breathed, "You!"

He nodded.

"But Alicia——"

"Darpool," the earl informed her, "would be devastated were his mama-in-law not to join him and his wife in their new home."

"He would?" The look was there again as the earl moved toward her.

"Devastated," he confirmed, his breath fanning her cheek as he stood close enough to take her in his arms and pull her close, looking down into her eyes.

"Oh." Cassandra tore her gaze away from his and looked down at her hand, encased in his larger one. His thumb was making circles on her wrist which must, she thought, account for the sudden jumbling of her pulse. "Well." She continued to watch his thumb. "I would not wish Mr. Darpool to be—devastated."

"No?" There was a soft smile on his lips as he gazed at the top of her head. His free hand moved to gently lift her chin until he once again could look into her eyes. "And me, Miss Worthington?"

"You?" she repeated. The lady gulped.

His soft smile grew. "Would you wish me to be—devastated?" His lips brushed her brow, and Cassandra gulped again.

"My lord——" she started, trying to make her voice firm. It did not work.

"I wish to be," he said. "I wish to be your lord and I wish you to be my lady. Would it be such a terrible thing, Miss Worthington, to be Countess of Wickham?"

"No," Miss Worthington stuttered; of course not. It was just that—that—"You could have your choice of so many talented young ladies!" she told him. "Beautiful women with money who could bring you such good connections——"

"I have already chosen." His smile was even more tender. "I

am only waiting for you to choose me back. I have no need of more money. And the connections I most want are with someone who will make me laugh. Someone known for plain speaking. Someone who reads Chaucer because she wishes to, and can discuss the book with a lively enthusiasm."

She was looking at him in bemusement touched with awe. "You must," she marveled, "be the only man in England who feels that way! No fear of a woman who reads Chaucer? No scheming for powerful connections? And money! I do not believe I have *ever* heard anyone in the *ton* say they have no need for more money!"

"Really?" He tucked her hand into the crook of his elbow and led her to a chair by the fire, gently placing her into it. "Obviously you have not spoken with the right people. Perhaps I feel this way because I know what it is to be without funds. So I also know when what I have is enough."

"My lord—" Miss Worthington began as he dropped to one knee at her feet, still holding her hand.

"Miss Worthington," the earl said, his formal tone belying the twinkle in his eye, "will you marry me?"

"Do you know, sir," she asked, anxiously watching his face, "that I am eight and twenty?"

"So old?" He appeared surprised, and it took her a moment to realize he was laughing at her.

"Come, Cassandra!" he said, smiling up at her. "Think a moment. It is a better age to wife two and thirty than is eighteen."

"Well . . ." She could not help but agree. "You *do* need someone who knows how to hold her own—"

"Yes!" He clasped her hand more firmly now.

"—for a more overbearing, stubborn—"

"Cassandra—" he began.

She grinned. "What will your grandmother say?" she asked, reaching out to tenderly caress the lock of hair that had fallen onto his forehead back to its appointed place.

"Thank goodness!"

Both Miss Worthington and the earl started up at the sound of a third voice where they'd thought they were alone. The dowager countess stepped from behind the large, heavily carved screen her grandson had brought back with him from India. She saw no reason to tell them she'd stepped into the library only moments before their arrival to fortify herself with a few drops of his lordship's fine brandy, and had been doing so when they entered. "That, my dear, is what I would say. Thank goodness! This is exactly what I wished for this Christmas!"

"Grandmama!" The earl glared at the old lady, and rolled his eyes when she laughed. "If you do not mind, I would prefer to do this in private!"

The dowager countess grinned and made him a regal curtsy. Not for the world would she have missed the sight of her grandson on one knee. Someday she would, God willing, tell her great-grandchildren all about it—and about how she, their great-grandmama, had given them the best Christmas gift ever before they were even born when she'd introduced their mother to their father one holiday season.

"As you wish," she told the earl, then smiled at Miss Worthington. "I started to tell you earlier, Cassandra—I wore that dress the night Edward's grandfather proposed to me."

"You did?" Cassandra fingered the material lovingly, and returned the countess's smile.

"It was very lucky for me." It was obvious from the soft tone and the faraway look in her eyes that the countess was reviewing something they could not see. After a moment she gave herself a shake and started toward the door, only to stop when she was almost there. She turned, claiming her grandson's attention with an "Oh, Edward." He looked up impatiently. "I have something for you."

Reaching into one of the many draped folds of her gown, the dowager countess pulled out a sprig of mistletoe and held it toward the earl. "I found this in your room," she said, frowning at him as he came forward to take it. "There was a lot of it there. A lot that used to hang in Wickly doorways, I believe." Cassandra laughed at Wickham's guilty expression.

"Make good use of this, Edward," the dowager countess said. She waited for him to open the door for her and gave a slight nod as he bowed her out.

"Now—" said the earl, coming forward purposefully. Before Cassandra could move, he had placed the sprig of mistletoe in her hair.

"You do love me, don't you?" he asked, his eyes anxious. "I thought—I hoped—"

"Yes," Cassandra said, smiling up at him as one hand

tenderly touched the worry lines in his forehead, smoothing them gently as anxiety gave way to joy. "Yes. I do."

He grinned. "Then," he said, touching the mistletoe he'd just placed in her hair in a most suggestive way, "it would be an undutiful grandson who did not follow his grandmother's direct order, don't you think?"

And Edward, not wishing to be thought undutiful, did.

The
Kissing
Bough

❉ ❉
❉

Martha Powers

✻
The Kissing Bough

GILLIAN FOSTER STABBED the poker into the logs and sparks rose like fairy dust to dance up the chimney. Heat from the fire pinked her cheeks. She reached up to resecure a chestnut curl that had come loose from the Psyche knot. Her eyes turned to her bedroom window, and in the gathering darkness, she could make out the crenelated roof of Maynard Hall, country seat of the eighth Earl of Elmore, Lord Chadwicke Kendale.

Chad.

A vision of dark, piercing eyes appeared in Gillian's mind and her heart beat faster. The very vividness of her reaction to the apparition was daunting. To break the spell, she cast her eyes on the travelling cape lying across the green velvet chaise longue. Picking up her candle, she headed for the door. The black skirt of her mourning dress swirled around her with the gentle hiss of silk. She left the bulging portmanteau leaning against the oak wardrobe and, without a backward glance, went out into the hall.

Even after two months, the emptiness of her father's room jolted her; each day she awoke with the expectation that it had all been a nightmare. But when she passed the open doorway she was reminded anew that her father was gone forever, and she tried to take comfort from her memories of the scholarly, absent-minded man who had raised her. Some days the pain was less intense. She set the candle on the table beside his bed. Stroking the soft nap of the comforter's brown velvet edging for the last time, she blew out the candle and left the room, closing the door firmly behind her.

She tried not to think about the evening ahead, but as she stood at the top of the stairs, her eyes were drawn to the kissing bough suspended in the center of the foyer. Apples tied to red satin ribbons dangled from the circle of rosemary. The candle she had left on the hall table flickered and the shiny apples swayed, caught in the errant draughts of the hallway. Her hand tightened on the walnut handrail as she stared at the mistletoe nestled in the heart of the greenery.

The kissing bough and apples and Chad. She had fought all day not to think about him, but he was wound up so inexorably with all her memories. The tall case clock in the drawing room chimed six. If he was coming tonight, he would not arrive until much later. Gillian sat down on the top step, tucking her skirts around her for warmth. Perhaps she needed to think about the past before she took the fateful step that inevitably would seal her future.

The First Kiss

GILLIAN SWUNG HER feet over the edge of the hayloft. Squire Bassington's barn was cold, but she was not uncomfortable since she was out of the cutting sting of the December wind. Her father had chuckled when she offered to go to the squire's for some apples for the kissing bough. Knowing it was her favorite fruit, he suggested she take two baskets.

She bit into the apple, sighing as the sharp flavor filled her mouth. She ate slowly, savoring every bite, her mind floating in pure sensation. When she finished it, she licked the last of the juice off her fingers with businesslike precision. She inhaled deeply, feeling contented. She loved the musty, pungent odors of the old barn. The squire's land was close enough that even in winter she could slip away to the barn when she needed to escape the confinement of the schoolroom. Both the squire and her father knew she used the hayloft as her hideyhole. It was a place to be alone, a place where she could think and plan, and best of all, a place to dream.

She heard the creak of the side door and stilled the motion of her feet. The voices were muffled beneath the loft. She hugged the basket of apples in her lap as she leaned forward to see who had entered. Recognizing Lester Wheatley, the son of the innkeeper, Gillian shrank back. She hoped he would not discover her presence. The heavily built boy was a bully, delighting in teasing the smaller village children until they cried.

Another boy came out from under the loft and she immediately identified the black hair and gangly body of Chadwicke Kendale, son of the Earl of Elmore whose land adjoined her father's small holding. Chad was older than Gillian, thirteen to her nine. She did not know him well, although he had been tutored by her father before he went away to school.

"What have you got in there?" Chad asked, pointing to the cloth bag in the bigger boy's hand.

"Wait'n you'll see." Lester opened the top of the bag. He reached in and brought out a small animal. Gillian caught her breath as Lester tied a long thong around the neck of a shivering kitten. Holding the loose end of the strap, he dropped the animal on the ground.

"Be careful. It's just a babe," Chad said, kneeling down to get a closer look.

"Don't be such a gudgeon. It's only a cat, that's what."

"I can bloody well see that. Wizard! Look at those ugly black patches on its back."

Bent on mischief, Lester was unimpressed with the outward appearance of the animal. He reached for a pitchfork leaning against the wall and tied the kitten's tether to the end of the handle. Gillian bit her lip, knowing she could not sit quietly in the loft and watch the boys hurt the cat. Her hand brushed the basket, forgotten in her lap, and her eyes narrowed. Her fingers tightened around the largest of the apples. Satisfied that she was well prepared, she waited calmly for the right moment to spring her attack.

"Have a care," Chad cautioned as the bigger boy tugged on the leather leash. "Don't pull on that!"

"Stubble it! I want to see if the cat can fly."

He raised the pitchfork and as the thong tightened on the kitten's neck, Chad threw himself at Lester, knocking the implement from his hand. For a moment the boy remained still, the only sign of his anger the flush of red that rose to his face. Then with a bellow of rage Lester's fists flashed out in a flurry of blows that knocked the slimmer boy to the ground. From the hayloft above, Gillian could see the dazed look in Chad's eyes and knew the fight was nearly over.

As Lester brought his fist back for one more punishing blow, she raised her hand and threw the apple with all her might. Gillian heard the bully cry out as the projectile hit him, but she did not wait to assay the damage. She continued to launch missiles with deadly accuracy, smiling grimly as finally the boy threw his arms over his head and raced out the open barn door.

"Oh, I say, that was well done," Chad said, voice tinged with awe as he looked up at her from his position on the ground.

"Are you all right?" she called down.

"Bloody nose is all." He brushed the tumble of black curls out of his eyes, his forehead furrowed as he stared up at her. "Who are you?"

"Gillian. Gillian Foster."

"Professor Foster's daughter?" At her nod, he grinned. "I remember you now. You used to have long red pigtails and your front teeth were missing. Can you still spit so far?"

"No." She shook her head with wistful regret. "My teeth grew in and it rather threw off my aim."

"Pity." His face was sad for a moment, but then his mouth creased in a smile that lightened his countenance. "At least your throwing is right on the mark. Good show, Gillian."

She returned his smile, feeling a glow of satisfaction at his words.

He stood up and brushed the dust off his breeches. Finished, he moved to stand just beneath her, one black eyebrow arched in question. "Would you like some help in getting down?"

Gillian was just about to tell him that she was quite capable of managing the wooden ladder when something strange happened. His face was turned up to her and she found herself staring into the most wonderful brown eyes she had ever seen. Surrounded by an almost girlish profusion of black lashes, Chad's eyes were deepset and so dark there were no pupils visible. Suddenly she could feel herself flushing and there was a strange quivery sensation beneath her skin. Without conscious thought, her mouth opened and she spoke in a breathless voice she barely recognized as her own.

"I would rather like a bit of help," she said. "The basket will be awkward on the ladder."

"Don't worry," Chad said. "I'm coming up."

He raced to the ladder and climbed it with the agility of a monkey. Gillian was barely on her feet before he was beside her, reaching for the nearly empty basket of apples.

"I shall go first so that you will not be afraid of falling," he said.

Although normally Gillian would have bristled at the suggestion she might be afraid, she contented herself with a nod of the head. She was impressed when Chad skinned down the ladder, setting the basket on the floor and returned to her side without evincing any sign of breathlessness.

"Can you handle your skirts?" he asked.

Until his mention of her clothing, she had not given them a thought. Normally she was alone when she scrambled up and down the ladder. Now, in his presence, she realized that her dress and petticoats represented a definite handicap to a modest descent. However, with newfound aplomb, she raised her chin and indicated that he should precede her. She turned her back to the open space and, gathering her skirts decorously to the side, she began to descend, steadying herself with her free hand.

"Don't worry," Chad called from below. "I shall catch you if you fall."

She was just about to snort in disdain when the heel of her boot caught in the hem of her dress. She had to clutch at the rung above her head to keep from tumbling backward. Her heart was hammering in her chest as she continued downward. She was almost at the bottom when hands grasped her waist and Chad lowered her the remainder of the distance. Carefully, he set her on the packed earthen floor. He was considerably taller than she, and Gillian had to tilt back her head to examine him more closely. A pitiful meow interrupted her scrutiny.

"Oh, the cat!" she cried. "Where are you, puss?"

Gillian spotted the end of the pitchfork and followed the leather leash behind a barrel of grain where the kitten was struggling to get loose.

"Poor darling," she crooned, untying the thong and scooping up the quivering ball of fur.

"It's not hurt, is it?" Chad asked, kneeling down beside her.

"I don't think so." Without the least bit of self-consciousness, Gillian turned the cat over. "It's a he," she announced.

Chad extended a finger and stroked the underside of the cat's chin, grinning at her when the animal began to purr. "What'll we do with him?"

"We'll get some more apples and then I'll take him home with me. He shouldn't be out on his own." She looked across at Chad. His face was dirty, his lip was split and puffy, and his nose had bled all down the front of his shirt. "I think you had better come home with me, too."

The boy cleaned up considerably better than the cat. In no wise could the animal be judged adorable. Unusual would be the best one could hope for. He was gray and white with a smattering of oddly shaped black patches on his coat. Aside from the strange markings on his fur, the chunk missing from one of his little ears ended any pretensions he might have had to beauty. Naturally, Gillian thought he was precious.

"Will your mother let you keep him?" Chad asked.

"My mother died when I was born. Papa takes care of me," Gillian said, her voice matter-of-fact. Head cocked to the side, she eyed Chad's bruises and bloodstained shirt. "Perhaps you should come with me while I talk to Papa. Looking at us, he will see how much trouble we had saving the cat," she said, flapping the skirt of her dress, which was liberally covered with hay and smudged with dirt.

The disheveled threesome knocked at the library door, waiting for the deep voice of Professor Ethan Foster to call admittance. Gillian was delighted to discover her father standing over the mahogany table that was spread with open books, one on top of the other in higgledy-piggledy fashion. She knew that when he was involved in his research he was less likely to scrutinize her requests with the attention he would give them at other times. She came to stand beside him and without looking up, Ethan put his arm around her, bringing Gillian close to his side.

She snuggled against his old tweed jacket that smelled of the woods and the smoke from the fireplace. She giggled at the surprised expression in Chad's eyes. His father must not be much of a hugger, she guessed. She had seen the Earl of Elmore at church and it appeared that the unsmiling man never forgot that he possessed a title. Thankfully Chad was not so puffed up in his own conceit. From the shelter of her father's arm, she winked at the slightly embarrassed boy, and immediately his face relaxed into a grin.

"How is your project going, Papa?"

"Exceedingly well," came the rather absent reply. "I have been able to trace much of Sir Hans Sloane's life. There are some gaps, of course. It is most vexing that I cannot find where he was the year before he succeeded Sir Isaac Newton as President of the Royal Society."

"Perhaps he was travelling," she suggested.

"Excellent thought, Gillian. Searching for more plants for his herbarium, I would wager. I'll have to check into that possibility. Was there something you wanted, poppet?" he asked, stroking her hair even as he leaned over to turn the page of one of the books.

"Chad Kendale and I rescued a kitten."

Gillian held out the scrawny cat for her father's inspection. Startled by such an occurrence, Ethan turned away from his books. He brought his face down to the cat's level to peruse the mottled furball in his daughter's hands. Unmoved by the scrutiny, the kitten stared back, his eyes never leaving the shaggy gray eyebrows that wiggled over the top of gold-rimmed spectacles.

"It doesn't look like much of a specimen," he declared.

"He's had a bad day," Gillian said, rushing to the kitten's defense. "I'm sure he'll be quite, er, handsome when he's older. Might I keep him, sir?"

Although less than enthused by the idea, Ethan took one look at his daughter's expression and rolled his eyes in defeat.

"I suppose it will be all right," he said. "Only keep it out of here."

"Oh, I will," she said, standing on tiptoes to give her father a grateful kiss.

"That's a good girl," Ethan said. He turned to show her to the door when he spotted Chad. "Hello, young sir. Have you arrived for a lesson?"

"Oh, no, Professor. I came in with Gillian."

"Excellent," Ethan said, an expression of relief crossing his face at the thought that his research would not be further interrupted. "Well, run along now. You best see to the cat."

"Who is Sir Hans Sloane?" Chad asked as they returned to the kitchen.

"Papa's writing a paper to deliver in London. Sloane was a famous collector. He was a doctor, too. And you'll never guess," she said lowering her voice to a whisper. "He treated sick people with live millipedes and crabs' eyes."

"You're bamming me," Chad scoffed.

"Am not. Papa read it to me right out of one of his books." She waited to see if he would challenge her, but when he shrugged in acceptance, she grinned and changed the subject. "Do you think Patch would be a proper name for the cat?"

Chad tipped his head to the side, his face screwed up in thought. "I'd say topping good," he announced. He edged over toward the kitchen table. "May I have one of the apples?"

Gillian started to shake her head but, caught by the eagerness in the dark eyes of her new friend, she relented. "But just one. We need the rest for the kissing bough."

She set the kitten on the hearth rug as Chad snatched an apple from the basket. He bit into it, the sound sharp in the otherwise quiet kitchen. His tongue snaked out to catch the juice that ran out of the corner of his mouth. Gillian watched in fascination as he devoured the fruit. It was obvious that he loved apples as much as she.

"Would you like to come to our Christmas party?" she asked. "We have one every year. People from the village are invited, and of course the squire and his wife. Some of Papa's students will be coming. The party's on Friday. There'll be ever so much food," she finished breathlessly.

She knelt down on the rug, lifted the kitten into her lap, and fussed with it, all the time waiting nervously for Chad's reply. Somehow an affirmative answer was most important.

"I'd like to come," he announced. Then with a casual salute he sauntered across the kitchen and out the door.

Chad did come to the Christmas party and, despite the fact he was heir to the Earl of Elmore, he fit in well with the other guests. While the adults congregated in the drawing room, the children were permitted to play games in the kitchen and the back parlor, with occasional forays into the dining room for sustenance.

The party wore on, becoming less formal. Chad and Gillian, along with the other children, took turns hiding behind the draperies in the foyer to watch as the ladies were kissed beneath the mistletoe. When the squire's wife took over the piano and began to pound out "Bernie Bough," the adults returned to the drawing room, much to the children's disappointment.

"Just when things were getting interesting," Chad said.

"There's still one apple left," Gillian said, staring up at the kissing bough.

"Go on, Gilly!" someone shouted. "Stand under it and pay the forfeit."

Gillian hesitated. It was not that she was reluctant. She'd had her eye on the apples all evening and felt one kiss was a small price to pay for her favorite fruit. However, she'd never been kissed before and was not eager for the other children to discover her ignorance.

Stalling for time, she said, "There is no one who can reach the apple."

There were giggles and a rustle of movement among the children. Gillian squirmed in embarrassment, wondering how she could get out of the awkward situation. Suddenly Chad stepped forward.

"I can reach the apple," he said. His voice cracked on the words, but he winked to indicate he was quite willing to save her as she had saved him a few days earlier.

Gillian relaxed, determined to enter into the spirit of the game. With exaggerated gestures, she sashayed across the hall, pantomiming the simpering young women she had watched earlier. She flipped her curls with one languid hand and fluttered her eyelashes outrageously in Chad's direction.

He played along, acting the part of the amorous gallant. Reaching into his pocket he pulled out a snowy white handkerchief. He fluttered it under his nose then made an elegant leg, sweeping the hand holding the handkerchief close to the floor. He straightened up, leaned forward, and kissed her with a resounding smack. On tiptoes he reached up and unfastened the apple, which was presented to her with great ceremony amid the cheers and applause of the other children and some of the adults who had come to investigate the cause of such hilarity.

Everyone said it was the greatest fun, almost like watching a play. Gillian laughed along with Chad, and it was only later when she was tucked up in bed that she had time to think about the evening. Her first kiss had been much different than she had expected. She was surprised that Chad's lips had been so warm and firm. More surprisingly yet was the funny, shivery feeling she had in the pit of her stomach when he kissed her. It was like falling; a curious but not unpleasant sensation.

The uneaten apple rested on the table beside her bed. She had found it in her pocket when she came upstairs. It was strange that she hadn't felt any desire to eat it. After all, she had earned it.

❄

The Second Kiss

GILLIAN THREW DOWN the rope she had been pulling and turned to glare at Chad. Her breath ballooned out in the frosty air. She stamped her feet on the frozen ground, wishing she had worn something more substantial than her half boots. She was inordinately proud of them, but the shiny red leather was ill-suited to hauling the Yule log through the woods. She had wanted Chad to see how well her boots and mittens complimented her new black cape with the military braiding. Excited about his own news, he hadn't even given her fashionable ensemble a glance.

Reminded of her grievance, she hurried into conversation. "I still don't see why you have to go up to London right after Christmas. From what Papa says, the town will be light of company."

"That's quite the point of it," Chad said. "Mother feels I need a touch of town bronze and since I have learned that it is pointless to argue with her, I will go. Besides I would much prefer to make my mistakes when not under the eagle eyes of the old biddies who line the walls at every ball. When the Season starts, I shall be up to snuff, ready to take my place in society."

"Piffle!" Gillian waved a hand, dismissing his pretensions to a proper place among the *ton* as if they were inconsequential. "You will miss the best of the trout fishing, is all. Now that you're the earl you've become a dead bore."

She knew part of her ill temper was due to the fact that she was feeling abandoned. Perhaps if Patch were still around to rub against her ankles she would not feel so friendless. For five years the ugly little cat had comforted Gillian when she seemed most inconsolable. A month ago she had found her furry friend lying dead at the edge of the woods, his unusual markings blending with the mottled colors of the autumn leaves.

And now Chad was leaving.

Since that winter day when she had taken him home, Chad had become an unofficial member of the Foster household. Not only had he become her friend, but he had developed a strong relationship with her father in the last five years. When he was home from school, he spent as much time with them as he did at home.

Gillian treated him with the casualness of an older brother, and they were privy to each others thoughts and dreams. They fished and hunted together, rode and walked in each other's company. On the occasions when he remained for supper, her father guided the conversation so that both Gillian and Chad were able to discourse on a broad range of subjects.

All of this had changed several months earlier when the Earl of Elmore was killed in a hunting accident. At eighteen, Chad was catapulted into a situation he had not thought to face for many years. No longer a carefree youth and heir to a title, he was now the eighth earl with all the responsibilities of his rank and fortune. He had estates to visit, tenants to contend with, and social obligations to fulfill.

Despite all of Gillian's carping at him, she was proud of the way Chad, after his initial shock and grief, had taken control. He had assured her that his change in status would not affect their relationship, but even at thirteen, she knew that nothing would ever be the same again. When Christmas was over, he would leave for London. Once he took his proper place in society there would be an unbridgeable gap between them.

Chad threw an arm around Gillian's shoulders and gave her an affectionate squeeze. "Have done with your sulking. It's much too cold to stand out here and argue. Miss Pennington promised that she would have sticky buns and cherry tarts for our party. I'm positively starving."

Gillian snorted. "You're always starving. I would be as fat as Squire Bassington's pig if I ate as much as you do. That's if Penny would let me eat as much as I wanted."

"Miss Pennington is an admirable woman." He picked up the rope she had thrown down on the snow and pressed it into her mittened hand.

"You only say that because she fair dotes on you. She's most impressed that I am friends with an earl."

"Hah!" Chad nudged her and they began to pull the Yule log, once more in charity with each other.

"I suspect it was your mother who suggested to Papa that I ought to have a governess to curb my hoydenish behavior." She peeked sideways to see if her guess was correct, but he stared ahead, his expression giving nothing away. "I vowed I would not like Miss Pennington, but of course I assumed she would be some starchy spinster who would make me learn stitchery and other useless occupations and would cry rope if I misbehaved."

"Oho, the truth is out," Chad crowed. "Miss Pennington has quite won your loyalty after only six months. What a paragon!"

Gillian grimaced in dismay. "I must confess that I quite like the woman. Although I blush to admit it, Penny even makes embroidery lessons interesting. And she was not horrified when she learned I was quite mad about fishing."

"I'm glad it has worked out. At your age it's fitting that you have another female to answer your questions."

"I believe the pictures in the book you stole from your father's library answered most of my questions."

Although Chad resolutely directed his eyes straight ahead, the tips of his ears reddened, much to Gillian's delight. She could feel the laughter rising to her lips and quickly dropped the rope to muffle her giggles in the wool of her mittens.

"What a horrid child you are," he declared archly.

The reminder of such a monumental transgression proved too much for him. Whooping in good humor, he scooped up a handful of snow and threw it at her. Gillian dropped her hands and her laughter rang out through the woods as she retaliated in kind. They pelted each other with snowballs until they were gasping for breath. Flopping down on the Yule log, they brushed the snow from their clothing, grinning companionably.

"I still remember my chagrin when I discovered that far from answering your questions, the pictures merely added to your curiosity." Chad noted the flush of color that rose to Gillian's cheeks and chuckled as he reached out to straighten the saucy red hat on her curls. "Your interest in my anatomy was nothing short of brazen."

"But as I recall you showed very little interest in mine," she complained. "It was quite the most lowering experience. Papa was very sweet when I came to him in tears. I told him that my body was nothing like the pictures in your book."

"So that's how my father found out. There was the very devil to pay. He caned me and sent me off to my loathsome cousin Waldo's for the remainder of the summer."

"Even though he did hire Miss Pennington, Papa was a dash

more understanding." Gillian's voice was soft in remembrance. "He took me into the library and showed me some of the art books he kept in the glassed bookcases. There were beautiful women in various stages of dishabille. He told me everyone's body was different, but that each one was beautiful. There was one woman in particular who was especially lovely, and she had no feminine curves at all. I remember I used to stare at myself in the mirror and think of her. It gave me hope that one day I might be pretty, too."

Chad caught the forlorn quality in her voice. Taking in the drooping shoulders and bent head of his friend, he said, "But, Gillian, you are going to be a beauty someday."

She peeked at him shyly from behind the cover of her lashes. "Do you really think so?"

"Of course I do," he declared stoutly.

Chad noticed with surprise how much her body had changed over the summer. The awkward coltish body was far more rounded now. Gillian's face had lost the plumpness of childhood, thinning out to hint at a more womanly shape. Set above the high cheekbones, her eyes seemed larger and more heavily lashed. All at once he recognized the truth of his words: Gillian was becoming a beautiful young lady.

With that realization, the tenor of his thoughts changed. He had never considered her as anything but his friend, and it troubled him that he had suddenly become aware of her as a young, shapely female. Staring down into her eyes, he noted the trust and innocence in the green depths and berated himself for his improper thoughts.

He stood up, making much of the snow melting on his Hessians. He pulled Gillian to her feet and, with a bluff camaraderie, he handed her the rope and encouraged her progress by chattering about the harmless details of his Christmas duties as the new earl. By the time they reached Gillian's house, Chad was able to speak to her in his usual bantering tone.

"Hello, the house," Chad called.

Miss Pennington opened the door and Gillian shouted her traditional greeting. "We bring the Yule log. Let the celebrations begin!"

Gillian apologized to her governess for the dirt and snow they dragged across the threshold, but the older woman waved her hand in dismissal. She helped them off with their coats and mittens, then set the kettle on for tea. Chad reached for one of the pastries and she smacked his hand.

"Not yet, young sir. There's more work before the feasting." She shooed him over to sweep the floor as she and Gillian set out the china and silver for their tea.

Christmas was Gillian's favorite time of year. She loved the secrets and the preparations and the traditions. She couldn't wait to see how Penny liked the evening's entertainment. Although Gillian had been angry when her father hired the governess, over the last few months she had become very fond of Penny.

Miss Pennington was tall and thin, with an elegance of manner that indicated she came from a refined background. She never spoke very much about herself, which lent an air of mystery to her that Gillian found intriguing. She never received any letters or packages. There were no visits home, and although Penny was invariably polite and cheerful, she did not encourage any relationships outside of the Foster household.

Gillian had originally fantasized that Miss Pennington had become a governess after a disastrous love affair. However, the brisk competence of the plain-faced woman suggested the real reason might be far less romantic. She was quite old, Gillian thought, perhaps even in her thirties. With her gray-streaked hair, unremarkable features, and her quiet demeanor, she was not unattractive, only self-effacing. Unless one noted her eyes. She had lovely gray eyes that looked at the world with an unruffled serenity that Gillian found soothing.

"Come along, slowpoke," Chad said. "Everything's ready."

His voice brought Gillian's thoughts back to the present. He had rolled the Yule log onto a long runner which he was dragging down the hall to the drawing room. Ethan had pushed back the pocket doors and folded back the carpet to clear a path to the fireplace. Chad did most of the heavy lifting, struggling to wedge the log into the fireplace. Gillian handed him the pieces of last year's Yule log that she had saved for kindling. While her father rolled out the carpet, Miss Pennington helped arrange three chairs in a circle before the hearth.

When the preparations were completed to Ethan's satisfaction, he indicated that the governess should take a chair while Gillian and Chad lit the candles around the room. When all the candles were burning except for the large red one on the mantelpiece, Ethan bid them to take their seats. Gravely, he shook Chad's hand. He kissed Gillian on the cheek, smiling at the shine of excitement in her eyes. Standing in front of the Yule log, he struck a flint and lit the candle on the mantel, then turned and smiled warmly at the governess.

"We welcome you, Miss Pennington, to your first Christmas in our home." Ethan bowed to her and handed her a small box topped with a red satin ribbon. "It is a Christmas Eve tradition in our family that a new guest at our table receive a gold coin so that he or she will not go penniless into the new year."

Penny's fine-boned face lit with pleasure as she rose to her feet to accept the present. She nodded graciously to Gillian and Chad but dipped into a very proper curtsy for Ethan.

When she was seated again, Ethan's deep voice rumbled in the quiet room. "In the village where my ancestors were born, at the time when Oliver Cromwell ruled, the town crier went door to door ringing a harsh handbell."

Chad picked up the battered iron cowbell that had been placed beside his chair. He remembered how thrilled he had been the second year he had joined the Foster celebrations when Gillian permitted him to ring the raucous bell. He had been a child of fourteen then. Now at the advanced age of eighteen, he thought he was too old for such juvenile displays, but he discovered the clanging of the bell seemed to break the bonds of tension that had wrapped him tight since his father's death. He wondered if he would grow to resemble the earl, but it came to him that the title did not have to confer arrogance and stiffness. It was up to him to take himself and his consequence less seriously. Vowing to remember that, he raised the bell again and rang it with abandon while Gillian shouted encouragement and the two adults covered their ears.

With a new awareness, Chad silenced the metal clapper with his hand, but the sound echoed in the corners of the room. He blinked to bring himself back to the present and his eyes touched Professor Foster's, and in their depths he saw understanding and approval.

"Thank you," Chad said quietly, his heart filled with happiness.

Ethan waited for silence and as the tension began to build again, he spoke. "The Puritan bell warned those within the sound of its clatter that no celebration of the Christmas season would be tolerated. In this household we welcome the holiday as a time of rebirth. We want all to know that our celebration has begun, and so we have found the sweetest sound to announce our joy and invite all to join us in our festivities."

With one hand Gillian raised a string of three bells, and with a slim metal rod in the other, she hit each bell in succession. The first chime was high, with a sweet clarity that held the attention. The second note was lower, complementing and intensifying the first. The third chime was lower still, adding the final ingredient to the rich blend of sounds. The tones rose to the ceiling, dissipating slowly and lingering in the memory long after the room was silent.

From the pocket of his jacket, Ethan took out a sprig of ivy and handed it to Gillian. "I give you this token, daughter, to indicate that a female will have the rule of the house in the coming year. Use your power with wisdom and grace."

"I will," she said. She accepted the cutting and carried it to the front door where last Christmas's ivy hung. She exchanged the two sprigs, returning to the drawing room to lay the old ivy on top of the unlighted Yule log. Grinning at Chad, she returned to her chair.

"With the fragments of last year's Yule log I will light the new one," Ethan said. He took a slender piece of kindling and set it in the flame of the candle on the mantel.

Gillian sighed in satisfaction as her father set the glowing end among the rest of the kindling. He blew on the wood and the fire caught and held. She peeked at Miss Pennington, delighted with the pleasure on the older woman's face.

Turning her head to the other side, she watched the flickering light of the fire playing across Chad's face. He had changed. It might have been the death of his father and his new responsibilities that made him look different. Whatever it was, there was a new maturity to his expression and his bearing. She had not noticed how handsome he had become, with his black curls and smouldering dark eyes. She could feel a lump rise in her throat as she wondered if this would be the last year he would join their festivities. He was an earl now and was going up to London to take his place in society. Would he come back?

As if he had heard her thoughts, Chad turned toward her and smiled. He reached into his pocket and withdrew a piece of paper. Gillian laughed, inordinately pleased that he had remembered to bring his letter to Father Christmas. She dug in her pocket for her own.

"Well, children," Ethan said. "Throw them into the fireplace and we shall see if you will get your wishes."

Gillian let Chad go first, watching as he threw his letter into the back of the fireplace. Wriggling with excitement, she followed suit, waiting anxiously to see if the parchment would be consumed by the flames. With a flutter of white, the two letters danced upward until the draft caught hold of them and pulled them up the chimney.

"Not even singed," Gillian bragged, hugging her father in her enthusiasm.

She smiled at Chad, noting with satisfaction the hint of triumph in his eyes. He was still not too old for such childish games. If this were to be their last shared Christmas Eve celebration, she was grateful that he could enter into the spirit of the festivities. She glanced up at her father and realized that he was aware that Chad's departure for London would change their relationship forever. She took comfort from the compassion in his eyes and raised her chin to show that she understood. Ethan patted her shoulder then took her empty chair. Gillian remained in front of the brightly burning Yule log, ready for her part in the proceedings.

"In his youth, Papa knew a man called John Newton," Gillian said. "He had not seen him for many years when he heard that a minister by that name was holding a lively prayer meeting in the Parish of Olney. Papa went to hear the preaching and found that it was indeed his old friend."

Gillian turned toward Miss Pennington, anxious to see her reaction to hearing this story for the first time. By the shine in her governess's eyes it was apparent that the woman was enjoying the evening very much. Since Penny was especially fond of history, Gillian spoke directly to her.

"The minister proclaimed that he had once been an infidel and a libertine. He had gone to sea, carrying items from Liverpool to Africa. He traded his goods for slaves. One night he couldn't sleep and went up on deck. It was Christmas Eve."

Ethan cleared his throat and Gillian grimaced at the lowered eyebrows of her father.

"Well, we don't know exactly what night it was," she said in defense of her fabrication. Then lowering her voice, she said, "It makes a better story, Papa."

"Nothing is as good as the truth, poppet," her father said. "Wouldn't you agree, Miss Pennington?"

"The truth is always best, Professor Foster," she replied formally. There was a twinkle in her eye as she noted the exasperation on her pupil's face. "However there is such a thing as dramatic license, Gillian. Perhaps you might just say that no one knows for sure what night it was but that it might very well have been Christmas Eve."

"Good show, Miss Pennington," Chad said, grinning his approval.

Slightly mollified, Gillian continued her story. "It seemed very cold on deck and John wondered if it might be Christmas Eve. It was a very dark night, and below decks he could hear the groans of the slaves. Suddenly he knew that it was wrong to take away anyone's freedom and he vowed to change his life. At journey's end he came home to England and became a minister. When he began to preach, he thought it was important for the people to understand that no life was so bad that it couldn't be saved. He wrote songs in the vicarage, late at night, when no one else was awake."

Hearing Chad's snort, she quickly added, "And sometimes he wrote during the day, although he never liked that very much. Papa went to the weekly prayer meetings when he could because he liked to visit with his friend afterward, but also because he liked to hear the music. Of all the songs he heard there was one that was his favorite. He thought it would make a wonderful ending to our celebrations."

Then without the slightest bit of self-consciousness, Gillian began to sing. Her voice was a sweet childlike soprano, perhaps all the more beautiful because it was untutored. Unaccompanied, the words were clear, catching and holding the attention:

> "Amazing grace, how sweet the sound,
> That saved a wretch like me.
> I once was lost, but now am found,
> Was blind but now I see."

When she finished the song, there was absolute silence. The perfection of the music had woven a spell of magic over the occupants of the room. Her father's face was filled with pride and Gillian went to him, pressing a kiss on his cheek as he gathered her into his arms.

"Merry Christmas, Papa," she said, snuggling close.

"And to you, daughter," came the gruff reply.

Gillian approached her governess, sensing that the sheen of tears in Miss Pennington's eyes was not from unhappiness but merely from the emotion of the occasion. "Greetings of the season, Penny," she said, kissing her on the cheek.

"Your song was lovely, child." The older woman hugged Gillian then beamed at the gentlemen. "What pleasure you have all given me tonight."

And finally Gillian stood in front of Chad. Every year she had kissed his cheek, but suddenly she was shy and the salutation did not come naturally. He was a peer of the realm and, what was almost more daunting, an adult. She could not bear the thought that he might think her actions childlike. She wanted to tell him some of this, but her awkwardness was so new she could not find the words.

As if he sensed her uneasiness, Chad stood up and bowed very formally to her. He did not kiss her but instead took her hand and led her over to the two adults. While he spoke with her father, Gillian went with Miss Pennington to the kitchen to bring in the tea. The pastry tray was piled with tempting confections and Chad's mouth stretched into a wide grin when he spotted the cherry tarts which were his special favorites. In honor of the occasion, Gillian was permitted to pour. Plates were filled as she passed around the tea.

"I fear I shall fall into a decline when I am in London," Chad said, licking a drop of cherry filling from the corner of his mouth. "No one makes tarts with as light a hand as you, Miss Pennington."

"Thank you for your kind words," the older woman replied. "Although we will miss you, I suspect your time in town will prepare you well for the rigors of the Season."

"I hope so but I wish I did not have to leave so soon. Tomorrow I will be tied up with my duties, so I will have to leave shortly. I know we do not normally exchange Christmas presents, but I wanted you to know how much joy I have found in this house." He stood up, crossing to the burled wood table in the corner. He removed three packages from the lower shelf, amused at Gillian's outraged expression. His tone was teasing as he returned to the tea table. "Admit it, Gillian. If you had known they were there, you would have badgered me all day to tell you their contents."

"I would not," she said, sniffing in high dudgeon, but she was much too curious and excited to resist the lure of the gaily wrapped presents. "Hurry and open your gift, Papa," she begged.

"Even at my advanced age I must admit I enjoy a surprise," Ethan said as he unwrapped the oddly-shaped present. He sighed with appreciation as he stared down at the soapstone carving in his hand.

"You will probably recognize Guandi, the God of War. I remembered you showing me pictures of some of the figures in Sir Hans Sloane's oriental collection. When I was in London earlier this year I found this copy and hoped you would like it."

"My boy, I could not be more delighted." The pleasure on Ethan's face was ample confirmation of his words. "The detailing of the carving is quite above the ordinary. Look at the precision of the miniature cuts in the battle dress. What an excellent gift. You are indeed a thoughtful young man."

Chad's face reddened at the compliment, and to cover his awkwardness he handed Miss Pennington her package. She opened the wrappings to discover a beautifully tooled leather book.

"Perhaps a book is not an original idea, ma'am," Chad said, "but I hope I am beforehand in giving you this autobiography. Despite the fact the man is from the Americas, I am to understand that Benjamin Franklin was a very interesting personage."

After accepting the pleased thanks of the governess, he turned to Gillian who was trying hard to control her impatience. Chad placed a small box in her hands and watched with amusement as she tore off the paper. She opened the velvet top of the jewelry box and gasped at the necklace lying on the satin lining. Suspended from a fine gold chain was a golden apple.

"I asked your father if it would be permitted to give you such an extravagant present," he drawled, pleased by the stunned look on Gillian's face. "I was sorry that I was not here when Patch died, but I thought this would remind you of the day we found the kitten and the great apple fight."

"Oh, Chad, it is beautiful," Gillian said, holding the necklace up for her father and Penny to see. She slipped it over her head, touching the pendant where it lay warm against her skin. Looking down, she sighed in pure happiness as the golden apple caught and held the light.

"I am glad you like it," he said. "I wish I could be here tomorrow to give you Christmas greetings, but I fear I must be going."

With little ceremony, he bade the adults a good evening. In the foyer, he accepted his hat and caped greatcoat from Gillian. His eyes were steady on her face as he wound a scarf high on his throat in preparation for the short walk to Maynard Hill. A smile touched his mouth as his gaze rose to the kissing bough.

"Don't be sad, Gillian," he said, hugging her with great affection. "It is not as if I will never return."

At the reminder that he was leaving, she buried her head against his coat. She squeezed her eyes shut, fighting back the tears that threatened to overwhelm her. She didn't want him to think she was a baby, but it felt as though her world was falling apart. Sniffing once she tipped her head to smile bravely up at him.

"I have already given you the apple, Gillian, now you must pay the forfeit," Chad said.

The leather of his gloved hands was cool against her skin, as he smoothed back the curls that tumbled around her face. Her heart quickened at the gleam in his eye. He bent his head and kissed her on the mouth.

Then he was gone. Gillian stood in the open doorway, watching as he strode down the snowy lane.

"This last evening will always be in my memory," she whispered. "Merry Christmas, friend of my heart."

The Third Kiss

"STOP TUGGING AT your neckline," Miss Pennington hissed.

"Why didn't I notice how low it was when I had my last fitting?" Gillian stared down at her bodice, appalled by the expanse of skin above the satin ruffle.

"It's not too low. Look around you, child, You are the height of fashion," the governess replied, nudging her young charge as they approached the entrance to Squire Bassington's ballroom.

"I'll probably catch some dreadful inflammation of the lungs. Or I'll lean over the buffet table and my bosom will fall out," Gillian finished gloomily.

"A proper young lady never mentions her body," Penny said. There was an archness to her voice that would have served as a setdown if the twinkle in her eyes had not belied the words. "Besides, by plucking at your neckline you will draw attention to it, which I assume is the very thing you are trying to avoid. Stand up straight and you will begin to feel more comfortable."

"Is that like, 'Close your eyes and think of England'?" Gillian asked pertly.

Penny stopped in her tracks, torn between shock and amusement. "My stars, child! Where on earth do you pick up such phrases? One would think I haven't spent five arduous years trying to teach you the art of ladylike behavior. After Christmas I shall have to set you to penning essays on the difference between feminine wit and coarse speech."

"Are you coming, Gillian?" Ethan said, holding out his arm to escort her into the ballroom. As she laid her hand on the sleeve of his jacket, he looked at her over the tops of his gold-rimmed spectacles. "Ah, my dear, just yesterday you were still in the nursery. Yet tonight you appear all grown up. Perhaps that explains why Robert Worthington has spent so much time at the house. And I thought it was just to show respect to his old tutor."

Gillian could feel the tide of color rising to coat her cheeks and prayed that she would not break out in nervous blotches. She tried to keep her voice neutral as she answered. "Mr. Worthington has always enjoyed your company."

"Mr. Worthington, is it?" he said. "It was Robbie when you punched him in the nose."

"I never did!" She looked around to see if anyone had overheard such a libelous statement. "Surely I could never have done such a thing."

"To my recollection, you have always been the model of deportment," was Penny's acerbic comment.

All at once Gillian had a clear vision of a furious Robbie, bloodied handkerchief clutched to his nose, threatening never to play with her again. She could not recall what had caused their argument, but it reminded her that her respectable behavior was of recent vintage. Until this year she had been more comfortable in the hunting field than in the drawing room. Her only interest in the young gentlemen of the neighborhood was as fishing companions.

Gillian squeezed her father's arm and gave Penny a wistful smile. "It is very difficult being eighteen." She grimaced at such an admission. "Some days I cannot believe how mature I have become. When I look at younger girls, I feel quite toplofty. A moment later, the rules of propriety tighten around me and I miss the freedom of being a child. I'm not sure I want to be all grown up."

"The realization that you do not know all the answers is the beginning of wisdom." Ethan chuckled. "Perhaps there is hope for you yet, poppet."

Hearing the pride of her father's voice, Gillian braced her shoulders, buoyed by his approval. She touched the golden apple on the chain around her neck. Since Chad had given it to her, she had worn it as a talisman. Thus fortified, she sailed into the ballroom and greeted the squire and his wife with a confidence she had not felt earlier. Once the amenities had been satisfied, she joined the younger set, searching out her best friend Nelda Bassington, the soft-spoken daughter of the squire.

"Greetings of the Christmas season, Nelda," she said, kissing her best friend on the cheek. "You are certainly in looks tonight."

Although they were the same age, Gillian felt like Nelda's big sister owing to the disparity in their heights. Gillian was tall for a woman, able to stand eye-to-eye with most of the men in the county. She had always felt like a veritable Amazon next to the petite, golden-haired girl with the enormous eyes of blue.

Gillian had not paid much attention to the squire's daughter in their younger days. Nelda was far more comfortable with feminine activities like needlepoint and sketching, while she preferred the rough and tumble adventures to be found in the out-of-doors. It was only in the last few years that they had been thrust together at neighborhood social affairs. Once they discovered a common interest in books and the theatre, they were soon nattering away like bosom bows.

"Everyone has been asking for you," Nelda declared. "Wherever have you been?"

"It was my dress. Do you think it is too revealing? Every day my chest seems to grow bigger," Gillian groaned.

"At least you have one," Nelda complained, looking down at her own neckline. Wide ruffles of soft lace billowed over the flat bodice of her yellow satin dress.

"Do not despair. Your body may change yet. Besides, it is most inconvenient. In another year I will be bubbling out of all my clothes like the opera dancers I have heard about."

"Who has been talking to you about such creatures?"

"Philip Favel-Chapenham. I think he wanted to impress me with how sophisticated he was. He was in London at the theatre and saw a woman with a dress of dampened muslin." Gillian put her mouth close to her friend's ear and whispered. "Philip said you could see her titties right through the material."

A rush of color flooded Nelda's face and she clapped her hands over her mouth to hold back a shriek of horror. Her eyes were enormous pools of dark blue above the white of her mittens.

When she could speak with some composure, she shook her head in despair and said, "You should not talk so. Just imagine if someone were to overhear."

"Penny is always prosing on about such a dreadful possibility." Gillian tried to look contrite but suspected such an expression was beyond her acting abilities. Diplomatically, she changed the subject. "Your party is surely a success. Everyone has turned out in fine state."

"Mama is in high alt," Nelda confided. "Her only disappointment was that the Earl of Elmore was unable to attend due to a previous commitment in London."

"She invited Chad?"

"Mama was hoping he might bring his future countess to Maynard Hall for Christmas."

Gillian snorted, then looked around to be sure Penny was not within hearing distance. Her governess had warned her about making such a vulgar sound. "Chad has been engaged for six months and we have not seen as much as the back of his carriage. I cannot think that he would invite Lady Chesterley here when he has not been home for Christmas in the last four years."

"I know that, but Mama always wants to ensure the social coup of the year. It would raise her consequence to extremes if she could be the first to introduce Edwina Chesterley to the county."

Knowing how important the battles for ascendancy in society were to Nelda's mother, the girls smiled at each other. They might have been less tolerant if the squire's wife had not been so reasonable in other things.

"I wonder what she is like," Gillian mused. "When I was growing up, Chad was my very best friend. I think of him so often. It came as such a surprise when I heard he was to marry. I guess I held out the hope that when he finally came home we would still be friends."

"You will always be friends," Nelda said, her voice crisply bracing.

"That's true, but it will not be the same if he is married." Gillian cleared her throat, blinking back a sudden rise of tears. Determinedly she smiled at her friend then let her eyes scan the ballroom. "With such a squeeze I just noticed that Robbie is not here. Where on earth can he be?"

There was no immediate answer to her question for the music was starting and her first partner came to claim her. She smiled with pleasure as they took the floor, for she loved the graceful movements and pattern of steps to each dance. Giving herself up to the expertise of her partner and the rhythm of the music, she thought about Robert Worthington.

Robbie had been one of her father's pupils. He lived only two miles away, so Gillian had known him all her life. She had always treated him with the most casual good humor, never thinking of him as anything but a friend. It was about a year ago that she first realized he was singling her out, making a point to speak to her at every social event. She knew he was waiting for some sign that she returned his affection, but for the longest time she had been unable to give it.

It was true when she told Nelda that Chad's engagement had come as a shock. She had been depressed from the moment she had heard the news. She supposed it was the sudden realization that her childhood was coming to an end. It was time to consider how she wanted to spend the remainder of her life. Much as she loved life with her father, she wanted a home of her own and children. For that she would have to marry.

The week after she had made such a momentous decision, Robbie called to pay a visit. The day was warm and they walked in the woods, cooled by the shading canopy of trees. They talked easily, as old friends. She noted Robbie's good-natured face and gentleness of manner. He had the ruddy complexion of a farmer and mischievous blue eyes. Best of all, he was at least a quarter of an inch taller than she. By the end of the walk, Gillian had given him to understand that she would not be against getting to know him better.

"I understand, young lady, that this is my dance."

Ethan's voice brought Gillian out of her reverie and she smiled a welcome as she heard the first strains of the waltz.

"Is it only because Robbie is not here that I am so honored?" he asked as he led her out onto the floor.

"Not at all, Papa," she cried. "It is a genuine pleasure to be so well partnered."

It was true. She was comfortable dancing with her father, for he had taught her all the steps. She remembered Miss Pennington playing the harpsicord while her father swirled her around the drawing room until they both were breathless.

"I assume Robbie will be here later." Gillian nodded and Ethan noted the blush on her cheeks. "No need to color up. He is a good lad. Perhaps not an intellectual giant, but not a dunderhead either. You could do worse."

"There is nothing for it, Papa. I would be at my last prayers if I waited for a man with your wisdom and learning."

A laugh rumbled in his chest. "True, my dear. But do not attempt to turn the subject by appealing to my pride. Robbie is a likeable young man. He has an honest heart and I see no meanness in his temperament. He has the advantage of being an only son. He will inherit a prime estate, close on to the area

where you've been raised. You would not have to give up family
and friends if you married thus. It would seem that the young
man is smitten. Do you return his affection?"

"He is a great friend of mine," she temporized.

"That's a good start, daughter. I would never consider giving
my permission to a match if there was not liking between you.
But is there more?"

"I-I'm not sure." She sighed and rested her head against his
shoulder, giving herself up to the movement of the dance.
"Before I came this evening, I thought I knew the answer to that
question. How can I know if I am making the right decision?"

Gillian stared up into her father's face, hoping to find some
clue in his expression. There was the gentlest of smiles on his
lips and the skin at the corners of his eyes crinkled with
amusement.

"It would be very easy to advise you, dear child," he said. "If
I did not have the greatest confidence in your judgment, I would
be tempted to guide you to what I think is the proper decision.
However, it is you who will have to live with the consequences
of your actions. When the time comes to give an answer, listen
to your heart."

Ethan returned her to Nelda's side and, after talking to both
girls for several minutes, he excused himself.

"Have you ladies saved me a dance?"

Gillian jumped at Robbie's voice so close to her ear. She
turned to him with a cry of exasperation. "You will frighten us
both to death, Mr. Worthington," she snapped.

"Fustian!" Giving her a look of disdain, he automatically
reached up to smooth the cowlick that threatened to break
through the control of his pomade. Not only was his hair the
color of wheat, it was almost as unmanageable. "You are no
simpering maiden, Miss Foster, subject to the vapors. Perhaps
Nelda here has sensibilities, but you are made of sterner stuff."

"Fiddlesticks!" She snapped her fan shut and slapped him on
the wrist before he could say anything more.

"Now what are you going on about, Gillian?" His tone was
aggrieved. "You are probably angry because I am late. I realize
I have missed the opening sets, but Nelda's father assures me the
musicians will continue late into the evening. Don't be cross.
My horse had a fall and injured his leg. I had to leave him at the
inn in the village. Despite my lateness, I hope you've saved me

a dance." He turned to include Nelda, who had remained silent throughout their wordplay. "Darling Nelda, intercede for me with Gillian and I shall sign any blank spots on your dance card. I am expert at the country dances, but I must admit my waltzing is considered far superior to most."

"There is nothing I can say to Gillian that you have not already announced," Nelda said. "But do sign my card, for I see Oliver Lancet coming to claim me."

With much good humor, Robbie signed her dance card then turned to take Gillian's. "What luck, my girl! You are free now. You must have saved this for me for I know you could fill your entire card without my assistance. Even though you love to dance, I'd much prefer to sit this one out. Couldn't we find a quiet corner? I would like to speak with you."

Gillian's heart lurched at his words. Could he be intending to make her an offer tonight? She was not prepared to give him an answer. She glanced sideways, catching the frown on his face as he scanned the room for a place to sit. In a flash, she realized he did not plan to swift her off to some empty room. If she hadn't panicked like some ninnyhammer, she would have known that he was much too proper to ask for her hand without first speaking to her father.

"There's a settee in that small bay. I suppose it's unoccupied because it's so close to the chaperons." Taking his hand, she led him around the periphery of the room. The alcove turned out to be nicer than it had first appeared. A profusion of plants from the squire's hothouses lent an air of seclusion that did much to appease Robbie.

"Not bad by half, Gillian. And right under the noses of the gossiping old biddies."

He handed her into a corner of the gold damask settee, then lowered himself, perching on the edge of the cushion as if ready for flight. Although Gillian was convinced he would not propose, she worried that he might declare his undying affection or something equally embarrassing. For once she could think of nothing to say. Her brain was numb. She cast about for a neutral subject, settling on horses as the least dangerous of topics.

"How is Pelligren's leg?" In the aftermath of such a sparkling conversational gambit, a bubble of amusement threatened to send Gillian into whoops of laughter.

"Pelligren?" It was evident that Robbie's mind was not focused.

"Yes, Pelligren. Your horse," she added for clarification. "You said you had to leave him at the inn."

"Oh, my horse. He's better. Had a bad fall and hurt his leg."

"Will there be any permanent damage?"

"To the horse?"

"Yes, to the horse." She giggled at his total inability to concentrate. "Who did you think I meant?"

"Well, I don't know, to be sure. You're the one asking the stupid questions. I don't want to talk about horses."

Gillian immediately felt guilty for finding amusement in his inattention. She knew why he was nervous, and she hoped he would not think she was making fun of him. "I'm sorry, Robbie. I should have asked you what you wanted to talk about."

"I want to talk about me. I mean us." He stopped, took a deep breath, then plunged ahead. "I'm going to London tomorrow on business. I'll be gone several days. When I return, I'd like to come for a visit. I would like to speak to your father, unless you feel that it would be presumptuous of me."

The words burst from Robbie's lips as if they had been rehearsed until he could say them automatically. She took note of the tightly clenched hands and the pained expression on his face. She hesitated. She liked Robbie very well, but did she want to marry him? Did she want him to speak to Papa? She remembered her father's words: when the question was asked, she would know the answer.

"It would not be presumptuous of you to speak to Papa," she said.

Her voice was so low that Robbie had to lean forward to hear her words. His face was so close that she could see the light of happiness that glowed in his eyes at her response. Perhaps in another setting he would have kissed her, but in the crowded ballroom, he could only reach across and squeeze her hand.

Gillian had not realized how nervous she had been at the beginning of the evening. Once her talk with Robbie was concluded, she was able to throw herself into a full enjoyment of the party. She had always loved dancing, and she had a bevy of partners who were more than willing to exhaust themselves on the dance floor. It was after a particularly vigorous country dance that Gillian decided to treat herself to a solitary respite.

She found a spot where she might see without being seen and, behind a screen of potted palms, she eased her much-abused feet out of her slippers.

Keeping a wary eye out for the ever-observant Penny, Gillian spotted her father and the squire just returning from the buffet table. Deep in conversation, the two men stopped, oblivious to the fact they were totally blocking the doorway. Gillian watched the rainbow of figures twirling around the dance floor, wriggling her toes in time to the waltz.

In a soft blur of satin, Nelda glided by in Robbie's arms. A golden ringlet lay against the girl's flushed cheek and Gillian thought her friend had never looked so fetching. She wondered why Nelda had not accepted any offers. She was well dowered, although even without it, Gillian suspected, her friend's sweet disposition and beauty would have drawn suitors from near and far. Nelda was popular but she treated everyone equally, never showing a preference for any of the young gentlemen who flocked to her side.

The music ended and Nelda dropped into a formal curtsy as Robbie bent over her hand. He raised her up and led her off the floor, seating her in one of the gilt chairs along the wall. Gillian smiled at Robbie's courtly manner as he bowed once more before turning away.

If Gillian had not been observing them, she might have missed Nelda's reaction to Robbie's departure. The girl's features contracted as if she were in the grip of intense pain. In an instant, her countenance cleared and a lovely smile appeared to give Nelda an air of quiet serenity. Gillian blinked. It had been such a fleeting change of expression, that for a moment she thought it might have been a trick of the light. With a sinking sensation in the pit of her stomach, Gillian recognized the flash of emotion she had seen in Nelda's eyes. Her best friend was in love with Robbie Worthington.

For a long time Gillian sat behind the potted palms until she was able to rejoin the party. When she said her goodnights, she schooled her expression so that Nelda would never know that her secret had been discovered. Only in the security of her darkened bedroom did Gillian shed a tear over the knowledge that she might lose Nelda's friendship when she married Robbie.

The next morning she slept late, talking little at the breakfast table. By late afternoon she was totally out of sorts. She read for a while and finally began to work on a new stitch for her sampler under Penny's critical eye. She did not have much enthusiasm for the work, so she was delighted when she heard the sound of a carriage arriving. From the window she watched as a hackney horses lathered from an extensive trip, stopped at their door. Her father let in the visitor and led him down the hall toward the library. After a few minutes, her father returned and opened the doors of the drawing room.

"Begging your pardon, Miss Pennington," Ethan said. "There is a gentleman here to see you."

He crossed the carpet and presented her with a calling card. Penny took it gingerly in her long fingers, tilting it toward the light. By the blankness of her expression it was apparent she did not recognize the name.

"Eldridge Thackery is a solicitor," Ethan explained. "He has come from London expressly to see you on a matter of business."

For the first time since Gillian had known Penny, the older woman appeared flustered. "What do you suppose it is about?"

Ethan smiled. "Mr. Thackery is a very proper gentleman and refused to give me any hint of the intelligence he wishes to impart. No matter what the information, however, I feel certain you will be able to deal with it. You are a woman with more sense than most men I know."

Penny blinked at the enthusiastic compliment of her employer. Her mouth twitched in amusement and her confident manner returned. "Thank you, Professor Foster."

"I have left Mr. Thackery in the library," he said, escorting the governess to the foyer. "If I can be of any service, I will be here trying to keep Gillian from listening at the door."

"Papa!" Gillian cried, glaring at him in reproach.

"No need to look at me so, poppet," he said, winking at her. "We will hear Miss Pennington's news in good time."

Although Ethan feigned indifference, Gillian noticed that he never turned the pages of the book he was reading. She held her sampler, but her mind was occupied with so much curiosity that she could not concentrate enough to sew. For almost five years, Penny had received no mail or visitors; she had never gone away to visit anyone. It was as if the woman had no family or past life. What did the arrival of the solicitor signify?

It was an age before the library door opened. Footsteps

sounded down the hall and Gillian caught a glimpse of a dapper little man who gravely shook Penny's hand before he left the house. When the older woman turned toward the drawing room, her face was so pale that Gillian cried out.

"Quickly, Papa, some brandy."

Gillian helped Penny to a seat by the fire, rubbing her cold hands until Ethan returned with a decanter and glasses. He poured the liquor, handing one to the governess and raising another to his own lips. Penny took a sip of the amber liquid. She gasped for breath but the color returned to her cheeks.

"Well done," she said. "That was just what I needed."

"Was it dreadful news?" Gillian asked.

"In actual fact, no." Penny shook her head as if she were having trouble coming to terms with the information she had just received. "Mr. Thackery informed me that a relative I did not know has died and left me a veritable fortune."

"Never say!" Gillian cried.

"What excellent news, Miss Pennington," Ethan said. He raised his glass in a salute.

"Mr. Thackery was my great aunt's solicitor. He is a dash older than I, and at first acquaintance appears to be totally devoid of humor. I do not know how well we shall deal together, since my every comment appeared to offend him. He was clearly expecting tears not laughter at such good fortune."

"What now, Miss Pennington?"

"The worthy solicitor has informed me that I have inherited an estate called Fieldings in some quiet village two days from here." Her imperturbable tone could not hide the fact that Penny was very well pleased.

"You will be leaving us?" Gillian wailed. She was ashamed of the tears that filled her eyes at the thought of her friend and companion's departure. "Oh, Penny, what a selfish beast I am! Please know that I am thrilled for you, but I am desolated at the thought of how much I will miss you."

Miss Pennington opened her arms and Gillian did not hesitate to accept the embrace. Over the last five years a loving relationship had been forged between the two of them. They cried for the imminence of their parting and the possible loss of their friendship. Even Ethan had to clear his throat several times before he could congratulate Miss Pennington anew on her good fortune. Eventually order was restored.

"Now, Gillian, knowing what a lively imagination you have, I fear this revelation will come as a bitter disappointment. There was nothing dramatic, sad, or mysterious about my becoming a governess." Penny smiled at the chagrined expression on her pupil's face. "I know that for years you have speculated over the romantic disasters that might have forced me into such a life. The reality of it is that I like children and I always wanted to be a teacher. When my parents died, I had no responsibilities except to myself. I decided to go out as a governess and see how I liked it. You and your father made my first post very enjoyable indeed."

Gillian was so fond of Penny that she was delighted to learn that her friend had not become a governess out of unhappiness. She had imagined such dire scenarios in her younger days that the very conventionality of Miss Pennington's wanting to be a teacher would have been a dreadful let down.

Penny took another sip of brandy and continued speaking. "All my life I have dreamed of opening a school, but of course I did not have the resources. Now I do. I am going to see if my new estate would be suitable for such a venture. If not, I will sell it and find something that is. The redoubtable Mr. Thackery will return to escort me to Fieldings. I know it is dreadfully short notice, but I would like to leave in three days time."

"So soon?" Gillian cried, tears threatening once more.

"If I were needed I would remain, but you have no need of a governess. And if I am correct in my assumptions, very soon after Robbie returns, you will not have any need of my services. At my age, child, there are not endless years ahead."

Once it was decided that Miss Pennington would be leaving, there were numerous details to consider. The next day sped by in a flurry of activity, but by teatime of the second day the frenzy had abated.

"How is your packing coming, Miss Pennington?" Ethan asked as he took a sip of tea.

"Most of my boxes are filled. It is strange how much one can accumulate in five years. I trust Mr. Thackery will have enough room for my things. He is already put out at my lack of propriety." She rolled her gray eyes in amusement. "He was most horrified when he discovered I would not be accompanied by an abigail. We will be two days on the road. I think he fears his reputation will be in tatters."

Both Gillian and Ethan burst into laughter.

"He could always bring his valet along for protection," Gillian suggested.

"Speaking of valets," Ethan said. "I ran into Chad's man Royce in the village. He told me the earl arrived at first light."

"Chad is home?" Gillian asked in surprise. "Why ever has he returned so close to Christmas? What do you think it means? Did he bring Lady Chesterley?"

"So many questions. I only wish I had the answers." Ethan's hand hovered over the pastries, trying to choose between the plum and the cherry filling. He decided on the plum, took a bite, and chewed with deliberation. His eyes twinkled at the impatience written clearly on his daughter's face. Patting his mouth with the linen napkin, he took a sip of tea before continuing. "All I know is that the earl came alone save for Royce. Though Chad's man was loathe to be caught gossiping, he did confide the fact that the trip was quite sudden. He also stated that Chad's fiancée would not be joining him. On my return from the village, I left my card at Maynard Hall with a note bidding him welcome."

"Do you think Chad will call, Penny?" Gillian asked wistfully.

The older woman glanced across at Ethan, seeing in his compassionate gaze a confirmation of her own suspicions. She sighed and patted Gillian's hand. "I don't know," she said. "We don't even know what has brought him home, quite unannounced. For the moment, you need something to occupy your time, young lady. There are books to be packed and some notes to be written, if you have a mind to help me."

"Of course, I will."

Gillian's voice was less than enthusiastic, but Penny pretended not to notice. "Excellent. After all, I would not want to keep the proper Mr. Thackery waiting. It is too bad that we will be gone before Robbie returns from London. That young man would find much enjoyment in meeting the little solicitor, would he not?"

Thus reminded of her suitor's impending arrival, melancholy settled around Gillian. She had spent the time while Robbie was away trying to decide what answer to give him. She had even gone so far as to list his virtues and his failings on a sheet of paper. The fact that his good points far outweighed the bad could be taken as a positive sign. Each night before she went to sleep, she reviewed her findings and made a decision. Unfortunately, it was never the same answer two days in a row.

Perhaps Penny was right. If she kept busy she would have less time to worry. With the firm resolution to banish all troubling thoughts from her mind, she rose to help clear away the tea things.

It seemed to Gillian that she did not have a moment of free time until she was ready for bed. Penny had kept her running most of the evening, and even her father had chores for her to do. She shivered as she slipped the linen nightrail over her head. It was cold in the room, but she opened the draperies so that she would watch the falling snow—the flakes a sharp white in contrast to the blackness of the night sky. Standing in front of the window, she glimpsed the lights of Maynard Hall, visible through the leafless trees.

Why had Chad come home?

She snuggled under the comforter, and as the warmth seeped into her body, she dozed, drifting in and out of a dream where she accepted Robbie's offer of marriage. The wedding was in the drawing room. Her father leaned against the mantelpiece, smiling proudly. Her bridal dress was beautiful, and she twirled to show off the lace medallions on the skirt. She raised her head, but above the bride's dress it was Nelda's blue eyes and golden curls that wavered and melted into the darkness.

Gillian came awake with a start. Her mind was fuzzy, still caught on the edge of the troubling dream, not yet fully returned to the reality of the moonlit bedroom. Something hit the window with a sharp ping and she jerked upright. For a moment she heard nothing, and then it happened again. Identifying the sound, she was not afraid. Someone was throwing stones at the window.

In a twinkling she was out of bed and across the room. She rubbed at the frost coating the glass until she had cleared a small patch. The snow had stopped and she could see a man, dark against the whiteness of the ground. She unlatched the window, sucking in her breath at the icy blast of wind. The figure moved and she recognized Chad.

"I'm coming," she whispered.

She closed the window, clenching her teeth to keep them from chattering. She slipped her arms into her dressing gown but did not take time to locate her slippers. Quietly she slipped out of her room, gliding soundlessly past her father's door. She wondered what time it was and, as if in answer to her question, the clock in the drawing room chimed two.

Guided by the light from the upstairs hall window, she found the walnut handrail and followed it downward into the darkness of the foyer. Sliding back the bolt, she pulled open the heavy front door. Chad quietly crossed the threshold and then helped her close the door. They tiptoed into the drawing room and closed the pocket panels so they would not disturb the rest of the household.

Without a word Chad handed Gillian into the overstuffed chair close to the hearth. She curled her feet close to her body and tucked the dressing gown around her for additional warmth. Noting the shivers that shook her body, Chad reached for the poker and stirred up the banked fire. He placed a small log on the embers, kneeling down to blow them into life. In the flickering glow, his face was all light and shadow, almost haggard. His eyes, hidden in dark pockets, gave him an air of menace that would have frightened Gillian if she did not know him so well.

"I probably shouldn't have come," he said.

"I'm glad you did."

There was something wrong. She heard a whisper of pain in the deep rumble of his voice. If they had still been children she would have asked what troubled him, but he was a man now and there was distance between them. They had lost their ease of communication.

He was twenty-three, she thought with some amazement. His life was in London now, and in the last five years she had not seen much of him. She wished the light was better so that she could see him more clearly. From what she could tell he was very tall and well proportioned. He had lost the soft prettiness of his youth. His face was unlined, and there was an elegance and refinement of features that marked him as an aristocrat.

"Tomorrow, or more properly, today," he amended as he glanced ruefully at the clock, "I will be leaving."

"Back to London?"

There was the slightest hesitation before he answered. "Yes. And from there I cannot say. I have bought a commission."

"I see," she said, although she was shocked at his words.

"Have you no questions?" He crossed to her chair, glaring

down at her. His face was harshly shadowed and there was an air of controlled violence in his stiffly held body. "Where is your facile tongue? Is there nothing you would ask?"

His tone was cutting but she did not flinch, keeping her eyes steady on his face. "No," she answered. She wanted so much to ease the hurt that was so clearly manifest in his voice. "Would it help to tell me?"

For a moment she thought he had not heard. He whirled to face the fire, then, as if he had made a decision, he flung himself down on the carpet in front of her. He eased his back against her chair and tipped his head back until it was resting on her knees.

She touched his hair, surprised at the softness of the black curls. She did not speak. Her fingers were gentle, lightly stroking his tense forehead. Like the ebbing of the tide, she could feel the tension draining away until his brow was smooth beneath her fingertips.

"You will hear eventually that Lady Chesterley has broken our engagement and that in despair I have joined the army. In part it is true. I do feel as if I were inconsolable."

Chad spoke without facing her, his eyes intent on the flickering blaze, his voice detached, almost indifferent.

"I have been away a great deal in the last several months. My other estates are not as well run as Maynard. I had heard rumors about Edwina's conduct in my absence, but I refused to give them much credence."

He laughed, the sound jarring in the soft glow of the firelit room. In the hush that followed, Gillian remained silent. The fingers of one hand stroked his temple and the other rested on his shoulder to remind him of her presence.

"Last week Roger Hornsby invited me up to his shooting box for several days of hunting. The second day the weather turned foul and we decided to give it up. I was anxious to return to London. Edwina had been put out that I would be missing a masquerade party. It was well into the evening when I returned. Stopping only long enough to change clothes and locate my domino, I left for the party."

"You do not need to tell me more," Gillian said, moving restlessly. At her words his body jerked and beneath her fingers his muscles tensed. Despite her reluctance to hear any more, she said, "Unless in the telling you will find some ease."

"Ah, Gillian, what a friend you are. I will give you no details that would offend your innocence." He leaned back against her, and she could feel him relaxing again.

"The man hosting the party was no particular friend of mine. Although nothing has ever been proved against him, there have always been rumors of his depravity. Edwina was frequently in his company and, when I cautioned her, said she found him amusing. I did not pursue it." He paused as if considering his own guilt in the matter. After a few minutes, he continued. "It was very late when I arrived, and I could not find Edwina. The party was very lively and had spread through the lower floor of the house. When I could not locate her below, I went upstairs to the private rooms."

Gillian closed her eyes, envisioning the scene, less from what he said than what he left unsaid. There was disillusionment and betrayal in his voice, and she wished she could take the hurt away as she had done when Chad was a boy. The ache of bumps and scraps were easily soothed away in the child, but the painful scars of the grown man were beyond her ability to heal.

"The proper Lady Edwina Chesterley was in a card room with the host and several of his friends. She was dancing on the table wearing only her shift. They were gaming for her favors, and although they did offer me a chance to enter the lists, I chose to absent myself. I called on her the next day and gave her the honor of breaking the engagement."

There was silence when he finished. Gillian did not insult him by offering sympathy. He reached up to touch her hand, and their fingers entwined. They remained thus, taking solace from each other until the fire began to burn low again. Moving stiffly, Chad stood up, turning to stare down at Gillian.

"You will catch a dreadful chill if you remain here." As she thrust her feet out from under her nightgown, he muttered. "Bare feet. Egads, Gillian, whatever are you about? Here."

Before she could protest, he reached down and scooped her up into his arms. She had always felt awkward about her height, but he made her feel like a veritable lightweight. He lowered her enough so that she could slide back the pocket doors. Once on the thick carpet of the foyer, he set her down. Gillian was used to being taller than most men she knew, so it was a surprise to discover that she only came up to Chad's chin.

"I'm sorry if my words have troubled you," he whispered. "I have missed you, and I could not leave without seeing you."

His eyes moved over her face, taken aback at how much she had changed. She was no longer a child. He had heard Robbie Worthington wanted to marry her, and he was pleased that she would make such a good match. Even in the moonlight he could see that he had not been mistaken all those years ago. She was on the brink of womanhood, her innocence and innate goodness shining with the brightness of the virgin snow outside. He wished that he could see her when she finally blossomed. He knew her well, and there was passion lying dormant within her.

"Keep me in your thoughts," he said.

"I will. And in my prayers."

She could not bear to see him leave. Her hands pulled at the lapels of his coat. She was grateful for the darkness that hid her blushing cheeks. Feeling like the most brazen of hussies, she raised her eyes to the kissing bough and waited.

Thankfully, Chad had never been a slowtop. He bent his head, covering her mouth with his own in a kiss of such tenderness that Gillian thought her heart might break. It was goodbye and she forced herself to let him go, although she knew that in his present state she could have held him.

And then he was gone.

The cold air that swirled around her ankles sent shivers up her spine. Her skin absorbed the chill until her entire body was frozen, and she wondered if warmth would ever again penetrate the empty corners of her heart.

"Come along, sweetheart."

"Papa, Chad was here."

"I know, dear. I heard him."

Ethan half-carried Gillian upstairs, removed her dressing gown, and tucked her beneath the comforter. He sat on the edge of the bed, holding her hand until the enveloping warmth eased the tremors of her body. In the stark moonlight, there was a stunned expression in her eyes.

"I didn't realize I loved him," she whispered.

"Does he love you?"

"No. He is the earl and I am only a friend from his childhood." There was no self-pity in her voice. She was far too practical for that.

"Robbie will be home in two days time," Ethan reminded her.

"I know. I dread hurting him, but I would not make him happy, Papa."

"You have always made me happy, daughter. And very proud."

Ethan rose and leaned over to kiss her on the forehead. He opened the door into the hall, then turned to the silent figure on the bed. "Perhaps you might remind Robbie of Nelda's attractions." At the gasp of surprise from his daughter, Ethan chuckled. "I may be old, child, but I am not blind."

Gillian made a sound that was halfway between a gurgle of laughter and a sob. "Good night, Papa. I love you."

※

The Fourth Kiss

"DON'T TELL ME you are breeding again," Gillian cried when Nelda had removed her fur cape. "How perfectly wonderful!"

"It is, isn't it?" Nelda folded her hands complacently atop the magnificent bulge at her waistline and smiled beatifically. "It's something I seem to be particularly good at. Three children in less then three years should gain me some sort of award. My darling husband is strutting through London, quite the cock of the walk."

"Well, if Robbie gets too full of himself just remind him that if he hadn't been so slow in offering for you he could have had four by now." Gillian hugged her friend and led her over to the silver-and-blue striped sofa in the drawing room.

Nelda shook her head. "I'd better not sit there. It looks entirely too soft and you will have to call for help to pry me out of the cushions. Here would be better." Once she was settled comfortably in the armchair, she looked across the tea table, her face set in somber lines. "My dearest friend, I cannot tell you how distressed I was not to be here when your father passed away. It was such a shock when I received your letter."

"Never fear, Nelda. I know full well how fond you were of Papa. It was very sudden. He did not seem to be ill, but he just kept getting frailer. Then one morning I found him in the library. I thought he had fallen asleep reading, but when I touched his shoulder I knew he was gone."

At her words, tears rose in Nelda's eyes, overflowing and

running down her cheeks. It was Gillian who found the hand-kerchief in her reticule.

"When I'm increasing, I am a veritable watering pot," Nelda said, dabbing at her eyes with the scrap of lace. "Pray, forgive me. It is I who should be comforting you."

"In the last two months, I have cried enough tears. I'm only glad that you've returned in time for Christmas. I was not looking forward to it this year." Gillian crossed to the bellpull. "Can you stay for tea?"

"My dear, I live for teatime," Nelda drawled, patting her stomach. "And lunchtime. And suppertime."

"How are the children?"

"Little Rob is a hellion and naturally the pride of his father. Olivia is absolutely exquisite. Even though I risk your thinking I am biased, I tell you she is the sweetest, most adorable child in the world. You will love her."

Gillian beamed across at her friend. It had been apparent from the moment of their marriage that both Nelda and Robbie were supremely happy. It was a pleasure to be in their company, because their joy in each other spilled out to enliven every occasion. For Gillian it had been that much more special since she had kept them as friends.

"I fear you will find us all deadly dull," Gillian said. "Your children will keep you from getting bored now that you are away from the excitements of London."

"Piffle!" Nelda said. "London can be boring. No wonder there is so much gossip. We always see the same people and go to the same balls and such. Any news helps to break up the monotony of the days."

"Well, I look forward to you filling me in on all the *on dits*. I am sadly behind in all the social news. I have not been to London in three years."

"And why not, may I ask? It's not as if you hadn't enough invitations." Nelda glared across at her friend. "Both Robbie and I have begged you to come, but you always fob us off with some shabby excuse."

Gillian laughed. "I was in London the year after you married, but after I had my surfeit of the theatre it began to pall. Ah, here is our tea. Thank you, Maddie."

The servant girl placed the silver tray in front of Gillian then busied herself setting out the napkins and silver. Nelda licked her lips in anticipation as she eyed the plate of sandwiches and pastries.

"The other day Robbie asked if I were going to have a pony," she said as she reached for a cucumber sandwich. "I am considerably bigger than I was with Olivia."

"Maybe it'll be twins," Gillian teased as she poured out the tea.

"Bite your tongue. With my luck it would be male twins. And believe me, my dear, boy children are a handful."

They chattered easily while they ate. After hearing all the local gossip, Nelda asked about Miss Pennington.

"She was terribly fond of Papa and quite devastated by the news of his death. We correspond regularly. In fact, I just received a letter from her." Gillian poured another cup of tea. "The school has been a great success. She started small; the first year there were only four girls, but this year there are twelve. She has tailored the entire curriculum not only to educate the young women but, more to the point, to teach them a trade. You know how Penny always lectured us on the fact that we should not depend on a man for our happiness. Now she is planning to turn out a whole corps of women who have learned to be independent."

"How revolutionary." Nelda pursed her mouth into a moue of distaste. "I am not at all sure that I approve of such ideas, although I can see by the shine of your eyes you are in full agreement."

"Yes, but then I had a very irregular upbringing. Papa himself gave me a copy of Mary Wollstonecraft's *Vindication of the Rights of Woman*." Gillian laughed at her friend's expression. "No need to look so appalled, Nelda. You are one of the lucky women who has a husband who respects and adores you. Your value in Robbie's eyes is not solely because you are a good breeder. He knows you have intelligence, and he encourages you to think for yourself. How extraordinary it is that so few men treat women this way."

"Well, I suppose you are correct that Robbie does bring out the best in me. I have seen other men who are constantly belittling their wives until the poor things become nothing more than a weak echo of their husbands. My apologies for appearing critical." Nelda's expression lightened. "Please give Penny my fondest greetings when you write her again."

Gillian wiped her fingers on her napkin. "In actual fact, I may be seeing her after Christmas. She invited me north for a visit, and I have been debating whether or not to go."

"I know that sidelong expression, Gillian Foster. There's more to the story than just a simple visit. I'm right, aren't I?"

"No need to act so smug. There is more, but at this point I haven't made any decision yet."

"Give over, do. I am fast losing patience!"

"No need to bully me," Gillian said. "Penny asked me to join her as one of the teaching staff. She thinks I need something to do now that Papa is gone. It is a relatively tempting offer."

"Don't be a looby!" Nelda said inelegantly. "You would traipse off to the north of England to teach a packet of runny-nosed girls how to get on in life? I begin to wonder sometimes if you have more hair than wit. You are missing Ethan and feeling downhearted at the thought of Christmas without him. By all rights I should bundle you up and take you home, but I know how stubborn you are. You would sneak out a window and walk back here."

"Ah, Nelda, how I have missed you," Gillian said, smiling warmly at her friend, who was trying desperately to maintain a vexed expression on her face.

"Just promise me you won't do anything until after Christmas. I would not want my dinner ruined."

"Heaven forfend that you should miss a meal!"

Gillian stared pointedly at her friend's girth. Nelda was just opening her mouth to reply when she caught the joke. Her blue eyes widened and she let out a great whoop of laughter. Gillian joined in, and they laughed until they were both breathless. It immediately returned the conversation to a lighter plane. Finally it was time for Nelda to leave. She had started to rise, when she clapped a hand to her forehead and dropped back into her chair.

"I almost forgot to tell you the most wondrous news. Robbie saw Chad last week."

"Chad is in London?" Gillian's heart was beating so heavily she could feel it in her throat. For a moment she could barely breathe. "Is he well?"

"Yes, except for a small scar near his temple. He was wounded at Waterloo, and I gather it took forever for him to get back to England. Some sort of mix-up. At any rate, Robbie said he looked pale but reasonably healthy. He's grown a beard."

"What kind?" was all Gillian could think to ask.

"Robbie didn't say. He was too busy giving the man news of our family. Chad didn't even know that Robbie had married me. Can you imagine, for all the time we have spent in London, this is the first that either of us have seen him." Nelda frowned across at Gillian. "We have heard much about him, and none of it good. When Chad was not off somewhere saving the empire, he was cutting a swath of devastation through the female population in London. I heard the whole corps de ballet went into hysterics on hearing he had been wounded."

Gillian had also heard rumors of Chad's conduct. Women, gaming, horse racing, and even violent behavior. She had never known how much to believe of what she heard. Eventually she had decided to close her ears and her mind to the gossip. She would think of him as she had last seen him. It was not that she doubted his ability for wickedness, it was only that she did not choose to dwell on it. If it were true, she hoped that the core of morality that was so much a part of Chad would eventually surface. She would have to pray that it would happen before he gave himself up to depravity.

"Is he coming home to Maynard?" Gillian asked.

Nelda didn't know and since the hour was getting late, they made their goodbyes. After her friend had gone, Gillian sat for a long time in the drawing room, thinking over all the news that they had shared. She was restless for the majority of the evening. She could not find a book that would hold her attention. She knew she did not have the concentration to work on her stitching. The night closed in and the drawing room grew cold. At midnight, she banked the fire, picked up her candle, and started up the stairs.

At the quiet knock on the front door, she stopped. Her skin tingled with presentiment and it took all her control not to dash down the stairs. For one moment she debated not answering the summons, but there was an inevitability to the repeated knocks on the oak panel.

It was Christmas again, and if her guess was correct, Chad had returned.

Her pulse beat in her throat and she tried to compose herself. She could hear the wind howling outside, and she placed the candle beneath a glass dome to protect the flame. Her hands

shook as she drew back the bolt. A cloud of snow billowed
through the opening, and when it cleared, she saw him.

How different he was, she thought. She could find only a
shadow of her childhood friend in the devastatingly handsome
man who entered. There were deep lines etched on either side of
a patrician nose and wrinkles radiated from the corners of his
eyes. His face was thin, and even in the flickering candlelight
she could see the pallor beneath his skin.

There was snow in his black hair, reflecting the strands of gray
at his temples. She liked the beard, which was neatly trimmed,
only covering his upper lip and his chin. The dark hair framed
his mouth, accentuating the generously sculpted lips and drawing her eyes like a magnet. The last time they had stood beneath
the mistletoe, he had kissed her. Her lips tingled in remembrance.

"I saw your light and I couldn't wait until morning. Robbie
told me about your father. I'm so sorry, my dear."

The compassion in his voice broke through Gillian's hard-won
self-possession. Tears filled her eyes, overflowing and spilling
down her cheeks. He pulled her into his arms, fitting her against
his body as if she belonged there. His voice was gentle as he
whispered words she could not hear for the sobs that wracked her
body.

The storm of weeping passed and she lifted her face. He stared
down at her, a smile of bemusement playing across his face. His
dark eyes sparked with an intensity that she did not understand,
almost as if he were seeing her for the first time. He brushed the
tumbled curls off her forehead and kissed her temples. Her skin
was sensitive to the silken brush of his beard and the firm texture
of his lips. She closed her eyes and relaxed as his fingers moved
to massage the back of her neck. He kissed her eyelids and her
cheeks. His lips touched hers in the tenderest of caresses.

She released her breath in a deep sigh of contentment. He
kissed the corners of her mouth—sweet, feathery kisses. Excitement raced through Gillian's body and she felt as if she were
going to swoon. Her heart throbbed in rhythm to the movement
of his mouth. A tension built within her as he repeated the
pattern, his lips blazing a trail of fire. Forehead. Eyelids.
Cheeks.

When he finally kissed her lips, she was jolted by the flood of
sensations that shot through her. The last time he kissed her, she

had tried to envision what it would be like to have Chad make love to her. She had wanted him to see her as a woman grown, and she had wanted his caresses with all of her heart. She had longed for him in the dark nights of her soul. Abandoning all reason, she gave in to the pleasure.

Her muscles relaxed and she pressed against him, the line of their bodies blending and flowing together. She moaned as his kiss deepened, but his mouth was different now. His lips, which had before coaxed a response from her, now demanded one. His hands moved over her body with a familiarity that was almost an insult. Suddenly aware of the inappropriateness of their embrace, she struggled to free herself.

Chad resisted her efforts to break away. For a moment Gillian feared he would not set her free, and she could not hold back a small cry. Although her physical struggles had not penetrated the passion that consumed him, he stiffened at the sound of her distress. With a muttered oath, he released her.

Gillian remained in place, her head bent, trying to control her rapid breathing and the agitated beating of her heart. Her face burned and she still could feel the imprint of Chad's hands and lips on her body as if he had forever marked her.

"Look at me, Gillian." Chad's voice was commanding, and she raised her head in obedience. He towered above her, staring down at her in silence. His eyes were dense pools of dark brown, unreadable in the shimmering pattern of light and dark that played across his face. "I did not mean to frighten or offend you. My experience has been with women of a different breed. You are an innocent and will need time to adjust to my loving you."

His eyes rose to the kissing bough. He shrugged in frustration and with a swirl of capes moved to open the front door, striding out into the frigid night.

"I will return," he said.

Gillian quickly bolted the door as if she could hold back the devil. She pressed her hot forehead to the icy oaken panels and listened to the echo of Chad's voice in her mind, the words more threat than promise.

❄

The Fifth Kiss

THE CLOCK IN the drawing room chimed eight. Gillian could not believe that she had been sitting on the stairs for two hours. When she stood up, she became uncomfortably aware of the aching stiffness of her body. The chill of the night had crept into her bones as her mind floated back through time to review her relationship with Chad.

Last night he had said he would return, and she knew he would come tonight.

She descended the stairs, smiling at the mistletoe caught in the flickering light of the hall candle. She was glad she had hung the kissing bough. Though strictly speaking it was not considered appropriate in a house of mourning, she knew her father would have been cross with her for neglecting tradition. Papa had loved the Christmas season, reveling in the feelings of joy and rebirth. Tonight she felt very close to her memories.

In the drawing room she set more logs on the fire and moved around the room, lighting the wall sconces and the candelabra on the harpsichord. She wanted no darkness to add to the sadness that threatened to engulf her. In the morning she would be leaving for the north to become a teacher at Miss Pennington's school. She knew she was running away and was ashamed of her cowardice. There was no alternative. Chad was a fire in her blood, and if she stayed she would succumb to his gentle seduction.

Chad was the Earl of Elmore, and eventually he would marry a titled lady who would give him the heirs he needed. She knew in her heart that, as the daughter of his old tutor, the only place she could have in his life was his mistress. Love him as she did, she could not accept such a position.

"Papa, keep me strong," she whispered as the knock came and she hurried to open the front door.

"Merry Christmas," Chad called as he burst through the door, carrying two wicker baskets. One was considerably larger than the other, but the tops of both were similarly covered with red-and-green checkered material and the handles were tied with large red satin bows.

Gillian eyed the baskets with misgiving before she had the courage to look up into Chad's face. Much as she had resolved to be strong, she was not proof against the infectious enthusiasm of his grin. She tried to keep her expression grave, but she could feel the corners of her mouth trembling with suppressed laughter. "Merry Christmas to you, too, Chad," she replied shakily.

Setting the baskets on the floor, Chad proceeded to brush the snow off the shoulders of his cape, smiling broadly when he showered her with some of the glistening flakes. He unfastened the cape and threw it over the newel post, dropped his hat on the hall table, then stripped off his gloves and stuffed them into the inverted crown. Finished at last, he picked up the baskets and led the way into the drawing room.

Gillian followed him, slightly flustered that he behaved more like the host than a guest. She watched as he set the baskets on the hearth rug, then, fingers of one hand stroking his beard, he surveyed the room. Without a word, he set about rearranging furniture. When it was completed to his satisfaction, two comfortable chairs were pulled up close to the fire with the low tea table between them.

"Sit here," he ordered, patting the back of one of the chairs.

Gillian knew she should resist Chad's maneuvering, but she was already caught in the spell he was weaving. Shrugging away her suspicions, she moved to the chair he held for her and sat down.

"My chef, Monsieur Hubert, has prepared a special feast for us. He was slightly put out when I would not agree to let him serve it, but I explained that his presence would be *de trop*."

While he was speaking, he whipped off the red-and-green checkered material that covered the top of the bigger basket. He lifted out a heavily embroidered linen cloth which he spread on the table. Then with military precision he set out china, crystal, silverware, and an array of delicacies that practically overloaded the table. In the very center, he set two shiny red apples.

"It all began with apples. Apples and a cat," he said as he uncorked the wine and poured the golden liquid into the wineglasses. "I explained this to Monsieur Hubert and, while not quite understanding why it should be important, he has done his best to oblige me in my whimsy. Everything here is made with or from apples, including this"—he displayed the bottle—"which is a special apple wine I discovered in France many years ago."

At Chad's thoughtfulness, Gillian could feel a lump rise in her throat and a film of tears forced her to blink rapidly. Despite her best efforts, one tear slid down her cheek to the corner of her mouth.

"You must not cry, Gillian," Chad said, his voice slightly ragged. "I discovered last night that I have little control where you are concerned. I cannot comfort you, because if I touch you I will not want to talk. And there is much I need to tell you."

"I'm all right." She gave a watery sniff and wiped away her tears.

Still keeping a cautious eye on her, Chad reached for his wineglass and raised it. "We will drink as old friends. And to prove my friendship, I will let you fill your plate first, although in all fairness I should warn you that I will be particularly offended if you eat all the meringues."

"I don't think I can eat anything," Gillian apologized. "You know we should not be here, alone in the house at this hour."

"Alone? My man Royce told me a maidservant lived with you. What have you done with the woman?" he asked accusingly. "You know the one. Aggie? Addie?"

"Maddie," Gillian mumbled. "I sent her to visit her sister."

"How very enterprising, my dear." At the speculative tone of his voice, her head jerked up and he chuckled at the flush of color invading her cheeks. "Why, Gillian, such a wicked plan. You knew I would come back tonight and you were planning to seduce me."

"I was not!" she denied hotly. "Maddie wanted to spend more time with her sister before we left."

Gillian's hand flew to her mouth as if she could pull back the words she had blurted out. By Chad's raised eyebrow and arrested movement, she knew it was too late. She raised her chin in defiance, refusing to flinch beneath his narrowed gaze. They remained thus, eyes locked together until he broke the contact by turning away. He walked to the fireplace, gently placed his wineglass on the mantelpiece and stared down into the flames.

Even if she could think of something to say, Gillian's mouth was too dry for speech. She waited, her body stiff with tension, until suddenly she heard the sounds of a low chuckle. She bristled with resentment that Chad could find any humor in the present situation.

"What an idiot I am," he said. He turned to her, shaking his head in chagrin. He dropped to his knees beside her chair and grinned roguishly. "Were you running away from me?"

"No." She let her eyes roam at will over his handsome face. She wanted desperately to touch his beard but kept her hands firmly knotted in her lap. "I was running away from myself."

"And why would that be?" When she dropped her head and did not answer, a frown appeared on his face and his voice took on a nervous edge. "You must tell me. Why were you leaving?"

"Because I love you."

"Ahhhh!" There was such relief in his sigh that she looked up in surprise. "For a moment, my dear, I was in despair. I have gone about this stupidly. If I am correct, you thought I planned to seduce you."

"Don't you?"

"No need to sound so disappointed." He held up his hand for silence when she would have spoken. "Everything in good time. In actual fact, I am much too tired for such exercise. I only just returned to Maynard Hall in time to pick up Monsieur Hubert's offerings and bring them here. I have spent the day in the saddle, completing three very important errands."

"What were the errands?" she asked, curious despite herself.

"The first one was to get a special license."

Chad's eyes glistened at the look of wonder on Gillian's face. He reached inside his jacket, withdrew a heavy parchment, and with great reverence laid it in her lap. With shaking fingers she opened it and silently read the contents. Her chin trembled as she tried not to cry.

"But I can't marry you," she wailed.

"What a contrary woman you are. Perhaps I will have to seduce you after all, because then as a fallen woman you will have to marry me. Come along now, Gillian, tell me you will."

"I can't. You have to marry someone with a title and an enormous dowry. You are an earl."

"So that's the reason. You must not be such a snob, my darling. An earl, indeed. First and foremost, I am a man. And I love you with all my heart. I think from the moment I saw you up in the hayloft, hurling apples to save me and an unprepossessing kitten, I've loved you. It took me a very long time to discover that fact, but now that I have, I plan to keep you by my side forever."

"Are you positive? You won't regret it?"

For answer, he rose to his feet and pulled her out of her chair into his arms. He kissed her until she was breathless, but managed to maintain enough control to place her back in her chair, out of temptation.

"You must be strong for both of us, my girl. We are going to be married very properly tomorrow evening. My second errand was to stop in the village and speak to the vicar, who has graciously agreed to marry us in the chapel at Maynard. Even now Monsieur Hubert is putting the finishing touches to our wedding supper. Thanks to Nelda and Robbie's assistance, everyone in the county has been invited. Have you any complaints as to the arrangements? Any questions?"

She beamed at him and he returned her smile. Without words, their eyes traded all the secrets they had kept from each other over the years, until finally Gillian ended the silence.

"What was the third errand?" she asked.

"To find you a Christmas present. That was what took me the longest," he said. He reached down to the small wicker basket, forgotten until now, and set it in her lap. "You will have to be an exceedingly good and loving wife for all the trouble I have taken to find you the perfect gift."

Gillian carefully pulled back the red-and-green checkered cloth. Nestled in the bottom of the basket was a kitten. The pretty red ribbon around the cat's neck looked incongruous against the gray fur dotted with oddly shaped black patches. Yellow-green eyes squinted up at Gillian, and with a cry she reached in to pick up the tiny animal.

"Patches must have paid a visit to every female in the county. I had hundreds to choose from, but this one resembled him most. Do you like him?"

"I love him. We shall have to name him after his father." She cuddled the kitten against her breast, smiling lovingly at Chad. "Thank you, my dearest friend. He is the most perfect Christmas present. I only wish I had something to give you."

He took the kitten out of her hands and returned it to the safety of the wicker basket. "Perhaps you do," he said.

"Chad!"

Amid the sighs and whispers, the kitten began to purr.

From the *New York Times* bestselling author
of <u>Forgiving</u> and <u>Bitter Sweet</u>

LaVyrle Spencer

One of today's best-loved authors of bittersweet
human drama and captivating romance.

___	THE ENDEARMENT	0-515-10396-9/$5.99
___	SPRING FANCY	0-515-10122-2/$5.99
___	YEARS	0-515-08489-1/$5.99
___	SEPARATE BEDS	0-515-09037-9/$5.99
___	HUMMINGBIRD	0-515-09160-X/$5.50
___	A HEART SPEAKS	0-515-09039-5/$5.99
___	THE GAMBLE	0-515-08901-X/$5.99
___	VOWS	0-515-09477-3/$5.99
___	THE HELLION	0-515-09951-1/$5.99
___	TWICE LOVED	0-515-09065-4/$5.99
___	MORNING GLORY	0-515-10263-6/$5.99
___	BITTER SWEET	0-515-10521-X/$5.95